losing it

BOOKS BY ALAN CUMYN

FICTION

Waiting for Li Ming (1993)
Between Families and the Sky (1995)
Man of Bone (1998)
Burridge Unbound (2000)
Losing It (2001)

NON-FICTION

What in the World Is Going On? (1998)

losing it

ALAN CUMYN

M&S

National Library of Canada Cataloguing in Publication Data

Cumyn, Alan, 1960-
Losing it

ISBN 0-7710-2487-8

I. Title.

PS8555.U489L68 2001   C813'.54   C2001-901029-X
PR9199.3.C85L68 2001

We acknowledge the financial support of the Government of Canada through the Book Publishing Industry Development Program for our publishing activities. We further acknowledge the support of the Canada Council for the Arts and the Ontario Arts Council for our publishing program.

This novel is a work of fiction. Except for references to public figures, the names, characters, places, and incidents are the product of the author's imagination and their resemblance, if any, to real-life counterparts is entirely coincidental.

Typeset in Janson by M&S, Toronto
Printed and bound in Canada

McClelland & Stewart Ltd.
The Canadian Publishers
481 University Avenue
Toronto, Ontario
M5G 2E9
www.mcclelland.com

I 2 3 4 5   05 04 03 02 01

For Suzanne

"You aren't going to throw that out," Lenore said, standing straight to stop it once and for all, this dreadful boxing business. She plucked the thing out, turned it around in her hands.

"What is it?" Julia asked. Sharply. Just like a daughter to know exactly how to say things to make it difficult, Lenore thought. Julia had been doing this all her life. Lenore remembered clearly: she never cleaned up. Always gave a hard time over food, clothes, whatever. This Lenore remembered.

"*What is it?*" Julia asked again. Lenore turned it around and around. It had a lever and holes in the side. Everybody knew what it was.

"It's a whatsit," Lenore said quickly. "You know what it is."

"I haven't the slightest idea," Julia said, too patient this time. That too was always a problem with Julia.

"You know what it is," Lenore muttered, turning it around. "It's for things."

"For *things*, Mother?" That tone again. Words wouldn't form properly. That's why she was using it. She always wanted to take over, wear her shoes, her lipstick, her earrings. Now this.

"If we don't know what it is, it's going out," Julia said. "You've had weeks to pack." Just the way she said it. "We only have a few hours left. It's time for hard decisions. There isn't much room in the new place."

"Ricer!" Lenore said suddenly, moving the lever up and down.

"A ricer?" Julia said. "For ricing potatoes?"

"Yes!" Lenore said in triumph.

"Well, you won't need that at Fallowfields. Meals are provided. Honestly, Mom, I've never seen you rice potatoes, and I've been around since 1969."

The ricer went in the Fallowfields box. A small victory. Everything else was going. Lenore knew which boxes to look for. Julia had written "*S.A.*" on them in green Magic Marker – *Salvation Army*. Lenore pulled out a faded dusty thing, green and white, read the side: it was a "cooky" press made of "micro-alumilite – electro-hardened aluminum." She pulled out her cheesecake-recipe book and her whatsit plates, which Julia said she had never used but which Lenore could remember using. When was it? It wasn't that long ago. Trevor was there and her brother and June and their kids. What were their names? Faces she was very clear on. In a way, anyway – she could remember some faces. But her brother's kids? They were just little then. The little ones. Before the one of them got big and killed himself. That was a disaster. On a motorcycle.

"When did you use the oyster plates?" Julia asked. Lenore looked at her, startled.

Lenore asked, "Who was it who died on the motorcycle?"

Julia said, "*What?*" That tone of voice.

"On the motorcycle," she repeated.

"That was Tommy," Julia said, boxing like a tornado. The blue china teacups and saucers. The English cutlery. The lace table flats. And all of her towels. Boxes and boxes of them. "Tommy died on the motorcycle," Julia said. "It must have been twenty years ago. Did you use the oyster plates then?"

"What oyster plates?" Lenore asked.

She wandered into the living room. Everything down from the walls now. So dizzy. There were strange shadows around the spots. Julia had packed most of the pictures, but on the flat thing an old one was lying out. Lenore read the print near the bottom: "*On the way home – off the track – Capt. Buzbie would like very much to know where they are.*" Captain Buzbie with his fur hat, driving his sleigh. And what's-her-name beside him. So pretty. Another beneath this one: "*Capt. Buzbie drives Miss Muffin.*" Lenore strained through her glasses to read the scratch on the back: "*During WWI I was convalescing at Dieppe – in the Hotel Bretagne I saw these 2 old Canadian prints. After prolonged bargaining with the hotel owner, who thought they were paintings, I obtained them. I showed them to an expert in London who told me they were of a set of 6 and very very well worthwhile.*" A shivering signature. Someone related to Trevor? Where did they get Capt. Buzbie?

On to the card drawer. Good thing Lenore was here. Just throw it out. That was Julia's solution. What about the bridge pads? *We They We They.* Felt covers with old Chinamen. You never see those any more. And on the shelf, two of Daddy's duck decoys, a red crystal pheasant, and a Chinese rooster. In the bottom of the drawer, almost hidden, was an old picture-paper. Lenore opened it to a peachy-cheek: "*Checked undergrads: a dream of a team for intra-mural and extra-curricular activities. Sweet and neat checks in all wool.*"

"Mother!" Julia called from the other room and Lenore looked up, shocked. Julia marched in like a two-year-old. She was going to say something, going to announce it. But then just like that the breath went out of her like a mudbath, and then the weird little noise. The *what am I going to do?* noise.

Trevor had a saying for this sort of thing, Lenore thought. But, of course, he was never there when you needed him.

ᔕ

"I don't see why there's all this rush all of a sudden," Lenore said bitterly in the new place. It smelled like that, a new place, all . . . smelly and such. Total confusion. First everything was going into boxes then there was such a mess and the boxes were going here and there and nothing was left in her house. What was she supposed to do with nothing left?

"We're not rushing all of a sudden," Julia said.

That jaw working up and down, and that strange look, as if Lenore had walked out of the change place without any clothes on in the middle of Pullman's. She remembered Julia holding her leg up one aisle and down the next. Up and down! All for that toy. That talking whatever.

"Well, I was living just fine, thank you very much!" Lenore said. Boxes going here and there. The smell was wretched. This new place. Like living in a hotel. Corridors and stink and wretched, ugly carpets. And old people, everywhere, wrecks.

"The house has been sold," Julia said, too tiptoe. She patted the bed, like it was, what? "Won't it be great never to have to cook another meal?" Like a piece of copper. "You know how much you hated cooking. And there'll be new people to meet . . ."

"Well, I'm not going to live *here*!" Lenore said. She stamped her foot and sat down hard on a box in the little space between *her* bed and *her* sofa in this silly thing they were trying to call her room. "I don't see why there's all this rush!" she said. Slowly, clearly, with no mistakes at all. "It's all just . . . a rush!"

"We sold the house, Mom," Julia said. Up and down. A little toy. Holding on to her leg like that, making such a scene. Lenore should never have given in. This is what happens. "The cleaners are finishing up, painters will be there tomorrow, and the new family moves in next week."

"I've never heard such broken eggs! Why did no one consult me?"

"We did, Mom. We've been over this again and again. We sold the house – you remember that. I wish I could take care of you but it's just becoming too difficult." Julia was back to patting the bed again, as if soothing a pet. "We can't give you the care that you need. Alex is in Calgary, he has his own life. And I have Matthew now; you know how demanding a baby is. I *know* you know that! You need people who can be here for you all the time. I'll be here *some* of the time, of course I will. But you have to trust –"

Lenore got up, sat down on another box, got up, put her hands over her ears, sat down, then got up again. Nothing was right, nothing! And why? All because of a stupid mistake with onions. Well, she was sorry. She'd never do it again. *Never*. So let's stop all this nonsense.

"Could you *sit still*, please?" Julia asked. Such a whiny little voice. About to cry. Well, let her. She wants to be a spoiled brat. Holding on to her leg. Up and down. Rotten behaviour. Trevor wanted pot roast for dinner, hated it being late.

A man came in then, a huge man. He startled Lenore so badly she lurched back and nearly toppled out of the window. What kind of place was this, they just leave it open so anyone could throw you out? They wanted the money. That was why. Lenore turned and the man was right there, lifting one of her boxes.

"Who's *that*?" Lenore demanded. A huge man, grunting, a shaggy black bear with grey hair at the temples.

That look on Julia's face again, as if horrors were upon them.
"*Well?*" Lenore said.

"It's *Bob*," Julia said. "My husband. Your son-in-law. Bob!"

"Hi, Lenore," the man said. "I know this is upsetting. How
are you feeling?"

A huge man, sweating big. She'd never seen him before in
her life. He lifted a box, moved it from here to there, then put
it down.

"There's still the dresser," he said.

"That's not Bob!" Lenore snorted. They were shifting
everything when she knew it all before. Perfectly!

"Of course it's Bob," Julia said. "Just take a deep breath. Relax."

"It isn't Bob," Lenore said softly. If Julia could be quiet, so
could she. "I'm sorry about the onion. It wasn't *my* fault!"

"Of course it's Bob!" Julia said. "And what is all this about an
onion?"

"This man is Bob?"

"Yes!" He was standing there like a labourer, sweating on the
carpet.

"Well, what does he *do*?" Lenore asked.

"He's a university professor," Julia said. Talking for him.
Because he wasn't Bob.

Her little girl, that puffing-up face.

"I think you're making this up," Lenore said.

"Who gave us the gold-trimmed placemats with the rose
patterns?" Julia asked.

Lenore laughed nervously. It was all a stupid, smelly dream.
If she just waited it out then everything would be marigolds
again.

"The gold-trimmed placemats," Julia pressed. "You organ-
ized our wedding. You used to know exactly who gave each of
our wedding presents. You *can* remember this."

"The Houghtons."

"*Yes!*" Julia said, hugging her. "You *see*? It's all in there still, you just have to access it!"

"Can I go home now?" Lenore asked.

ഗ

There was one time, Lenore remembered – in a wispy way, for the most part, though it came in strong as nails sometimes – they were driving in a snowstorm. Trevor, of course, was at the wheel. Driving and smoking, his brow creased in concentration. Outside, snow – the blinding white against the black of night. There was a bridge party, with . . . with what's-their-names. Who had the little boy who committed suicide. And that was before what's-his-name – the man – went off with that young woman from his office. It was before all that. Trevor would have nothing to do with him after, and Babs – that was her name. Babs and Dougie. Babs fell apart. It was before all that. It was just bridge and everything was happy.

Except for the snow. Trevor smoking, worrying, peering out the windshield of their old car. It was new then. The wipers went *whap! whap!* furiously clearing the snow, but new blurriness always returned right away. *Whap! Whap!* Lenore could tell Trevor was getting a headache. The tires were spinning. The new car was clumsy in the snow. It was so heavy, the backside slid around.

"Why didn't you put on the snow tires?" Lenore asked and Trevor gave her his King-of-the-Castle look. He *was* King-of-the-Castle anyway. He didn't have to give her that look. Smoking and peering, the tires spinning, everything vague in black and white.

"For God's sake!" Trevor said everything sharply. "I just wanted to play some bridge!"

This was what it was like in the new place. Lenore wandered around peering, but it felt like snow and gloom behind a windshield. I'm ready to go home now, she thought. Sitting on a box with the telephone on her lap. Sitting in her slip with a sweater on and the blackness pressed hard against the windows. She called up Julia and told her about the bridge, about the snowstorm with Babs and Dougie. Then Julia wasn't there, it took the longest time to figure out – some problem with the phone. But nothing seemed quite right these days anyway. So Lenore punched in the numbers again. One after another. It was better if she didn't think of them. That was the funny thing. As soon as she thought straight at the numbers they went away.

It rang and rang and rang. Then – Trevor! But she didn't want to talk to him, not now. She asked him, very politely, if she could speak to Julia.

"*Who?*" he said, but in an odd way.

"Why won't you let me speak to her?" Lenore said. Then she added, "I am sorry about the onions. I won't do it again!"

He hung up. Drunk! Lenore punched the numbers again immediately. Just with her fingers. It rang and rang and rang again.

"Uhn-hn!" said a woman. Then, "Yes? Hello?"

"Julia?" Lenore said.

"No," said the voice. Then louder: "*NO*. Wrong number! God, what time is it?"

"But that's not possible," Lenore said. She was trembling.

"There's no Julia here. I'm sorry," said the voice. But she didn't go away. Lenore said, "Well, could you *give me* her number?"

"*Who* is it you're calling?"

"I told you. Julia!" Lenore said.

Nothing. The phone was working badly. Lenore tried again.

"We're not in right now," a voice said. "But we'd like very much to respond to your call. So please leave a message after the tone."

Lenore waited, then said, "Why won't you talk to me? I want to go home! Why can't you understand that? *Has everybody gone nutmeg here?*" Lenore cried for a bit, then talked some more, but no one replied.

As soon as she put down the receiver it rang, a huge jangle that made her leg jump. She snapped up the phone.

"Julia?" she cried.

"*Who* have you been talking to?"

"Well," Lenore said, "you're not the only one in the world who has friends."

"*Friends?*" Julia said.

"Yes," Lenore said, proudly. The box was starting to dig into her back. Why couldn't they give her some decent furniture? "I'm meeting lots of new friends," she said. "Lots and lots." She added, "Ever so many!" but Julia couldn't keep up her end. "Are you there?" Lenore asked finally.

Julia yawned and said sleepily, "Oh, I'm sorry! I had an itchy nose."

"Well," Lenore said, "that means you're going to kiss a fool!"

"Does it?" Julia said absently. Then, "It's time for bed, Mother. Time for sleep," so gently, with so much tucked wool, it reminded Lenore of something, she could almost put her finger on it.

2 ↫

"My mother and Matthew hath murthered sleep," Julia murmured, stretching to replace the phone. Bob had turned over, was huddled in a mass at the edge of the bed, a spare pillow wrapped around his ears. His hairy back was slightly exposed to the chill so Julia pulled the blanket up for him. But he recoiled at her touch as if expecting to be hit. He was muttering something in his sleep: *fathom, farling, fucking?* She couldn't make it out.

Matthew was asleep now too, though he was still latched on to her breast. He was almost two, felt enormous on her front, and she knew it was time to wean, well past time. He was too strong, suckled like a wolfhound, left Julia's breasts wrung out and wrinkled, rubbed raw. And he had teeth now too. He knew, for the most part, not to bite, but would forget sometimes in his enthusiasm and send Julia howling. But how to say no to those sky-blue eyes, the drool and gleam, the way he'd quiver in the second or two it took to latch on? He drank like an addict, drained her of energy even while bloating himself stupid with satiation. Now they were both lying like addled lovers parted after the storm, Matthew too thick to move, Julia too fatigued.

"Bob," she said and kicked him gently on the back of the leg. He didn't move. "Bob!" she said again, kicked him harder.

"*Feeling, foaming*," he mumbled, and turned over even further, was going to fall onto the floor in a second.

"Bob, could you put Matthew back to bed? Please, honey?"

"Huh," he said, then flumped over the edge. She expected him to get up finally, take Matthew off her chest. But he stayed where he was, wedged between the wall and the bed, snoring, most of the blankets having gone with him in the collapse.

Now it was cold. Julia struggled upright, held on to Matthew, swung her legs over the opposite side of the bed, stood up groggily. She carried Matthew into his room, fought to keep her balance as she leaned over the bed and put him down gently. Probably he needed a change, but she wasn't going to bother. He was asleep, that was good enough. She tucked him in, started to tiptoe away, then returned and kissed him softly on his sweet hair.

He opened his eyes and she nearly swore, but then they fluttered closed, soft as butterfly wings. Julia crept away.

"Mama!" Matthew cried and she froze, held her breath. "Mama."

"Shhh, baby," Julia whispered. She stood rooted.

"Mama," he said, but softly, dreamily. She didn't reply but waited, counted off one hundred and twenty seconds until she could hear his breathing, deep and even. Then she took another step.

"*Mama!*" he yelled and started to cry, a choking sob.

Julia turned. "Matthew, *no*, it's time for sleep!" she said. He was starting to stand in his bed, was holding out his arms and wailing as if he'd been abandoned in the dust with wild dogs circling. "It's time for sleep! This is ridiculous! God, you're exhausted, why don't you sleep?"

She took him in her arms, held him, swayed back and forth as he sobbed into her shoulder, his breath choking and strained. "Oh, you are wet, you are soaking," she said in her soothing voice. "I'm sorry. I'm so sorry. There, there." The crying subsided gradually into a low-gear, throbbing moan, and she carried him over to the changing table in the corner of the room. But as soon as she put him down he wailed again, as unnerving as a siren. "Shhh!" she said, picked him up again, clutched him.

Matthew reached inside her nightie. She could see that his eyes weren't really open, he wasn't quite awake.

"No!" she said. "No, mister, no way! You've had enough. You've already drained me for tonight."

"Yes, nubbies," he said. Eyes closed but burrowing his face between her breasts, looking for the opening.

"No nubbies. We've done nubbies. I'm going to change you and then you're going back to sleep!"

But he was relentless, all yearning hands and mouth. She tried to put him down on the changing table again but he squirmed and fought. He was too strong. She knew she could drop him if she wasn't careful. So she retreated to the rocking chair by the dresser, pulled her nightie off her shoulder and let him have some more of her right side. "Careful, oh, gentle, sweetie. Don't chew!"

He calmed down. He wasn't really hungry. This was just psychological. After a time his lips went *glip glip* in a funny little pseudo-drinking motion. He liked having his hands on her breast too, it seemed – to be in control, tilt her this way and that. *Glip glip*.

Gently, with Matthew still attached, she reached around and pulled down his plastic outer lining, then expertly undid the two pins. The cotton diaper was soaking but the diaper pail was several feet away. She got up awkwardly, held Matthew with her left hand, and leaned back to balance him while she fought with the lid, then dropped the wet diaper into the pail. She could hear her mother's voice – her old, sane, real voice – implanted in the back of her head. "No diaper service in my day. No disposables! I soaked them in vinegar and washed them in boiled water and hung them out on the line white as lilies. It's no wonder you love me so much!" Julia could almost feel her mother's fingers reaching for her sides – a teasing, pinching kind of tickle.

"Matthew, honey, I have to wipe you," she said, and moved to return him to the changing table. But he wouldn't let go. He clamped his teeth around her nipple and she was forced to lean all the way over so he could still suckle while he lay flat. "Ow! Come on, let go!" she said and wiggled her finger between his lips and her skin. The vacuum was broken but his jaw stayed firm. "Matthew. Matthew!"

He wouldn't let go. She had to strain and twist to keep her breast positioned on top of him while she grabbed a fresh diaper, wrapped him up, fought the safety pins into place. It wasn't snug but would have to do. She stood him up rudely. For a few seconds he was shocked into letting go of the nipple, too stunned even to cry. She took advantage and hustled him into a dry plastic lining, then just as he opened his mouth she plugged him onto the left breast so that his scream was muffled, went deep inside her.

Back on the rocker, she pulled an old blanket around them, tried to tuck her cold feet underneath her, but it was a tight fit, uncomfortable, so she left them down. She closed her eyes and rocked and sang little snatches of nursery rhymes. "*To market to market to buy a fat pig.*" She had a funny memory of her mother deliberately mixing up the words of old songs.

Hush little baby don't you cry,
Mommy's gonna bake you a wishbird pie,
And if that wishbird pie won't chew,
Mommy's gonna make you a daydream stew.

That Scrabble-champion gleam in her eye, always ready to score and total and find herself ahead. "Well, I don't understand what the problem is," her mother used to say, gazing over Julia's shoulder at some wearisome bit of homework, the square of the lesser angle or the Diet of Wurms. "When I was in school it was just a question of remembering!" She gave parties for forty, she wrote the book-club newsletter for thirty-five years, she remembered exactly when you'd last worn a particular sweater and what boy was a nuisance and what bill had been paid when and from what account. She knew the origins of weird words – *ergotism*, a disease in grasses that also means quibbling, arguing, wrangling. When was that? A year and a half ago at Christmas she'd brought that out to put Bob in his place. He was pontificating – about what? About the role of the artist in a world gone mad with materialism, something like that, and she'd cut right in with, "What an ergotist," which had stopped him flat.

"Egotist?" he said finally. "Don't you mean?"

But she insisted on *ergotist*, and she knew what it meant, and he didn't. "A lifetime of crossword puzzles must be worth something," she'd said.

She was shutting down even then but they didn't know it. They'd all thought it was just the peculiarities of age. After Julia's father had died, her mother had settled into her routines, her toast and tea for breakfast, walking to Pullman's, to the bank, to Lilian's for her hair on Tuesdays. Things were coming apart, in hindsight it was obvious, but four months ago she was still driving – to the library, to bridge club, to the dry cleaner's. The living-room table was a disaster: papers piled in odd clumps sorted according to no decipherable order, bills mixed with garage-sale flyers and strange articles carefully clipped, obituaries and wedding announcements of people her mother had never known, ads for weight loss and used cars, unopened letters, and of course her messages scrawled on scraps of paper that she'd forget about then rediscover. *"Left in cheesecloth,"* she'd read, squinting, and turn to Julia. "What does that mean? Why did I write that?"

Looking to Julia for the answer, increasingly for every answer, for who it was who called and what he was asking for, and where the insurance papers went, and what had happened to the damn radio that was *always* in her kitchen, thirty-one years on the same shelf, the brown one with the silver knobs and honest grease, perpetually set to the classical-music station.

The phone rang. Matthew started awake but Julia cuddled him, pulled the blanket up by his ears to deaden the noise. It rang and rang. She's being looked after, Julia thought. She's safe, she can't hurt herself, she's already called twice since midnight.

It kept ringing. Why didn't the answering machine cut in? Matthew must have switched it off again, the way he liked to play with any button within reach. After a while Julia started to count, let it go to thirty before she finally got up. Then it stopped, of course. So she put Matthew in his bed and this time he took, but now she was wide awake. She walked back into her bedroom and stared at the naked bed, the shadowed, blanketed lump of husband on the floor. She found her robe, stuffed her aching cold feet into a pair of woollen socks, shuffled downstairs. It was 4:38 by the microwave clock. She turned on the overhead light – oh, she thought, I *hate* the way this kitchen looks. It was so dingy. The floor especially was a disaster. Layer upon layer of linoleum, cracked, dirty, falling apart. She hadn't decided on a colour. The floor guy was coming tomorrow – *today* – and she still hadn't decided. She didn't want to think about it.

She hadn't written anything for months, could hardly remember the last time she'd had what felt like an original thought. "Telling It Slant: The Indirections of Emily Dickinson." That was her last paper, returned in the mail months ago, and now she could only remember Dickinson in snippets, as if encountered in an almost forgotten dream of a time when ideas, when words on a page, seemed to be at the centre of what the world was about. The onset of motherhood had wiped out most of that, the old concerns lost in the midst of the extreme physical changes, the sleep deprivation, the all-consuming drain of nursing and attending her son. It was just a phase – she knew it, everyone said – but at the moment she couldn't believe it with any conviction. Her own mother never gave in to motherhood like this. Julia remembered as a little girl lying stiff and alert in bed in the middle of the afternoon, tucked in to within an inch of her life, while her mother shut the door, and the *click click* of her heels went down the hall, nap time inviolable. She remembered her mother so often buried in a book, irritable at any interruption, with her cigarette (oh how she hated to quit later on) and her coffee cup stained with lipstick and her invisible shield of defence: you are the child, you play over there, and I am here, we will each amuse ourselves.

How Julia swore she would never be like that with her own child.

She plugged in the kettle now, waited, poured herself a cup of tea. She took a blanket from the sofa in the living room – there were blankets everywhere now, thanks to Matthew – and sat in the darkness, gazed out at the street. All the quiet houses.

Someone had a light on down the road, upstairs. But all the rest of the houses were dark and the street was deserted. A white cat slunk across the lawn two houses over, disappeared into a hedge. Julia sipped her tea. She had an odd memory, just fell into it, of watching Bob in the classroom. He had a beard then, was animated the way that he gets, was wearing a black shirt with a dark tie and had taken off his jacket, was pacing as he talked, flinging his hands this way and that. She'd written page after page of notes but now she stopped, or rather she kept writing but lost track of what it was.

He was playing to her. She knew it suddenly, it sent heat straight through her – her professor, twice her age! He was pacing and gesticulating, weaving his stories the way he had all term, looking everywhere but at her. But now she knew, it all made sense: the personal notes, the long chats in his office, the lunch they'd had that time when they were supposed to be talking about her project but instead he'd asked her all about her family, her other courses. Suddenly it all made sense. He was performing for her, had worn the black shirt for her, was going to chat with her at the end of the class about something. She didn't know what it would be. Some little thing. He always did it. After ignoring her the whole period, just as she was leaving he'd say, "Oh, Julia," and then the little thing would come out. The book he'd brought for her. The article he thought she should read. The poem he'd forgotten to bring last time, here it was. The little thing he wanted to mention.

And there he was in Julia's memory, talking away, and it was like it was happening again, she flushed just thinking of it. Because he looked at her at precisely that moment. She *knew* and then he looked and everything stopped. For the first time in ages, it seemed, he looked at her in the class and surely everyone else knew then too, it might as well have been announced. They were locked in this lover's gaze, she couldn't turn away, didn't want to, was thrilled through and through.

Then the bell went and he swivelled suddenly, gaped at the clock, this exaggerated, funny expression. "*Already?*" Everyone laughed. They stood and gathered their books and Bob finished the story, whatever it was, wrapped it up in another sentence or two while Julia stared at the floor, her face burning. She could barely breathe, felt trembly and out of control. She didn't want to go but her feet moved her towards the door. Bob was talking to a couple of the students who had cornered him, were asking him about something. He couldn't see her go but her feet were taking her, not slowly either. Some boy asked her something. She could hear the words clearly but didn't reply. She was listening too hard for something else.

"Oh, Julia!"

Bob's voice, across the classroom.

"Julia! Could you wait just a second?"

Stopping everything. Everyone looking once again.

"I have a little thing," he said, and smiled, and that was the day she knew.

~ 3

Bob's special package arrived in the mail in a plain brown padded envelope. The mailman handed it to Bob on the porch along with a water bill, a postcard from one of Bob's ex-students written in the south of France, a flyer for discount muffler inspections, and a free pouch of shampoo called Lumio. The mailman was shorter than Bob but younger and carried himself straighter, and made a habit of looking each of his householders in the eye as he said, "Good morning." Bob looked him right back but made a funny noise in his throat – "*ghnihhr*" – when he realized what had finally arrived.

"A bit cool today," the mailman said. It was grey and many of the chimneys in the neighbourhood were showing smoke for the first time that fall. But the mailman was in walking shorts and had worked up a sweat. His face glistened and Bob thought, How can he still be so fat? Walking like this every day.

"Hope you finish before the rain," Bob said, holding the special package and the discount muffler inspection in just the same way, as if all pieces of mail were created equal. He allowed himself a quick glance. The company logo, *Lighthouse*, was discreetly stamped on the top left, and the package was addressed to *R. Sterling.*

"Anything?" Julia asked when Bob stepped back into the house, an old, solid, respectable home that Bob had bought with his first wife, Stephanie, when he'd landed tenure. He had loved the solemn bearing of it then, but it was dark on sombre days. The windows were original, with diamond-shaped panes set in lead. Bob was stiff from the night of bad sleep. He turned back into the hall and suffered a moment's awareness of how closed-in the place made him feel. Though Julia had managed her best with it before the baby – she'd done over the living room and had had a wall taken out upstairs to open up the master bedroom – it reeked of Stephanie still. Her mirror in the hall, her wallpaper with the iris pattern in the den, her hand-stencilled border linking room to room.

"I'm just about off," Bob said. His briefcase was right there in the hall beside his packed bag and he knelt to click it open quickly and put his package inside. But his fingers fumbled with the combination. Calm down, he thought, and he tried to breathe deeply. He put the package and the rest of the mail on the oak floor to give the lock his proper attention. But Matthew erupted from the kitchen pulling a thumpy plastic elephant that scattered the mail.

"Shit!" Bob roared and the boy flooded into tears, ran back to Julia, who hugged him quickly, smoothed his brown curls.

"*Bob*," she said softly, but with an edge so that he understood perfectly.

The taxi pulled up in the driveway and honked. Bob opened the case, retrieved the package from the floor, put it inside and snapped the lid shut again. "I'm sorry," he said, straightening. "I'm sorry, Matthew." He nuzzled the boy's neck. Matthew kept his face buried in Julia's front. "I *wish* I didn't have to go,"

Bob said, and kissed Julia on the cheek, nuzzled her earlobe. He felt a wave of tenderness for her as she stood in her frayed yellow sweatsuit, the sleep still in her warm brown eyes, her blonde hair, not natural any more, but the colouring suited her, wisps tucked behind one ear and straying over the other – a surge of love and appreciation for her beauty. Little as she tried, she was still striking.

She turned for a proper kiss but the taxi honked again and Bob had already stepped away to pick up the rest of his luggage.

"Hey," she said at the door. Bob was halfway down the steps but stopped, took three strides back to her, and kissed her on the mouth.

"I wish you could go with me," he said. His voice was gentle and deep, his eyes soft with what he knew was a look of self-mocking, a sense of the absurdities of the world and his own position. "Next time," he said and kissed her again.

"You'll get lipstick," she said and wet her thumb, rubbed it off his lips.

5

It wasn't a long ride to the airport. The route skirted the university and along the Rideau Canal. Ottawa was subdued, the colours muted and wet, the sky choked with gnarly clouds and the vague threat of winter, a dull chill, a starkness where the leaves had left the trees, the sudden thickness of people's clothing. The roads were congested with workaday government and high-tech types on their way in for nine o'clock. Bob studied their faces: doomed-looking, numb-eyed men and women clutching their coffee cups, rolling forward a few feet then stopping, their shoulders hunched already, backs aching.

The taxi driver said the forecast was for rain then and Bob made an appropriate reply, his face composed, as if there were no special package in his briefcase. As if he hadn't ordered it from an Internet company five weeks ago and conducted a detailed correspondence to tack down his measurements – hip point to hip point, belly button to base of the spine, the average size of his penis and testicles (measured in bath water, resting) – his skin colour (porcelain-beige, pale), his pubic-hair type (basic black, mince, but with traces of heather-brown). Bob asked, "Does your business pick up in the rain?" and the driver told him all about it. It wasn't such a simple thing. It depended on what type of rain it was, what time of day, what season. A really hard rain in the morning in the summer might mean that people decide to call a cab to get to work, or they might just stay home. A light rain in January that made everything icy slick . . .

"Yes," Bob said, following him and not following.

"All I know, the really heavy rain, the traffic is *crap*," the driver said, and Bob nodded in solidarity.

"We should all stay home in a heavy rain," Bob said. "Stay home and take taxis!"

ら

She was waiting for him by the ticket counter. It had all been arranged, and yet when she stood up he felt giddy and a new sense of awe. She was tall and wiry and womanly and twenty-one, in black hip-hugging pants that twenty-one-year-olds used to wear when Bob was twenty-one. With flared legs and rounded, pocketless bottoms and even damn near the same ridiculous cloggy skyscraper shoes from the olden days. And her maroon leather jacket was open to reveal a clingy black top several sizes too small. Nobody could get away with clothes like that. Except if you were twenty-one and immortal.

"Professor Sterling," she said, stepping towards him. She had sunglasses tipped high on her head, holding back her shoulder-length black satin hair. She looked like she belonged in a glossy magazine, a certain kind of immortal of the instant. But more than that, Bob knew this girl had an intensely intriguing spirit. She was Sienna Chu, half-Chinese, half-Irish, and her eyes were ever-so-slightly crossed so Bob couldn't tell if she was looking directly at him or away.

"Please, call me Bob. Everyone in the department calls me Bob." He touched her arm briefly, put his briefcase down – he was dragging his main luggage behind him on little wheels. "Well, isn't this marvellous!" he exclaimed, gesturing vaguely so that he might mean the occasion, the day, the airport, or perhaps just life in general.

"I am so excited! I've never been to a Poe conference before." She blushed, it was endearing, and she had no further need to be endearing, he was already teetering on the edge of total endearment.

"Where's your ticket, Sienna?"

Helen in the English-department office had booked her into economy, which was ludicrous. Bob marched her straight to the booth to upgrade her to business class. "Some things in life are not worth stinting on," he said. "If we're going to die a ragged, awful, cruel death, then it should be in great comfort, with plenty of leg room, a champagne glass at our lips, and smart, good-looking attendants to look after our every whim."

Bob waited for her reaction, but she apparently chose not to react, looked away instead like a princess who doesn't have to listen if she doesn't want to. But she did let Bob pay the difference, then take her to the restaurant to buy her a proper breakfast: two eggs and sausage, toast, hash browns, coffee. "You can't trust the food on the plane," he said. "*Even* in business class. Alcohol, certainly, but I have a friend in catering and the stories he tells me!" She gobbled down her food like a starving child. He tried not to stare at the soft taper of her fingers, the smooth heaven of her throat.

"They say the same about residence food," she said.

"Don't get me started on residence food!" he exclaimed, too loud. People looked at them from other tables. But he couldn't help it, he was utterly alive, he felt like shouting. "Don't get me started," he repeated in a more normal voice. "I have seen them taking the bodies out at night. Poor, anonymous freshmen who paid the ultimate price for coveting the custard pie. It's scandalous, there's been a cover-up for years. The parents are bought off by the multinational that owns every college catering company in the Western world!" He was babbling but couldn't help himself.

"No wonder you like Poe so much," she said, and pulled out the conference brochure. "I *really* want to hear Solinger on Poe's concept of women," she said.

"Oh, Poe and his women. *Don't* get me started!" Bob said. But it was too late, he was already started. There was Eliza Poe, Poe's actress mother, who outshone her shiftless husband so badly and died so young, penniless, a charity case after having played more than three hundred parts. And Poe's wife and cousin, Virginia – *Sissy* – fourteen when they married, who lingered for years on her deathbed, the relentless cough of the white plague, tuberculosis, her skin pale, deathly beautiful, tinted with night sweats, too pink in pallor. The poor dear, saddled with Poe, a dead-poor, luckless, mercurial poet, scathing critic, inventor of the detective story, author of all those cryptic tales, wildly ambitious, jealous, driven, haunted, alcoholic, unstable, brilliant, morose, half-starved, bitter, possibly mad.

"Curiously," Bob said, glancing at his watch – he didn't want to miss the flight, and giddy as he was he could see himself doing it – "Curiously enough, one time Poe *almost* got a government job. It was as if the gods were playing with him. Prominent writers used to get cushy jobs back then –"

"Yes, you said," Sienna cut in. "I remember you mentioned this in class."

"Did I?" Bob asked. "Yes, probably. My God, the old professor has started repeating himself."

She might have interjected something about him not really being old, but instead she said, "His name was actually published for the post, wasn't it?"

"Yes! Well, it was *Pogue*, under the list of new appointments, and Poe inquired and was apparently told the name was his, garbled by the press. He was all set for the swearing-in. *At last, a government job!* He waited and waited . . ."

"Should we get going, Professor Sterling?" Sienna asked. "*Bob*, I mean."

"Yes, we should," Bob said, but stayed a moment more just to look at her. Then while they were walking to the departures gate they passed a mirrored wall at which Bob couldn't help glancing. He was struck, as he had been several times lately, by a feeling of being an impostor, but quite a good one: solid-looking, squarish, fleshy, yes, but tanned, too, and prosperous and well turned out. She was gorgeous, a real head-turner. But he too had a presence, didn't look hopelessly drowned beside her.

There was an annoying delay in the customs line-up which Bob hadn't figured on. Being Canadian, he found it hard to consider the United States an entirely foreign country, and he'd forgotten about this small matter. Time really was pressing now, so he sent Sienna into another line down the row. Then he waited patiently while a young woman with an English accent and seven rings in her cheek showed her passport, answered one question, then was let through. She was followed by a raggedy, intense man with a sickly pale face and dust on his jacket who squinted at the customs officer like a known criminal, also said only a few words, and was similarly waved through.

"Next!" the customs officer said, staring at Bob. He pulled his luggage up to the yellow line, stood with his briefcase under his arm.

"Name?"

"Uh, Bob Sterling. *Professor* Bob Sterling."

"From?"

"From here. From, uh, Ottawa."

"Destination?"

"New York City."

"Purpose of trip?"

"Oh, uh –" Bob couldn't seem to get the rattle out of his voice. He felt suddenly and completely guilty. "I'm going to New York for the Poe conference at Columbia University." Then he added, "Edgar Allan Poe. The writer."

"You'll be there for how long?"

"What's today, Friday? Till Sunday." That was better. His voice sounded more normal. The customs officer was a plain-looking woman, her uniform puffed-out and sexless, her face quite blank: pale blue eyes behind wispy brown lashes. In her identity-tag photo she looked as if she was being busted for drug possession. Rebecca Williams.

"Do you have anything to declare?" It was a standard question, and it may have been the way she ran all the words together that made Bob pause to consider that, given his age and stage and position, perhaps he had, or at least ought to have, things to declare. She didn't mean it in a philosophical way, of course, and he realized it nearly right away, but for an instant he tried to think what he could possibly say to excuse himself, as if she had seen into his soul and was demanding some sort of justification or analysis.

"Uh, no," he said, finally.

She asked something else, too quickly to catch, and again Bob had to ask her to repeat herself.

"Could you open your briefcase please?"

"Oh, I, uh, I just have the one piece of luggage," Bob said, turning to gesture to his suitcase behind him. She was staring at him so hard he finally looked – clown-like, he thought – down at the briefcase tucked under his arm. He'd been clutching it so hard he'd forgotten it was there. "Oh gosh, yes!" he said, smiling and blustering. He almost started to explain about absent-minded professors, how he could be walking down the street completely absorbed in some thought or other . . .

"Your briefcase, sir," she said, rather harshly. "Could you open it?"

"Oh, this!" Bob said, still clutching it.

Sienna was waiting for him now beyond the customs line. People of all stripes were turning to look at her as they filed past.

"Here it is," Bob said softly, and placed the briefcase on the inspection table, fiddled self-consciously with the lock. Finally, after too much effort, it fell open.

Rebecca Williams flicked through several things. "What's this?" she asked. She held up the special package.

"That's nothing," he said quickly. "I just threw it in there. It came in the mail today."

"What is it?" she asked slowly, enunciating every syllable, as if talking to a second-language learner.

"It's a tape of a famous lecture on Poe's view of poetics and transcendence, in light of his struggles with the Transcendentalists," Bob said. Then, meeting her blank expression, he added, "It's an academic cassette."

"Value?" she asked finally.

"I'm sorry?"

"What's the value?"

"Oh, uh, it's completely useless to almost anyone. But to me –" And then he stopped himself. She was looking at him with near-malice. "Twenty-five dollars," Bob said.

There was a terrible moment in which it looked as if she was going to open the package anyway. She'd hooked her sharp thumbnail under an edge, and at the same time was eyeing his suitcase. Bob willed himself to appear absolutely calm and innocent, despite his rising panic.

"Could you open your other bag?" she asked, and closed the lid of the briefcase, leaving the special package unopened inside.

Bob hoisted the suitcase onto the table. Sienna gave him a bright smile when he looked up, terror-stricken.

The customs officer unzipped Bob's bag and rummaged through his things: spare shirts, trousers, and socks, the Silverman biography of Poe, and an old copy of the complete tales and poems too bulky for his briefcase. Then she got to the padded black lace bra and panties, the nylons and purple silk slip and red satin corset at the bottom of the bag. She didn't hold them up but simply fingered through them, pausing with each new discovery.

"Those are, uh, some of my wife's things," he said, feebly. His face was flushed crimson and he was aware that his breath rattled in shallow, rapid little wheezes. He tried to calm himself but couldn't.

"Your wife?" Williams asked, deadpan.

"She's uh, she's waiting for me. Over there," Bob said. He pointed slightly in Sienna's direction.

Rebecca Williams – small, pasty-faced Rebecca Williams with the limp brown hair and washed-out eyes – looked at the stunning Sienna for what seemed to Bob like thirty or forty years. Finally she turned back to him.

"All right. You can go," she said. Not a flicker of light behind those eyes. *"Have a good stay."*

Bob zipped up his bag, collected his briefcase, and wandered, dazed, to where Sienna was waiting.

"Boy, she really put you through it," Sienna said.

"I need a drink," he said.

〽

Bob had a moment of nausea right before liftoff. He let Sienna have the window seat and tried to study his hands and breathe deeply. A video screen two seats in front of them showed calm, responsible people in life jackets sliding down an inflated rescue chute into . . . what? An angry ocean below? A sea of flames and death? Into the abyss off the screen.

"I just . . . I am so moved by this," Sienna said. "It's a miracle, the earth so still below. Whenever I'm taking off I have a sense of how large the planet is. It seems smaller when we're on the ground."

She was trying to be sophisticated and Bob felt more sophisticated just knowing that. She had also, some weeks before, given him a sheaf of poems to read. They were in his briefcase and he planned to discuss them with her on this trip. They were extraordinary. Everything about her, in fact, was extraordinary, but for the moment Bob had to concentrate on mentally pulling the plane away from the ground, to grease the connections and hoist up the wheels and ensure the electronic system didn't catch fire, to clear the pilot's neural pathways to allow for correct decisions.

It was an odd thing, this flight anxiety, a minor case he'd developed only after the break-up with Stephanie, although his near-disaster at customs was now contributing as well. It was as if he were being reminded that the end – *death* – was not just a theoretical, logical outcome, but inescapable and, quite possibly, imminent. Little mistakes erased entire lives. Valves gave out. Veins blew up to the size of balloons then burst. An argument in the morning with an ex-lover and a drink too many, a finger on the wrong switch, someone asleep at the air-control tower because the union failed to negotiate rest time and management squeezed an extra dollar . . .

In large part the feeling went away after they levelled off. His breathing eased, heart rate subsided. It wasn't so bad, after all, as far as anxiety could go.

He ordered a Scotch for himself and Sienna took a brandy and sipped it competently, her lips leaving a small red mark on the edge of the glass. Bob took her hand and squeezed it gently, then let it go. "You are an astonishing poet," he said. "I've been meaning to tell you. I am just . . . well, I was amazed by many of the poems. Really *striking* work. We'll go over it in detail, if you want. But I just meant to tell you . . ."

Oh, how she blushed! There is nothing a poet would rather hear more and Bob knew it, but he meant what he said, and his words made him feel even more deeply.

"You have a *talent*, Sienna, and it's something that can't be taught. I mean, one can get people to think more deeply and carefully about how they use words. But there's a *sensibility* that simply is there or it isn't. A lot of students show their work to me, I can't tell you. I'm happy to look at it. But most student writing is, well, dross. But *your* writing . . ."

How she hung on his words. He could feel her heat rising. It was heady and he had a sense that he had to be careful, for himself as well as for her.

"Well, I don't want to go on about it," he said. "But you have a resonance, a sense of complexity of life and spirit." He fumbled under the seat to pull up his briefcase, fought again with the combination before freeing the lid. There was the special package, still, thank God, wrapped in its thick brown envelope, and there were his conference papers, and there on the bottom was Sienna's poetry. The first poem was "Nighttime in Cellophane," which Bob read quietly out loud:

nighttime in cellophane
                                        crepuscular slopes
cement mixed eggish hot-blooded high-tops
                        she dips
                                                drags her slit-purse into
                organdy   *by which*
                                there are no confectioneries here
your pores reek
                                blister-juiced
                        curvilinear   *barely toff-topped*
                my poster-lock in leather pants
                                we are satellite debris
                                                cumulonimbus nipplewort
                                Pocahontan preening with clogs
collared, kites /
                        cut by the wind, knuckled in the primrosed path
                                        slideless, turfed in the juvenilia
                        of our lakefront list we
                                        are thunderslips and aphids
                                periscope mornings, niacinamide and
                                                riboflavin
                silting the leg-lorn ozone
                        i arch my back and you curl
                        centuries like this, your pickle

my precambrian mastoid process
no sugar no
artificial sweeteners

"It's very . . . evocative," he said, fighting for a proper word. "I'm having a hard time describing it. You know, when a brain gets older it calcifies. That's why it usually takes young people with nimble, unconventional minds to string together words like this. 'Thunderslips and aphids.' Wonderful! It's nonsense, on one plane, and yet it has a resonance of received wisdom. Do you know what I mean?" She nodded but looked at the poem, not him. "'There are no confectioneries here.' It's Joycean. I don't mean to puff you up, but it took him years to string together words like this, the layers of different meanings. 'Cumulonimbus nipplewort.' Beautifully playful. And then: 'kites / cut by the wind.' Extraordinary!"

"I like doing things with reality," she said. "I like cracked lenses. Throwing words, the way they go together."

"Precisely! You've taken the words and put them together. And nobody else on earth would have done it the same way. It's authentic, completely unique. Mystifying, and yet –" And yet what? He took a breath, then said, "Poe was also one of the few people in his day to realize that in poetry the words, the sounds, are far more important than their mere meaning." He paused, then began reciting: "'Once upon a midnight dreary, While I pondered weak and weary, / Over many a quaint and curious volume of forgotten lore –' You see, the sound *is* the beauty of it. 'While I nodded, nearly napping, suddenly there came a tapping, / As of someone gently rapping, rapping at my chamber door –'"

Her smile was the sun blessing the earth as seen from an airplane miles above the ground and Bob was acutely conscious of his good fortune, to be with her, to be him, in his skin, his privileged position. It must have been something like what Poe felt at those private parties in his honour when he would stand in the middle of the drawing room holding a glass of wine and recite the entire eighteen verses of "The Raven," the words spilling so felicitously one to the next, the eyes of all riveted upon him, every female wondering what it would be like to be married to a famous poet, a sensitive, *suffering* soul, a genius mind, wayward boy.

They talked easily, comfortably, with an energy that did strange things to time, made Bob unsure, at one point, whether the flight had just begun or had lasted weeks and weeks. It was an unsettling state because he felt as if he had no control. He gave in to it, and then was ripped awake, back to the old reality.

"I'm sorry," Bob said, closing the briefcase and standing abruptly. "Back in a minute." He didn't want to appear flustered, but his digestion was delicate and there was usually little warning. He was halfway down the aisle when he realized he'd brought his briefcase with him, and had an idle thought that he should return it, but decided to keep going. Bob struggled into the little cubicle, locked it, then lowered his trousers and backside in one efficient movement that almost ended in disaster since the toilet seat had been left up. But he caught himself in time using the handrail on the right side, managed to reach behind and drop the seat, then settled down . . . to an expulsion of gas, that was all. Still, it would've been embarrassing enough.

He stayed to coax his bowels, idly opened his briefcase and took out the special package. It felt insubstantial, not something for which one would pay $149.95. Bob opened it gently. The object was encased in plastic bubble wrap and, once freed, looked at first glance like a woggly sea creature not meant to be exposed to the light of day. There were three long dangly straps, like tentacles, and in the middle puffed-out balls of pubic hair – too light; they didn't quite get the colour – and an ancient, irregular . . . *mouth*.

This isn't the right time and place, he thought, and refolded it in its bubble wrap. He then tried returning the bubble wrap to the envelope but it didn't want to go. It had been tight to begin with and now the bubble wrap and purchase had somehow become too big to fit back in the envelope. The more he tried the more the envelope ripped.

There was a sheet of instructions.

Welcome to your new Lighthouse® Portable Vagina®. The PVII® has been design engineered using the finest latex and synthetic hair to bring the closest possible approximation to natural, working female functions. Please follow the installation and maintenance instructions carefully so you can enjoy your new vagina for years to come.

Bob looked at the diagrams. They showed, in stages, two detached hands, large, but with longish, almost female nails, wrapping the straps around the hips and under the pubic area, then fastening them behind with discreet metal hooks. Another pair of detached hands tucked the penis and testicles into a pouch that rested behind the vagina. An insert showed how a man, properly fitted, could pee while sitting down using the latex vagina.

Great care has been taken to ensure that when worn properly all normal female urinary functions can be performed using the PVII®. Please note that, as with a natural vagina, you will have to wipe yourself after peeing. The PVII® should also be soaked daily for thirty minutes in warm water and baking soda and then rinsed with fresh water and lightly towelled dry after use. To ensure a long and full lifespan for your PVII®, do not wear it more than five hours per day.

Bob looked at his watch, peered at the instructions again, and half stood, to get a better sense of how the thing would fit. The pouch for his male organs felt firm and secure, and the straps had just enough elastic to pull it all comfortably, but not so much that his circulation was at risk. The hooks were not so easy. He fiddled, got them the wrong way round several times before it finally felt right. When it was all in order, thin, smooth latex flaps neatly folded over to hide the hooks. The skin colour was remarkable, and Bob liked having lighter pubic hair – it looked younger.

But oh my, to glance down at a beautifully discreet vagina, to feel so tucked-up and transformed! It was wonderful. He looked at himself in the ugly, dully lit mirror of the airplane washroom. Or rather, he looked at the vagina, fine as it was, perfectly passable, and with a trick of the mind didn't focus on the trousers and underpants wrapped at his knees, at the hairy belly button, the ponderous suit, the tops of his shaggy legs.

He sat again. It felt . . . remarkable. A little cramped. He couldn't push his thighs together too harshly. My new toy, he thought, and chuckled to himself in the safety of the little wash-room thirty thousand feet above the ground. Every vibration of the airplane was magnified in the tiny chamber and the smell of disinfectant and other people's waste products should have been nauseating, he thought. But this was a bubble of magic, a pause outside the normal, like sex or a compelling dream.

He had a pee. It was extraordinary. It took the longest time to allow himself to release, then when he did there was a moment of horror as the urine went . . . well, somewhere, but not out his new urethral outlet. It seemed to get caught up in the tubing of the mechanism. But after a pause there it was, gushing out in a series of fine streams, exactly with a feminine peeing noise: *wshhh! wshhh!* He had to be careful to tilt his pelvis downward and direct the stream, and to keep his thighs apart so that he wouldn't make a mess. He dutifully wiped the latex and artificial hair with toilet paper. It didn't feel at all like his own tissue – it was rubbery and dead. But the illusion was striking.

Someone tried the door then and Bob froze. But the door was locked, of course it was, and right away he could hear the sound of the adjacent door opening and then the lock being rattled shut. The shock startled him enough, however, to make him remember that Sienna would wonder why he'd been gone so long. He stood up then and reached around to fiddle with the clasps at the back of the PVII®. Just as he managed to unhook one of them, the pouch holding back his penis and testicles released, and with it a shocking amount of urine fell onto his trousers and underpants. He was too surprised to curse, right away. Then he did curse, and reached down to stop the last drips, but brushed the contraption instead and released a last rain of pee. He almost ripped the hooks, then, trying to get the thing off, and the tension of his last tug sent the creature whirling crazily and spraying a mist around the cubicle, on the mirror and door, his trousers and shoes and jacket.

"Oh, for God's sake!" he said, and flung the vagina into the sink. His trousers were soaked at the crotch almost as badly as if he'd peed himself without any artificial help. He pulled up his shorts and pants but realized it was no good, there was a dark, wet, smelly stain down his front. He took off his shoes then –

the floor of the cubicle was wet and he shivered with revulsion – and stepped out of his trousers and underpants. At that moment the airplane tilted and Bob was thrown against the wall and bonked his knee hard on the handrail. The airplane levelled and Bob picked up his trousers, which now had grit stains on both legs to go with the urine and water marks. He took a deep, calming breath, then said *"Shit!"* seven times in succession.

The seatbelt light began strobing and there was a gentle knock at the door. A flight attendant said, "We will be landing soon. Could you please return to your seat and buckle in when you're ready?"

"Certainly," Bob said, his voice somehow sounding calm and deep and unconcerned. Landing *soon* did not mean *right away*. He looked at his watch. He would have at least fifteen, maybe even twenty minutes, he thought. No need to panic. Though he could feel the tilt of the plane, had to adjust his balance as he washed off the portable vagina and dried it carefully on paper towelling. He reinserted it in the bubble wrap and then spent a bit too long trying to fit it back into the torn envelope. He forced himself to focus and prevail. Finally, when the package was safely back in his briefcase he allowed himself to check his watch again. My God! It didn't seem possible. Nearly six minutes had passed already. He picked up his urine-stained trousers and ran tap water over the crotch, briskly rubbed in liquid hand soap and rinsed. He tried to wet just the worst-stained section but the plane dipped and much of the rest of the trousers got soaked. Little bounces of turbulence followed and Bob fought to keep from ending up in the toilet himself. He barked his shin against the seat, stepped back and tripped over his shoes, then sat hard on his opened briefcase. One of the supports snapped and a clasp bit him on the buttocks like a rat.

"Jesus!" he shrieked.

"Are you all right, sir?" the attendant asked outside the door, her voice superficially calm but infused with concern. Bob didn't answer right away and the attendant pressed, "*Do you want us to come in?*"

"*No! No! I'm fine!*" Bob asserted, trying hard to sound fine. He clambered back to his feet, grasped the door handle firmly in case they tried to open it. Of course they could unlock it from the outside if they wanted, he thought.

"You should return to your seat immediately, sir. The landing light is on."

"Yes. Thank you. I'll be finished in a minute," Bob said.

He picked up his drenched underwear then, stuffed it in the waste bin and wrung out his trousers in the sink. They were almost entirely wet now, besides being stained and badly wrinkled. He looked around for a hot-air hand dryer but there wasn't one, there were just paper towels from the bin. Useless, practically, but he pulled out several, spread them along the legs of his trousers, then rolled the trousers and pressed down to squeeze out the moisture. He could feel the precious minutes sprinting away.

He quickly unrolled his trousers, withdrew the damp paper towelling, stuffed it in the waste bin, then brushed at the many wet flecks of brown residue left by the paper. Five minutes left, perhaps seven. He took the last of the dry paper towels and repeated the process, rolling and squeezing. His ears popped as the plane headed earthward. He swallowed hard three times, furiously unrolled and brushed at his trousers. Awful, sodden disaster. He twisted one last time, harvested a few more grudging drops. Trapped, he thought. There was nothing else he could do. Reluctantly he stepped into the sorry pants, pulled them up. The plane began rattling as if the wings were going to fall off. He zipped and buckled himself, then shoved his wet socked feet into his shoes and tied the laces. His briefcase was ruined. He could force the top down but then the back left corner would spring out.

"Excuse me, sir. Please take your seat *now!*" came the flight attendant's voice outside the door. "Are you okay?"

"Yes! Yes!" he said. He unlocked the door so that the occupancy light would go off. But he took an extra moment to examine himself in the mirror: he was dishevelled, filthy, pale with panic. He splashed water on his face, ran his fingers through his hair, smiled bravely. Then he propped his broken briefcase on the tiny sink and pressed the various corners in a final effort to make things right. He was still fiddling with it when the plane touched down on the runway, bounced once before all wheels smoothed onto the tarmac. Bob was thrown in the air and jammed his hand against the light fixture on the ceiling before he came slamming back down. He felt his back wrench and then when the engine thrusters reversed to slow the plane he caromed off the toilet and into the far wall. "*Hnnn*," he said, like a hockey player slammed against the boards, but too dopey by now to react any more sharply. Despite himself he laughed.

Finally the plane stopped. He could hear people gathering their belongings. He picked up his injured briefcase, clasped it under his arm to keep the contents from spilling out, looked at his reflection one last time.

There was nothing else for it. He pulled open the door, stepped out cautiously.

A young flight attendant was upon him at once. "Are you all right, sir?" she asked. She was tall and slightly heavy, had dark red hair pulled back severely and overly anxious make-up.

Bob held his briefcase in front of his trousers, pressed it closed in the corners with his hands. "It's okay," he muttered, then he brightened, gave her a clear-eyed smile. "I'm fine," he said.

The aisle was jammed with people waiting to deplane. Sienna stood, looked at him with concern. Bob gave her a hurried wave, then began wedging his way back to his seat. He was full of the oddity of the moment, a precarious sense of how the next step might change everything, take him over the precipice he'd been walking so long he'd almost forgotten it was there. He should have been terrified, but he had an oddly detached thought. In my shoes, right now, he thought, a twenty-five year-old would flee in panic; a fifteen year-old would kill himself! But I'm fifty-four.

And there she was, gorgeous, confused, twenty-one, looking at him with such a questioning gaze. "It's just madness," he imagined saying to her. Calmly, soothingly. "It's just a little madness."

"There you are!" she said. "Are you okay?"

"I'm fine." And really he was. "It was awful!" he said. "You wouldn't believe it. I turned on the tap –"

"My God, you're all wet!" she said.

"– and water started spraying everywhere. It was ridiculous. And the door was jammed so I couldn't open it."

She started laughing. She was magnificent. Her teeth looked as if they'd been stolen from a toothpaste commercial and her eyes shone dark as a northern lake in August under a wild moon. Stop it, he thought. Stop being so damned irresistible.

"I've *never* –" he started to say, but he had, of course, and he would again. And he didn't need to finish, either, because the line was moving now, he just had to put one foot in front of the other and keep his face composed.

4

It's hard to know where you are or what you're supposed to do. If only they'd tell you! But they don't. They put things in the food. It's the brown stuff. And the drunken man with the puffy lips takes your food. Reaches right over. Doesn't speak English. Why do they let these people in? They drool and his hands shake like . . . like nothing will ever stay still for ever and ever amen.

This is what they do: they put you in the bad place. When you make a mistake. Over just stupid things. It isn't fair. She could take the stitches out and try again. She had the book. And Mary Hoderstrom would help her because she never makes mistakes.

"I want Julia," Lenore said. The Italian man laughed at her, reached again for her brown thing. She took her fork and poked it at his fingers. All because of one silly. She put the stitches in the wrong way but there were things you did to make it right. She could tell you in a minute. She had to get the book.

"Are you finished, Lenore?" the fat woman asked her. Everyone was brown or Italian or smelly or fat. This girl was all of them at once.

"Yes!" Lenore said. "I'm finished!"

"Then I'll take your plate. How did you like your breakfast?"

Lenore was already up and started to say but then stopped, because if you make a mistake, that's it.

"Did you like your sausages, Lenore?"

If you don't answer then they can't take points off.

"What about your toast?"

Lenore pushed in her chair and the droolly man stabbed her last sausage. They don't have them in Italy. Because of the war.

"And your toast? Did you like your toast?"

"I'm going to call Julia," Lenore said. "This is ridiculous! Mary Hoderstrom could have helped me!" She started walking down the hall. Nobody tried to stop her. It was all in the book anyway.

But where did they put her room? Her books were in her bedroom, on the shelf with the pictures. You go down the hall, past the bathroom and kitchen, past the spare room and the kids' rooms, past the pictures of Julia and Alex, past Capt. Buzbie and Miss Muffin. But they changed it. Vaguely, Lenore could remember Mary's room being something like this. But why would they put her back in Mary's room? It was so long ago. Nobody told her what was going to be on the test.

She tried one door and another and another. Some of them were locked and some weren't. In one of them an old bat said, *"You aren't supposed to play cribbage!"* and dashed her foot against the bed. She was stark naked and her breasts drooped like a witch's. Lenore drew herself up and said, "I can play cribbage with *anyone!*" and left.

"Can I help you, Lenore?" someone asked. The Italian woman who smelled nice. It was a pity, so attractive! But she'd have a hard time finding a husband.

Lenore said, "I'm trying to find the book."

"What book?" the Italian woman asked.

It wasn't a trick question but it was hard and she had to think it through. It was like walking where Daddy used to take them fishing. They'd walk and walk in the dark in the morning and their boots would slip and squelch. Daddy would say, "Shhh! Goddammit!" and suck on his pipe. "The fish can hear you!" You put your line in and wait and wait but you have to be quiet or you won't get that niggly on the line.

"What book are we looking for?" the woman asked again and Lenore said, "Shhh! Goddammit!" but whispered and kind, so she'd know.

⌢

Julia was coming. Very soon. Lenore paced up and down the hall. She had her purses and her coat and was ready to go to Pullman's.

But where was Julia? Pullman's was going to close soon. You have to go at the right time. Lenore paced up and down. It was a smelly hallway. The carpet was green, it was ridiculous, and there were bright, sunny pictures all along. Cows and such. What a frightful expense. To put her up in a hotel like this when she just wanted to go back where she knew the kitchen.

Lenore said, out loud, "Capt. Buzbie would like very much to know where they are." Nobody heard her. She walked to the door clutching her purses and her coat. She pushed to open the doors.

The Italian woman – the pretty one, unmarried, it was such a shame – said, "Where are you going, Lenore?"

Lenore said, "Julia's here! She's right here!" and then some old wreck fell on her side and the Italian woman had to look after her. So Lenore pushed at the heavy doors, pushed and pushed, but they wouldn't open.

Lenore walked back down the hall into her room, right past all the boxes. It didn't look like her place but there was the big picture of Julia and Alex, and there were Capt. Buzbie and Miss Muffin. Not even on the walls! Well, that explained it. Why the door didn't work. Because you had to use the window. You had to bend double, it was so stupid, these modern places! Lenore never in her life thought she'd end up like this. She had to squeeze and kick hard to loosen it up. They were all rusty, in terrible condition, falling apart. She had to hang on. Pull her coat through, her purses, it was all such a mess. But Pullman's was closing!

So she had to do it.

ᔕ

"I'm not sure which bus is which," Lenore said. The young woman at the bus stop had a baby in a stroller and looked up in a friendly way.

"Where do you want to go?" she asked.

"To Julia's house."

"Which street is it on?"

"I tried to get to Pullman's," Lenore said. "But it was closed." Then she pointed. "I think it's down that way. One of those streets. Julia's house."

"Maybe the 108," the young woman said uncertainly.

"She was divorced," Lenore said. "A terrible thing."

"I'm sorry."

"It was after the motorcycle accident, with what's-his-name. You know."

The young woman brushed a fly away from her gurgle baby.

"She was nasty after that," Lenore said.

"Ah," the young woman said.

"She always had a bad temper. Like Trevor. Always getting lost. In the snow."

Lenore looked down the street, first one way, then another. Her wool coat was too hot for the afternoon but it would be too much to carry.

A bus approached and she caught her breath. Lenore stepped up to ask the driver.

"Julia's house?" he said. "Where's that?"

"It's – well, I think it's down that way," Lenore muttered. It didn't matter. She'd sit by the window and when she saw it she'd get off.

"Fare, please!" the driver said, but not at her, he just said it.

So hot! The wind blew in the open window like it was from a furnace register. Nothing looked familiar, the shops, streets, buildings. Switched so cleverly and quickly.

She turned to the bald man beside her with the awful breath. "Do you know if this bus is going to Julia's house?" she asked politely.

He looked at her. "Where do you want to go?"

"Fare, please!" The driver was a stuck parrot.

They were all looking at her but nobody knew. Not the bald man, not the skinny woman with brown eyes, not the black boy with the knapsack. It all went rushing by. She should have been able to remember the name. Damn it!

Of course, her address book. Which purse? The white one. But first she had to take out her raincoat, her little umbrella, the scarves and lipsticks, a whole pile of whichever and other things, coffee mugs, strange notes. The ricer! What was it doing there? She made a heap on her lap but soon things fell on the floor and people leaned over to help.

"Excuse me! Oh, I'm sorry. So silly of me. Sorry!"

Then something caught her eye. On the street. That shop looked familiar. She craned her neck but the flapping bit slipped out of sight. A hardware? Kitchen store? Whatsit? When she stood up to get a better view, everything slid off her lap. In seconds Lenore was on her knees on the bus scooping. The ricer started to roll away but got stopped by its own handle. Too many people bent down to help.

"Please! I'm so sorry! It's so silly!" she said again and again. Everyone had to wait while she decided where went what. If she got it wrong then she'd never find anything again. The brooch from Aunt what's-her-name. With the green stone. Now what was that doing there?

Such a fuss. The driver even pulled over, stood up, helped her put her raincoat back in the white purse. Was that the right one? She was just not sure. So she got off, clutching, walked away. It was so hot. She looked back at where the hardware should have been. The one that Trevor used to disappear in. But it wasn't there any more. They must have moved it. An older man worked there, very gentle. He always knew what you were looking for. You didn't even have to describe it very well. He knew. He could go get it for you. And a good thing too, because that store was packed to the sky with screws and nuts and . . . and odds and such. You couldn't find anything on your own. Which was why the man was there.

And that's why it was so disappointing to look back and find he wasn't there. Where do stores go? Lenore walked across the street, slowly so the cars could stop for her. Stood for a long while looking at the spot where the hardware should have been. It wasn't fair. She longed to go in and have Trevor say what to do. He was a great man for that. He always knew. Not a moment in his life when he didn't know exactly what to do. It wasn't always the *right* thing but he never had any doubts at the time.

"Hello?" Lenore said the word in her funny voice that made everybody laugh. Usually, anyway. But this boy wasn't laughing. He didn't seem to know about anything. It was so noisy, Lenore was trying to get away.

"Are you all right, lady?" he asked. His hands were shoved in his pockets and his hair was sick yellow. He must have a disease, Lenore thought sadly.

"*Hello?*" she said again, even funnier, letting him know it was all right. She was fine, except for the noise.

"How'd you get here?" he asked, stepping between the branches, just a little closer. It was very thick.

"I think I'm finished now," Lenore said, pushing at one. It pushed right back at her.

"Do you need some help?"

"Off the track," Lenore said, pushing at the branch. "I think I'm finished."

"Here," the boy said and stepped over a log, bent low under something thick, squeezed past some others. They shouldn't keep it this way, she thought.

"How did you get here?" the boy asked. There was still a nasty bit between him and Lenore. He looked like he wasn't sure he wanted to go through it. He hesitated as if Lenore might be able to pick her own way out.

"It's a lovely day," Lenore said.

"Where are your shoes?" the boy asked. It *was* uncomfortable. Stickies on her nylons. And mud. What was Julia going to say?

"Did you lose your shoes somewhere?"

"I think I'm finished," Lenore said, sitting down. It seemed the only thing to do. There was a bit of a fallen-down thing right there, but it started to give way as soon as she sat and then she had to get up again. It's all being looked after very badly, she thought.

"Give me your hand," the boy said, reaching through.

"I think I'm finished."

"We have to go back this way to get to the path," the boy said. "Just give me your hand."

Lenore reached out to him and stepped halfway over and straight into the stickies. Everything was so badly managed. She clutched at her purses with her free hand but the blue one swung and got caught again and again. The boy started to break the branches with his hands. Carefully, as if they had all the time in the world.

"Did you get lost?" he asked.

"You never know," she said, half-laughing. The hooks tore at her coat and tried to keep her purses. It had been a long time since she'd felt so cool on her toes.

"I saw some shoes by the river," the boy said, pulling her. Gently. Almost like what's-his-name. "Are those your shoes?" he asked.

It was no good. She wouldn't make it this way. Honestly, anybody could see that. Lenore let go of his hand and dropped to her knees. Had to be careful to keep her coat out of the way and hang on to her purses, which dragged on the ground. Hooks in her hair. If you just keep your head down. She crawled through, tugging, keeping herself together.

"Don't tell Julia," she said finally, straightening up, wiping at the mud on her knees. The trail was right there after all. She wasn't so far off. It was just so noisy.

"I won't," he said, walking beside her. Gentle, gentle. Something about him reminded her of someone. A real gentleman.

"You can call me Miss Muffin," she said then and laughed, her first real laugh in a long time. Of course he didn't understand and it was so hard to explain. Though the water was cold, it felt nice to wash her feet for a bit and listen to the river slipping past the stones.

"Can I take you somewhere?" he asked and Lenore bit her lip. She wanted to keep hold of the nice part. It never lasted these days, always went away. "Is there someone to call?" he asked.

"Sometimes there is," she said, hugging her knees, trying, trying to keep hold.

5 ⌒

One problem was colour. The home-decoration book Julia
had borrowed from the library was full of Grecian blues and
greens that looked fabulous in glossy print, but would they
work in this kitchen? She gazed around forlornly. There was an
open feeling – she liked having the landing to the basement
right there, by the back door, and no divider shutting off the
stairs going to the second floor – but everything was cramped.
The floor looked terrible: ugly chipped beige linoleum tiles
glued, sloppily, over buckled green linoleum tiles, so there were
waves and holes. And the walls were a very dull, stained white,
the minuscule counter a tacky fake chopping-board brown, the
sagging cupboards false oak and falling apart.

She couldn't manage a kitchen renovation. Julia knew this in
her marrow. Yet rationally, logically, she felt she should have
been able to get something else done in a given day besides
looking after Matthew and dealing with her mother. She had a
master's degree, had held a research job, had submitted articles
to some of the finest publications.

Matthew pulled open the bottom drawer of the oven,
slammed the pots and pans, sent the lids rolling down the hall,

one of his favourite games. Julia flipped the pages of the library book. Gorgeous summer hues, rustic, artfully primitive. A turquoise chair, shimmering violet door, a window trim of ancient blue opening onto a summer meadow with a bottle of white wine in the foreground, some grapes and bread. Why not go to Greece in the spring break? Bob would love it. Bathe their bodies in olive oil and salt air. They hadn't been anywhere since France. Since Matthew.

Everything was either Before or Since Matthew. Before Matthew was sleep, regular, ordinary, plentiful as water before the drought. It was so much sleep they took it for granted. It was staying up till two in the morning with red wine and *Hamlet*, Julia and Bob alternating parts. It was making love everywhere from this tiny kitchen counter (Julia sitting pretty, wrapping her legs around Bob's shaggy torso) to the attic among Bob's dissertation drafts and the bags of clothes that they'd pull out, wrapping one another in silks and old ties. Before Matthew was dining in dimly lit restaurants on rich little combinations of feta cheese and black olives, on tandoori chicken and satay and sushi with black bean sauce. It was talking about inconsequentials, about George Eliot and Franz Kafka and Bob's obsession, Poe, about how a poem can change the balance of your life, one certain slide of words delivered at a particular time with the suddenness of love or the weight of received truth when there was no such thing any more for those too old for it, how odd and humbling and electrifying to read something and have it stiffen you or melt the cold feeling in your centre.

Before Matthew was Sunday mornings on the sofa with Bob rubbing her feet, books and magazines and newspapers spread all over the floor. It was going from one to the other with something rich on the stereo, an old, bluesy Ella Fitzgerald album found in vinyl at Ackerman's second-hand downtown, with

Mozart and Brahms and Gershwin and Patsy Cline in the wings. It was long, lingering *New Yorker* articles on obscure cartoonists who died tragically, on forensic geology and charting fashion trends by obsessively reviewing store-security videotapes.

Since Matthew was the odd smell of stale milk on her breasts. It was dribbling from her front in the middle of the afternoon when he'd slept too long. It was staring down at him on the changing table through blurry, sleep-deprived eyes while he wiggled, gurgled, played with her hair, then fountained his pee straight into her downturned face as soon as she'd loosened his pins. It was phoning the diaper service in a panic when their delivery was an hour and a half late and she had no extras on hand. It was rubbing him with talcum powder and playing with his toes in the bathtub, then hauling him out after a sudden and hilarious shit. It was reading him "Jack and the Beanstalk" four hundred and seventeen thousand times, morning, noon, and night, bugging her eyes out whenever she said, "Fresh boys on toast!" just like the giant.

Since Matthew was making love mechanically, after the news and before collapse, once every few weeks if she could remember. It was feeling her body go cold as a milkbag. It was only wanting to wear the same tired sweatsuit, not wanting anyone but Matthew to touch her breasts, to make any physical demands. It was letting the hair grow on her legs and underarms, as if in permanent winter, and getting it cut on top that once quite short. It was lying on the couch with Matthew asleep, drooling on her shoulder, and floating on a sticky, warm, milky current of love that made her want to memorize every dimple of his fat elbows, caress him endlessly, fall into his eyes, closed or otherwise, they were utterly endearing either way. It was going on endlessly to bored friends about trivialities, the feel of his hair, a little wool sweater for sale at the second-hand store, hand-knit by someone's grandmother, with elephants and monkeys and teddy-bear buttons and what a little mister he looked like when he wore it. It was endless sodden wool in her brain so that she could stare for hours at a book of colours and not be able to make a decision one way or the other. To not *care*, really, except on a rudimentary level wanting to stop the physical nausea brought on by the ugliness and disrepair of the kitchen.

"Matthew!" she said, because he had somehow climbed on top of the end table in the living room and was poised to hurl a steel pot-lid at the antique cabinet of crystal figurines moved from her mother's house. "*Matthew, get down!*" She moved towards him. The floor man was going to come at any moment and she'd accomplished nothing, had been unable to don a decent set of clothes, had failed to run a brush through her hair, which was growing out again now, needed attention she was unprepared to give it.

"*Get down now!*" she said to Matthew, "*or there's no Dormy!*"

"*Yes*, Dormy!" Matthew said. He had wonderful balance and a strong arm and he wanted everything exactly *when* he wanted it.

The lid left his hand, but Julia caught his arm before the follow-through, so the projectile merely dinked off the cabinet door then fell to the floor. Matthew laughed as he twisted.

"*Bad!*" Julia said and shook him once before she regained control of herself. "Oh, Matthew!" she said, trembling with anger even as she hugged him. "Just for once, *please* obey me!"

Matthew patted her back gently. He really could be a gentle boy. He said, "There, there," and put his hand inside her sweatshirt.

"Not now," she said. The kitchen man was coming any minute.

"Yes now!" Matthew said. Fiddling with her bra, trying to pull her loose. "Nubbies now!" he said and tweaked her left nipple with his soft little fingers. He pulled up her sweatshirt and tried to bury his face in her front.

"All right. Quickly!" she said and hoisted him over to the sofa, cradled him. He was so heavy! She would hurt her back sometime if she continued to lift him like this.

The knock on the door came only a few minutes later. Julia's first instinct was to sink down into the sofa, to try to hide. Maybe he'll go away, she thought. Matthew usually hated being interrupted in his feeding. She thought, I could phone someone else. I'm not ready anyway. I look like shit and haven't even chosen my colour.

The knock came again. Julia could see him on the porch through the side window. Then he looked and saw her and still something in her mind said, Maybe he'll just go away.

But he wasn't going to go away. Julia stood up and swiftly detached Matthew. There was no storm. He was asleep. She held up a single finger for the floor man through the window. "Just a minute!" she mouthed, and carried Matthew upstairs, laid him in his little bed. He was soft oblivion, like Bob after an orgasm, the same mouth-open, happily stupefied slumber.

While she was upstairs she changed into a pair of dark pants that were sharp-looking but comfortable – a combination rare enough to find since her pregnancy – put on a nice blue shirt and sweater, retouched her lips, fixed her hair quickly. Then she hurried down to open the front door. "Donny, is it? I'm *so* sorry to keep you waiting," she said. "Won't you come in? I'm Julia Sterling. Professor Ruddick highly recommended your work."

He was not large but he had the strong, blunt hands of a workman. His face had strange marks on it, small welts and pimples, his nose twisted. His hair was wiry and sparse and his eyebrows joined in the middle of his forehead. He looks like a toad, Julia thought. A kindly, gentle sort of toad.

She said, "Don't bother about your boots," which were mud-spattered, and he immediately kicked them off. His right big toe was sticking out of his black sock, which was inside out.

"No, really, the house is a mess," she said.

"It's a beautiful house," he replied. "Just needs some attention."

"Wait till you see the kitchen."

They walked through to the back. He didn't seem to know what to do with his hands, whether to clasp them in front or behind or shove them in his pockets. But when they got to the kitchen he squatted expertly and inspected the sorry tiles. He looked like an old-time woodsman reading tracks in the mud or a farmer touching the soil.

She explained what she wanted, as far as she knew, about pulling up the tiles to the pine floor below, about wanting it repaired and sanded and then painted and varnished. She even got as far as the Mediterranean colours, but the way he was looking at her was unsettling and she found her words faltering.

"It's Carmichael, isn't it?" he said finally, straightening up, only slightly taller than Julia's five and a half feet. "Julia Carmichael."

"Yes. That was my maiden name," she said.

"From Brookfield."

"High school. Yes," she said. "Did you go there?"

He swallowed before answering and his face suddenly went red. "Donald Clatch," he said, moving his head up and down as if coaxing her. "Donny."

"I'm sorry. You *did* go there?" she said.

"I sat behind you in homeroom. Every year."

"*Ah*," she said, her face brightening instinctively, but she couldn't remember him at all.

"Mr. Wigs. He wore that brown suit every day, the same one, with either the brown tie or the green. Clatch. I was right behind Carmichael. Every day from 9:00 a.m. to 9:10."

"Oh yes, of course," she said, nodding now, but still uncertain.

"You don't remember me," he said.

"Yes, I do. Of course. Hi!" she said, and thrust out her hand again. "I was just – well, I was never a morning person," she said. "Homeroom was a blur. *Mr. Wigs.* Yes, of course. I wonder whatever happened to Mr. Wigs?"

"He died of testicular cancer two years ago," Donny said. "I kind of kept up with the family. I used to hang out with Bill until he went out west to work on the rigs. His son Bill."

"Oh. Yes."

"He didn't go to Brookfield, he went to Hillcrest. He didn't want to be in the same school where his dad taught. But I knew him through hockey. We played together from squirts to midgets."

"Hmmmm," said Julia.

"I remember you," Donny said, his face very red now, eyes bright. "There was a scent you used to wear. I'd get to homeroom early and wait for you to sit down. It was . . . I don't know what it was. But I just couldn't wait. It was like, the start of my day."

Now Julia was flushed.

"I smelled a touch of it just now when I walked in. I thought, shit, what's that? Is that ever familiar! And then, you know, when I saw you. *Julia Carmichael.* You are still –"

He didn't finish the thought. Julia didn't want him to finish it.

"So you do – you do floors, is that it?" she said.

"I do everything," he said, proudly. "I do walls, and bathrooms, I do landscaping and painting. I've done roofing, it's not my favourite. Basements! I'm great on basements." He paused. "You knew that Billy Marcello was killed?"

"Uh," Julia said. "Was he?" She had a vague idea who Billy Marcello was. Perhaps.

"In prison," Donny said. "He'd murdered a man seven years ago. It was a bar in Hull, he was drunk, it was predictable. And then in prison he got stabbed himself. I know his sister Ramone. She's doing great now, she works for a lawyer, has four kids, and has this business on the side selling cosmetics. She really does well. She could come by, you know, if you like buying things out of catalogues. I'm sorry. I *never* got to talk to you in high school, I was too shy. So I guess it's just pouring out! So what does your husband do?"

"That's sweet, Donny," Julia said softly. She thought maybe now she remembered him. He *had* tried to ask her out once. At least that's what she thought he was trying to do. He'd ended up muttering something in the general direction of the floor until the bell rang for class change, at which point he'd fled. "He's a university professor," she said. "In English literature. That's where I met him."

"God," he said, staring at her.

"Anyway," she said, "I'm sorry I'm going to have to hurry us along but I need to see my mother very shortly. So what I want, really, is to get rid of this floor . . ."

"Julia Carmichael," Donny said, shaking his head and whistling softly.

6 ↰

There's a trick to getting through most of life's absurdities, self-imposed or not: stay still, keep breathing, and eventually terrible moments turn into less extraordinary ones, then are in the past. Calmly, without panic, Bob retrieved his luggage and, in the safety of an airport washroom that did not lurch and buck at crucial moments, changed into new underwear and clean, dry trousers and socks.

Sienna was waiting for him outside the washroom. She stood tall and straight and bright as a beacon, had strong shoulders and luminous skin. "That's better!" he said as he approached her, limping slightly from his wounds, pulling his luggage behind him, clutching closed his broken briefcase.

"You should complain," she said.

"Absolutely!" he exclaimed. "That kind of mechanical failure is unconscionable! I'm going to send them my dry-cleaning bill and an invoice for, well, what can we call it? Psychological trauma! What if I'd had a weak heart? Or some kind of serious medical condition? Trapped in the washroom with water blasting out at me. Did you know there are no seatbelts in the washrooms? What are you supposed to do –?"

And on and on, all the way to the cab. New York was sunny and cool and settling into October with steel-grey clouds massing on the horizon, ominous as traffic build-up before rush hour. Feeling better now, Bob watched Sienna across from him in the taxi sitting wide-eyed and silent, taking in the sky-scrapers, the dirty ones and the gleaming, the rivers of cars, buses, taxis (it looks like a reverse volcano, Bob thought, the lava flowing up into the hulking crater), the occasional, surprising tree, leaves thinning, pale yellow or washed-out red at best, not the vivid colours of home, but somehow in New York any colours at all seemed unusual.

"Have you been here before?" Bob asked.

"I was born here," she said. "But we left when I was five, so I don't remember much."

"Ah."

"My father was an illegal immigrant. He came from Shanghai on a boat, in secret, and worked three restaurant jobs for seven years to pay off his debt. He was a mechanical engineer and had taught himself English from BBC broadcasts during the Cultural Revolution when he was sent to the countryside. He always wanted to go to England."

She nodded slightly as she talked and her jaw tightened so that Bob could imagine her father had impressed upon her what it meant to escape Mao's China, to take on menial labour in a strange land.

"And your mother?" he asked. "You told me once she was Irish, I think."

"Yes. She was a nanny. She would come to one of my dad's restaurants on her day off and spend hours at the window writing home."

"She came to see your dad where he worked?"

"Well, he started working there and then after a while he owned it. I'm not sure how that happened. But it happened more than once. He ended up with all three restaurants by the time he was ready to leave. My mom was supposed to marry a rugby player back home, but Dad wooed her with won ton soup and ginseng tea. She maintains that I was conceived after she had eight bowls in one afternoon. Supposedly it had nothing to do with my father – he was just the guy standing by at the right time to marry her."

"Are they . . . still together?"

"Oh God," she said. "Like two barnacles on a boat."

They were immersed in the streets of Manhattan by then. An immense billboard showed a thin, blonde, washed-out-looking model in the act of pulling down her panties for reasons unexplained but apparently having something to do with a particular brand of soap. Bob let the unfamiliar streets and traffic pass through his consciousness like a series of waves that he would not try to grasp or control in any way. Their taxi driver, Ravjinder Singh, whose blurry face stared at them from the identification card on the sun visor, and whose immense blue-turbaned head seemed to take up most of the front of the car, would bring them safely to the Central Heights Hotel.

"How about you?" Sienna asked. "How about your . . . wife?"

Although he wore a wedding ring, Bob had never mentioned Julia. Not in any of the notes he had exchanged with Sienna, starting in early September when she had come to see him about his course and building when she submitted her project outline, then her poems; not a word about Julia during their quick lunches at the cafeteria, sometimes with other students and faculty, lately not; nothing about her or Matthew during their several long walks in the park at the edge of campus in the late afternoon. It wasn't, as far as Bob was concerned, a deliberate omission. Julia simply wasn't part of that universe – if that was the word – the *universe* that Sienna brought with her. It was one of poetry and light, of energy and youth and dreams and potential, the *possible*, as Bob thought of it, nothing ground down or stuck in the mundane mould of reality. Nothing of bills and groceries and weekends spent traipsing from home store to home store looking at tiles and glazes, cupboards and counters, doorknobs, sinks, pantries, faucets, on and on ad nauseam to repair the allegedly disgraceful kitchen. Nothing of laundry and garbage, no recycling, no lawn to tend, no muffler that sprang a hole one turn of the dial past the 10,000-kilometre warranty. There was no middle-aged spread, no decay, no brain cells falling out overnight.

And no touch. It was pure that way. They walked and they talked of Heidegger, Proust, of Orwell in Spain and Hemingway in Africa, of Jane Austen calculating the winds of courtship, of Melville and Hawthorne and Poe. Such talk. Pure and full of energy and life, of history and literature. There was no touch, no ignoble sweating in back rooms, no furtive kisses instantly regretted, no dresses stained with executive semen.

"Bob?" Sienna said.

"Ah," Bob said. "You asked about my wife. She is a very . . . capable woman. Quite a good . . . mother and, in her day, an . . . able scholar."

"You have children?"

"One. Yes. A boy."

She asked his name and he told her, felt quite uncomfortable. Home was home, a different sphere, distinct, important in its way, vital. But it would be wrong to have the two intersect. They were like the positive and negative worlds of some science-fiction novel, simultaneous and opposite, not meant to know of one another. Explosions would result and it was dangerous to talk of these things, to risk disaster; the real world was tiresome and inflexible and unable to cope with ambiguities the way one could safely within one's personal privacy.

Bob had no problem keeping the two worlds separate in his own mind. But he *was* having trouble keeping Sienna in her small space. She was overwhelming that way; by far the most beautiful, original, and approachable of the undergraduates he'd taught in the last several years.

Since Julia, in fact.

"My wife and I," Bob said, "have been married seven years now. It's a very – well, it's a conventional union," he said.

"Conventional?"

"We're doing the things we *ought* to be doing," he said, with something of a sigh. "And for now, that's how it feels."

"Conventional."

"Yes."

Poe betrayed Virginia too, Bob thought. As soon as she was dead he downplayed any love he'd felt for her. It was so easy. Bob wanted Sienna too badly. He wanted to stay in the bubble of her universe. He didn't want it to hold him but he wanted to stay and so the words had come out in a tone of voice that gave the impression all was not well with his marriage, not as it could or should have been. He hated himself for doing it but didn't stop himself either, then didn't correct the impression afterwards.

I'm a slumper, he thought, and slumped in his seat, in self-acceptance and resignation.

But then at the Central Heights Hotel, a tall, bright, impressive building with an atrium in the lobby and glass stretching to the heavens, Bob felt much less of a slumper. Of course, they had booked separate rooms, on separate floors even. His was quite small, a generic North American hotel room but on a corner, with windows looking out on traffic in two directions. There was a miniature plastic bottle of Scotch in the courtesy bar that he drank down immediately to help stop the slumping. Then he carefully took his special package – his ludicrous Internet purchase – wrapped it in a plastic bag and stuffed it in the wastebasket along with the female clothing he'd brought with him.

Enough slumping, he thought.

The courtesy bar contained vodka as well as the now-empty Scotch. It would be stupid to mix the two, Bob knew. Especially in the middle of the day.

Still, the Scotch had gone down very smoothly. They were such small bottles. And it was going to be a heavy afternoon.

ᔕ

"So, briefly, it would be useful to recapitulate, to rough out the broad outlines of Poe's situation in that doleful, contradictory January of 1849," Bob said. He cleared his throat, shifted his weight, took a careful gulp of water from the glass provided and leaned close to the microphone. His notes lay open on the lectern in front of him, typed up several years before by the departmental secretary, Helen. He had delivered this lecture at several forums over the years. Occasionally he looked down at the notes and noticed something he'd quite forgotten, but for the most part he simply spoke from memory. This was an accomplished group: the feminist Solinger was there and the critic McMurphy, the French scholar Jean-Yves Rémy, who worshipped Baudelaire as well as Poe, Christopher Hindle from Yale and Dorothy Turman from Harvard and Columbia's Professor Windower, the conference organizer. Hindle was looking a little dotty. His head bobbed badly and his mouth yawned, as if the old man had lost control of it. A new professor from Oxford was there, Saddle-something, a double-barrelled name. And many others he didn't know, the younger generation of Poe enthusiasts.

Sienna sat in the front row. She had changed at the hotel into a micro-skirt and ankle boots, and was not always managing to keep her long legs together. Sometimes she shifted in her seat and revealed . . . well, a darkness that Bob refused to stare at but which occupied his thoughts nonetheless, fuzzy as she was beyond the range of his reading glasses.

Something wasn't quite right. He couldn't put his finger on it, but perhaps it had to do with his traumas at the customs booth and in the airplane. The universe felt tilted in a way, nothing exactly where it should have been. His breathing was a little ragged; he was more nervous than usual delivering his lecture; he had a feeling that something dramatic was going to happen but he didn't know what.

"Poe's wife and young cousin," he said, "Virginia – *Sissy* – dies of consumption in early 1847. They had been living in abject poverty with Sissy's mother, Muddy, in the little cottage at Fordham. Muddy was a frequent visitor to publishing houses begging for money for the family. After Virginia's death, Poe, who has just turned thirty-eight, is lost for a time, then seems to shift gears and quixotically starts to court three different women more or less simultaneously: Jane Locke, Nancy Richmond, and Sarah Helen Whitman, then later a fourth, his old flame Elmira Royster. He is clutching at straws, hoping a good marriage can provide him the financial stability that has eluded him his entire life. And yet, being Poe, nothing is simple and he seems to throw himself in all directions at once, to create the conditions in which, as Silverman has pointed out, failure is the only possible outcome. Jane Locke writes to him expressing sympathy for Virginia's death. They correspond, feel one another out. Poe thinks she's a widow but can't be sure. He goes to visit her in Lowell, Massachusetts, and to his horror finds her matronly and middle-aged, married to an attorney, mother of five, a doggerel-writing parlour poet desperately fantasizing about him. So he flees to their friends the Richmonds and here he does fall in love with Mrs. Nancy Richmond, also married but twenty-eight, beautiful, tall, simple, a Christian, charitable woman, mother of a three-year-old girl. Her husband, a paper manufacturer, does not seem to mind having this vagabond poet of uncertain reputation sit by the fire night after night holding hands with his wife. She becomes Poe's 'Annie,' his ethereal creature."

Bob took another sip of water. Hindle was completely asleep, his eyelids fluttering now and again from some dream. It was a bad sign, but the rest were with him. He had, usually, a natural ease in telling a story. His voice was deep and resonant and he loved his material. Sienna was hanging on every word, rocking slightly with the rhythm of his delivery.

"If Jane Locke was a mistake, then, and Nancy Richmond unattainable, Sarah Helen Whitman – *Helen* – remained Poe's best chance at a favourable union, one with an intellectual peer, a poet and critic in her own right, a bona fide widow six years his senior but handsome, with financial security enough for the two of them. She lived in Providence and they carried out a careful, oblique correspondence. Helen had survived a difficult marriage already, was in poor health, and did not necessarily feel up to any sort of new romantic attachment. She was also part of the Transcendentalist movement, of whose members, like Emerson, Thoreau, and especially Longfellow, Poe was so contemptuous. Her friends were his enemies, and no one seemed to have accumulated enemies quite like Poe. But, I am digressing."

He was indeed falling off track. Sienna's legs were now tightly wound together, and as she rocked, so slightly, she seemed to be, discreetly, massaging her right nipple. Every so often she closed her eyes for longer than necessary and ran her tongue lightly over her bottom lip.

"The letter I have come to talk about – *ghnihhr*," Bob said, and cleared his throat, then took time to sip more water and stare blankly at his notes. Sienna stopped rocking. Perhaps her fingers were just lightly resting on her bosom. It was hard to tell through the haze. "The letter I have come to talk about, of course, is the Whitman letter dated January 2, 1849, long believed to be lost, which I, through good fortune, managed to find –" Bob almost said twelve years ago – "in a box of misfiled Rufus Griswold papers in the archives of the Boston Public Library. Griswold, of course, was Poe's literary executor and, as has been amply shown, a rival and sometime enemy. You will recall –"

At that moment Bob could not recall anything much because Sienna separated then recrossed her legs, leaned forward a little and squeezed her leg muscles together, then released them and closed her eyes. Her breathing, though nearly silent, became deeper.

"You will recall," Bob said, trying to concentrate, "Poe's first meeting with Helen at her house in Providence. Both Poe and Helen were nervous. Her hand trembled when he grasped it; her voice faltered. She had a domineering mother who strongly objected to Poe's advances. And what mother wouldn't? He was notorious by then for his drunkenness, his temper and vindictiveness, his constant lack of money. And yet they talked, Poe and Helen, of past grievances and disappointments, of writers and poets, literature and learning. Then on a long walk in the Swan Point cemetery he declared his love – 'now – for the first and only time –' possibly kissed her, and proposed marriage, after having known her in person for only two days."

There was a titter in the audience, a nodding of heads from the more experienced scholars. This was an old story, Poe drowning and desperate. But for the first time while telling it, Bob himself felt something of the same throbbing incoherence. The words were leaving his mouth but he didn't seem sure, beforehand, what he was going to say. And then for periods of time he wasn't sure what he *was* saying. Sienna was looking at him, her eyes were demanding something of him, he didn't know what. She seemed to be beaming a message of longing and need and invitation. Bob looked everywhere else in the room, at the cinder-block walls painted grey, at the rows of auditorium seats, the screen to the side – What about my slides? he thought. He had brought slides of the Whitman letter.

But he wasn't talking about the Whitman letter. Try as he might to approach the subject, the wind of his rhetoric pulled him further off topic. He was telling the story of Poe and Helen's conditional engagement, how Helen's mother had forced him to sign away any right to property or money from the marriage, how Poe had agreed never to taste wine or spirits again, then broke that condition almost immediately. How Poe continued to court Annie even while swearing his love for Helen, how he seemed to desperately want out of the marriage even while doing his damnedest to secure it for himself. Then Bob got caught on a long and convoluted tangent regarding Poe's later rantings about the cosmological world, his Eureka lectures on the origins and fate of the universe. The audience shifted nervously. People in the back started consulting their programs and sliding away.

"At any rate," Bob said, checking his watch. What time was he supposed to finish? He looked up at the auditorium clock and then down at his watch again and failed to register the time. He was panicking. He felt dizzy. Not enough to fall over, but when he looked at his notes, just for a moment, he couldn't make out the words. He knew the words were there, could see them, but it was as if he'd entered a dream in which everyone was speaking a foreign language close to English but not quite right. None of the connections were making sense.

"Maybe you could show us your slides, Bob," Professor Windower said. The conference organizer was thin and ramrod straight, white-haired, his face red from some condition. Alcoholism? Not likely; perhaps just a too-earnest approach to life.

Bob said, "Yes, of course. How much time have I got?" and checked his watch again. Once more, the oddest feeling, seeing the numbers and the hands but not being able to collect it all into meaning.

"If you could wrap it up in a few minutes," Professor Windower said, not unkindly. His hands were open, as if apologizing that so little time could be afforded such an important lecture.

Bob stepped over to the machine. He had given the technician his carousel of slides. But where was the operator now?

"Just click the first slide," Professor Windower said. Bob looked at the buttons. In his present state he could barely manage to get his shaking hand to try any of the buttons. But he stabbed at one blindly. The first slide appeared – upside down. There was laughter, and Bob shook his head briskly as if to clear the cobwebs. Sienna appeared at his side. She touched his shoulder and said, "I'll help. You're doing fine."

So Bob backed off. In an instant Sienna had the slide right way round. Page one of the Whitman letter. The closely packed words, the careful, nervous hand. "*My Dearest Edgar. I am writing you now to confirm what I am sure you must know in your heart of hearts, that there can be no union between us . . .*"

"If you could just sum up, perhaps," Professor Windower said, gently, looking at his watch again. Bob took a deep breath. Such a strange disorientation. He thought, Have I had a stroke? A mild heart attack? But here he was, still standing. Many eyes remained on him. He'd been safely on the rails one moment, badly off them the next. He skipped ahead in his notes to the final page and read, word for word, what was there in the last paragraph, relieved that the words at least were filtering into his brain and out of his mouth.

A strange case of nerves, he thought.

And also this: she unbalances me.

There was perfunctory applause at the end. Bob hurried to gather his notes, wanted to leave quickly. His brain felt, suddenly, crystal clear and achingly sensitive, aware of every nuance of this unfolding failure. He heard Hindle, awake and climbing the stairs, say, "Bloody unfocused!" to a colleague, loud enough so that everyone could hear.

"That's too bad. You ran out of time," Sienna said. "I thought you were doing very well." Saddle-something, the young Oxford guy, was right beside her. He had a goatee and bushy eyebrows and in the English academic tradition looked like he'd bought his tweed jacket at a garage sale in the rain. He was obviously smitten with Sienna.

"Fascinating about the letter," Saddle-something said. "Would you have your lecture notes, by any chance? Maybe you could e-mail me?" He held out his card. Bob took it hesitantly.

"I published my findings, and the letter in its entirety, in *American Literature*," Bob said, trying not to sound stiff and off-balance.

"Excellent! Perhaps you could send me the reference."

"*Ewan Suddle-Smythe*," the card read. "*D.Phil., English Literature, Oxford University.*"

"Volume 63, number 3," Bob said. "September 1991."

"Very good!" Suddle-Smythe said. "Yes, excellent!" He had longish hair and his eyes were too big and watery and green, they shed too much light and seemed excessively full of laughter. "Would you care to come for a libation of sorts?" he asked, not of Bob but of Sienna, in a voice only slightly lowered.

"Well," she said uncertainly. "You'll come with us? Bob?"

"Yes, of course!" Suddle-Smythe said then, too hospitably, too effusively. "There must be a British pub somewhere in New York. You'll come?"

"No," Bob said, falling on his sword. "You two go ahead."

They had to hurry out of the hall because the next speaker, a professor from the University of Chicago, was ready to start. She was to speak on "Poe and the Worship of Death" and looked white-faced and ghoulish, as if she'd spent weeks buried alive in a tomb as part of her research. Already more people were streaming in than had attended Bob's muddled effort.

Sienna was up ahead, nearly out the door, when she looked around at him. Sorry, her look said, and he forgave her – of course he forgave her, as age must give way to youth. A dark beer would go nicely now, he thought. Warm, heavy beer in large quantities, but not with a dazzling young woman, not in competition with some English charmer. Did she notice Suddle-Smythe's wedding band? Bob felt somewhat fatherly in his concern.

Outside the auditorium he remembered his slides and went back for them. The University of Chicago ghoul had already set them aside as she loaded her own. Bob collected his apologetically. Professor Windower caught him on the stairs near the exit and shook his hand too warmly, a gesture of pity and concern rather than appreciation. "Perhaps something fuller on the Eureka lectures next time, Bob? Is that what you're working on?"

Bob wasn't, but he nodded and gave Windower the impression that he was, in fact, putting together a full treatment of Poe's warped and misguided view of the cosmos, and that was why his lecture on the Whitman letter had run off course. It was one of the last things Poe worked on, when he was falling in and out of coherence and suffering a grandiose delusion regarding his ability to piece together universal laws based not on observation and experiment but on intuition and instinct. It might be an interesting project. But then again, it might be best left to the historical dustbin.

"Maybe we could post your notes on the conference Web site?" Windower suggested, in consolation, it seemed, for Bob having fumbled his lecture.

"Yes," Bob agreed. "I'll just have to do them up . . . properly."

"Oh, of course!" Windower said. "You can e-mail me later. Isn't this a *fantastic* era we're living in?"

"Fantastic," Bob said, taking his leave, smiling bravely but feeling old and left out, shabby and entirely unfantastic.

ഗ

There was a message from Julia on the telephone in his hotel room.

"Hi, Bob," she said. "Listen, I don't know when you'll get this. And I'm not even sure if there's anything you can do. But

I needed to talk to you. Mom has disappeared. If you can believe it. Those idiots at Fallowfields let her out somehow. I had to get there myself before they realized she was gone. I'm just . . . *beside myself.* I don't know . . . I'm sorry to call. There's nothing you can do. I'm sorry to worry you. Just – call if you can. Bye."

There was a second message. Julia again: "I'm sorry. I just – I hope the lecture went well. I *wish* you were here. Bye."

Bob phoned immediately but got himself on the answering machine. He wasn't sure what to say. "It's me, I'm at the hotel," he said. "You can call me, I won't go out. I'm sorry I'm not there. Do you want me to come home?"

He put the phone down and sat on the bed.

He turned on the television and flicked through the channels. He was feeling thick-headed, defeated. It was late afternoon and three outlandish transvestites were telling a talk-show host why they had chosen to live as women. "I was trapped!" one of them said, a black she-male in a blonde wig, dressed, like the others, as a hooker in skimpy, gaudy clothing ratcheted tight, folds of flesh bulging wherever it was unrestrained. "I was a man trapped in a woman's body!"

Bob turned it off. Another tiny bottle of Scotch had appeared in the courtesy cabinet of the hotel room. He poured it into a glass and drank it down as slowly as he could.

The phone failed to ring.

It was strange to be scrambled like this. He thought again of the feeling in front of everyone of being suddenly lost in fog, especially of looking at his watch and at the auditorium clock and then back at his watch, and not having it register. Chilling, how quickly it can all fall apart.

Bob ordered room service. Filet mignon with mushroom

sauce, bleeding rare, with green beans and baby roasted potatoes and a proper red wine, a French Merlot that would not
leave a headache. He cleaned his plate, drank the better part of
the bottle, and still the phone didn't ring. He called Julia again
but got the machine once more. He said, "My lecture was fine.
I ran out of time, but I think it went over –" and he hesitated.
He was going to say he thought it went over well, but really, it
hadn't, and while it wasn't a disaster – well, not an unqualified
disaster, as academic lectures go. Some of the droners he'd
attended over the years . . .

The thought got lost and he hung up. He waited, and still
the phone didn't ring. It wasn't that he was concerned about his
mother-in-law. She'd always been a bit batty, in Trevor's
shadow. Trevor was a flinty old bastard. He could argue about
anything, about whether it was raining right now where you
stood. Bob never got along well with him, except when they
were drinking; then things were bearable. Otherwise, Bob was
the married older professor who'd abandoned his wife and
taken up with their precious daughter. They couldn't see
beyond that: it was pure scandal for them, dirty and shameful.

Alcohol helped.

But Lenore was always nervous and flighty. This illness was
unfathomable, better not thought of too deeply. The abyss that
might be awaiting any of us. Still, Bob wasn't worried about
Lenore. Whatever the present crisis – and they came up at least
three times a week with Lenore these days – it would pass. But
he felt deeply the need to talk to Julia, to reconnect with
someone from home. He was deracinated here in this soulless
hotel room eighteen floors above an outrageous city. This was
the problem, he decided. He was too far from Julia, from the
department, the things he knew and loved. Sienna Chu was

poisoning his thoughts. Bewitching him. It wasn't his fault. He was a terrible slumper. Julia kept him straight but she wasn't there. She was ages and miles away.

And the phone didn't ring.

7

Julia was running now, clutching Matthew, dodging pedestrians, lowering her shoulder to force her way through the idiot wind that blasted free on every street corner she passed. She had to get to Pullman's before closing. It was a traditional store, didn't stay open past 5:00 on a Friday night. A neighbourhood store, with a tiny parking lot so full Julia had had to drive the van around the back streets, vainly searching for parking, drifting farther and farther away. That's why she was running now, to get there in time. It felt good, somehow, to punish herself with intense physical effort for having left her mother in such shoddy care. They'd lost her within a day. How was that possible?

There wasn't enough air, because of the wind, probably. Her lungs felt ripped raw, but she had to keep going. She was cramping now, but she didn't want to stop. She missed the young woman on Rollerblades. She missed the old lady, but not the man in the blue suit. Thumped straight into him from behind, then collapsed because that's as far as her legs would take her. As she fell she twisted herself around trying to save Matthew, place him as softly as she could on the ground. But the pavement scraped her wrist and knee. The man in the suit, blindsided in the middle of the sidewalk, cried, "*Jesus fuck!*" and folded like a tent, but in slow motion, all in a heap. Julia tried to get up but her body wouldn't obey her. There wasn't enough air.

More slow motion.

"*Fucking moron!*" the man in the suit said. He was on his feet now. Didn't seem to see Julia at all but was bearing down on . . . Donny! Donny Clatch, who was there all of a sudden, unaccountably holding Matthew.

"I'm so sorry," Donny said.

"*What the fuck do you think you're doing?*" the man in the suit said. Fists doubled. Looming over little Donny and Matthew. Julia started to move but everything was so slow.

"I'm very sorry, sir," Donny said.

"*What do you think this is, fucking Roller Derby?*" He was going to punch Donny. He was going to punch Matthew! Julia lost sight of them as she was fighting her way to her feet, and then the man in the suit was on the sidewalk clutching his knee. Donny remained standing, still holding Matthew.

"Matthew!" Julia sobbed and Donny held out the baby for her. Matthew was calm as a Buddha in his arms but burst into tears as soon as Julia took him back. So they wept, clutched together.

The man on the ground said, "*Jesus Christ!*"

"I thought you were going to hit the baby," Donny said. "I'm very sorry."

"*You've broken my fucking knee!*" the man said.

"No. I just kicked it out from behind you. It'll be okay."

Matthew was crying and screaming. Julia had to take him away. She could hardly keep hold of him. Everything was scrambled. There wasn't time to think it through. She had to get to Pullman's.

"Are you all right, Julia?" Donny asked. "Hey, don't go."

"Why are you following me?" she blurted.

"I'm not. I wasn't!" he stammered. "But I saw you running. It looked like, I don't know, someone had stolen your purse."

Her shoulder bag hung off her elbow, big as a baby. But it didn't matter. What was the point of trying to make sense in an idiot wind? "Quiet, Matthew," she said, stroking him.

"It looked like you needed help."

"It's my mother," she said, and started crying again. How could she explain it? "I've lost my mother!" she said.

ᔕ

Of course, she wasn't going to be there. All that time, wasted! Now it was nearly 5:00. Julia and Donny – he was calm as a rock, she felt better having him there – walked up to Pullman's. Swirling pockets of wind buffeted them first from one side then the other. Julia had to turn to keep Matthew away from the dust. Donny just kept walking.

A thin girl with a sardonic smile was tending the door. "Sorry," she said, not sorry at all. "We're closing."

"Listen, this is an emergency!" Donny said. "Julia's mother is missing. Did you see her here today? What does she look like, Julia?"

Julia told Donny and Donny told the girl. "We're looking for an older woman, hunched significantly, with white hair, pretty frail, suffering from dementia. Did you see anyone like that this afternoon in your store?"

"You just described half the clientele," the sardonic girl said. She couldn't help smiling at her own joke. She looked at Julia, then smartened up. "Maybe someone inside saw her. I'll get Mr. Peters."

Mr. Peters was thin and nearly bald, a careful, dapper man whose flesh had sunk with age. His skin had an undertone of grey and the form of his bones showed in relief like some fossil emerging on an eroding cliff.

"Mrs. Carmichael!" he said, as soon as he heard the name. "Lenore, yes, she was a regular customer for many, many years."

He hadn't seen her, though he was very sorry to hear about her declining health. His hands trembled as he spoke.

"She would come Tuesdays, and Wednesdays, and often Fridays as well," Mr. Peters said. "I would put aside some things for her which I knew she'd be interested in. She liked the Dutch biscuits, if I remember, and certainly any silk scarves that came in. And I could usually interest her in towels."

"If you see her," Donny said, handing over his handyman card, "please give me a ring." He seemed confident, in charge, like a detective on the scene.

"I remember she used to bring you in when you were small!" Peters said to Julia. "Not as small as this young man, perhaps!" he said, meaning Matthew, who was hiding between Julia's legs. "But a little lady."

"Yes," said Julia. It felt better somehow just to be in Pullman's, even without her mother. The lunch counter was still there, the sides of the stools gleaming with chrome, and she could smell toasted cheese and bacon. Ladies' socks were on sale three pairs for $7.99, and the support-garments section had, if anything, grown over the years, now took up three aisles.

"And *Mr.* Carmichael!" Peters said, animated now with the memory. "He was a man's man. He *hated* it in here. I remember him lost in lingerie, wandering around helpless!"

"Anyway, if you see her," Donny said.

"I said, 'Can I help you? It's Mr. Carmichael, isn't it?', and he said, '*Where does a man get a drink around here?*' There was one time –"

"Thank you," Donny said, trying to turn them away.

"– but perhaps that was someone else," Peters said.

They walked outside again. It was already starting to get dark. Julia scanned the area. The tiny parking lot was empty now because the store was closed. The other stores up and down the street, in this older part of town, were glum in this light. An old woman on a street corner was begging for change, her clothes tattered, hair matted. One leg had a grotesquely purple, oozing wound. She held out a sorry Blue Jays cap and kept her eyes on the ground.

"That's not her?" Donny asked.

No. No. Julia had a sudden vision of her mother wandering on the Queensway, eight lanes of angry traffic screaming by, weaving to avoid her, honking their horns while she panicked. Doomed in another second and a half.

"So you checked all around Fallowfields," Donny said. He was wearing just a light shirt. Why wasn't he cold? "Their staff are out looking. The police are out looking. You've scanned the obvious places . . ." Ticking all this off in his head methodically. Like it was some . . . kitchen job! "So, she might be found *already*. It might just be a case of going back home –"

"She's not," Julia said, with conviction. "This is my mother. Nothing is straightforward with my mother."

ᔕ

There was one other place to try. Tellman's Groceries was several blocks away. It had changed enormously over the years, was no longer a crowded little butcher-and-greens shop with a crate of vegetables in the front. It was now a sprawling, shiny vault of food that covered acres, having swallowed two restaurants, a bank, a gift shop, a photo store, and a pharmacy. Her mother had hated going there in recent years, often complained that she no longer knew where to buy her Dodds biscuits, her Valentine's sandwich bread and Mr. Doodle's cheese. The biscuits could be in aisle three one week and aisle eight the next. They were constantly changing the plastic wrap and the Boston cream pie. You just couldn't count on anything. None of the old staff were there any more. Mrs. Stephens, whose son became the president of whatever it was and whose husband died in the garbage compactor at work, gone long ago. Now it was all teenage girls who couldn't even give proper change without a computer telling them what to do. And they packed the bags all wrong, with eggs on the bottom every time, and mixed meat and vegetables together without a thought.

Her mother's voice drilled into Julia's head even before they entered the store. For how long had she blamed everything that went wrong on changes at Tellman's? For ages, it seemed. Before they knew what was happening. When she was just eccentric, a bit confused.

Now Julia felt exactly the same way. It was an overpowering store, the lights jacked up to megawatt brightness, twenty-one check-out cashier's booths stretching into the distance. A few desultory shoppers pushed huge gleaming carts, the food-shopping equivalent of minivans. Aisle upon aisle of products, relentlessly packaged, hyped in colour. The fruits and vegetables looked drugged up, on steroids, too vivid and robust to be believed.

Everyone looked lost. Bent-over old ladies wandered aimlessly, their eyes glazed, limbs trembling. They weren't her mother. Julia knew she wouldn't be here but she had to look, for her own conscience. It was all her fault. If only she'd moved her mother earlier so she would have adjusted better, instead of waiting till she couldn't cope with any change at all.

She remembered her mother pulling her along by the wrist as they walked down the narrow, cramped aisles of the old Tellman's, where the shopping carts were too tiny even for little girls to ride in. She professed to hate shopping, brooked no child-caused delays in getting it over with. And yet there was also this sense of her being queen in her own domain. Behind the meat counter, the butcher's white apron was forever smudged with blood and grime, but no one cared. How he brightened when he saw them. Her mother was pretty then, trim, always well dressed, she wore scarves often and would fix her make-up in the car mirror, oblivious to the swarming traffic. "*Mrs. Carmichael,*" the butcher would say. "You've brought your beautiful daughter, but I can't wait for her to grow up. Are you still married?" His drooping hound-dog expression and her business-like attitude, secretly pleased.

"Is there any prime rib left, Oscar?"

"For you, Mrs. Carmichael, I will go kill the cow right now!"

Somebody was staring at her. Julia turned and saw Stephanie, Bob's first wife, only a few feet away. Julia's stomach knotted in alarm. Stephanie was stocky now and had done something awful with her hair – it looked as if she'd tried to dye it red but had ended up with near-purple. Her face was chalky white and she was wearing dark glasses in the middle of the store and thick, red, garish lipstick. Julia wouldn't have known her except for the malevolence.

Donny was in another aisle checking out old ladies. Matthew was holding Julia's hand and reaching for a feminine product in a silvery package. Julia said, "Hello, Stephanie." The other woman's expression didn't change. Again Julia said, "Hello." Then she noticed that Stephanie wasn't staring at her at all, she was staring at Matthew. She looked so miserable. Julia said, gently, "How are you?" and Stephanie hissed, "*He didn't want children with me!*" Then she turned and rattled down the aisle, her heels going *clack! clack!* Every footfall driven into the floor. At the corner her sunglasses fell off her face and clattered in front her. She didn't pause but kicked at them furiously, just the once. Half missed, and kept going.

"Who was that?" Donny asked, coming up from behind.

Julia picked up Matthew and hugged him ferociously. When she put him down again he tore away from her grip and went after the sunglasses. There was a near-collision with a store clerk pushing a convoy of the massive shopping carts too fast. He wouldn't have been able to stop in time, but Matthew had surprisingly good timing and balance. He reached down for the glasses and spun out of the way in one athletic movement. Julia's heart trampolined. "Matthew!" she said. "*Matthew!*" as he turned to smile at her.

One of the lenses had slipped out and was scratched, but Donny was able to fit it back in and Matthew looked like royalty with them on. People turned in the store to smile at him perched in Donny's arms.

"Oh, take me home," Julia said, a bad headache that instant coming on.

8

They made you walk and walk even when your feet were wet and dirty. And it was so hot. Where was the camp? Miles away! She was sure they were lost. She and Capt. Buzbie. He was completely out of uniform and was making her carry all the bags. They should have stayed with the horses.

"It's not too much farther," he said, but not the way he was before. One spot of trouble and he got discouraged. Bad-tempered. All walk-walk. It wasn't her fault.

She asked him, "Who's going to look after the horses?"

He replied, "It's not too much farther. Do you like toast?"

"I would have stayed with the horses," she said. It was easier to look at the ground, hard and black. He was so high up.

"Do you know any of these streets?" he asked.

"All my life," Lenore said. Jesper Street, she meant to say. All her life on Jesper Street, until that next one. When Daddy lost the business that one time. And William whatsit, the tall one, lost his finger. What was he doing? Snowing.

"Where do you normally stay?" Capt. Buzbie asked. He'd shaved off his moustache, looked quite different.

"You should know," Lenore said.

"Is it in this neighbourhood?" he asked.

Hard, black ground. Lenore's feet were so tired. "Where are the horses?" she asked. Her bags were so heavy, and it was hot. Why did she have to do all the work?

"Were there horses here?" Capt. Buzbie asked. Such an idiot. "When you were young?"

"We *had* horses," Lenore said, stamping her foot, "just a few minutes ago! For God's sake!"

"Horses?" Buzbie asked, inanely.

Walking and walking. One foot and then the other. At least there'd be a swim at the lake. Trevor would make the martinis. He was such a good-looking man. Nice hands. He'd say, "Where the hell have you been? Next you're going to ask me to make my own dinner!" He'd say, "It's Cleopatra, risen from her sleep!" Drunk with it.

"This is it," Capt. Buzbie said.

At last! Lenore was shivery from the heat and bother of it all. She wanted a swim badly. Then a martini, then she'd get to dinner.

"My mom's not home, so we're going to have to wait for her," Capt. Buzbie said. "Careful on the steps. Do you want a hand?"

Lenore didn't need a hand with anything, thank you! Just show me to the lake, she thought.

"I'll get the door," the captain said.

"I really think I need a swimsuit," Lenore said.

"A what?"

"Well, you don't want me winter-dipping, do you?"

"No," said the captain uncertainly. The poor man was shocked! Well, what do they teach you in the army?

They went in the cottage. It was substantial, lots of stairs.

That's too bad. Not really on the lake at all, Lenore realized. What a silly place to build.

"Would you like some toast?" Buzbie asked.

"You must have a hard time with the docks," she said. It wasn't the black ground any more. It was wood and carpet. Darker though, and it smelled of something. So hard to keep clean.

"The what?"

"Docks!" she said. It was the right word. She hadn't made a mistake in a long time.

"What docks?"

"I would like a martini," she said proudly. It was the proper thing to offer. "Before my swim."

The captain was nervous. He couldn't seem to settle down. He'd probably never been with a woman before. Even though she was married. They were very secluded in the military. Made a lot of mistakes. His uniform was sloppy. The cuffs of his trousers dragged on the ground.

"How about some juice?" he asked. "Or do you drink milk?"

"I think I made myself perfectly clear!" Lenore said, snappishly then. Probably too much yelling in the military. Softened the brain. Or perhaps –

"Were you overseas?" Lenore asked.

"Overseas?"

"That Jones boy was," she said. "It was terrible! They found out from the little paper. The whatsit."

"The whatsit?"

"Yes," she said. His brains had been softened. That's why he couldn't make a martini. "Well," she said, straightening up. "Enough of this! Say hello to everybody!" She walked off, glad to be on her way. Enough chitchat, when our boys were off. She walked to the door and opened it. But it didn't lead outside at all, it led into a bunch of clothes.

"Oh for heaven's sake!" she said.

"I think you should stay till my mom comes home," the captain said. Nerves shot through.

"I have never been so stupidly –" she said. She became flustered and the words wouldn't come right. Her brain went hiccup.

"My mom will be home pretty soon," the captain said. "I hope. Sometimes she doesn't get home till late, though. It depends on the buses and what's happening at work."

Lenore backed out of the fake door and turned around uncertainly. She was alone with a captain in the barracks after hours. How did that happen? The dance had gone on and on but she didn't remember getting here. Sometimes they slipped things in your drink. Betty Jane told her that. They slipped things and then you got pregnant and it wasn't your fault but who would believe you? Alone in the barracks after hours.

"I think I would like to go home," she said. Men respected compost. If you lost it, they didn't respect you at all. "Right away, please," she said.

"But where do you live?" he asked. Silver-tongued devil. Those were the ones to look out for. In sloppy uniforms, who lured you.

"Home! Just take me home!" she said.

"If you could tell me –"

"I did tell you! For God's sake, stop all this –"

"Maybe your address is written in your purse," he said. He reached for her and she backed up, nearly spat at him.

"Don't touch me!" she said, straightening her shoulders.

"Okay, okay!" He backed off.

"I believe," Lenore said, pressing her advantage, "I asked for a martini!"

"Well," he said. Carefully. He'd never been alone with a woman. No wonder he was so crinkled. "I'll see what I can do!"

Indeed. Lenore watched him go into the other room. Then she walked quietly to the door, turned the handle, and slipped away, closing it behind her.

Into darkness. Night already? But a thick darkness, smelly, hard to turn and see anything. No moon, no stars. Just thickness. If only she wasn't so hot. She could put down the bags. She'd carried them all so long. And her coat. It really was too hot. Dinner could wait, Trevor was fine as long as he had his drink. Lenore took off her coat and her blouse, laid them neatly on the shore. It was hard to move, it was so dark and thick. She took off her skirt and shoes and nylons. It would be better to swim by moonlight. But sometimes there just wasn't any. She wriggled out of her underwear. That felt better. The only way to swim, really. So free. Not . . . *held up.* Girdles especially. She kneeled to try to find her way but the rocks were lumpy and uncomfortable. She could hear the water but couldn't find it.

The lights went on then, it was so sudden she screamed. "Trevor!" she shrieked. He did that just to embarrass her, shone the big flashlight when he knew she was skinny-dipping. You could see clear across the lake with that light.

"Jesus!" Trevor said. But it wasn't Trevor, it was Capt. Buzbie. Then it went dark again. Lenore felt for her clothes but it was hopeless, nothing was where she'd left it.

"*What are you doing?*" Capt. Buzbie asked. Terrified.

"Don't turn on the light!" Lenore commanded. The stupid man. Drugging her like this back to the barracks. "Bring back my clothes!" she said.

"*I don't have your clothes!*"

Too excitable. You come back with crust in your head.

"I will not stand for any more of this!" Lenore said. "Who is your commanding officer?"

"*My what?*"

"I am going to report you to the authorities!" Lenore said. "Now bring them back immediately!"

It's compost. Either you have it or you don't. If you don't then they ride clodhop. Take your clothes and get you pregnant. But if you do they bring your clothes back. Hand you your dress while they turn their heads away in the light. Like a gentleman.

"It's my mother's," Buzbie said. "She'll be home soon. I promise!"

It's what they tell themselves when they don't know anything. They've come back crust-in-the-head so you have to be kind.

The dress fit badly. Lenore tugged it and tugged and it would have to do. Silly things. She was just trying for a skinny-dip. Before the stitches went all wrong.

"It's not my fault," she said.

9

The phone didn't ring. Bob flipped through the evening television news, a forgettable blur of murders, fires, earthquakes, and football scores, and one oddball story of a man so upset about cockroaches that he started throwing furniture out the window of his twelfth-floor apartment onto the street below. Bob turned it off as the camera was panning the crowd on the sidewalk chanting, "Jump! Jump! Jump!" He skimmed the conference binder. Tonight he was missing the ritual reading of "The Cask of Amontillado" and the Alfred J. Kiddleton memorial lecture entitled "Edgar Allan Poe and Stephen King: The Confluxes and Divergences of Cultural Sub-Texts." Tomorrow morning Yamada was speaking on "The Doomed Writer: Poe's Shadow in the Twenty-first Century," and later there would be a panel discussion on Poe's controversial place as critic and promoter of early American letters.

Bob opened his *Complete Tales and Poems* at random and read, "During the whole of a dull, dark, and soundless day in the autumn of the year, when the clouds hung oppressively low in the heavens, I had been passing alone, on horseback, through a singularly dreary tract of country, and at length found myself, as the shades of the evening drew on, within view of the melancholy House of Usher." How many times had he lectured on that particular opening sentence? The relentless repetition of tone in elegant, haunting variations: *dull, dark, dreary, oppressively low, alone, in the autumn, shades of evening*, finally leading to the culmination of despair, the *melancholy House of Usher*. Bob read the sentence again and again. The rest of the story was almost superfluous; it flowed entirely from the ache of that beginning.

The phone still did not ring.

He was very good. He reread "The Poetic Principle" and "The Rationale of Verse" in the small stuffed chair by the phone under a mediocre light. He started to read a graduate paper somehow connecting James Fenimore Cooper to the Transcendentalists but stopped himself after a few pages, his cynicism rising. Anyone who could bear to read large tracts of Cooper's tortured, incompetent prose was obviously cursed with a second-rate mind; and yet that too was the famous dismissal of people too interested in Poe, whose prose was usually far finer but whose life was a disaster.

He paced the little room. The night sky pressed against the window, which wouldn't open. The fan rattled annoyingly, not a loud noise, but whining, like a dentist's drill that became more annoying as the evening wore on. He turned off the fan and the air hung dead. No matter how he fiddled, the lights were either too dull or too bright.

He ordered a bottle of Scotch from room service. He didn't ask the price. It would be outrageous. Helen would find a way to hide it on the expense account. *Incidentals* perhaps. *Necessities* more like it.

The phone still didn't ring.

The Scotch came and Bob poured himself a glass too quickly

then didn't drink it, just looked. Sienna's poems were in his broken briefcase. He took them out and fell to reading one of them, called "Decision 21":

scissor-lean my limpid limbs
river-rut my boiling pot
village-hut my aching horn
my livid-cave

my
gentle rot
shadow-tilt and binding-bait
my hunger-hole my
weariness
I will float I will
drowsy-drop
molten-melt to razor-glop
lap it up and
lapidate
lighten like a
lie.

He read it again, out loud, the words falling into one another, pure sound, little niggles of half-sense, suggestions of meanings. "My hunger-hole my / weariness." He wanted her so much. That was the truth. Bare and desperate. He was blessed with a fine wife and a new son, a satisfactory life, a good life, compared to most, a great life. But he wanted more. He wanted Sienna Chu. He wanted her youth and her mind and beauty. He wanted her and Julia and the boy; he wanted his position and his salary and perks. He wanted everything, he thought. The more he had the more he needed. This ragged desperation. Dull, dark, dreary, oppressive, melancholy want.

He wanted Julia to call, but she was too wrapped up in her own things. Her mother's latest crisis. One call would make so much difference. He was having his own dark night but she didn't care. She was preoccupied, taken up, consumed by her immediate concerns, by Matthew and Lenore. Bob had done his genetic duty, now had been tossed aside. Just stay quiet, pay all the bills, don't ask anything in return.

He needed her and she wasn't calling and he'd be damned if he would call again. That much was certain. He looked at the phone and at his empty glass – now how did that happen? He didn't remember drinking it. He poured another and this time concentrated so he would remember. What was the point of paying an arm and a leg – of having the university pay an arm and a leg – for a bottle of Scotch if you didn't remember drinking it?

Incidentals, he'd tell Helen. He'd hosted a small gathering of senior Poe scholars. For networking purposes. Christopher Hindle and Bill Windower and Jean-Yves Rémy, who got drunk and started quoting Baudelaire. "Don't put that on the expense form," he'd say to Helen. She'd understand. There's black and white for a tiny percentage of human endeavours, shades of grey for everything else. Helen did the forms, the black and white, but she understood grey.

Bob salvaged his portable vagina from the wastebasket, which hadn't been emptied yet. The clothes were still there too. Garbage was once a day, he thought, courtesy bar twice. He pulled the vagina out of its bubblewrap and dangled it. $149.95. It smelled now of airplane soap, was still a little wet. What a huge amount to pay for such a dopey little thing! His deformed octopus. What was the James Bond movie? *Octopussy!* Bob said the word out loud and it was suddenly unbearably funny. As he laughed the labia jiggled as if mouthing the word. He laughed and laughed, rolled against the side of the bed, fought for oxygen. Windows shut, no air! A tomb!

It was too funny. Too funny for the hour, for such airlessness. He clutched himself in painful paroxysms of laughter.

He took off his shoes and socks. Of course, he was going to throw the damn thing out. What was he thinking? But he might as well try it properly. He took off his trousers – his clean, dry trousers – and hung them up for tomorrow. There was an iron in the closet, he could press his other pair, but they were soiled. The overnight dry-cleaning service! Of course. He'd send for them right away. No, not right away. After.

He turned the lights low, made sure the heavy drapes were properly closed, the door latched and bolted. Privacy at last. This is what he lacked. There was no privacy at home. Julia was liable to walk into the bathroom when he was having a shit, for God's sake. That's the kind of family she grew up in. No wonder Lenore's screws were loose. Her whole family had no sense of privacy, of mystery and personal space. Ha! Matthew destroyed all space anyway, whatever Julia hadn't yet taken. He was all-consuming. Couldn't even make it two minutes into a meal without upsetting something, his milk or biscuits or a bowl of applesauce. You couldn't think straight, there wasn't a moment's peace. Open a book and there was Matthew crawling up your leg. *Daddy has nothing to do!* After working all day, in the quiet hours needed by an academic to stay fresh, to view the chaotic madness of the world from some sort of safe perspective . . .

The glass was empty again. At home Julia harped on him about his drinking, but she wasn't here, was she? She was far away and deliberately not calling despite his present crisis, so he would turn to whatever it took to get him through. That was his right. It was his dark hour, he could get through it any way he chose. He poured another glass, not to drink but as a gesture of independence. From Julia. From the oppressive pressures of his everyday life.

He took off the rest of his clothes. It was warm already in the room, it felt good to shed all encumbrances. He walked into the bathroom to do this right, to have a hot bath first, soak in oil. But the light in the bathroom was glaring and rude. There was his body suddenly in three mirrors all around him: huge, hairy, paunchy, old. He didn't want to see himself that way so he turned off the light. Why weren't candles provided in hotel rooms? A candlelight bath would be perfect.

He skipped the bath, went back to the bed, and put on his vagina. He was much more adept this time. The floor didn't tilt suddenly and throw him into the ceiling or wall. The clips meshed easily. His fingers knew by now. It felt the same as before, snug and interesting, nearly natural. The manufacturers had taken care. He closed his eyes and felt himself. The artificial hair, the gentle opening . . .

When his penis hardened the vagina didn't fit so well any more, so he had to put on a pair of panties quickly to keep everything firmly in place. He fished a black pair out of the wastebasket and stepped into them, then he put on the pantyhose he had slipped from Julia's sock drawer: Whisperline, in a silky tan colour. They stretched prodigiously, held everything in, felt feminine beyond words. His black hair underneath the nylon made almost a fishnet effect. He walked to the full-length mirror to view himself from sideways, from straight on, and from behind. Ignore the shaggy legs and torso and there was a female form in panties and nylons, almost like in one of those glossy department-store flyers that arrive at the door.

The corset was more of an adventure. It was another Internet order, flashy red satin with black furry trim, and a bodice that he couldn't fill. It really didn't fit. He had to turn it back to front and pull hard to get the clasps to reach. Each one was a terrible effort, and there were twenty or more. He was sweating by the time he'd finished, but he was no longer hard, so the vagina fit better once again. Then he had to pull the corset around so that it faced properly. He must have put on weight recently, he thought, because it was arduous. When he was finished, though, there was a sense of having a waist. This was the discipline of being female, he thought. This feeling of encasement and support. He couldn't bend or even walk very well; sitting was very difficult. He did it anyway, sat on the edge of the bed then crossed his legs. Flabs of belly bulged out the bottom of the corset, but that was a pair of panties covering a beautiful dark triangle framed in shimmering Whisperline thighs.

Breathing was difficult. He couldn't keep the corset on long. But he had to try on the slip. It was a purple silk one he'd bought for Julia the Christmas before she was pregnant. It was too big for her and, he had discovered, too small for him, but silk was strong, it would stretch and hold. He stepped into it, pulled it carefully over his bottom. He had to adjust the straps for maximum length, but eventually his arms and shoulders made it through.

It looked hideous. Even in a darkened room, looking at himself in the mirror, he knew what a joke he looked like. Or part of him knew. But it was a part he wasn't interested in. Sections of him looked respectably female. Or at least it was enough for his imagination to take over. It was dress-up. He'd never played when he was a child. Not dress-up as a female. It would have been too much a taboo. Too outside of himself. But that's what he wanted now, to be someone else for a time. Not for always, not even for more than a hour, and not for public, just private. He didn't want to go through horrendous months of operations and hormone treatments to change his identity. He just wanted to have a short holiday from himself, to play make-believe, to sink into the basement of his psyche for a little while.

And the silk felt wonderful. He couldn't get it on without the corset, that was the terrible thing. The corset squeezed him so badly he felt he might keel over. But the corset made the silk possible, and the silk was a flashlight down the path of being a goddess like Sienna Chu. Perfect breasts and skin, youth, tender folds, royalty of sorts. What were all the feminists squealing about no power for women? What about the terrible power of beauty?

Bob felt himself through the silk. He walked slowly this way and that, sometimes past the mirror. Like a little girl imagining breasts and dresses, nylons and high heels, lipstick and perfume and everything sophisticated and female. It was just this moment of . . . transcendence. Of being something pure – not heavy and male and hairy and old, but someone thin and young and stunning. Just for this moment.

The phone rang. Bob's heart leapt, a moment's panic, privacy ripped. But it was just the phone. He composed himself, tried out his voice. "Hello?" he said, practising in front of the phone. "Julia! God, I've been waiting for you to call!"

He picked up the phone. "Hello?"

"Professor Sterling," the voice said. "Bob! I'm sorry. I'm not used to calling you Bob."

"Hi, Sienna," he replied, as calmly as he could, although he was trembling from excitement and the pressure of remaining in the corset.

"I hope you don't mind that I'm calling," she said, and paused as if gathering her wits along with her breath. She seemed unusually nervous.

"Not at all," he replied lightly, though it was hard to breathe. He caught a glimpse of himself looking like a fuzzy joke in the mirror, a figure from some drunken Hallowe'en party.

"Well, I just, uh – *huhhh*," she said, sighing suddenly.

"What's the problem?" he asked.

"I think I need to see you," she said. "I need to talk to you about some things. Is it too late? I'm sorry . . ."

"No, no," he said, not knowing what time it was. "Come right up."

"You wouldn't mind? You weren't in bed?"

"No, that's fine," he said.

He was going to add, "Just give me a couple of minutes," but she hung up on him before he could get it out, as if the sheer act of making the call had consumed all her reserves of confidence and grace.

"*Jesus!*" he said, panicking, slamming the phone down. He tore the strap of the silk slip while trying to get it over his shoulder. Then, bunched around his hips, the slip stayed stuck for an agony of time while he fought to get it off. But that was the easy part. The corset now seemed welded in place. It took an enormous effort to twist it around back to front so he could get a decent look at the hooks and clasps, which were multiplying, now seemed to number a hundred or more. His big fingers fumbled incompetently under pressure. He'd had too much to drink! "*Damn!*" he said and stamped his foot, the breath squeezed out of him by the corset.

There was no way to rip it off. The clasps were too strong. He sucked in his gut, strained to push the fabric together, then tried to pinch the tiny hooks and clasps with his fingers.

He didn't know how much time he was taking. The room began to spin slowly. Too much to drink, not enough air.

Trapped! The window was sealed shut. He flicked at the fan button but nothing happened. He looked at it for the longest time in disbelief. It had been working before!

One clasp and another. Now he was getting the hang of it. If he fought hard enough. Sweating now, his heart racing, one clasp and another and another . . .

There was a knock at the door.

"Yes!" he said, too excitedly, not his professorial voice at all. "Just a minute!"

One extraordinary heave and he squeezed the half-hooked corset past his hips and to the floor. His panties and pantyhose came halfway, then he ripped them the rest of the way. He tore his trousers off the hanger, stuffed his legs in. Pushed himself into a shirt.

"There in a second!" he said and excitedly gathered up the torn slip and corset, and from the wastebasket the black lace bra that he hadn't tried on. He knelt to shove them under the bed, but there was no under the bed. The bed was mounted on a wooden box, solid to the floor.

Into the closet. Doors pulled shut. He fought some socks onto his feet, for propriety, pushed the Scotch bottle into the courtesy bar cabinet.

He reeked of alcohol.

"Bob?" came the voice. Timid and uncertain. A different Sienna Chu.

"Yep!" he said and stole into the bathroom, hurriedly yanked the plastic wrapper off the top of the complimentary mouthwash bottle. In his haste he mistakenly swallowed half a mouthful then spat it out uncontrollably, all over the mirror and sink. He washed his mouth out quickly with water. Nothing on his trousers and shirt, thank God.

"Sorry!" he said as he opened the door. "I was just . . . on the phone with Windower, the conference organizer. Did you go to the events this evening?"

She was wearing the micro-skirt from earlier, the same tight black top. But she looked, somehow, more vulnerable and thus absolutely magnificent. She dipped her eyes as she walked past him. "I couldn't think very well," she said in a little voice.

He looked behind him at the room in sudden terror that he might have left something incriminating out in the open. But it looked very innocent: the chair turned sideways by the phone table, the pillows propped on the bed where his books and papers were spread, evidence of serious and legitimate pursuits. Her poems too were on the bed. "I've been reading some of your work again," he said. "It's extraordinary. I can't say it often enough –"

"Bob," she said, turning to him, owning the centre of the room. Her eyes were darkly luminous. "I'm sorry," she said. "I am so confused about everything."

"What?" he asked, and took her hands because it seemed like the thing to do. She responded immediately, held him behind his neck and kissed him deeply.

She backed away, pushed her hands through her hair and stepped to the window. "What am I doing?" she said.

"It's all right," he said softly and walked towards her. But she didn't want him to approach her. She wanted to talk it out.

"I can't believe I'm here," she said.

"I'm glad you're here."

"These last weeks," she said, not looking at him. Her face was badly flushed. "I've been trying so hard to keep myself from doing that."

"That's all right."

"I kept telling myself, *he's my professor, he's off limits, he's a friend at most!*"

"I've felt it too," he said.

But it was as if she hadn't heard. *"He's married!"* she said. *"He's got a kid!* Although you never talked about that. And we never *did* anything, it was just talk. But wonderful, wonderful talk, and I thank you for that."

"Oh, Sienna," he said, stepping forward.

"No," she said, motioning him back.

"Sit down," he said quietly. There wasn't much choice, either the bed or the chair by the phone. She took the chair. He carefully moved his papers and sat on the bed. "Sienna," he said.

"I have just been torn up about this," she said. "I'm not –"

"Sienna," he said again. "There's so much –"

"– the kind of person who –"

"– I have to say. It has been ripping at my –"

"We need to be –"

"Yes," he said.

They both stopped talking. She looked at him with such need and want. A child, yes, but a woman too, far beyond him, he knew it in his blood. Still, an innocent, not the seductress his overworked imagination had conjured during his lecture.

"Yes," he said again.

"Oh, Bob," she said. She wanted him to come over, to bridge the distance. It was as clear as if she'd commanded him out loud. They understood!

"Yes."

But he didn't move. Something inside him knew. It wasn't for him to move. How did he know that?

"I want to say this first," she said. Clear-eyed now. She was the stronger. He'd always known that. "I have always treasured our conversations. They have meant so much to me. I don't want to lose that. No matter what happens."

"We won't lose that," he said in a soft, gentle voice, in precisely the right words and way, now that she'd given him the clue. That's what maturity gets you, he thought. She was about to offer herself – she might not even know it, but he knew it, and he knew enough to stay back on the bed, to appear the reluctant one, Mr. Responsible. He felt a speech coming on. "Sometimes," he said confidingly, "souls – if you believe in that sort of thing – just connect, naturally, on myriad different levels. You recognize it in a glance across a crowded room, a first touch of the hand, an innocent remark. What is it? I don't think anybody really knows, and a lot of people ignore it, they stop looking for it." He paused. He felt strangely dizzy, caught up in his own words, perhaps, in anticipation. He took a deep, clearing breath. He felt deeply conscious of the fact that he was still wearing the portable vagina. "That knowledge withers," he continued. "It can be best that way. If you can dull yourself, just focus on the day-to-day, much better than being open to the ravages of an extraordinary love."

Tears were now welling in her eyes. "Oh, I knew –" she began to say.

"Shhhh." She was going to throw herself at him. He could almost count it down. He stood, not swiftly, not slowly, not as a motion towards her but towards the bathroom. The floor was not as steady as it should have been. "There's a great, great deal more we need to talk about," he said humbly, and he held up his finger, a simple gesture of restraint. "Back in a moment." Then he stepped heavily into the bathroom, locked the door as silently as he could, flicked the switch, recoiled from the nauseating brightness. He breathed deeply, steadied himself, undid his trousers deliberately, not rushing, unhooked the vagina and looked to see where he might hide the thing. He didn't want to feel anxious, yet the room was slowly spinning. Then – and it was cruelly sudden and unexpected, overwhelming – he began to empty his stomach, as quietly as he could, into the toilet. He tried to be silent, to be neat and controlled, but the heaving was riotous, unruly, rude. Everything had to go, not just the Scotch but the filet mignon and mushrooms and red wine, the other drinks from earlier in the day, even parts of lunch and breakfast. He could taste certain undigested bits as they rushed past the wrong way. His body was left in a cold, trembling sweat.

Ages later there was a little voice at the bathroom door. "Bob? Are you all right? Professor Sterling?"

"*Ghnihhr*," Bob said. He wheezed a couple of times, ran warm water in the sink, and wiped his face in the dark with a cloth.

"Can I help?"

"No," Bob said weakly. "No. I'm sorry." He ran more water.

Still later came a click of the door and she was gone. Bob cleaned himself up, took off everything, wandered out of the bathroom and fell back into bed. He meant to call her right away. In his mind he was up and dialling the number. The phone was ringing in his ear. "Sienna," he was saying. "I'm sorry." In his mind. But his body stayed on the bed and he slept, badly, the rest of the night.

10

Julia's head was splitting. Little cracks were spreading along the base in the back, and one major rift gaped down the front between her eyebrows to the bridge of her nose, a ragged wound of pure pain that nonetheless left her free to sit, very still, by the telephone and talk to the executive director at Fallowfields. Mrs. Watkins was breathless with concern and apology – Fallowfields had never had a patient go missing before, not from the secure wing. But there was positive news: the police had interviewed a bus driver who had picked up Mrs. Carmichael close to Fallowfields and had let her off near the park at Hog's Back Falls at 2:49 p.m. A dozen off-duty Fallowfields staff were that instant helping police personnel search the park, and Mrs. Watkins was expecting to hear good news any moment.

"Hog's Back Falls!" Julia said. "My God, she's fallen in the water!"

"We cannot assume the worst, Mrs. Sterling," Mrs. Watkins said gravely.

"Oh my God! Oh my God!" Julia said when she got off the phone. Donny was in the den playing with Matthew, who hadn't been changed in hours and should have been cranky with starvation but seemed entranced with his new friend. All the things to do at once, faster than at once, lined up in Julia's mind: change and feed Matthew, feed herself, take some pain pills, drive to Hog's Back, find her mother's dead body in the freezing, violent water.

They were in the van in under six minutes. Donny drove. There was no question about whether he wanted to continue to be part of this domestic drama, it was simply the way it had to be. With her head like this Julia couldn't drive. She could have called for a cab; she could have called any one of a dozen friends scattered in different parts of the city; she could have spent half an hour or more trying to arrange a babysitter. But Donny was the nearest and quickest help and she had switched into vital-efficiency mode. Her mother might be dying. Any extra minute could be the difference.

She closed her eyes and held her temples in the van, gently rubbed the base of her skull, the top, and along the sides. More food might have helped, but the fault was hers, she'd left things too long. Matthew was quiet in the back in his baby seat. Donny was talking but his voice sounded like elevator music, something that didn't need to be paid attention to. He was naming people from Brookfield and what had become of them. Some Julia recognized, most she couldn't or didn't want to remember.

"You could go faster," she said without opening her eyes. As soon as she said it he speeded up drastically. "Just don't get us killed," she said and he instantly slowed down again.

"Do you remember Ray Jenkins? You won't believe this. He sold his little Internet company for three hundred million dollars. Can you believe that? Just before the crash. Where did I hear that? I ran into someone a month or two ago. Oh yeah, Willy Leach. Do you remember Willy? . . ."

Fading in and out. A gentle voice, just by itself it seemed to be mending some of the lesser cracks in her skull. Despite herself she thought of Ray Jenkins, with his scientific calculator in his shirt pocket, the bad acne and greasy hair, the way he couldn't look any girl in the eye. At least not Julia. There'd been a whole squadron of Ray Jenkinses who would start to sweat when Julia walked by. She used to take slight pleasure in their discomfort. Mostly they were annoying, not worth thinking about.

Donny had been like that too. She was beginning to remember him: a shy, thin, nervous boy behind her, all elbows and ears. Now here he was driving her to Hog's Back, where they were going to find her mother's body face down in the shallows below the falls, her legs drifting lifelessly, her eyes open and tortured, little bits of reed and river filth in her hair.

Police cars huddled at the entrance to the park, their doors open, lights flashing. No ambulances. Julia's heart sank then rose again. No ambulances meant she hadn't yet been found, but also that she wasn't dead yet. There was still hope.

"I'll carry Matthew," Donny said but Julia countermanded him. It would have taken extra energy to explain, so she didn't. But she *had* to carry Matthew herself. Julia had a front-loading strap-on baby carrier that she hadn't used for Matthew since he was much younger, but she fit him in now, wrapped her coat around him.

"Want to see!" Matthew said but Julia said "*No!*" in her new way that Matthew seemed to understand really did mean no: no way, absolutely not, impossible. You are not going to see your grandmother's twisted, bloated, drowned body caught in the mud and rocks.

"I'm the mother!" Julia announced when she walked up to the nearest officer, then corrected herself. "She's my mother!" she said. "I mean I'm the daughter. It's my mother who's lost."

"We're not sure, ma'am, that she's actually here," the officer said. He was enormous, his holster, boots, and truncheon bar gleaming black in the headlights, his bulletproof vest a duller, heavier black. "We're cordoning and searching the trails and the surrounding bush," he said. "They feed into the river, but we don't think she's there. We've already had a team go up and back and the view is pretty open for the most part." He had a fat head and small, dark eyes, and either didn't know what he was talking about or was trying to spare her feelings: she knew exactly where they were going to find her mother. She knew too, suddenly, with a certainty that seemed to swell from her cells and tissue, that she would be the one to find her, that it would be gruesome and inevitable.

"If you'd like to stay here, ma'am, I'm in radio contact with all the search teams," the officer said.

"No," Julia said without hesitation. "I have to do this." She thought, but didn't add, that otherwise they might be there all night. This was her duty. It was unavoidable, just as she had to carry Matthew, which was part of her punishment. She took the flashlight that Donny silently offered and strode down the trail that led directly to the falls, which she could hear roaring somewhere in the black. That's where her mother would have gone, the quickest route to disaster. The ground was muddy and wet. With Matthew on her front she felt pregnant again, heavy and earthbound. Every step sank into the dirt. The light from her flashlight carved dim tunnels out of the night, which wasn't as black as it could have been, she thought, would have seemed greyish without the artificial light to keep their eyes from fully adjusting. She could see other beams in the woods, could hear the teams calling for her mother. Behind her, Donny was scanning his flashlight back and forth, checking the bushes which loomed so suddenly in the blank light.

Useless, she thought, but she didn't tell him to stop.

There was no point going to the falls themselves, a body would be quickly carried downstream by the violent pull of the current. There was a safety fence, but Julia knew her mother would have found a way around it – she'd gotten out of Fallowfields, hadn't she? She'd probably crossed the bridge on Hog's Back Road, paused to look down at the roiling fury, then had fallen over right there just from the awful pull of it. From this angle down below Julia could see the jutting grey cliffs, the hump of rock in the middle of the maelstrom, the swirling, foaming, roaring tonnage of falling water.

"Scared!" Matthew said.

"No, you're not," Julia snapped.

"Yes, scared!"

"Just go to sleep!" she said, knowing he wouldn't. He started to whimper. "Shhh!"

"I can hold him," Donny said, but Julia refused again. She couldn't possibly entrust him to anyone else tonight. Then it occurred to her that she'd forgotten about her headache, but with the thought it came surging back.

"Slow down!" Donny said, but what was the point of that? They were only postponing the inevitable. Her head would just burn, burn from the inside, become completely unbearable. Better get it done now. "We might miss her!" he said, farther behind than before. He could look back in the bushes, uncover every twig if he wanted.

There was the water now, calmer, almost subdued at the base of the falls. She turned off her flashlight, weak as it was. Better to let her eyes adjust, watch the black water turn grey, the sky lighten to dark blue, purple. Shadows of trees, the murmuring of the ripples. In many spots here the river wasn't more than a few inches deep. But her mother still would have found a way to drown. This Julia knew: it was the final punishment for selling the house and moving her, for not taking her in herself. This horrible death, with no doubt about who was responsible.

"Do you see her?" Donny asked, coming up from behind. He shone his flashlight up and down the river. The light beam reduced the field of vision considerably. Everything outside of it disappeared in black.

"She's here. I know it!" Julia said.

She waded into the water. It was frightfully cold. Her running shoes were soaked and frigid in an instant. She let out a harsh breath then kept going. It had to be done. You carry the child, let it take over your body for nine months, then you have to squeeze him out. There's no other way, either you do it or you die, or you let some doctor cut it out of you like a tumour or a stone. You don't think your legs can spread wide enough, you feel like it's going to rip you from your vagina to your throat, but you do it. Drugs help but it's still impossible and yet must be done. Like this. One step after another, slimy rock and silty bottom. You cannot fall; your child is strapped on; you're walking for two.

"Do you see something?"

Julia took a step, balanced on a small rock, then took another step and sank down to her knee. There were even deeper sections. That's where her mother would be, she thought. Dragged under by the current, her twisted body. A rock wobbled and Julia nearly went over. She fought upright, drenched the other leg in stretching for a more stable perch.

"What do you see?"

Something silver in the water. A hand? Julia bent over, so carefully, with Matthew's enormous weight on her front. It would be so easy to fall over. She could feel her back resisting, complaining. A hand? No. Something else. Not a body part.

Julia was relieved and disappointed. It could just be a tin can. Deeper than it looked; she had to lean and hold herself back at the same time. Her knee buckled slightly but held. The water was screaming cold on her arm but she stayed silent, the way she had in the hospital with Matthew. What's the point in yelling? You have to go through it. It's a debt that must be paid.

"What did you find?" Donny asked, shining his light, temporarily blinding her.

She started screaming then. It came from her bones and shook the night.

"What? What is it?" Donny yelled.

"It's the ricer!" she wailed, waving it around, unmistakable proof. "My God, oh my God, it's my mother's ricer!"

ဢ

There were blankets on the shore and searchlights, men wading in the frigid waters, poking with sticks, police dogs sniffing up and down the shore. It was out of Julia's hands. She was wailing now, inconsolable. She shook with cold and fright and exhaustion, with hunger and fear and the dread of night. The big officer stayed with her and patted her shaking, huddled body from time to time. At any moment the men with the sticks were going to pull up her mother's body. It was going to be black with muck, lifeless. The sight would sear itself into Julia's soul. She'd been entrusted with her mother's care and had sloughed it off to incompetents in order to save money.

Why hadn't she spent more time observing the security precautions at Fallowfields? One afternoon's visit was hardly enough. She could've asked for references and followed up, phoned the relatives of some of their other residents. She was a researcher, it wouldn't have been too difficult. A little effort, some imagination, and all this would have been avoided. What a pitiful dishrag she'd turned into: one small child and her world had sunk into mush. She pictured her mother wandering stupidly, blindly, all alone on the bridge, mesmerized by the pull of falls, no one around to hear her screams. In the middle of the city, in the middle of the day! Losing her balance, falling over, slamming her head on a rock on the way down and then the merciless current rolling her light frame, her fading little body, sweeping it away in slow motion while no one helped.

What had Julia been doing? Taking forever to get Matthew ready to go out. Planning her kitchen renovations! She retched suddenly but nothing came up; there was almost nothing in her stomach.

Julia heard a commotion in the distance – dogs barking, men yelling – but she couldn't look. It was the body. They'd talked about this very thing countless times over the years, that strangely serious though mocking tone that her mother would adopt whenever they passed by a feeble, wretched old soul. *"You will not let that happen to me. I'm telling you now, if I'm drooling in bed and muttering, you have my permission to take me in the backyard and shoot me. Just bury me in the back garden by the rosebush. Not the rhubarb, I don't want you making jam out of me later on!"* Smiling at her little joke, at the way Julia couldn't figure out whether to take her seriously.

"Ma'am?" the big officer said. "Mrs. Sterling?"

"There's your father's shotgun, he taught you to use it for a reason. If I'm ever moaning about my lost knitting like Mrs. Abelnorth, if it ever comes to that, you'll know what to do. That's a darling. Did you write to Mrs. Henley? You should thank her for the hairbands she gave you at Christmas."

"Mrs. Sterling!"

"Huh?"

"I just got word from one of the hospitals. A woman has brought in someone who fits your mother's description. Pretty disoriented. Her son found her wandering around here this afternoon. Do you want to come with me to check it out?"

Julia looked at him the longest time. It was *so* cold!

"I think I need to stay here," she said dully. Then suddenly, "Where's Matthew?"

"I have him. He's fine. Sleeping away!"

Julia looked up without comprehension, finally said, "Donny," as if practising his name.

"You should come with me to the hospital," the officer said again. A persistent grip on her elbow, she had to rise. But this is where they were going to find the body! What about the dogs? What had they been barking at? Julia peered into the gloom to see what the dogs were doing.

"We can come back here if it doesn't pan out," the officer said.

II ↰

Julia Carmichael. Three years ago, when Waylun Zhi said to choose a personal word pattern for the microcosmic meditation – something relaxing yet powerful, full of grace, energy, redemption – the first words to leap to Donny's mind were *Julia Carmichael.* He'd been standing in Waylun Zhi's little studio in the tree-hugging position, knees bent modestly, back straight, arms rounded in front of his chest as he tried to relax, to focus inwardly, to channel the energy of the universe through his own sacred vessel.

Julia Carmichael.

The in-breath, when the energy wheel in his middle source opened like a petal to the soft heat of spring, was *Julia.* The out-breath, when the wheel tightened like a ball being squeezed in all directions at once, evenly, not hurried, as if wringing out all the bad energy and toxins accumulated in the body – that was *Carmichael.* He said the words, and although he was supposed to be standing without mind, in emptiness, he usually thought of a specific image: Julia Carmichael in tight, faded blue jeans and a velvety-soft, form-fitting purple sweater, with her dead-straight, shining blonde hair combed down her back-side, standing outside the gymnasium before the Christmas term History exam, two pens and three pencils gripped lightly in her small right hand, and who gave a shit what Mr. Wilkens was going to ask anyway?

She was sitting beside him now in the squad car, older, with shorter, more ordinary hair and a thicker body, suddenly much more human and approachable than that younger version. Her child was on his lap and Donny was breathing with the cosmos, thinking *thank you, thank you* with every tingle of energy that squirrelled up his spine, circled his brain, dripped down his front to his middle energy reservoir buried behind his navel. Waylun Zhi said that he should have faith, that if he repeated the sacred patterns daily, worked towards no-mindedness without hurry, without ambition or goal or desire, but faith-fully, with an open heart, then balance would be achieved and great channels of life vision would open up to him. His health, his disposition, his energy for work and love, all would improve. Good things would happen because of his positive thought energy. You couldn't predict exactly what they might be, but a diligent practitioner would be in a steady, peaceful state, ready to accept the gifts of universal harmony.

Julia was holding her temples, now, drying her eyes. She was full of a seasoned, more vulnerable beauty than when he'd sat behind her every day and rehearsed, fruitlessly, snatches of nervous conversation. *Did you get the assignment done for Billings? What's happening with your science project? Are you going to the ___?* The ___, the whatever it was – the football game, the fall dance, the Christmas concert, the event, the non-event, the nothing, the excuse. *Will you go with me?* Five words, impossible to articulate, but whirling inside his head day after day.

Now here she was, in a different lifetime almost, so small beside him, her head leaning on his shoulder, everything up to him.

"It's all right," he said. "I think we're probably going to find your mom is fine."

She didn't respond.

"What do you call your grandmother?" Donny asked Matthew. "Do you call her Nana?"

"Gamma Lenore," the boy said. "She's bongo."

He was younger than his friend Ramone's kids, was full of spark and kick. His eyes were never still but constantly roamed over everything.

"She's what?" he asked.

Julia shifted slightly, didn't look at them but seemed to be listening.

"She eats nappies!" Matthew blurted.

"What's a nappy?" Donny asked.

The squad car pulled up in front of the hospital's main doors. It was a sprawling, weathered, brown brick building covered in ivy turned rusty now with the cold weather.

"It's a napkin," Julia said, getting out. "My mother poured her wine on her napkin a while ago, put it on her plate, and then started to cut it with her knife and fork. For Matthew it was a real highlight."

They followed the police officer into the dull corridors of the aging building. The officer was tall and rectangular and had a head that looked as if it had been carved out of a tree trunk. Like Ian Lambton, who used to play for Brookfield and then went on to four seasons at tackle with the Rough Riders before they went under.

"Has your mother gone missing before, ma'am?" the officer asked.

"No. Never. It was my fault," Julia said. Her voice stretched tight.

"It was?"

"I was late going to get her," she said bitterly.

Up the stairs, down one corridor, around the corner. Through two heavy security doors, past the sign that said *General Psychiatry*. The officer addressed the desk nurse first.

"Julia Sterling is here with her husband to see the confused elderly woman who was brought in earlier. They want to make an ID."

"He's not my husband," Julia said.

Donny thought, It's Carmichael, Julia Carmichael. Sterling is all wrong.

"Sorry. You're not the husband?" the officer said to him.

"No. We're not married," Donny said. He hesitated, realized that it sounded like he was trying to tell the world they were just living together. "I'm doing the kitchen," he said.

The nurse looked from the officer to Julia to Donny. She was a heavy woman, used to knowing everybody's business.

"My husband is away at a conference this weekend," Julia said. "Donny is just helping me. Where's the woman you think might be my mother?"

"I have to warn you," the nurse said, "she's been sedated. She was very agitated when they brought her in. A woman and her son found her."

The nurse stood and led them down the hall. "This can be a bit of a shock," she said. "Has your mother been hospitalized before for her condition?"

"She just wandered off!" Julia said. "I don't think she needs to be hospitalized!"

A young woman in a light-blue hospital gown, with pale skin and dark smudges under her eyes, limped down the corridor, her brown hair falling in front of her face, her lips trembling in a constant muttered explanation. Donny tried to distract Matthew from behind but the boy's eyes followed her in wonder. They passed an open door where a rail-thin man in his late thirties, perhaps, with a shaved head and sad eyes sat in bed, turned listlessly to watch them go by, then peered without interest at a magazine.

Finally they came to a locked heavy steel door with one small window.

The nurse said, "Maybe, Mrs. Sterling, you could leave your baby with your friend here, and we'll just go in alone."

"Matthew has seen his grand–" Julia started to say, then she stopped and handed Matthew over to Donny. "Thank you for this," she said, and it was her old Julia Carmichael velvety voice that sent a wave through him, warmed the roots of his hair.

"Come on, Matthew," he said. "We'll go for a walk."

The boy was so light, he fit easily into the crook of Donny's arm and snuggled against his shoulder. They walked back up the corridor while Julia and the nurse went into the locked room and the police officer remained outside the door, his feet spread apart, hands clasped in front of his flat belly, as if standing at ease on a parade square. Donny could feel Matthew turning to look at the policeman even as they walked away.

"Have you ever been in a hospital before?" Donny said to Matthew.

Matthew was looking at the sad-eyed thin man in the bed with the magazine.

"Ever been in a hospital, Matthew?" Donny repeated.

"No."

"I bet you have! I bet you were born in a hospital! Do you remember that?"

"Oh yeah," Matthew said.

"You *do*? You remember being born?"

"Daddy flover."

"What's that?"

"Daddy flover!"

Donny asked several more times then said, "Your Daddy *fell over*, is that right?"

The pale woman with the lank brown hair walked by them again, still muttering. Donny thought she said, ". . . detergent in a whorehouse."

"Flover boom!" Matthew said.

They made three more trips up and down the corridor, then Julia came out of the room. She was having a heated discussion with the nurse while the police officer looked on. He couldn't seem to make up his mind whether or not to pull out his pad and take notes – his hand kept going to his pocket, then withdrawing, then going back.

"I would like to take her right now!" Julia said, near tears. "I can't believe you would sedate her like that and tie her into her bed!"

"Mrs. Sterling –"

"Oh, Matthew!" Julia said and reached for her baby.

"What's the problem?" Donny asked.

"I want them to release her to me right now but they're refusing –"

"Mrs. Sterling," the nurse said. "We need to keep her under observation at least through the night. When she was brought in to us she was very agitated and distressed, she kept taking her clothes off –"

"Oh *please*," Julia said. "This is my mother!"

"She might have suffered a stroke, we're not sure. We need to keep her at least overnight to run some tests. Then I would suggest you can bring her back to Fallowfields –"

"I am *not* going to return her to that place!" Julia said. "Oh, God," she said to Donny, "you should see her in there. When I left her yesterday she was full of spit and fight –"

"Maybe we should go back," Donny said. "You should get a good night's sleep."

"Oh. Bloody likely!" Julia said, then almost immediately, "I'm sorry. I'm sorry! You've been wonderful. You've all been . . . very helpful."

"This is upsetting, I know," the nurse said.

ᔕ

They returned to the parking lot at Hog's Back in silence in the back of the squad car, Matthew asleep at Donny's shoulder, Julia staring blankly out the window at the night, Donny breathing little sips of microcosmic energy. The police officer drove swiftly but not recklessly, his radio bursting forth from time to time with news from the underside of the night. Donny remembered the night Billy Marcello killed that guy in Hull, the swarm of cruisers around Billy's parents' house, the crackle of fear in the air, the odd light of the rotating red lights. He used to play road hockey with Billy in the neighbourhood. Billy had a terrible temper even then, used to pick fights, and when he got older carried a knife.

The parking lot was dark, deserted; all of the other squad cars were gone and the searchers had left. Julia was distracted, exhausted – she didn't even thank the police officer but walked dully to the van, strapped Matthew in his seat, and got in beside him automatically, without thinking.

"Is she going to be all right?" the officer asked, and Donny said she'd be fine, that he would take her home.

It was silent on the drive. Matthew was asleep and Julia stared out the window. Then in her driveway she got out of the van without a thought for Matthew but walked, heavy-footed, to the door, then fumbled with her keys. It took her quite a while.

Donny got the sleeping Matthew out of his car seat, closed up the van, and carried the child to the porch. "I think you'll find your mother is in very good hands," he said to Julia. Then: "Are you all right?"

Julia didn't answer. She walked inside, her shoulders slumped, head drooping. Donny carried Matthew in, closed the door. Julia kicked off her shoes, let her jacket fall to the floor without hanging it up. She seemed to be almost in a trance. "Just put him to bed," she said, not looking at either Donny or Matthew. Donny hesitated, meant to ask if that's really what she meant, but she left, half-asleep, trudged wearily up the stairs. So Donny carefully stepped out of his own shoes and followed her. Julia walked past the baby's room without looking, but said numbly, "Just come and rub me when you've got him down. I have a terrible headache. I think you should sleep downstairs tonight."

"Sorry?" he said.

"Just do it," she muttered and walked into her bedroom.

Donny was left standing in the hall with the child asleep at his shoulder. He could hear her undressing, then a moment later all was still, and he could hear her breathing on the bed. He stepped into Matthew's room then. There was a nightlight and he gradually figured out the set-up: the changing table was on the far side, the clean diapers were stacked neatly on the shelf near the lamp, the wet ones went in the big white plastic pail. Donny struggled with the first pin, but he had good hands for close work and learned quickly. Matthew didn't even wake up. He stirred slightly when Donny put him in his bed, stretched his arms out briefly, made a sucking motion with his mouth and opened his eyes, just the once. Settled back into sleep.

Donny stepped out quietly, stood in the hall for several breaths. Microcosmic energy. She wasn't in her right mind, he knew. She was exhausted from the trauma, dead on her feet, didn't know what she was saying.

He put one foot tentatively into her bedroom. "Julia," he said, then shifted his voice immediately into a whisper. "I'll say goodnight now," he said.

He waited for a reply, then stepped back and pulled the door softly closed.

"You have to come rub me," she said then.

He waited, then opened the door a crack again. "Pardon?"

"You have to come rub me. Just for a minute. My head is splitting."

He knew he shouldn't, but somehow his feet wouldn't turn away. He hesitated, then stepped cautiously into the darkness. His eyes adjusted slowly. It was a large bedroom with a thick carpet on the floor, two massive dressers, a wide bed in the shadows. Donny felt something soft through his socked feet, nearly tripped trying to step around once he realized it was Julia's clothes. There she was, face down on the bed, naked under the sheet.

"Julia –"

She pushed herself up on her knees. Her eyes were closed, she was facing away. Donny could see part of the outline of one of her breasts.

"Just at the base of the skull," she said sleepily. "Like you do."

Donny knelt on the bed, took a breath, then put his fingers in her soft hair. Massaged up and down her neck and head.

"Oh that's good. Oh," she said.

He looked down at the carpet in the shadows, felt just with his fingers. The scalp and neck, then around to the eyebrows, pulled them apart nine times like Waylun Zhi had them do in self-massage classes. Down the sides of her nose, reaching from behind, leaning over her but trying not to press his body against hers. Then he touched her shoulders and she eased herself flat against the bed again. "Oh that's good," she murmured, her eyes closed.

She had wondrously soft shoulders, and he tried to be gentle, not press too hard with his fingers. Then down her arms and squeezing her hands, the special points in the palms. "Don't stop," she said when he started to pull away, so he started on her back, went up and down her spine and then out to the sides, gently massaging her muscles. He pulled the sheet down to the small of her back but no further, and when he had gone up and down several times, and revisited her head and neck and shoulders and hands, he tickled lightly down her back with the tips of his fingers. She responded with moans of appreciation. He didn't want it to end, so he stayed a long time. But finally, when her breathing was deep and even and contented, he stepped away. He was careful to avoid her clothes this time and had almost made it to the door when she said something. He stopped, sure she was asleep, but she repeated it.

"How was the conference?" she asked.

"Good," he said softly, before he left.

He'd left his truck downtown, at least an hour's walk away. He thought about calling a taxi, but it seemed too much trouble: he might wake Julia with the noise, and besides, the walking suited him. It was his own quiet brand of devotion. He didn't want to be a bother, or even particularly noticed. She'd wake in the morning and remember, and he hoped she'd think well of him. Finally. Years and years too late, perhaps, but at least it would be something.

And he could think about her on the walk.

12 ⤳

Bob woke from a deep fog, looked at the blurry red numbers on the hotel alarm-clock radio. The room was black and, for a moment, he receded into an odd, dreamy but bitterly real-seeming death struggle with Stephanie over the burgundy couch. She wanted it for her retirement but Bob couldn't let it go; it used to be his mother's, and there was all his loose change in the cracks. As the dream began to clear he went over everything as a pilot might check the facts of his aircraft before takeoff: Stephanie and I are now completely divorced, he thought; there is no burgundy couch; his mother would have wanted to give it to Stephanie anyway; there's no loose change.

And Sienna Chu was here then left, probably for good.

Bob's eyes hurt, even closed. His back was stiff and his knee throbbed from the debacle in the airplane yesterday. His head felt leaden. He pulled himself closer to the clock so he could read the numbers: 10:18. The morning sessions had started at nine. He'd meant to call Sienna. He remembered having had the thought and also having not moved a muscle. He sat up, reached, and opened the heavy hotel drapes a fraction then turned away from the glaring sunshine. "Awful," he said as he got up, limped to the bathroom. His back felt like concrete. The rubber vagina was twisted on the bathroom floor like a dead rodent. He gingerly stepped over it and into the tub. He stared for a moment at the unfamiliar faucet control. It was a single round pull-knob with no apparent markings for hot and cold.

He stepped out of the tub then pulled the knob and let the water run. There should have been a lever or something to switch the water to the shower but Bob couldn't find it. He also couldn't find the plug for the bathtub. The one lever that was there didn't seem to do anything. Finally, Bob stuffed a wash-cloth down the drain and let the tub fill up with water, then eased himself in.

I need to call Sienna, he thought. I need to tell her . . . what? To explain to her that he'd been sick, a bit of food poisoning. Everything was all right. Marvellous, in fact. She had come to him. It was a miracle.

Slowly, the tub filled. The hot water soothed his aching parts.

The phone rang.

He was out of the bath in an instant, grabbed a towel, ran into the other room. He let two more rings go by as he stood at the phone, dripping, trying to compose himself. "Hello?" he said finally.

It was Julia. "Oh, Bob! You are there," she said. "I thought I'd be too late. I slept in badly. I miss you so much!"

"Oh, honey," he said. "I miss you so much too. You wouldn't believe –"

"I had the most amazing dream," she blurted. "It was so powerful. It was about my mother. We were at the lake. Have you got a few minutes?" And she told him all about it, a garbled tale of her mother in a papyrus boat being unable to bring it to dock because of the slightest of winds. So Lenore had dived in to pull the boat along, and Julia – who was only a little girl in the dream – watched while her mother's friends played bridge in stuffy clothes, and wouldn't look up when Julia ran to them to tell them her mother wasn't surfacing. Then in the morning, Julia's father had come down for his swim, had started yelling, so Julia dove in, and there was her mother, just a few feet from the surface, reaching up, with a little chain dangling from one ankle.

"It shouldn't have been enough to hold her down," Julia said. "It was horrible."

And while she was talking, Bob was reminded of the thousand chains holding him in place – and how wonderful they were, how lost he would be without this woman holding him to a semblance of normal life.

"What's happened with your mother?" he asked.

"She's all right," Julia said, and she explained it all: her mother wandering in Hog's Back, the ricer in the water, how she was sedated in the horrible hospital room. "There were scratch marks on the walls," she said, "and it smelled like old urine, my God, you'd think they never cleaned the place. It would drive anybody crazy to be there. And Fallowfields is so incompetent . . ."

There was a sound at the door, someone fiddling with the handle then a quick knock. "Housekeeping!"

"Oh no. Excuse me, Julia," Bob said, and draped the skimpy towel over his middle. "Please come back later!" he shouted in the direction of the door.

It opened anyway and a sturdy-looking Latin American woman poked her head in.

"Please come back later!" Bob repeated.

"Oh! Yes, sorry!" she said, and took a good look nonetheless. Sienna was right behind her in the hallway, evaporated the thousand chains in a single glance.

"Julia, listen!" Bob said quickly into the phone, panicked and almost dropped the towel as the door closed. "My colleagues are here and I have to get going. I'll call you, all right?"

"*Oh,*" she said, an ocean of disappointment charged into one syllable.

"I'm sorry. I'm sorry!" Bob said, and had the phone halfway down before he pulled it up to his mouth again and said, "I'm so sorry about your mother. I'll call you later!" But the line was already dead.

"Sienna!" Bob took two strides towards the closed door then turned to the dresser and threw on a pair of pants and a shirt before sticking his head out in the hallway. She wasn't there any more. The cleaning woman was halfway into someone else's door, her vacuum and cart behind her. Bob walked down the corridor in his bare feet, looked around the corner, saw the elevator waiting area was empty. He pressed the button to go down. He waited, and in the hall mirror he saw an unshaven, aged, hungover-looking man in shirtsleeves and pants with no shoes or socks. His hair was wet and uncombed, his face looked ghastly.

Before the elevator arrived he turned and walked back to his room. He felt a momentary surge of panic when he realized the door had closed and locked behind him. But his card key was in his pocket from yesterday. I'm lucky, he thought. Despite myself, someone is watching over me.

∽

Bob made it to the conference hall just as people were getting out of the panel discussion on Poe as critic. He scanned the faces emerging from the auditorium: mostly greying, time-worn men and women like himself, talking in clumps of twos and threes, conference binders clutched to their sides.

"So," a voice said behind him, and he turned to see someone familiar, but whose name escaped him. "How is the conference treating you?" what's-his-name asked. A very solid, pear-shaped man with drooping jowls and a shiny pink scalp.

Davis, that's who it was. What's-his-name Davis. Who taught at –

"I'm fine, fine!" Bob said, shaking the man's hand. Penn State. Penn State? Or was it Arizona?

"Started to lose me, I'm afraid," Davis said, shaking his head. "Once we get post-postmodern I have a hard time keeping up. I thought Lewis was right on, though, when he talked about our culture's mortal fear of primordialism."

"Gosh, it's been a long time," Bob said.

"It certainly has. I'm sorry I missed you yesterday," Davis said. "I heard you got a little flummoxed by the slide machine. Are you still – where are you, anyway? You're way up in –"

"Ottawa, yes," Bob said. "And you're –"

"Rice, still. Assistant head of the department, actually," he said, and made a little noise in his throat, a trumpeting burp as if to make it sound at the same time insignificant and monu-mental. "I've published a new book, as it turns out," Davis said, and while he explained Bob didn't listen. He was scan-ning the crowd for Sienna. Minutes later he was aware of Davis still talking about his book. "I see it as a real bread-and-butter, middle-stream reassessment. You might think about it for your freshmen."

"Yes. It sounds good," Bob said.

"I could send you an order form," Davis pressed.

She wasn't anywhere. Bob saw Suddle-Smythe, but he was talking with some other woman, a tall brunette with black horn-rimmed bifocals that she kept on a neck-strap, somehow making them look elegant.

Bob relinquished his business card and clapped Davis on the shoulder as he took his leave.

"We'll have to have you down to give a talk," Davis said. "I heard you were working on the Eureka theories."

"Just some preliminary thoughts," Bob said.

He stepped among the bodies, strained to see. She would stand out in a crowd like this. Suddle-Smythe approached him and introduced the tall brunette, Elizabeth Jersey, a nineteenth-century specialist from UCLA. Bob shook her hand pleasantly and asked Suddle-Smythe straight out if he'd seen Sienna.

"She was here this morning," Suddle-Smythe said, looking around. "That stunning undergrad," he explained to Elizabeth. "She has a first-rate mind," he said to Bob.

"She was here but then she left?" Bob asked.

"She can't have gone far," Suddle-Smythe said.

But she was nowhere to be seen. Bob waited in line at the cafeteria for lukewarm soup and plastic-wrapped crackers, and sat through a dreary meal with a stolid grey-suited man from somewhere in the Midwest who'd thoroughly researched Poe's periodic bouts with plagiarism, and with a tiny woman in an olive-green dress and with a terribly receding chin whose father had read her "The Pit and the Pendulum" every night for a year as her bedtime story.

"He worked on an assembly line. He liked to do things over and over," she said. "He could recite whole paragraphs feverishly. I think he would have done well in amateur theatricals. Are you looking for someone, Bob?"

"No. Yes," Bob said, caught out, reddening slightly.

She wasn't there in the cafeteria, and she wasn't in the afternoon seminar on Poe's tortured relations with his sometime-wealthy adoptive father, John Allan. Bob felt himself grow more agitated and restless as the afternoon wore on. Elizabeth Jersey approached him in the break and asked if he was all right. "You look quite pale," she said with concern, and he did feel that way, sickly, nearly faint.

"No, no. I'm fine," he said. "I'm just, I'm fighting something. I think it was a bit of food poisoning from the airplane yesterday."

"Maybe you should sit down," she said, but he insisted that he was better off on his feet for a while.

"There's a very pretty atrium down this way," she said, and so he went with her, along a corridor and up some stairs and then around a corner. It wasn't a large space, but there was room for a stand of tropical trees, some marble benches, and a glimpse of now-grey sky.

"The secret police in Canada are called CSIS," Bob said as they sat on one of the benches, which was much warmer than he expected, passively heated by the morning's sunshine. "Canadian Security Intelligence Service. They have a beautiful new building in east Ottawa, out in the country, and they put up a very impressive central atrium around some trees that were there. But they paved around the roots, or something, and the trees died, so they glued on fake leaves. You have to get pretty close to tell. A friend of mine from political science was doing some work for CSIS and he couldn't help himself, he jumped up and grabbed one to get a good feel."

"These are real," Elizabeth said, and closed her eyes for a moment, breathed in the warm air. She had very large hands, a bit bony now; they would have been elegant in her youth.

Most of her fingers and both thumbs were ringed, except for the fourth finger on her left hand. She caught him looking and said unexpectedly, "Yes, that's right, I am newly divorced."

"I'm sorry," Bob said.

"Never marry an academic," she said, smiling sharply. Her eyes were painfully bright and she held herself unusually straight.

"Your ex-husband's a professor?" Bob asked.

"He's a serial philanderer," she said. "He cannot resist young skin. At one point he actually made reference to himself and Clinton. You know how Clinton claimed he was the chubby one in school, never popular with girls? And so when he got in a position of authority and attraction he couldn't help himself."

"I'm sorry," Bob said uncomfortably. The air seemed much warmer suddenly, his tie too tight.

"You don't remember me," she said softly, and Bob was gripped with a terrible thought – did I sleep with her? It might have happened years ago, in the wild days. She must've been a beauty. But no, he would've remembered.

"Have we met?" he asked haltingly.

"It was in San Diego. You brought your wife, Julia. I got to know her better than I did you. She and I had some wonderful long chats, walking in the evening. I remember she was so nervous about her paper. What was it on? Poe's sense of the feminine, I think."

"Oh, yes," Bob said, brightening, and he almost said, "She wrote that for me, I was her supervisor," but caught himself. Instead he said, "I think I remember you."

"She *has* something, you know," Elizabeth said. "A real spark. Well, you know. She has so much energy and passion, she must be doing wonderful work now. Did she finish her Ph.D.? Is she teaching somewhere?"

"She's taking a break," Bob said, looking around to see if there might be a means of easy escape. "We have a child now, a little boy," he explained. "And she's completely into it, as you might expect."

"Oh, congratulations!" Elizabeth said. A warmth flooded her eyes and seemed genuine. "You must be so proud!"

"Yes. Yes," Bob said.

"We never had children. Burt didn't want them, he thought they'd take up too much time, destroy our careers. Then I found out what was taking up all of his time."

"I'm sorry," Bob said yet again and he looked at his watch. "Probably we should –"

"I understand you've come to this conference with a stunning undergraduate," Elizabeth said then, dangerously. "Can I just ask you something?"

Bob's eyes jumped. "Uh, probably we should be heading back –"

"Just for my own edification. For my own struggle with truth," she said. Her lips were pulled tight now and she was suddenly working hard to maintain her composure.

"The next session is just about to start." He glanced wildly at his watch and started to rise, but she jerked him back down by the tail of his jacket.

"I'd just like to know, would you ever consider driving over Julia with your car?"

"*What?*"

She was furious now, her eyes hard buttons of accusation. "I mean, you are heading out of your driveway and there she is, standing with her back turned. Would you ever consider just ploughing her over?"

"No!" Bob said. He did get to his feet this time, stepped

away to look at her in surprise. She was crying now, holding herself, her thick brown hair mopped across her face.

"Would you ever . . . take her by the throat and throw her down the stairs?" she asked.

"What are you talking about?"

"You know what I'm talking about," she said, not looking at him. "You just don't want to *think* about it!"

Bob turned and fled. He didn't know where he was walking, it was just away, anywhere away. Along the hall, down the stairs, turn the corner, along another hall, up some more stairs . . . Not to the conference room. It was some kind of academic wing, lecture halls to the left and right. The air was draining away and the centre of his vision was filled with a bright, hard light. He stopped to rest against a pebbly, painted wall, tried to gather himself. What was happening with the air? He loosened his tie, sank down to a squatting position, closed his eyes, but the hard brightness only seemed to grow, and now someone was pressing a needle in his chest, a sudden hot point of pain, and he felt his left side grow numb. Not now, he thought. *No.* And struggled back to his feet.

Relax. *Relax!* He puffed his cheeks and blew out, out, out. Shook his shoulders, rubbed his eyes till the brightness subsided, the needle receded. This had happened before. It wasn't a heart attack. It was anxiety.

He massaged up and down his left side, stretched his leg, stepped tentatively down the hall and took a series of deep breaths.

It was all right. Everything was fine.

13 ⤳

"I don't understand why you're holding me here." Lenore couldn't remember being angrier. She was belted into bed in a filthy room that smelled of urine and had nothing else, *nothing*, besides the bed, a barred window, a hideous door, and walls scratched with disturbing messages. *Die, You Fuckheads. Why are you persecuting me? See you again in hell.* And, strangely, *I love you Loxi.* She had a sharp pain in her bladder and the doctor, a young man she'd never seen before – his eyes were magnified enormously behind thick glasses, she would have remembered that – was spending more time looking at her chart than he was at looking at her. He was a tall man with sloping shoulders and a goatee. Why couldn't men shave any more? "The operation is over, isn't it?" Lenore asked. "You *are* going to let me go to the bathroom, aren't you?"

"Do you feel like getting up?" the doctor asked.

"Well, if you must know, I'm ready to burst!" she said. "Untie me, for God's sake!"

The doctor looked at her curiously, made a note on the chart – he had to hold it quite close to his face to be able to see it – then undid her straps.

"Where are my clothes?" Lenore demanded.

"You should probably stay in your gown while you're here," the doctor said.

"What's your name, by the way?" Lenore asked. She sat up briskly.

"Dr. Halloway. Are you feeling better, Mrs. Carmichael?"

"I'm in considerable pain. Please turn your head if you won't give me my clothes." There was no curtain, even. This was the oddest sort of hospital room.

Dr. Halloway blushed suddenly, hesitated, then turned his head. Lenore struggled out of the bed, pulled off a blanket and wrapped it around herself, then hobbled to the door. She was so stiff and sore! It must be from the operation.

She tried the handle.

"*Why* have you locked me in? Do you *want* me to wet myself? No wonder it stinks in here!"

"I'm sorry! Of course!" Dr. Halloway said and hurried to unlock it with his key. "You're feeling . . . quite a bit better, then?" he asked.

"Oh, for God's sake, I have to pee!" Lenore said. "Which way?"

The young doctor led her down the hall. It was a madhouse. A ghastly relic of a man with vacant eyes and a permanently opened mouth – and no teeth, for that matter – sat in a padded chair repeatedly tapping the floor with his cane. A young woman in a stained, torn yellow sweatshirt twisted her hair around and around a pencil, appeared completely and lumpishly bound to her wheelchair until she turned to look at Lenore, then got up suddenly and disappeared into a room. A boy, barely a teenager, with a shaved head and sunken eyes, was staring gloomily at the wall of his room.

"I have private insurance, you know," Lenore said to Dr. Halloway. "You didn't have to bring me here."

"The bathroom is this way," he said.

"This is what health care has come to?" Lenore asked. "It was a success, wasn't it?"

"Uh, health care?" the doctor asked.

"My *operation*!" Lenore said.

Dr. Halloway looked at his chart again. He doesn't know what I'm in for, Lenore thought. They've bungled my file.

"You didn't have an operation, Mrs. Carmichael," the doctor said uneasily. "But you do seem to be much better than you were last night."

They found the washroom then and Lenore hurried in. It had a single toilet and a sink but no lock; she was sure one of those psychological patients was going to burst in on her at any moment. So she hurried, felt great relief when her bladder released.

"Is there someone I can talk to?" she asked politely, when she got out. "Somebody who has *some* idea about what's going on?"

"I think I can fill you in," Dr. Halloway said. He started walking back towards the prison room, but Lenore stopped. She didn't want to go anywhere near it again.

"You're obviously very junior," she said, trying not to be cutting. "You don't even know about my operation, and you seem to have me confused with someone else."

"I actually admitted you late yesterday," Dr. Halloway said. "And I have consulted with your regular physician, Dr. Beamus. He was here last night to examine you. Do you remember that?"

Lenore bit her lip and tried to remain calm. He towered over her, it was unsettling.

"I came in last night with my husband," she said firmly. "The operation was this morning. I do remember that very clearly. I counted backwards from one hundred, got to ninety-six before the gas took effect. Dr. Beamus did not perform the operation – he's not a surgeon, is he? It was a different doctor. I'm afraid I can't remember his name at this exact moment. But Dr. Beamus recommended him. When my husband comes back he'll straighten you out. In fact he'll probably want to pop you on the nose for your impertinence. Can you please get me my clothes? I really feel I should go."

She clenched her jaw and looked at him hard with her head tilted resolutely. Her mother used to look that way; Lenore remembered learning it, practising in the mirror.

"Mrs. Carmichael, you *haven't* had an operation!" Dr. Halloway said. Again he looked at her chart, as if confused. "You *are* much more coherent than last night, however," he said. "Dr. Beamus has put you on a new drug, thorazinol, and it appears to have had a dramatic impact. Your speech is much better, your awareness of the present moment."

"Young man, are you *refusing* me my clothes?" Lose your temper and no one will take you seriously. Daddy always said that. Lenore straightened up as much as she could – oh, but she was sore. Quite something to be on her feet after what she'd been through.

"Your daughter is coming to get you this morning. Why don't you just rest until she gets here?"

"My daughter? My *daughter*?" Lenore said. "My *daughter* is eight years old!" And she turned in disbelief, in disgust – these broken people wandering the hall, the smell of this place, of disinfectant and lives coming apart. "There must be some mistake," she said quietly, clutching the blanket around her.

"You are doing much better than last night," the doctor said, gently touching her arm.

It was like a bad dream. Lenore closed her eyes, waited for it to clear, but it didn't clear; when she opened her eyes again it was exactly the same. "May I please have my clothes?" she asked again with as much dignity as she could muster.

"Yes. All right," he said uncertainly.

They walked back to the prison room. It really was like a cell, with the hulking great door, the tiny barred window. Dr. Halloway reached under the bed and pulled out a sorry-looking plastic shopping bag, like something you'd see a vagrant carrying on the streets.

"What's that?" she asked.

He took out a dirty, wrinkled, beige dress that obviously wouldn't fit her, it was so large, and anyway she never wore beige, her skin was too light.

"This is what you were wearing last night when they brought you in," he said sadly.

"*Oh!*" she said sharply and she didn't know where to turn. "You've taken my clothes!"

"This is what you were wearing –"

"Can you imagine *me* in something like that? It's a tent, for God's sake!"

"Your daughter will bring some better clothes, I'm sure," he said. "How about some breakfast. Are you hungry?"

Lenore stood for what felt like the longest moment, so still and tense she thought she might shatter. It must be a dream, she thought again. If I just wait . . .

"You can put these on your feet," the doctor said, handing her a pair of paper slippers. She'd never seen anything like it. Numbly she put them on. Her feet were marginally warmer but they made a slidey, rustling noise when she walked, and she felt as flimsy, as insubstantial as they were.

"I think I'll just wait," she said.

୨

Lenore sat motionless in the tired green three-seater with the chipped wooden armrests and flattened, tired cushions. The blanket was still pulled around her. A television was on across the room but she ignored it, as did most of the other patients, it seemed; they retreated into their own separate spaces while the broadcasting noises swirled around them like so much mist. Lenore fixed her mind on this thought: Trevor is coming soon to pick me up. He will have it out with the insurance people, who will sue the hospital, and justice will be done. It wasn't the money; she simply didn't want this to happen to anyone else.

He'll be outraged, she thought. He'll want to hit somebody. All that boarding-school boxing, you never got it out of a man, they were always doubling their fists and ready to lash out. But he'd be gentle with her, oh so gentle, he'd be loving and kind and after he got her home he'd bring her tea in bed with honey, a hot water bottle, would rub her feet and kiss her neck. Maybe it will be like that time, she thought. When she's feeling better, when she's completely over the operation. That one time she remembered so well. It was after Alex was born, a month or so, and Trevor had been so attentive, but there were his needs, you couldn't get around it. He was a real gentleman, but the time comes.

But she'd been sore still. It had hurt to pee, to walk quickly, everything was so sensitive. It was a Saturday, no, a weekday; it seemed so long ago. He was home from work, had a touch of flu or something, but that was just an excuse. The baby was asleep in the next room and Julia was playing downstairs – oh, how she would organize those dolls, they each had a separate existence and character. Trevor was lying on the bed in his blue pyjamas, the old ones he didn't like her to wash, they were already worn so thin and smooth, he was afraid they would fall apart. She'd just had her shower, walked into the room in her robe, let it fall off her as she closed the door.

It wouldn't lock, wouldn't stay closed. They had to be so quiet.

How he loved to look at her. You could tell in a man's eyes. They could hear Julia singing something in the distance, stopped once because they were sure she was on her way up the stairs. But she wasn't and they started again. It was just the way she wanted it and in the end she couldn't keep quiet, she sobbed on him, it felt so good, and he laughed. He thought it was so funny, he laughed and hugged her, lit a cigarette, giggling, and stayed where he was, let her fall asleep on top of him.

She almost had the feeling again. She was within smelling distance of it, somehow, it seemed so close and real. He was coming to get her and he'd be gentle again because of what she'd been through. He might even try cooking a can of soup, serve her in bed with toast and a martini glass of milk. Lenore held herself in the blanket and waited for him to arrive.

ᕐ I4

Every time a yellow taxi went by, it blurred, became a smudge of yellow, worse when Sienna opened her eyes wider. Nothing else smudged, just the yellow taxis. It was hard to tell where one ended and the others began. She was sitting stock-still on a bench by the sidewalk in front of the hotel. She had her notebook open, the bitter taste was in her mouth, and her skin was very thin, waxy; if she moved suddenly everyone would be able to see directly inside her. So she didn't. She had her notebook, had written down *"Central Heights"* and *"life without a remote,"* had done a quick sketch of a non-smudgy, parked taxi with a long, beautiful female leg poking out, a doorman in uniform standing by, face turned away but his eyes peering down at the leg. In the margin of the page, running sideways, she'd written *"Ricky knows,"* and by *"Ricky"* she'd drawn an iris with petals opening like labia.

She couldn't draw without being waxy. That was the funny thing. When she wasn't waxy her drawings were muggish. Smuggish? Druggish. They were druggish when she wasn't waxy and crystal gone when she was. Crystagalon.

On another page in her notebook she wrote:

The grit in my limbs and the ache and the pull
the letter of groceries and the slow sink of drains.

She crossed out "*drains*" and wrote "*blood*" and looked at it.

There was something about Bob. Sienna couldn't put her finger on it. Something twisted and unusual and somehow attractive, if that was the word. Bob as suit. Bob's eyes looking out. Ridiculous, wanting to be caught. Affectionate. Bob both comfortable and uneasy. Bob reaching for his lines. Bob as subject, unaware and yet self-conscious. Bob both ways. Bob the mysterious who seems to be had and then slips away after she's already (almost) counted him. Bob the slippery fish. Not this and not that. More intriguing somehow, not what you'd expect, although he seems to be (he looks like the whole package, but he isn't).

The man behind the man behind the man (behind the suit).

She wrote in her notebook: "*I'm not sure who he likes, the GIM or LGQ.*" Then in the margin she printed in block letters "*Goddess in the Mirror*" in one direction and "*Little Girl Quiver*" in another. It was hard to know. She hated this stage, almost more than anything. The uncertainty, her own flimsy. Who was studying whom? That sort of question. She thought Goddess, she wanted Goddess, but Quiver was winning. The yin side, how powerful is that?

She smelled him first. Turpentine and blisterine. Blisterine? Neoprene. Yards and years ahead of him. It took ages for the rest of him to get there. She sat waxy still, knowing decades ahead of time what was coming. Unable to move. He could see right into her. She didn't bother to close her notebook, he could see right through the cover. He had those eyes. He smelled like he was from another karmention. Killingly and kaustically karmonized.

"Do you have a problem?" she asked, with some effort. He was in a filthy blue greatcoat, torn woollen pants, and battered black military-style boots, had a matted white beard, and skin that was flaking off in a kind of red snow. Not cold snow but warm, human snow. Skin snow. No two flakes the same. Each one a genetically imprinted piece of personal rot.

A smudgy taxi went by, *zoooooong*, like the sun drawn in melting crayon. His fingers were red and puffy and there were blisters all over him, his face, lips, neck, wrists, every part that was visible. Some were purple welts, some red and split, some whitish, perhaps healing. His eyes were silvery and runny.

That was clarity for you. It came in a little tinfoil packet and tasted like it might burn a hole in your tongue if you left it there too long. So you didn't, and except for the blurry taxis everything else was lined in precise silver etchings. Even when they weren't silver. Or etchings. It was lined and exact.

"You're a model, right?" he said.

"Yeah, I'm Cindy Crawford," she said. "Don't tell anybody." She kept her head very still, didn't want the wax to crack and fall. Just barely moved her lips, saw him out of the edges of her eyes. He grinned, showed three brownish teeth. He was very fluid, looked like he might wash away any moment, as soon as his surface tension was disrupted.

"No," the man said. "You are *somebody* though. I know you!"

"I told you. I'm Yoko Ono."

"I saw Yoko Ono. You are *not* Yoko Ono."

"I had the surgery, you know," she said. "I can afford it. Nobody recognizes me any more."

"Oh shit," the man said and put his hand on her knee. She slapped it off but didn't get up. He was the whole history of New York, every bit of smudge on the street. He was immigrants on Ellis Island and Joe DiMaggio kissing Babe Ruth, kissing

Marilyn. He was Dillinger blowing cover to see Myrna Loy in *Manhattan Melodrama* and getting shot; he was King Kong and Fay Wray and her dad slicing ginger root and pouring tea; some grimy back street in the Bowery and Donald Trump's erection and haywire graffiti; he was a wandering soul oozing on the sidewalk, smelling like chemical death, like dry-cleaning solution, like Sid and Nancy at the Chelsea Hotel. He was all of it at once and the wax was very brittle. She had to melt it before she could move very far. There was only one way to do it.

"I want you to show me what's in your bags," she said, going on the offensive. The only way to melt the wax.

"No," he said abruptly and turned his head away as if she'd slapped him there.

"Was it before Lennon was shot?" she asked, and he took a moment to follow her. When he saw Yoko, of course. One little prick and he'd flood away, wash into the sewer.

"No," he said. "After."

"Did you ever see Marilyn?"

"Three times!"

"Bullshit," she said. Her head so still. Like a mannequin.

"I saw her when her dress went over her fucking head."

"You did not," Sienna said.

"I did! She was naked. They surprised her. I was right there."

"What's in your bags?"

"I saw Reggie Jackson," the man said. "I saw him with Wilt the Stilt and Muhammad Ali. They were walking along Fifth Avenue."

"I want you to show me what's in your bags."

She was doing him. She knew it and she couldn't help it. It was self-defence. One little prick.

"I saw Reggie Jackson hit four home runs in the World Series."

Sienna stopped talking, looked at him the way she could if she kept very still. If she didn't move a muscle, just looked. Pure yin.

"I saw Yogi Berra and Mickey Mantle one time. I saw –"

She just looked. Yinned him.

The man stopped, rubbed his leg, turned his gaze away, made a snorting noise in his nose. The words died in his throat. He was etched in silver, like everything else except the taxis. He sighed, seemed to be about to get up and move along. Finally he pulled one of the shopping bags out of his cart.

"This is my bed," he said, and gently took out an orange-and-red polyester sleeping bag, neatly rolled, but ripped, stained in spots. It was waxy but it wasn't. She could do both better than anyone she knew. Be here and there. Have the taxis go *zooooong* but stay with it, play both sides.

"What else?" she asked, doing him.

He took out another bag that had an ancient, dog-eared copy of *GQ* magazine, a metallic green flashlight, a plastic mug, several batteries, a filthy T-shirt, some letters, a can of Lysol, a lone sock, a cracked radio, a book with a torn cover.

"What's the book?" she asked. He hesitated, then handed it over. *Jaws*.

"Who are the letters from?"

"No," he said, and grabbed back the book, started returning things to his bag. But he left the letters till last. She stared at him until he gave in.

"They're from my daughter," he said.

"Read one of them."

"No," he said and stood up, made as if he was going to leave.

"Please," she said. She didn't want to but she reached out anyway, touched his puffy hand. She was getting meltier anyway.

"I don't read those," he said, eyes on the ground.

"You read one for me," she said. "You can tell your friends. You saw Yoko Ono." She smiled and he couldn't resist, she knew he couldn't. It was almost too easy. He stayed standing but pulled out one of the letters.

"'Dear Snakehead,'" he read. Then he looked up and said, "That's kind of like her pet name for me." He looked at the letter again, then read: "'I am in a laundromat in a shithole town somewhere in Louisiana. Conrad still has your boots, he's sorry about the rug, he told me. So now I'm telling you. We heard about a place down the road so we're going to try there. Just wanted to let you know how fucking brilliant everything is. See you, Deb.'"

The man put the letter away. Sienna held out her hand and at first he tried to ignore her, but finally he relented and handed it to her.

"Why does she call you Snakehead?" she asked.

"It's on account of a tattoo," the man said.

"That you have?"

"No, it's one I did for a man who wanted a snake running up his neck and around the top of his head. So some people started calling me Snakehead."

Sienna asked him if he had any tattoos on his own body, but he said no, his mother taught him never to get one. "I just do other people."

"Could you give me a tattoo?" she asked.

He wiped his nose on his sleeve. "Of course," he said. "What do you want?"

"I want a naked woman in chains," she said. "I want you to put her on my right cheek." The man looked at her face and she laughed, everything melty now, it was fine. She said, "Not there." Then he blushed suddenly. His face was already red, now it looked purple. Just for a moment. "In a black hood and high heels. Can you do that?"

He nodded his head. "I've done worse," he said.

"Where's your shop? Can we go there now?"

The man paused to consider, finally said, "All right."

"First you have to tell me about Deb," she said, and she waved the letter, which was still in her hands.

He sat down again. He didn't want to do it so she yinned him till he had to start talking.

"Deb's my daughter," he said. "She's a singer, you should hear her. Fucking beautiful voice. I was a businessman, you know, I wasn't always like this."

"What was your business? Tattooing?"

"All kinds of stuff. I did moving concerns, I was in catering, I was a technician for the Rolling Stones."

"For the Stones?"

"Mick Fucking Jagger. He hired me himself. I did all the lighting, everything. I knew people. My God. Everybody came to see us."

"What about your daughter?"

He was studying the ground. "She got into some bad shit," he said. "You know, the way it happens. But I'm going to hear her on the radio someday. You can't keep some people back. Not with a voice like that. She does that song, amazing, like nobody else. Fantastic."

"What song?"

"That Nancy Sinatra song. Everybody knows it."

"'These Boots Are Made for Walking'?"

"Yeah, that's it. Just like Nancy Fucking Sinatra." And he started singing, right there on the sidewalk. People crossed the street to avoid him, but Sienna laughed, it was the right thing to do. She laughed and clapped and so he sang louder, stood up and did a little dance step, started showing off his old boots.

"What else do you do?" she asked. People were stopping to look at them now, some near the entrance of the hotel across the street, and on this side by the Indian restaurant and the deli and the takeout sushi place. She knew how odd it appeared but she stayed very still, poised – very yin. "What else do you do?" she asked again.

He did "New York, New York" and "The Impossible Dream" and "Blue Velvet." He did "Feelings" and "Mandy" and the theme from *Cats*. Sienna watched and prodded and goaded until the crowd was all around them, pressing in, and the man was Topol singing "If I Were a Rich Man," and people were tossing coins into his bag, laughing, cheering, singing along, and Topol was drunk with himself, with this moment.

Then she slipped away, kept the letter in her notebook because she could.

ら

She walked quietly into the auditorium, sat in the back by herself with her notebook on her lap because there were no little writing surfaces attached to the seats. The wax was gone now, there was no more blurriness, everything was becoming unjuiced. Still hyper-clear, but without clarity. Clarity was drifting away, the way it can so suddenly. She'd been back to her hotel room, had changed into jeans and a white turtleneck sweater, kept her jacket on her shoulders because she was chilled from the walk. There'd been no messages from him.

She was surprised, a bit hurt. Men. What a study! She didn't know what he wanted, what sort of special words, whether to make him on the Goddess or Quiver. Maybe it would take both before he'd crack open.

The auditorium was only quarter full. Almost everyone was down close to the front. There were four panellists: a red-haired bloated face who looked stuffed into his suit like a penis in a condom; a short, balding, pathetic ponytail in sandals and denim; a wiry black man in a dark jacket trying to be dangerous; and a grey-haired, thin-lipped, post-fucking stage-of-life woman who'd shovelled herself into drab, olive pants and a tired beigy cowl-neck sweater.

"The thing we have to remember about this period in American letters," the woman was saying, "was that there was no international copyright law, so American publishers were simply stealing British books and magazine articles, flooding the country with cheap reprints, and thus keeping the monetary value of American writing artificially low. As you know, Poe was very involved with the fight for an international copyright, and he would have been a wealthy man if he could've cashed in on the popularity of some of his works, like 'The Raven,' for example."

"And it would've been interesting to see what kind of shift might have happened in Poe's writing," the stuffed man cut in, "if he'd had sufficient income. It's quite possible, of course, that if he'd had ready access to a well-stocked liquor cabinet he'd never have lasted as long as he did or been anywhere near as productive." There was a titter in the audience, a light squawking of birds. "Some people are beyond a doubt the authors of their own misfortunes. But just to get back to the focus of this discussion . . ."

Sienna scanned the heads below her. She couldn't see him.

"Writers today are every bit as hungry as Poe," the ponytail said, "if you think about it. There are hundreds of literary journals in this country and they don't pay even the equivalent of *Graham's* five-dollar page in Poe's day. I mean, today it's still five dollars a page, maybe ten, although many literary journals pay nothing – you're lucky if you get a couple of contributor's copies. Poets, of course, consider themselves lucky to be paid in toilet paper. Hardly any mass-market periodicals publish short stories any more . . ."

He wasn't there. He hadn't bothered to phone. He wasn't waiting for her here. She opened her notebook and on a blank page wrote:

spiral trains and aeroplanes
sinking like a lung
like a poet on morphine
on a microphone
on a talk show explaining
this is x this is y this is y u fled

She heard the auditorium door open and shut behind her and felt a jolt of adrenaline. She knew but she didn't turn her head. She wanted to be absorbed in something when he found her. There were footsteps, muffled by the carpet, but from a heavy man. She knew it was him.

this is y this is when this is you and that was then

Steps. She focused on the page, wondered if he'd walk right past her, not see her because his eyes were adjusting to the darkness. So she looked up, just as he gazed at her.

But it wasn't him. It was a tall hawk-faced man with enormous hands and patches on the elbows of his sports jacket. He saw her just as he was stepping past and he stopped in mid-stride, pulled his foot back like it was something private hanging out.

"Is anybody sitting here?" he asked, indicating the seat beside Sienna. There were hundreds of open seats all around them.

"Well," she said, and stiffened.

"I want to be able to duck out," he said, and even though she hadn't given her assent he added, "Thanks."

He was enormous and bony and didn't seem to be able to slide past her without rubbing against her legs and examining her chest. Then when he was seated, his elbow took most of the shared armrest.

"So, any fireworks?" he asked and looked at her notebook, which she closed immediately.

"I got here a little late myself," she whispered.

"Larry Barclay, from Berkeley," he said, and held out his enormous, bony hand, which she took reluctantly. His fingers were cold.

"Sienna Chu," she said. "Ottawa."

"Ottawa! I was there, when was that? It must've been 1977. Your prime minister was a rock star or something. What was his name?"

"Pierre Trudeau," she said. "He wasn't a rock star. His wife hung out with rock stars."

"That was it!" he said, too loud. Heads far down below turned to see who was causing the disruption. "You probably weren't even born in 1977," he said.

"I read about it." Sienna sighed, tucked her chin in, clutched her notebook to her lap.

Larry Barclay from Berkeley listened to the panellists for a few seconds, then said, in a slightly lowered voice, "You know, a lot of this is crap."

"I'm trying to listen," she said.

"Yes, of course," he said quickly and leaned back but looked sideways at her, not down at the speakers.

"Do you have a pen?" he asked, after a time.

Sienna bit her lip, then felt in her purse and pulled out her spare pen.

"Thank you."

The ponytail was saying, "I think Longfellow is the exception that proves the rule. That's why Poe was so jealous of him. He married marvellously, was independently wealthy, and made money through his poetry not only by being popular, but also because he invested in publishing himself. He didn't *need* the money the way that Poe did. *Voices of the Night* sold forty-three thousand copies. Poe was sick with envy. But it didn't stop him from currying favour with the great man."

"Excuse me," Larry said, laying his hand on her arm.

"What?" Everything was too clear, that was a problem. Every re-entry was different. She wished she'd taken something else. That stuff that Ricky put in chewing gum that tasted like cherry. You could blur by anything, just hit fast-forward. But not now. She was stuck in crystal mode.

"Do you have a piece of paper?" he asked.

Sienna pulled her arm free, tore out a sheet from her notebook, and handed it over. He took it, thanked her, but had nothing solid to use as a backing. Finally he used the thin armrest, which meant having to rub his shoulder against hers. She leaned away as far as she could.

The woman said, "I think we need to recognize that the excesses of the Longfellow War are symptomatic of a deeper imbalance within Poe's psyche. He attacked Longfellow in print both as himself and posing as other people. He even pseudonymously praised Longfellow so that as Poe he could respond in the negative. These are all signs of extreme disjunction, the juxtaposition of his desperate literary ambitions with his agonizing struggle with poverty and the dreadful realities of the writing life."

Larry Barclay from Berkeley bumped Sienna's elbow. She looked at him with impatience, wondered, What now? He handed her back the piece of paper.

"*What are you doing after this?*" he'd written.

"I think if I can interject," the black man said. "Lorraine, you have to admit that Longfellow was a very popular but tepid poet, perhaps the equivalent in his day of a Robert Frost or a Rod McKuen . . ."

There were noises of protest in the audience and the stuffed man said, "That's just opening a can of worms, isn't it?"

Sienna looked at the piece of paper, felt her anger rising.

"It was certainly a strong part of the debate during Poe's day," the black man countered. "Even if we condemn Poe's methods . . ."

"*I was hoping I could sleep with you,*" Sienna wrote back. When she handed the note over she caressed his forearm briefly. She could feel his gaze but kept her eyes trained on the speakers below. His hand immediately felt her thigh, but she stabbed him quickly with her pen.

"Ow!" he said, but it was lost in the hubbub of the debate.

Sienna ripped out a new sheet and wrote, "*You don't touch me. Not here.*"

Again she handed it over without looking, but didn't brush his arm this time.

"I don't see why we need to bring the name of Robert Frost into this discussion," the woman was saying. "Or Rod McKuen for that matter. The point is that Poe engineered most of the Longfellow War as a desperate bid to build himself up by . . ."

"*Where?*" Larry Barclay from Berkeley wrote back.

"*Tell me what you like first,*" she replied.

Out of the corner of her eye she could see him pausing for a moment, looking at the immobile side of her face. Then he set to writing as if completing a momentous essay in the dying moments of an exam. A minute later he handed over the sheet. She turned ever so slightly away, read his scrawl coolly.

"*Is that all?*" she wrote on a new piece of paper.

"Poe was out of control at the time," the ponytail said. "People commented on it. He wrote a review of Elizabeth Barrett's *Drama of Exile* that was almost schizophrenic, he was so cutting and so gushing at the same time."

He wrote something else, quite crude.

"You can certainly see the same sort of loving hatchet job showing up in today's criticism," the stuffed man said. "Writers can be consumed by ambition and jealousy as much as any professionals, and it's usually frustrated novelists or poets who do the reviews. Somebody did a review of my book last year . . ."

"*I didn't think you would be so conventional,*" she replied.

All four panellists started squawking at once about rotten reviews their books had received.

"*What do you like?*" he shot back, and she smiled softly, took her time composing her reply.

Sienna ripped out another sheet.

"*I want you nearly cracking,*" she wrote. "*I want to know what REALLY turns you on.*"

"She as much as confessed in the article that she didn't like books by men!" the stuffed man said, his voice finally drowning out the others. "And then she proceeded to trash *my* book! I know it has nothing to do with Poe and nineteenth-century conditions, but all I'm saying is this sort of thing goes on today. This woman – I'm not going to bring up her name, she'd probably sue me for slander – she's a fine essayist, a brilliant mind, but there it was plain as day in her review."

Larry was writing in a blur now. He filled a page and handed it over, started on another, then handed it over as well. She could feel his heat and strength, the stupid, thrilling danger of the moment.

"I don't think this is quite the forum for discussion of sexist reviews of current literature," the woman said. "But I can tell you in no uncertain terms that I have had books absolutely dismissed by male reviewers, *when they get reviewed at all*, which by the way is a far more serious, if less blatant, sort of sexual discrimination."

"*You wait here for me,*" she wrote. Then she got up without looking at him, stuffed the sheets of exchanged notes in her purse and walked off, knowing that if she bolted he would chase her, but if she simply walked at a certain speed, without looking back, he would wait and wait for her long after the lecture hall was deserted.

15 ᨆ

"Just leave your seatbelt alone, please. We'll be home in a few minutes," Julia said. They were in the van. Julia reached over with her right hand and snapped the clasp back in place. Her mother immediately started to fiddle with it again.

"I would just like to know where you're taking me!"

"Home! We're going home. *Please*, Mom."

"But this isn't the way! I don't recognize *any* of this!" She was trying to open the door now, pawing the unfamiliar latch, which Julia had automatically locked from the driver's side.

"We're going to *my* home. You're not used to the route, that's all. *Please* leave the door alone."

"I think we should ask for directions. There's somebody!" And she started knocking on the window as they drove past the man. "You didn't stop!" she said. "Now we'll *never* get there!"

"I know how to get to my own home. Just relax, will you?"

"*There's* somebody!" her mother said excitedly. "We could ask him. Oh, *why* won't you stop?" Her fists were doubled and then she started to cry.

"Mother. *Please*."

"You *never* listen. You *never* stop to ask directions. I don't recognize anything. Why don't we just ask? There's somebody!"

They were stopped at a light now. Julia flicked on the radio to light classical music. "Why don't you just listen for a minute?" she asked soothingly.

"Hello! Hello!" her mother said, knocking on the window. The man, sleepy-eyed, wearing a blue tuque and a black nylon hockey jacket that said "*Hawks*," was standing at a bus stop just a few feet away with a white plastic grocery bag in his hand.

"We're okay. I know where we're going. I don't need to ask directions."

"Hello!" Her mother's left hand was making futile rolling motions, over and over, where the window roller would have been on an older-model car. The man looked up, started to walk over. "Oh, here he is!" her mother said. "I *can't* get this window. Blast it! Here he is!"

Julia leaned across, waved to the man dismissingly. "It's okay. It's all right!" He turned his ear in question, motioned to her mother to put down the window.

"I can't get it. Oh, this is so annoying!"

"Fine," Julia said angrily and she lowered the window from the driver's side.

"Hi, there," the man said. He had a day's black stubble on his cheeks.

"Yes, hello," her mother said, very politely. "And how are you?"

"Fine," he said, and smiled. "Do you need help?"

"No thanks," Julia said.

"Well, it's very kind of you to offer," her mother said.

"Where are you going?"

"We don't really know."

"It's all right," Julia said.

"We've been driving for hours and hours, and we thought *you* might know."

There was a horn blast from behind them. The light had turned green.

"Thank you. Thanks!" Julia said and drove off, pushing the button to raise her mother's window. "We're almost there," she said hotly. "*Just relax.*"

"How can I relax? Honestly! I don't know where we're going, you won't ask directions, you won't tell me anything!"

She's not in her right mind, Julia thought. She always thrived on crisis anyway, there's no need to take the bait. Julia focused on the road ahead.

"Why can't we ask somebody?" her mother pleaded. Then, "There's someone! Stop! Stop!" And she started to pull on Julia's arm.

"You're going to cause an accident! Just stay in your seat, please!" Julia didn't think it would work but her mother took her hand away suddenly, sat back, and made a little miffing noise with her nose. Now they were stopped at another light.

"I don't understand any of this," her mother said bitterly.

"I know. I know. But if you could just trust . . ."

"We're driving around aimlessly for hours and hours –"

"We have been driving precisely fifteen minutes." Don't respond! Julia thought even as she was blurting it out. How could she not, she wondered? Confused as this woman was, altered almost beyond recognition, those blue eyes still reached deep into Julia's childhood, those thin shoulders had carried her long before memory, that frightened, uncertain gaze still belonged to her mother.

"And we don't know where we're going. Everything is strange and unrecognizable. I have never been able to get you to ask for directions. Never! This is so typical!" Her hand was making the circling motion again, turning in the air fruitlessly. "And you are such an ass sometimes. Drinking in front of the children!"

"*What?*"

"I asked you not to, but you wouldn't listen!"

Julia stopped herself from responding. The light turned green. It was slow traffic, late Saturday afternoon in the Glebe, an old residential neighbourhood near downtown. The sidewalks were crammed with shoppers, young mothers pushing strollers, elderly couples looking in the shop windows, traffic stopped at every block. Julia edged the van forward into the intersection, but she wasn't certain she could clear in time for the next light because of a bottleneck up ahead.

"You never took me seriously," her mother said. "As long as I had your martini ready, that was all that mattered!"

Inching forward. The light turned red and they weren't quite through the intersection. But there was nowhere else to go. Nothing was moving up ahead. A pick-up truck turned left and crowded in behind them.

"I think I can ask this man!" her mother said suddenly, and then the door was open.

"Hello! Hello!" her mother said. She waved, then wrestled with the seatbelt, which would not let go, then waved again. "Excuse me, sir, could you help us?"

"Close the door!" Julia snapped. She leaned over her mother's lap but the door was too far to reach.

"We've been driving for hours and hours!" her mother announced.

Julia threw open her own door and ran around the front of the van to her mother's side.

"What's the problem?" the man asked. He was an older, fairly short gentleman in a black felt coat.

"Hours! Just hours! And we can't find our way!"

"It's all right. It's fine!" Julia said and pushed her mother's arm and leg back in the van, locked and shut the door.

"Where do you want to go?" the man asked.

"She has Alzheimer's. I *know* where I want to go," Julia said and sprinted around to her side again. Cars were honking behind them; the traffic had cleared ahead and the light had turned green. She drove another block with her mother fighting for release from her seatbelt. Finally Julia parked the van on the side of the road and turned off the engine.

"We are almost home," she said through tense lips.

"I don't believe you!"

"Look at me." And she held her mother's shoulders. "Look at me!" But her mother's eyes wouldn't be still, they roamed constantly from one thing to the next. Julia took a deep breath, tried to calm down. "Look at me. Relax. Look at me."

"You must think I'm crazy!"

"No, you're sick, that's all. But you have to trust me. I know what I'm doing. I trusted you when I was little. When you were taking care of me, I trusted you. Now you have to do the same with me."

"It's all gone strange!"

"Please, stop moving your head for just a moment. You have to look at me." Julia tried to steady her but her mother fought it, grew even more panicky. "It's all right. Shhhhh. Be still."

"*Why won't you let me out?*"

"Shhhh."

"I need to get out! I can't just sit here for the rest of my life!"

"Fine. It's all right. We'll get out." Julia unbuckled her mother, unlocked the doors. Now her mother couldn't figure out how to open the latch so Julia went around to her side and let her out. "We'll just walk for a bit."

"Let's not waste any more time!" Her mother put her head down and started to walk along the sidewalk. Julia closed the door and had to hurry to catch up with her, take her arm. They covered a block, then came to a red light, which her mother didn't seem to recognize.

"We have to wait a minute," Julia said.

"Well! What in God's name for?"

So they crossed at right angles with the green and continued along a back street. The houses were formidable age-darkened brown brick structures that pushed the boundaries of the small lots, with tiny huddling front lawns and gardens sombrely waiting for winter. Her mother didn't look at any of it, was simply intent on walking with her head down in any direction. Julia steered them around a full block and back onto the main street. It was a grey, chilly afternoon and the coat she'd brought for her mother wasn't going to keep her warm long.

"Here's the van," Julia said. "Why don't we get in?"

"Oh! I thought we'd never get there!"

Julia opened the door, helped her mother into her seat, buckled her securely and shut the door. Then she went around to the driver's side and climbed in, hit the autolock, put her key in the ignition.

"Where are we going now?" her mother asked.

"Home to my house. We're very close – five minutes. Can you last that long?"

"But we've been driving for hours and hours! Endlessly! I think we should ask directions!" Her hand had started the rolling motion again, and she was looking out the window for someone to bother.

Julia pulled into traffic again, was halted immediately at another red light.

"Just hours and hours! Nobody listens to me! You never listened to me! You and your stupid poker nights! I told you not to go, but you lost hundreds, hundreds of dollars! And the stains on the rug! That was Mother's rug, she got it in Belgium before the war. But you didn't care. Anything to get out of the house. You said you weren't going to bet. And you came back with holes in your pockets, the windows all broken. What was I supposed to think? In front of the children and everything. The drink is ruining us! And you know it!"

The light turned green, but now there was the sound of a siren behind them. Julia looked in the mirror – fire trucks. She pulled over into a metered parking space. Her mother was rattling away, head down, talking just for the sake of it, it seemed, the same way she'd walked around the block.

"You told me there'd be plenty of money for a vacation this year, but there wasn't, was there? You gambled it away! Admit it! You gambled and you drank and now there's nothing left but holes in the furniture. I asked you to fix the sewing table. You said that you knew someone. That was last month! Now I find holes and more holes, and what have you done? You went down the sewer just like your pals at the club. You're all the same."

Julia turned off the engine. The fire trucks roared past.

"I went down to the cleaners to pick it up and they said, 'I'm sorry, madam.' I looked and there were holes all through it. It was awful. I didn't know what to say."

"Mom," Julia said gently, but her mother didn't seem to hear.

"And then there was that other thing, you know what it is, that thing –"

"*Mother!*" Julia barked, suddenly aware that it was her own mother's voice she was using, the clarion call to lunch, to stop fighting with her brother, to pay attention this instant. Her mother looked up suddenly, her eyes wide, amazed.

"Shhhh," Julia said, and put her hand over her mother's mouth, very gently, as if she were stilling a trembling limb. Her mother pulled back slightly but didn't say anything. Julia started to tickle her down the side of her face. It was one of the things she always loved, light tickles. "I had a dream the other night," Julia said softly, near tears, this was so difficult. But the tickling helped. Her mother stopped squirming somewhat, made pleasant, almost cooing noises in her throat. "Close your eyes, Mom."

"But there were holes everywhere –"

"Lenore!" Julia said. "Close your eyes."

"Everywhere . . . ," her mother said again. But almost dreamily. She closed her eyes.

"Do you remember the gentle place?" Julia asked. "I was a little girl in the gentle place, you were the mommy. Do you remember?"

"This is lovely," her mother said.

"Whenever I had nightmares you'd come sit by me in bed. You'd tickle up and down my arms and hands, my neck and scalp and back. Just like this. Do you remember the gentle place?"

"Mmmm."

"It's a meadow on the edge of the woods. In a clearing. You used to tell me all about it. We'd walk through the woods and then emerge in the sunshine. The grass was so soft, we'd have to take off our shoes and walk barefoot down to the willow tree. Do you remember the weeping willow? So big. The leaves rustling in the wind, the sunlight dappling through. It had magnets, that tree, you just *had* to walk to it, lie down underneath it, the grass was so soft. There'd be the heat of the sun and the cool of the shadows, and the sounds, do you remember the sounds?"

"Mmmm," she said, rocking slightly, her head drooping. Just like Matthew. So suddenly running out of energy.

Gentle fingertip tickles along her mother's papery cheek and neck, along the edges of her ears, gone soft with age like vegetables slowly wilting in the fridge. In a few minutes she was asleep, her head slumped forward, jaw still absently working up and down as if worrying something out of constant habit and need.

Julia stopped talking, continued to tickle so gently her mother's face and neck. Just barely brushing.

"Thank you," Julia whispered. "Thank you for the gentle place. All those years ago. It's wonderful to still have it."

Julia restarted the engine, turned slowly, eased back into traffic. "Huh!" Her mother said suddenly, startled awake. "*Where are we?*"

"Oh no!"

"I don't recognize anything! For heaven's sake! Where are we going?" And she started to fiddle with her seatbelt clasp again.

"Home! *My* home! Oh, Mother," Julia said.

16

Bob shoved the padded lace bra and panties, the corset, slip, pantyhose, and the latex vagina into a small black plastic Central Heights Hotel garbage bag, and stuffed the package in the wastebasket once and for all. Then he emptied his broken briefcase, put all his papers and books in his main luggage, and leaned the briefcase carcass against the wastebasket, since it wouldn't fit in. He did a quick last tour of the room to make sure he hadn't forgotten anything: checked around the bed, behind the drapes, in the closet, in the bathroom. Then he returned to the bed, zipped up his bulging suitcase, and put on his coat. He glanced at his watch: 6:10. It was growing dark outside already. It would be good to get going, to put this horrible trip behind him. Julia would be surprised, elated to see him home a day early. Saturday night! He'd pull up by taxi, it would be like that time he came back from Vancouver, after his flight had been delayed by a freak snowstorm. He'd had a cold for two weeks before that, she wouldn't let him near her, but when he'd walked through the door that time she burst like a dam, they stood in the hallway and kissed and kissed, starving for one another.

That's how he felt now, starving for Julia. She was always more attentive when they'd been apart for a while; it was one great thing they could always count on. When she'd gone to Calgary to visit her brother's family – he remembered it suddenly. She was seven months' pregnant, had trouble walking to the baggage-claim area, her hip was so sore. He wanted to find a wheelchair for her but she refused. Then when he got her home she jumped him – her word for it – wouldn't even let him get upstairs to the bedroom. It was right there on the living-room rug, the fat lady on top – again, her expression – and she climaxed in seconds, the only time it ever happened that way.

Bob picked up his suitcase, walked to the door, opened it, looked behind him one last time to check the room, and nearly ran over Sienna, who was standing with her knuckles raised, ready to knock.

"Jesus!" he said.

"Oh, Bob. Oh, there you are!" she said, and stepped back slightly and then forward again, almost into his arms. He should have embraced her. Clearly she wanted him to, but he stopped himself, and she stiffened. "You're leaving?" she asked.

"It's an, um, emergency," he said.

"What's happened?"

"It's something with my mother-in-law. I have to get back, Julia needs me." Julia. The first time he'd used her name in front of Sienna. It worked like a talisman. *Julia.* Now she was real and the sugar-castle world he'd constructed would be washed away, as it had to be.

"I'm sorry. I'm sorry to hear that," Sienna said. He stood with the door half opened, leaning against his back. "When does your flight leave?" she asked.

"In an hour and a half," he said. "But I have to go now. Who knows what the traffic will be like?"

"Yes," she said, and they looked at one another in silence. She seemed nearly in tears. Bob looked away. Just get down the hall, he thought.

"I'm sorry to leave this way," he said abruptly. "We'll talk next week, all right?"

"Next week?" she said, her voice brittle. She'd have to move for him to get by. Or he'd have to touch her.

"Yes. Is that all right?" He looked at his watch again.

She said, "Fine, sure," but didn't move.

"Could I get my poems back at least?" she asked finally. Her eyes were puffy and the "at least" hurt.

"Oh. Yes, of course!" Bob said. He started fiddling with his suitcase zipper, but was cramped for room. "Here," he said finally, "come on in," and he pulled the heavy bag back into the room and onto the bed. Then he unzipped it, found the folder with her poems, and handed it over. "They're really wonderful, as I said. I'm sorry we didn't get a chance to talk about them properly. Maybe next week. I'll send you an e-mail."

She took the folder wordlessly, hesitated, then sat in the small stuffed chair by the telephone, pulled her knees to her chin and hugged them in a childlike motion. Even in her simple jeans and white turtleneck she was lovely. Bob zipped up his suitcase again, turned to go.

"If you have two minutes, maybe –" she said.

"No, actually," he said quite sternly, and then she was crying.

"Oh, Sienna. Listen." He stepped towards her. She held her face in her hands now, was bent over, her long black hair curtaining her face. "Listen," he said again, and touched her shoulder. Then he got on one knee and kissed the top of her head. Just the once, for comfort.

She tried to say something but couldn't mouth the words. He rose and went to the bathroom, returned with the tissue box. "Of course I have a couple of minutes," he said, handing one to her. "Of course I do."

She took the tissue without looking, blew her nose, wiped her eyes, then picked up another and wiped her eyes again. "I'm okay," she said, took a third tissue and blew her nose again. "Did my eyes run?" she asked.

"No. Your eyes are perfect."

"It's just –" she said, and then she broke down again. Bob looked at his watch.

"I know. I know," he said, and kneeled once more, took her in his arms, gave her a fatherly hug. She really was terribly young, he thought, and he was too old for this stuff. "We'll talk about it in a couple of days," he said.

"Yes. Okay," she said, and stood up so that she towered over him for just a moment. Then he regained his feet and she embraced him, in a daughterly way. He patted her back soothingly. He tried to let go, but she increased the pressure and so he hugged her some more. Then she did let go, turned for a moment, and rushed to him again, kissed him on the mouth. "I know I'm not going to get to do that in a couple of days," she said.

He couldn't find his voice right away, but finally he said softly, "No, no you won't," so they kissed again.

"Oh God. Oh," he said weakly, when they broke apart.

"I know. I know," she whispered.

"Sienna, I can't do this," he said.

"I know. Shhhh," she said, and put her finger on his lips. Then they kissed again. She slid her lips down to his neck, kissed him lightly. "I had this feeling," she whispered, "that we would be different. That we would connect on a whole other level."

"Yes," he said, closing his eyes.

"I'm not . . . I'm not like a lot of women," she said, and kissed his mouth again. His hands roamed up and down her body, he couldn't help it. She was moving against him, was rubbing the inside of his thigh with her own. "I don't like . . . straight-forward men," she whispered.

"No," he said.

"I like . . . twists," she murmured, dipping slightly so that the pressure of his leg increased for a moment between hers.

"Mmmmm."

"I just had a feeling . . . that you were the same."

"Oh," he said. She backed him against the telephone table and began rocking gently against his leg.

"Do you?" she asked.

"Oh. Yes," he said. Then: "What?"

She moved away slightly, looked at him with a flushed face, tiny smile. "Do you like things . . . a little different?"

He probably weighed twice what she did but he had the feeling that she was far stronger, had him surrounded, could crush him if she wanted. He needed to look at his watch, get himself moving forward, out the door, into the taxi, back to his own world. One glance at his watch would set it all in motion, but he didn't feel he could raise his hand.

"A little offbeat," she said, and rubbed him with her small, warm hand right down his front. "Unconventional. Just for private."

"Mmmm," he said, his eyes closed. It felt too good to stop.

"I like things that way," she said. "There are a few . . . *unconventional* things I like a man to do with me. But you have to trust someone so much, don't you? To let down your guard. Let them in."

She unzipped him gently and he let himself lean back. There are other flights, he thought.

"If you had something," she said, "something so private, would you tell me?"

"Uh-huh," he whispered.

"Would you?" she asked again.

"Yes!"

She pressed her body fully against him and nibbled on his ear.

"Tell me," she sighed.

"Oh."

"Tell me. You can. Just say it."

"Oh. Oh."

She pulled her hand away slowly and Bob felt himself caving.

"I don't like macho men," she said, and bit gently the edge of his lip, kissed his closed eyes. "I like to be in charge, whatever it is."

"Yes."

She rubbed him once, swiftly, then stayed very still immediately after. "I bet you like to lose yourself," she murmured.

"I like –" he said, and the words caught in his throat. I need to leave, he thought. I need to get out of here.

"Yes, what do you like?"

He couldn't say it. No, of course he couldn't. But she wouldn't let up. "It's something, isn't it?" she asked. He felt flushed, over-balanced, as if the glue were dripping from his seams. "Please, oh please!" she pleaded. But he wouldn't say. No, of course he wouldn't. It would've been beyond this life. So it wasn't his voice, not his at all that he heard.

"I like to be . . . slightly . . . feminine, sometimes," the voice said, and she smiled, oh, what a smile, the relief and joy that seemed to sweep over her, it reverberated inside him as well. It was all right, it really was just fine.

"I knew that," she said. "Oh, I knew that about you!" and she kissed him so deeply then. "It's clothes!" she said, almost too loud, he felt like putting his hand over her mouth, but really, it was safe, they were in private. "Lingerie," she said, lingering over the word. "I bet you like lingerie!"

"Oh," he said, all resistance crumbling.

"I can't believe this. This is so wonderful," she said. "I am so . . . turned on by this," and she stepped back, looked at him from arm's length with her eyes bright with tears. "Will you do this . . . will you do this with me?" she asked.

I will lay down my life for you, he thought.

"I couldn't bear it if you won't," she said, her face suddenly uncertain, as if he could refuse.

"No. No, of course!" he said, and stepped towards her again. But she kept him at arm's length.

"I want to do it right." She beamed at him. "Oh, I want to do this so right. But not now. You've got your plane –"

"I could take another one."

"No, no, there's Julia, you have to get home to her," she said. "This will be outside all that. Completely separate. It'll be just for us. And we'll have to prepare."

"Oh, Sienna," he said, and had a hard time finding the words. "You can't believe how long –"

"No, no," she said. "Don't tell me now. You haven't time. We need to do it right. I'll do the shopping, all right? But you need to –"

"The shopping?"

"Well, you don't have your own things, do you?"

"No. No," he said quickly. "No, of course not."

"I'll get some things together. But you have to do something too. Can you?"

"Yes! What?" He was nearly bursting.

"You have to shave, of course!" she said excitedly. His hand went instinctively to his face but she smiled, so sweetly. "Not just there!" she said, and kissed him again, playfully.

"Everywhere. We're going to make a stunning lady out of you. It's what you want, yes?"

He could hardly speak. His heart was hammering. "You wouldn't believe how much I've wanted . . . ," he breathed.

"And I want you naked in your skin. For me. Will you? For after class on Monday? Will you? I'll do *everything* else!"

"Yes!" he said suddenly, excitedly. "Oh God. Yes!" It was too much, too much to ever hope for.

"Go. Go!" she said, turning, grabbing his suitcase for him. He was muddled, could hardly think where to put his feet to step in the right direction.

"Bob. Wait!"

"Huh?" He turned back, took hold of the handle of his suitcase.

"You're sticking out!" And she laughed, oh it was glorious, she laughed and tucked him back in, gingerly, it was hard to make him fit. Carefully pulled up his zipper. They kissed again and it was like nothing else.

"Go!" she said, and pushed him towards the door.

⤳ 17

For the last twenty minutes Julia had let her mother worry the stairs. She would start up muttering to herself, get about halfway, then look around in bewilderment. Sometimes she would come down again and sometimes she'd continue up a few more steps before pausing once more. It was well past Matthew's bedtime but he wasn't going down, not with his Gamma like this. He stayed at the bottom of the stairs calling to her until she turned around, then he'd laugh and hide his eyes. But she didn't seem to recognize him. Before reaching the top she'd start back down saying, "Bloody rot!" or, sometimes, "Why on earth would they ever, ever, ever?"

It was exhausting, nerve-straining to watch, to not say anything. When is she going to fall? Julia wondered. She imagined it over and over, the terrible *thud, thud,* then her mother smashing onto tiny Matthew.

Yet, on the other hand, Julia thought, her mother was pretty good with stairs and may simply have entered into a harmless loop that kept both her and Matthew if not happy then at least occupied. Once she interfered her mother would just get onto something else. So Julia held off as long as she could. Finally, when she couldn't stand it any more, she said, "A drink, Mom? A martini?"

"Oh! A drink!" Sudden delight.

The door opened then and Bob walked in, dragging his suitcase. Julia stood stunned in the kitchen.

"Hello! I'm home!" he announced, and for a moment she was paralysed by two simultaneous thoughts: he takes up so much room, and, I've lost an entire day. He looked at her expectantly, then in disappointment, puzzlement. "Is everything all right?" he asked, struggling out of his coat, banging the narrow shelf in the hall but not knocking it down like he sometimes did. "I came home early. It just didn't seem right to stay away when . . ."

"What day is it?" Julia blurted.

"Saturday," he said. "Of course."

"Oh, thank God," she said and she started crying. It was silly, but the wave broke and there she was, sobbing into a dishtowel.

"What is it? What's wrong?" Bob enveloped her in a hug.

"Who are you?" her mother asked halfway up the stairs. "Where's my drink?" Matthew ran to Julia and grasped her leg and told her not to cry.

"I'm all right," Julia sobbed. "I'm all right. It's so good to see you," she said to Bob and pulled him close, kissed him hungrily. "And I'm not going crazy," she said later, quietly, when they came up for air.

∽

Julia closed the den door slowly, crept away, breathed easier when she got back into the living room. Bob had lit a dozen candles, was sitting on the sofa in the shadows with a glass of wine.

"She's down. I think she's exhausted," Julia said, and curled up beside him, fit like a cat beneath his arm, head on his warm chest.

"Do you think she's going to sleep?" he asked. He started kissing her hair. His hand fell naturally to her breast, which was so tender from all the feeding. He was very gentle.

"She just zonked out. But she's been so agitated, poor thing. You should have seen her in the car. I got her to sleep. I do this whole routine, something she used to do with me . . ."

He started kissing her again, she had to stop what she was saying. He'd just lifted her until her mouth was against his and it was like falling into an oiled bath, her whole body felt turned to lotion inside and out.

"You missed me," she whispered. He'd been drinking on the plane, the Scotch was on his breath, but she could smell a slight perfume on his skin – the hotel soap, it made him seem different.

"Oh," he said, and grabbed her too hard, pulled her body right against his middle. "Did I ever."

Afterwards he would tell her all about the conference, who was there, who wasn't, who said what, who argued with whom. Not now, but when they were lying puddled in bed, satiated, bloated with after-happiness – a strange word; she'd read it somewhere, couldn't remember where. *After-happiness.* When they were lying hot and still, snuggled yet separate, he'd start to talk, to tell her everything, all the stories. Where he went for dinner. Who's sleeping with whom. Whose book got trashed, who got a big grant. All of it. He was always this way when he got home, wound up, flushed with the energy of the conference. Any other time he'd just fall asleep like most men.

"Slow down," she whispered. He was going so fast. He seemed delirious with need. Not this time, she thought. Not so fast. Let me be the one delirious with want.

And she was, she'd been half-mad with anticipation all through feeding and cleaning and getting Matthew down, then dealing with her mother, steering her into her nightclothes, washing up, putting her to bed in the guest room off the den. Holding her, tickling, singing to her till her eyes closed in peace and exhaustion.

"Christ, I am in need," he said. He'd negotiated several of her key buttons already.

"No – upstairs," she said. He stood and lifted her in one motion. His hands on her buttocks, she wrapped her legs around his waist and they kissed deeply again. She closed her eyes, just wanted to be carried like this forever.

"Excuse me!" her mother said then, her voice like cracking glass. "But I don't think you should be doing that in church!"

"Lenore!" Bob said, and Julia twisted around, slid off her husband, frantically adjusted her clothes.

"It's bedtime," Julia said patiently, and stepped towards her. "Why don't I just help you back to your room?" She turned back to Bob and whispered, "Could you blow out these candles and wait for me upstairs?"

"Here we are," she said when they were back in the guest room. "You must be exhausted. Here's your new bed. It's a lot nicer than the room you had last night, isn't it?"

"I *hate* this room," her mother muttered.

"Let me tuck you in."

She climbed docilely into bed, turned her cheek to let Julia kiss her, then put her head on the pillow. "It was an awful birth," she said. "Just awful."

"Shhhh. It's all right."

"They pulled the baby out with a rope!" She sat up suddenly, looked around in agitation.

"No, no. Just be calm, please," Julia said. "For tonight, please."

Her mother looked puzzled for a moment, then it was as if she'd decided something, and nodded her head sleepily. Julia started in with the walk through the woods, the clearing, the soft grass, the big willow tree in the distance. Her mother eased noticeably, then shot out of bed with surprising speed and power. "I won't sleep here!" she said, taking three or four quick paces towards the door.

"It's all right, calm down!" Julia rose, tried to keep the frustration from her voice. "Everything's fine. It's time to sleep. You'll feel better."

"There are *snakes* in there." She was headed out of the room.

"No, no, Mom, there are no snakes." Julia said. But her mother was pounding up the stairs now, stiff-legged and much louder than before. "Shhh! Don't wake Matthew. Please, come down here. Please."

Her mother kept going and Julia followed, not knowing whether to grab her. She seemed so tense she might try to fight back, so Julia held off. Her mother walked straight into Matthew's room, snapped on the light. Julia turned it off again immediately. Matthew's face remained unperturbed, serene in slumber.

Her mother made the little snorting noise again, marched out of Matthew's room, and then into the master bedroom. Bob was sitting up in bed in his black silk robe; he'd lighted candles on the window sill, dresser, and bookcase.

"My God!" her mother said, and stopped short, stared at him. "He's going to burn the church down!"

"Lenore, it's just me," Bob said.

"Well, Just-me! I'm Cleopatra!" Then she turned on her heel and walked past Julia out of the bedroom.

"I'm sorry. I'm so sorry," Julia said to Bob. He looked grim, didn't smile at her reassuringly or tell her it was all right.

Tramp tramp tramp. Down the stairs again, Julia following briskly. "Would you like a drink, Mom?" she asked.

"It's about time."

"A martini? Would that do it?"

"That would be a wonderful start. Don't give any to the minister."

"I won't. You sit here, all right?" Julia pulled out a kitchen stool for her. "I'll just be a few seconds." She grabbed a martini glass and some ice and soda, walked to the cabinet in the dining room, came back with the bottle of gin. Her mother was already up and wandering again.

"Wait!" Julia said. "I'm just pouring it. Come back!" She tipped a double shot of gin, added a whisper of soda, nearly spilled the glass hurrying off with it. Her mother was fiddling with the front-door handle.

"It's been splendid, simply wonderful," she said, turning the knob and pulling, turning and pulling. "I don't have the code."

"Here's your martini." But her mother didn't take it, she was intent on opening the door. "Don't you want your martini?" Julia asked.

"No, thank you," she said politely, and nodded her head.

"I've never known you to turn down a martini."

"You're very kind. But I really must be going."

"Where are you going?"

She didn't answer, just repeatedly turned the knob while Julia stood behind her, holding the glass and watching.

"Why don't you come stay with us for a little while?" Julia asked finally. "I have your room all made up. It's late. We can sit for a moment and have a drink and then go to bed."

"Oh, dear," her mother said with a sigh, and her hand dropped from the knob in apparent resignation.

"It's time for a drink, then bed," Julia said. Gingerly she steered her mother back to the bedroom, sat beside her on the bed, handed over the drink. Her mother took it brightly, closed her eyes in pure pleasure with the first sip.

"It's been such a nice visit, dear," she said, took another sip, then leaned over and kissed her daughter. "I am so looking forward to Bermuda."

"Are you?"

"Lovely. Just lovely," she murmured, and sipped again, moved her head slowly from side to side as if in a trance. "You know we went to Bermuda on our honeymoon."

"I thought you went fishing in Quebec."

"It was gorgeous, the sky was just like tonight. Black!" She tittered at her joke. "Trevor was terribly nervous, you know. I can tell you, Mary, you're all right, you know about these things. Don't tell anyone else."

"I'm Julia. I'm your daughter."

"He'd never done it before, you know. Never. Well, except with some cousin, once, by the lake, apparently. And with the minister."

"The *minister*?"

Her mother smiled suddenly, her face full of mischief. "Did I say minister?" she laughed.

"That's exactly what you said."

"Well, I didn't mean the minister. I don't know what I meant. What did I mean?"

"You said Dad slept with his cousin and some other one."

"Oh, not Daddy!" her mother laughed. "*Trevor!* Daddy slept with maids and maidens."

"*Did he?*"

"Oh yes, everybody knew! He couldn't help himself!"

"Isn't that interesting. But, Mom, finish your drink, will you? I have somebody waiting."

"You do?" her mother said, and took a stiff swallow.

Julia whispered in her ear. "Can you keep a secret?" Her mother nodded. So Julia said, "The minister. He's upstairs!" And they both laughed uproariously; it seemed like the funniest thing ever.

"The minister!" her mother said, and spilled some of her drink on the rug.

"It's okay, don't worry," Julia said, and took the empty glass from her, eased her into bed. "I'm going to lie down with you, just for tonight, to help you get used to things. You go to sleep, I'll be right here."

"What about the minister?" her mother asked, giggling, and Julia said, "Don't worry, he'll wait for me!" She turned out the light, kept a reassuring hand on her mother's shoulder, then climbed in beside her and held her frail body. It didn't seem like her mother, not like this, in the dark and quiet, this tired, drooping sack of flesh.

"What does the minister like to do?" her mother asked, chortling. "Does he prefer the missionary position?"

"Enough! Please!" Julia said, and hugged her, tried not to laugh too loud. "Go to sleep." She feathered her fingertips down her mother's arm and the palm of her hand, spent time on her neck and cheeks, felt the old body relax, her breathing deepen.

"Trevor was always a gentleman when I had my period," her mother said dreamily.

∽

Back up the stairs. Slowly, quietly. It wasn't that late. Not yet. Just before midnight. Julia was tired but still tingling. The third stair from the top had a terrible squeak; she stepped over it, slid past Matthew's room without even a breath's noise. The bedroom door creaked and she froze half a minute, but the baby remained asleep, there was no sound from downstairs. She walked in.

The candles were low but still burning. Bob was asleep on his side. He looked so peaceful, but she could always wake him for loving. She shed her clothes quickly. It was cool. She stepped into bed naked, snuggled him from behind.

"Hey," she murmured. "My mother thinks you're a minister."

"Uh?" he said sleepily, and then he said, "Oh, Sienna," and rolled on top of her, had her legs spread in an instant and was hard inside her.

"Oh, *who*?" she asked.

"*Oceana*," he said quickly, his eyes bugging out. "Oh God!" he said. "It was the lost city. I was right there in a dream. There were mermaids everywhere."

"Oceana isn't a lost city," Julia said. "You're thinking of Atlantis. And those mermaids must've been hot, mister."

"*You* are hot. My God, are you hot," he said, and started to thrust, was over-excited in a minute and had to slow down.

"Shhhh. Shhh," she said, stroking him. "Slowly. Gear down." And he did, he breathed out, kissed her deeply, stayed wonderfully still while she rocked and slid beneath him.

"Mama," Matthew said, a whisper in the night.

"*Shhhh!*" Julia said and froze.

"Oh no," Bob moaned.

It was utterly silent. She counted to thirty, breathed, counted to thirty again. Bob was shrinking inside her, it felt so lonely all of a sudden. She tried squeezing with her vaginal muscles, but that seemed to hasten the decline, turned him into a soggy noodle. He pulled out, rolled over with a terrible sigh.

"He's asleep," she whispered. "He was just dreaming." Bob's back was to her now; he was curled up and his hands were covering his head as if he were expecting bombs to fall. "Hey," she said, and felt his nipples through the silk of his robe. Both at the same time; he couldn't resist that. He tried to pretend he was almost back asleep, but she persisted and then he was on top of her again, resurrected.

"Could you get a condom, please?" she asked. He leaned way over to the bedside table, pulled open the drawer. She could hear the rustling of the package as he tore at it, watched while he unrolled the rubber onto his penis. But he was already flagging. In seconds, it seemed, he was limp and small again.

She sat up and kissed him, rocked him, started to feel for his nipples once more.

"Mama!" Matthew said, with intent this time, there was no mistaking it.

"Damn it," Julia muttered. Bob ripped off the slippery condom, threw it bitterly onto the floor in the darkness.

Matthew started to cry. "Mama!" he said. "Mama!"

"It doesn't matter," Bob groaned, and rolled over stiffly, taking most of the blankets.

~ 18

"Donnnn–ny." His mother's voice came down the stairs weak and tremulous, and yet thorny as a scrabby old bush growing out of garbage and gravel. Donny immediately lost his *sung* state of peaceful awareness, though his shoulders remained soft for now, his breathing deep and full, his arms rounded protectively in front of him.

"Did you get the coupons, dear?"

His tongue remained lightly touching the roof of his mouth just behind the teeth. His fingers were spread, but not rigid, in the "beautiful lady hands" posture, the thumbs and forefingers slightly stretched, the other fingers relatively more relaxed. His spine was straight, shoulders rounded, his pelvis tilted slightly, his knees bent, toes lightly curled. His eyes were open to the fullness of the cosmos, but not focused on anything in particular.

"Food Plaza is open right now, but the coupons won't be there all day," his mother said. "I need lemons and eggplant. Did you hear me?"

His spine was subtly stretching and compressing with each breath, exercising the three "hinges of power": the base of the spine at the pelvis, the middle where the chest opened and closed, and the "gate of heavenly awareness," where the spine meets the skull. Each co-ordinated stretching and compressing was designed to pump life-force energy from the "lower well of power" to the middle and upper wells and back again, to balance out his state, smooth out the edges, harmonize darkness with light. He needed to be in a state of complete awareness and relaxation to make it work. His jaw, however, was clamped tight and now he could feel his shoulders knotting.

"Are you hugging the tree again, Donny? Didn't you do that yesterday?"

"I'm almost done, Mother," Donny barked, his voice rougher, his anger stronger than he expected.

"It's just the coupons, dear," she said.

Eighteen breaths, three times with his arms rounded in front of his chest and face, elbows lower than his hands, the energy portals of his armpits open, not squashed closed. *Julia* on the in-breath, *Carmichael* on the out-breath, his energy wheel expanding and tightening.

"I don't mind so much about the lemons," his mother said. "It's more the coupons. I don't know how long they're going to last. Maybe they'll be there all day. I don't know. But I would think there'll be a terrible rush. You know how the Food Plaza gets on Sundays. It's best to go a bit early. And I would like the eggplant. Though it's horrible for my digestion. Are you listening, dear?"

Eighteen breaths, three times through with the arms up, then eighteen breaths, plus nine more, with the arms lowered, hands palm up in front of the abdomen, holding the energy in the lower well of power. With each breath, cosmic energy is drawn through the body's portals of connectivity: the top of the head, eyes, nostrils, palms of the hands, soles of the feet. Draw in fresh life-force, then on the out-breath expel the toxic refuse built up in your energy channels.

"I don't see why you have to hug the tree today when you just did it yesterday," his mother said. "If you found a girl you wouldn't have to hug the tree any more, or do any more foot-stamping or those snaky things with your arms. Whatever happened to what's-her-name? Do you ever see her any more?"

Julia on the in-breath, absorbing the fresh energy of the universe. *Carmichael* on the out-breath, releasing the toxic grubbiness of this dark little house.

"I don't see why you can't *talk* to me, Donny," she whined. "I'm stuck up here. I'd go get the coupons if I could. I did it for years and years. I know that they don't last. That's all. I don't mean to bother you. Could you *answer* me?"

Julia . . . Carmichael. Julia . . . Carmichael.

"Donnnn–ny!"

He tried to stay focused. She said, "I don't know where you go at night. I wish you would tell me. I worry so much. There are so many stupid things men can do at night."

"I'm not doing stupid things, Ma. I'm just walking, that's all. I like to walk."

"You go off in your truck!" she said. He stayed very still, his breath slipped in and out like a single strand of silk being pulled smoothly from the cocoon, no jerking, no sudden, abrasive –

"I said, you go off in your truck! Why won't you talk to me?"

"Because I'm meditating!"

"I don't understand why you can't meditate and talk at the same time."

"It's not like knitting, Ma."

"Well there, you're talking now. You see, you can do it!"

There are many ways to kill somebody, Donny thought suddenly. A quick blow to the front or side of the neck. A knuckle to the temple. Collapse the sternum. Overwhelming force to the solar plexus. Anything like that. One reflex spasm. You go from reptile-brain readiness to catastrophic action and then back to readiness. Like a crocodile exploding out of a muddy hole to pull down a young water buffalo. That's reptile brain. Donny thought of Waylun Zhi demonstrating it: this scrawny man in glasses rounded his shoulders, spread his fingers, widened his stance, became very still and dangerous. Not angry, that wasn't it; a crocodile isn't angry. It's just coiled and loaded on a hair-trigger. *Bam!* Set to go off.

"What was her name, anyway? That last one. Renatta? Rhoda? Reisa?"

"Ramone," Donny barked.

"Oh, *Ramone*. I remember her now. She wasn't right for you. Too – what was it? She wasn't right. She was too –"

"Married, Ma. She's too married!"

There were other terrible, terrible things you could do to someone. A quick blow to the side of the knee, *snap!* It didn't even have to be much pressure. Or stamp on their foot, that will get their attention, collapse their arch. Or a palm strike on the front of the chest, then drag your hand downwards quickly, inflicting great pain and disrupting their energy flow. Someone like Waylun Zhi could pour overwhelming energy into any vulnerable spot on your body, just through touch, a particular grip. On the elbow joint, for example. Donny had seen him knock out a senior student that way in a demonstration. One minute standing fine, then a little squeeze of the elbow and the legs buckled, the eyes rolled back as the body collapsed.

"Not for you!" his mother said. "I knew it as soon as you told me about her. But what about this new one? The one you were out with till all hours. She's married too, isn't she? Don't you ever learn?"

It's easy to get sidetracked, to focus on the violent aspects. You don't want to become a psychopath in order to protect yourself from psychopaths. But it's difficult not to think about it. Waylun Zhi called it sneeze power: pouring everything into one focused explosion, then letting it go, relaxing again. A whiplash through the whole body, making every point of contact a weapon. He could've used it on that guy on the street the other day, the jerk who was so furious after Julia knocked him over. He actually wanted to strike the baby; he was crazy with it, drunk with rage, but stiff as a ladder; Donny just swept his leg out and the guy toppled over. He could've done much worse: kicked him in the groin, or poleaxed the guy with his elbow as he charged in. He could've chopped him in the neck and killed him on the spot. If Donny hadn't stayed calm, hadn't been equal to the situation.

"I said, don't you ever learn?"

"No, I don't, Ma," Donny said. "I never learn." He lowered his hands, blinked several times, walked around the dim living room slowly. All the furniture was old and ratty, had been bought nearly fifty years before. His mother used to keep the plastic cover on the sofa in case of accidents, until the plastic was ripped and shredded. Now the sofa itself was coming apart. The cushion covers had split their seams; the arms were beaten down, exhausted; the whole thing sagged in the middle and looked as if it couldn't support more than one light person at a time.

It was dangerous to just leave off like this, raise and accumulate the life-force without circulating it throughout the major organs and limbs, balancing it properly, then storing it again in the wells of peace. But it would take several other exercises to finish and he couldn't manage them anyway, not with his mother in this kind of mood. He'd probably get angry, with his energy like this, but there was nothing else for it. He walked to the base of the stairs.

"Her name is Julia Carmichael," he called up. "I used to go to school with her. She's married now, has one son. I was helping her out the other night because her mother was lost, and I'm going to do her kitchen floor tomorrow. That's all. I'm going out now to get the coupons."

"How could her mother get lost?"

"It just happens sometimes."

"What kind of woman allows her mother to get lost?"

"She's just lucky, I guess," Donny said.

"What was that? What kind of joke was that?"

"I'm going to get the coupons, Ma."

"What about my kiss?"

He could hear her struggling to get out of bed, to drag the walker closer.

"I'll just be gone a few minutes, Ma."

"Not without my kiss!" she said, and then he heard her clump-thumping across the floor. He started up the stairs.

"I'll be back in ten minutes, Ma."

She got almost to the bedroom door, then quit and sagged against the support. Donny climbed the stairs quickly, took her gently in his arms, lifted her as if she was nothing, which she was, practically, light as a thorn bush.

"Don't you ever leave without my kiss," she said.

He put her back in the little bed. The drapes were closed; the room was gloomy and airless. It didn't take long for his mother to make it feel like it had been shut up for decades.

He kissed her on both sagging cheeks.

"I'll be back in about eleven minutes," he said. "What was it you wanted besides the coupons? Lemon and something?"

"I *wish* you weren't in love with this Julia person," she sputtered. "I don't see any good coming out of it."

"I'm not in love with her. For God's sake!" he said, with too much force, he could feel his body ugly with it.

"Of course you're in love with her. You never mention the name of any woman you're not in love with!"

"That's not true," he said.

His mother looked at him. "Why couldn't you just be *normal?*" she asked.

"Because I'm taking care of *you*," he whispered, and took her hand gently, so softly. He had a horrible, fleeting image of his fingers on her tiny throat, but it was gone in a second. "Let it go," Waylun Zhi was always saying in class. Whatever it was, that stupid, profound, amazing, passing thought. Let it go and it will not harm you.

19 ↲

Bob stepped out of the house. It was a chilly, uninspiring, dull morning, but the cold air seemed to him at least fresh, vital, and as he walked away he felt as if released from bondage. It wasn't just the near-sleepless night, it was his mother-in-law endlessly fussing at breakfast, his son scattering sugar-frosted cereal all over the kitchen floor, his wife distracted, helpless to cope . . . and the anticipation of all that awaited with Sienna tomorrow, blessed Monday. It couldn't come too soon. He'd avoided a fight, had handled himself with restraint, had walked the knife-edge of wordlessness and acquiescence for the sake of domestic non-violence. Now he was out and almost away.

But the front door squeaked open. "Honey," Julia said in a unthreatening, reasonable, and completely commanding voice. "Honey, *could* you take Matthew. *Please?*"

Bob had a wild thought – he could just keep going. Get in the car, drive away, never be heard from again. He could pick up Sienna at her residence then drive south. They'd be in the States in an hour, could go all the way to Florida in three days. Two if they pushed it, but they wouldn't need to push.

They'd be together. Wherever they were, it would just be them.

They were always looking for professors in Florida, he thought.

"I'm sorry to ask you," Julia said, pleading this time. She was leaning halfway out the door in her old terry-cloth bathrobe, her hair a mess, face drained and puffy with strain and fatigue. He could hear Lenore's voice from inside, whining about something. "But it would probably save a life if you just took him for a bit. I'm *not* asking you to take my mother," she added, and he knew one word of disagreement from him – one syllable of protest, of non-compliance – and the detonator would go off. Part of him desperately wanted to do it anyway, to say, "I'm just going to the drugstore," and then watch the mushroom cloud rise.

"That's fine," he said instead, though not cheerfully, not willingly.

"Oh, *would* you? Oh, thank you!" she said, and if he'd been at the porch still she would have hugged him. He knew that and stayed where he was, feeling brittle, resentful. "I'll just get him changed. I won't be a minute. *What is it, Mother?*" she said, then disappeared, the door closed.

Bob stood on the walkway, shoved his hands in his pockets. She wasn't ready in a minute. He knew she couldn't accomplish anything in a minute. But she wasn't five minutes, either, and then she wasn't ten, which seemed like an hour to Bob anyway as he stood in the chilly air suspended where he was like a puppet. He hadn't put his sweater on, just his light jacket, because he knew he was just going to be in the car and then the store. He shivered, paced a bit up and down the walkway. The maple tree in the front looked naked and dead. In just a few days most of the leaves had blown off. There they were, lying on the lawn, one more thing for him to look after.

He didn't want to go back in. Chilly as it was, being outside still felt better than being in the madhouse.

When fifteen minutes had passed, Bob almost decided to leave. He could probably be back before Julia had Matthew ready anyway. He'd say, "Too late," as he walked in the house with his little bag from the pharmacy. "Too late," he'd say, and watch the meltdown.

But when twenty minutes had passed he stepped back onto the porch, put his hand on the door handle, and watched, both knowingly and in amazement, as the inside door opened and Julia thrust a hat-and-mittened, jacketed boy at him. "I'm sorry, it couldn't be helped," she said crossly. "I'd be happy to take him if you want to stay here with *her*."

"No," he said calmly, reasonably, as sweet-naturedly as he could summon. He took the baby in his arms. "Matthew and I will have a good time."

"There are a few other things I need you to get," she said in her way. A few other things. Bob rocked back on his heels as she produced the list. "We need the children's multiple vitamins," she said, "not the dinosaur ones, he won't take those, but the robot ones in grape, not cherry. We need toothpaste, too, both a new tube for us and one for Mother. She uses Longworth's tooth powder, there's only one place that has it, it's the McIntyre's downtown on Rideau Street. Do you know the one I mean? I'm sorry, if you can't manage I'll do it myself later. I just thought that since you're going –"

"I didn't say I couldn't manage it," Bob said stiffly.

"Well, you gave me your look."

"What look?" he asked. Ten seconds to meltdown. He could feel the detonation building.

"Your look," she said lightly. "Like you're putting up with me."

Bob tried not to look at her that way.

"I'm sorry. Anyway," she continued, "I need sanitary napkins. I know you don't like to get them but it would save me a trip and I do get condoms for you. I like the Daisy Clear but not with the wings. You might as well get the bulk box. I love you," she said, and handed him the list, leaned out the door, and caught his ear with a kiss that was close to being a bite. "*I adore you,*" she whispered. She gave his bum a very familiar squeeze, right there in the doorway, and as he turned away she said, "Oh, and diapers, please. I think we need him in disposables at night. Check the weight to get the right size! He's twenty-nine pounds, if you can believe it!"

Bob smiled numbly as he turned away. His feet were cold from standing so long. Matthew started gurgling about a squirrel and Bob opened the van door, put him in his baby seat in the back. "A five-minute errand," he said to the boy as he buckled him in. "Do you see how this works? You want to go out for a five-minute errand and you end up with a yard-long list that takes you all the way to Rideau Street buying sanitary napkins!"

Matthew said, "Kwirrel! Kwirrel!" and pointed out the window.

20

"Hello," Julia said into the phone. She was in the master bedroom, had shut the door, did not, at that moment, know exactly where her mother was or what she might be doing. "Is that Lisette Tremblay? Oh, wonderful, you're there. Yes, hello," she said, and introduced herself, her voice sounding foreign, as if it belonged to some other daughter whose neck was not wooden with strain, who didn't have what felt like an arrowhead buried deep behind her left eyebrow. "We met in the summer. I'm sorry to call you on the weekend, but you'll remember that my mother, Lenore Carmichael, is looking for a room in a full-care facility . . ."

Lisette Tremblay did remember her, and Julia remembered Rideau Gates, with its tired carpets, bored-looking attendants, the vague odour of vomit in the elevator. It had been "no, thank you" then, but now she was desperate, and Lisette Tremblay had seemed like a caring, competent person who wouldn't choose to work somewhere that wasn't worthwhile. It was hard enough to get hold of anybody on a Sunday, but of those Julia could get answers from, the waiting list at Rest Haven was a year and a half, at Tanglewood almost two years. And under no circumstances would she take her mother back to those incompetents at Fallowfields.

"Yes, yes. And are you still looking?" Lisette Tremblay asked. A lilting French accent. "Your mother does not need full-care though, does she?"

When they visited in the summer, they'd just been looking for a smaller place for her mother, for a bit of extra care; they didn't know then that her mind was in the process of rapidly falling apart. So Julia told the woman the story of the diagnosis and explained what had happened at Fallowfields. Low noises of surprise or empathy came over the line – Julia remembered from their summer meeting how this woman would suck her teeth when she concentrated.

"She must be kept absolutely safe. There is no negotiating this," Julia said. "She must be well fed and looked after by competent professionals who've been properly trained in dealing with Alzheimer's sufferers."

"Of course. Yes!" Lisette said, but added, "You know, Fallowfields really has an excellent reputation."

"You have to understand," Julia pressed. "I can't leave my mother there any more. I have no *confidence* . . ."

"Absolutely," Lisette said, as if she understood. But how could she? It hadn't been her mother wandering in the wild waters at Hog's Back. Suddenly Julia thought, they stick up for one another, these old-age-home workers. Probably residents at Rideau Gates wander loose all the time too. She was so angry that she had to stop and ask Lisette to repeat what she'd been saying, which turned out to be a variation of what Julia had already heard elsewhere: "It's just that full-care, you know, it's a much longer waiting list. There are so many now. I think it would be best if you brought her back to Fallowfields. If she still has a bed there."

"Thank you. Thank you anyway," Julia heard herself say. She pressed the phone back on its cradle while her pen dug deep black lines into the pad balanced on her knee.

I can't look after her, Julia thought. I wish I could but I'm just not a saint! And she remembered how her mother would spit out those words at her father. How majestic she could be. "You must have married the wrong woman. I am just not a saint!"

Julia let her eyes linger on a picture by her bed of her sitting with her parents on a big rock in front of a waterfall. Her brother, Alex, had taken it. Her father and mother were on either side of her; little Julia, about ten or eleven, with short-cropped hair, a sun dress, white knee socks, an underbite that orthodontics would soon erase. Although it was a holiday – they'd been hiking in Vermont – her father was wearing a shirt and tie, long pants freshly pressed, polished leather shoes. He was balding already, had his ubiquitous cigarette between his fingers, but down by his side, away from his daughter. He looked confident, all-knowing, vaguely bored. Her mother was in a skirt and stockings and a pale sleeveless flowered blouse, with low-heeled pumps, though not completely flat. No one would wear them for hiking now. But she looked normal, herself, an arm around her daughter, her mouth set, but just for a moment – she seemed to be on the verge of telling Alex how to take the picture. The falls were behind them, mostly mist and fuzz with this focus and angle. And it was just a trick of the angle, too, that made it seem that they were all on the verge of falling over, were standing innocent and unaware, flushed from the hike so far, had no idea how close they were to the brink.

In the picture her mother looked like a woman of her generation, but who'd had her children somewhat late and reluctantly, a woman who knew seven different recipes for pâté, who folded the napkins like flowers in the wine glasses and was aware of her partner's strong suit even if she didn't always lead to it. A woman who planned birthday parties with the organization of a military campaign, who knew in her bones the minute you failed to brush your teeth or wash your hands or put soiled linen in the laundry hamper, who borrowed guide books from the library months before a vacation and within days of the return had the best photos pasted in an album with cheery captions printed below: *"Alex finds a leaf!"* *"Trevor looking handsome."* *"Lost in a good book."*

She was the backwards-spelling champion of her elementary school, and at breakfast used to torment her daughter with elaborate tests of mental arithmetic, impatiently tapping her fingers on the table while Julia tried to work things out. This brainy, glint-eyed woman who had all the answers but never quite seemed to know what to do with her life. How pathetic she would appear to Julia just a few years later – constantly starting this course or that, on the verge of being saved by Intro to Sociology, the Art of Pottery, or the Bible in Modern Thought. Unable to make up her mind, to commit to something while the whole world was changing.

Too late now, Julia thought. Somehow decades had gone by. She picked up the phone again to give in, to call Fallowfields, but then put it down. It was her last option really, but she didn't want to think about it now. She carried the framed photo downstairs, where she found her mother squatting on her heels in the den, pawing at the rug.

"What's the problem? What are you looking for?" Julia asked.

"Nothing!" her mother said, pawing, pawing. It was a strangely animalistic movement, as if she were digging, or cleaning herself off.

"Here, I've found something," Julia said and put her hands on her mother's to make them stop.

"I believe I have too!" her mother said.

"What have you found?"

"It's really something," she said. "I don't know what it is. I've lost the word. How does that happen?"

Julia stayed with her, squatting, holding her hands, until her mother stood up suddenly and announced, "It's been lovely!" and started walking away. She walked to the sofa and pulled up one of the cushions, examined it intently, then threw it aside and pulled up another.

"Mom, I've found a photo of all of us from many years ago that Alex took in Vermont. Do you remember when we went hiking? Here, leave that and come have a look."

"Is there anything I can get you?" her mother asked. The second cushion went on the floor on top of the first and she uprooted the third.

"No. Please leave that and come sit with me for a moment. I've got this photo to show you."

Her mother took the photo in her trembling hand. "Trevor is going to be so annoyed."

"No. No, he won't," Julia said. "Do you remember this trip? Daddy broke the clutch outside of Stowe and we rode down the hill all the way to the garage. Do you remember that?"

"I do remember that. I remember it very clearly," her mother said.

"And the little motel where we stayed? A deer came right up to the window in the morning. Daddy wanted to go get his gun but you wouldn't let him do it. He was just fooling anyway. He hadn't even brought it. The deer was so tame he ate out of my hand."

"And we lost the baby," her mother said sadly.

"No. No, there was no baby."

"The wolf came. It was *awful*. I remember the sandwiches. Sand, and garlic, and old worms. Just awful."

Julia put down the picture. "I'm sorry," she said, and tried to give her mother a hug, but she pulled away.

"It's terrible what they've done. I think they should put a stop to it immediately!"

"Don't worry," Julia said. Her mother was making a rolling motion with her hand again as if she were in the car trying to open the window. She looked about anxiously. "Are you getting hungry, Mom?"

"Awful! Just awful!" she said and got up, walked back to the front door. "I don't know where I've put him!"

"Who, Mom?"

"The little one!" she asked.

"You mean Matthew? He's gone with Bob to do some shopping. They're getting some tooth powder for you. Do you remember Longworth's? I bet Daddy never went out to buy you sanitary napkins."

"That's what I mean!" her mother said. "They go off! Just for anybody! You have to watch them like a wolf!"

ら

Alex called sometime later from Calgary. Julia was surprised – he could go weeks without inquiring after their mother, and Julia had not yet phoned him about the current crisis. She summarized quickly now, downplaying the problems, then left her mother in the den with the phone to have a half-cracked conversation with him. Julia didn't have the heart to try to make her make sense, or interpret for her brother, whose concern did not run as deep, she knew, as his relief in not having to handle the brunt of the responsibility for their mother. While they were talking, Julia took the picture back upstairs, picked up the Fallowfields executive director's card again, put it in her pocket. She gathered the dirty laundry from the hamper and from Bob's closet, brought it down to the kitchen, where she paused to look at the dishes piled in the sink and overflowing from the dishwasher, and to look at the ugly floor. She thought, a colour, I need a colour. Then there was a loud crash and Julia dropped the laundry, raced into the den to find nothing. Her mother was gone. She looked in the bathroom and the living room, then finally in Bob's office, the door to which she thought had been locked. But her mother was there looking out the window to the back garden, and Bob's large brass stand-up lamp was on the floor.

"It's lovely," her mother said, her face nearly pressed against the window. "It must be beautiful in spring."

"Are you all right?" Julia asked. She picked up the lamp. The bulb was smashed, but the rest seemed intact.

"Just gorgeous," her mother said.

"Where's the telephone?" Julia asked.

"Oh, that. It wasn't working. I threw it out."

"Threw it out! Where? In the wastebasket?"

"Yes," her mother said, distractedly. "Oh, robins, it must be cold for them," she said.

The phone wasn't in the wastebasket. It wasn't under the pull-out couch in the den or behind Bob's desk or on any of his shelves. Julia scanned the kitchen cupboards, looked in the oven and the freezer and the fridge. Finally, she went to Bob's fax machine, which was on a different line, and dialled the home number. The upstairs phone rang but not the den phone. It didn't seem to be anywhere and her mother was no help; she was entranced by Bob's office and the view of the dead back garden, the trellis and patio stones and the wicker chairs they still had to bring in before winter.

Julia looked in the downstairs linen closet, in the bathroom wastebasket, and then in the toilet. She knew as she was lifting the lid that it would be there. She knew because she knew her mother, and because this was the worst possible place it could have gone. Even before she saw it she had a sense of things falling away, soundlessly, terribly, without reason, just falling away, and there was nothing to do but fall as well.

She heard Bob come in the house. He walked right up behind her – she was on her knees, staring into the toilet – and he asked, "What are you doing?" Then, without waiting for an answer, he said, "We didn't get the grape robot vitamins, and the girl at McIntyre's said these sanitary napkins don't have wings, so it's her fault if they do. McIntyre's is on *Richmond*, by the way, not Rideau. What *are* you doing, anyway?" he asked again, so she pulled the phone out of the toilet and held it out to him as if he had a call waiting. He was carrying Matthew, and his gaze betrayed a momentary suspicion that the family madness had spread to her as well. He started to ask what was going on, then stopped.

"I can see *you've* had a good time," he said instead.

21 ⤴

lustre like lost ligaments
        of aching, rotting, fallen flesh
  photomarts of family pets
      this tired day this
              laundromat
                  blowing lost as leaves of grass
        as mustard gas
         as alcatraz
    scissor wings and wounded-ness
       lizard-wet, blackened jet
     I saw you at the five and dime
         the dollar store
             the shopping whore
I saw you there in black and white
I saw you spread your wings for flight
I saw you in the dead of night
I saw you kiss the knife so bright
I saw you slither in delight
I saw you slit your tongue

Ricky entered the tiny residence room. Sienna put down her pen and looked at her: the hacked red hair, purple now at the ends, with blonde-black roots, a very cute little diamond in her nose, the tiny gold ring on the edge of her lip. She was carrying groceries in a brown paper bag, had on her big green army jacket, thrown open, and sloppy black pants, a tight top that showed her belly-button, also ringed, and wore her black heavy boots.

"And now, ladies and gentlemen!" Ricky said, her face alight as soon as she saw Sienna. "Just back from New York – *Ms. Sienna Chu!*" She threw her grocery bag aside and launched herself at Sienna, who was sitting on her desk chair, swivelled around so that her legs were stretched out on her bed. She was wearing one of Ricky's giant T-shirts with black fleece tights and no shoes or socks. Ricky landed somewhat roughly on Sienna's lap and the chair rolled backward and bumped the desk so that they both bounced and laughed.

"Did you get the stuff?" Ricky asked, "Did you get it?"

They'd talked on the phone the night before. Sienna had told her everything, and she nodded now. "I got it," she said.

They were on Sienna's side of the tiny room: books stacked on her desk shelf by height, clothes away, bed made, shoes and boots in the closet by the sink. Even her fashion magazines were arranged in an orderly way on her desk: a symmetrical, semicircular fan, *Elle* on top ahead of *Vogue* and *Cosmopolitan*, *Paris Match* and *Vanity Fair*, a cornucopia of pouty bee-stung lips, plunging necklines, thong panties, impossible eyes. Ricky's side was a pandemonium of papers, textbooks, boots, shoes, bicycle parts, two computers on her desk, spent printer cartridges, boxes of diskettes, a CD burner, scanner, a nest of cables and all the boxes piled higgledy-piggledy, bits of foam and plastic packing peeking out.

"Let me see, let me see!" Ricky said, squirming with excitement, but Sienna refused. "Come on!" Ricky pleaded. She was short and solid, almost heavy, quite strong. She wouldn't let Sienna look away.

"It's for research," Sienna said finally, so Ricky snatched the poem from the bed, said, "All right, then I'll have to read this!"

"No! It's not finished!" Sienna said, and though her arm was longer she couldn't reach it, Ricky whizzed it around so quickly.

"Let me see the stuff!" Ricky insisted. Sienna bucked and twisted then, upended Ricky onto the bed, and though the paper tore a little when she took it away, the damage wasn't serious, only part of an unmarked corner was ripped. She sat back again and Ricky grabbed her ankles, started whirling her on the wheeled chair. Sienna shrieked and laughed, and in no time they were on the floor in a heap together, Sienna on top, both of them breathless with hilarity, kissing but not being able to keep it up, having to gasp for air.

"You *promised* you'd show me," Ricky said, and she tweaked Sienna's right nipple till Sienna tweaked hers. Then Ricky lifted her booted left foot and lodged it against Sienna's stomach, threatened to launch her if she didn't show her everything she'd bought.

"It's private. It's for research," Sienna said.

"Bullshit," Ricky said. "I think you like this one."

Sienna shifted her weight back stealthily, then suddenly cleared herself away from Ricky's foot, which didn't move. Ricky remained on her back on the thinly carpeted floor with her leg raised. Sienna wiped a bit of dirt from her front, stepped back, looked inside the big paper bag that Ricky had brought: saltines, cheese, some tired red grapes, a mickey of rum, a small packet wrapped in foil.

"I think you like him," Ricky said, propped up on her elbows now. "I think he gets to you."

"It's research," Sienna said. She took out the saltines and started to eat. She kept her eyes down, hated it when Ricky got like this, aggressive and jealous. Sienna held out three crackers but Ricky stayed where she was. Her legs were wide open and she had that teenaged-boy look in her eyes.

"What's so different about this guy anyway? I don't understand," Ricky said. "You can tell me. That was part of the deal, anyway."

"The deal was I'd share my findings," Sienna said. "I'm not finished yet, so I can't share them, can I? It would be premature." And she slid her bare foot along Ricky's leg, watched those eyes narrow, turn into glistening slits.

"You're avoiding the question," Ricky said after a while, but she didn't turn away, didn't stop Sienna's foot. When Sienna reached the middle she turned her foot to the outside edge, eased it back and forth, then stirred the pot gently. Ricky put her hand on the foot then and began to guide it, increasing the pressure then decreasing, along the edges and down the middle and then pressing sweetly at the top until Ricky's eye-slits were closed, her head thrown back, the small of her back arched in such a pretty way.

"I think you like old fat men who tell good stories," Ricky then said bitterly, ruining it. This whole thing is getting dangerous, Sienna thought. "I think you like a big hunk of red meat every so often," Ricky said.

Sienna withdrew her foot, wheeled her chair back to her desk and sat down again. She had another cracker, examined her feet, which were quite ugly, she thought, too long and thin, bony, and her ankles were lopsided and large.

"The inscrutable Sienna Chu," Ricky said from the floor.

Sienna picked up her poem from where it had fallen, put it in the bottom drawer of her desk, then flipped open a textbook at random and peered at the page. "When the relation of aggregate consumption to national income is in a state of disequilibrium, payments to the factors of production can fluctuate unpredictably, depending on several variables. Consider figure 3.21, which charts the maximizing behaviour of individual economic agents."

"She shuts you off whenever you try to get too close," Ricky said. "We had an *agreement*, don't you remember?"

"Don't you have any assignments due?" Sienna asked.

"I'm supposed to be done tomorrow," Ricky said. "But I don't have all my data ready, do I?"

"I don't know, do you?"

Ricky did a funny walk on her knees over to Sienna and turned her around in her chair. "I thought of a line for you," she said. "For one of your poems." She buried her face for a moment between Sienna's legs, made a funny blowing noise. "'More twisted and beautiful than rain.' Do you like that?"

"It's nice," Sienna said and pushed Ricky's head away, crossed her legs. "But it's not for me."

"No," Ricky said after a time. She was looking too closely into Sienna's eyes, it made Sienna uncomfortable. Ricky knew it too; she looked just long enough for Sienna to squirm, then she got up and walked over to her own desk, had to clear some books and papers just to get at her keyboard. "You know I hate this," Ricky said in a little voice, almost as if she didn't want Sienna to hear.

"Hate what?"

"This – thin ice," Ricky said. She turned on both of her computers. The screens started to come to life.

"What thin ice?"

"You know," Ricky said, so sadly. She could go like that, be thirty feet down in half a conversation. Sienna wondered for a moment if she was on something. It was sometimes hard to tell.

"Do I?"

"Two months ago I didn't even know you," Ricky said. "Next month you'll be on to somebody else. You can have anybody you want. And you know it, it shows."

"I want you," Sienna said, and walked over to Ricky's chair. There was a sudden noise outside the door, it sounded like a gravel truck roaring down the hall, with yelling and screaming, pounding on doors. "Water fight! Water fight!" people shouted, and they could hear the sounds of spraying and laughter, girls screaming and cursing. Then a few seconds later the fire bell started.

And Sienna and Ricky started kissing. "Help! Help!" some boy yelled right outside their door. Sienna had a quick picture of him in her mind: two hundred and twenty pounds, on the football team, razor cut, thicker in the neck than the head, more alcohol than blood in the brain.

"Did you lock the door?" Sienna asked Ricky.

"You check," Ricky said quickly, so Sienna walked to the door. As she pushed in the lock the door shook and the frame groaned. "Help! Help!" the football player yelled. "I'm being raped!"

When Sienna turned back Ricky had drawn the drapes, was standing naked on a pile of grubby clothes, her skin almost green in the glow of the monitors. Her pubic hair was still orange, her breasts were still small and mostly chocolate nipple, she was posing like a movie star turning her profile up for a big screen kiss.

"Your bed or mine, darling?" she asked.

"Mine, of course," Sienna said, and rechecked the door.

"Would you put lipstick on?" Ricky asked, springing onto the bed in a sudden, comical charge under the covers. "I just love it when you wear lipstick."

~ 22

Night took forever to arrive. Bob plunged himself in work all afternoon, or at least he barricaded himself in his home office and pretended to be working. His computer was on, his notes were spread around him on the desk, he made a show of getting up and consulting one or more of the books on his shelf. But he had a hard time concentrating. Matthew invented a game of rapping on the window of his door with a little truck and then closing his eyes to hide, and if Bob didn't immediately call out "Who's there?" or "Hello? Hello?" then the boy would either rap harder or begin to cry.

Lenore too seemed fascinated with Bob's office door, and would wander along periodically and rattle the delicate glass-handled knob. She seemed to have lost all sense of appropriate force, would break the handle, he feared, if she continued for long. So he'd get up and open the door gently and say hello, explain patiently that he was working and didn't want to be disturbed. She responded well to politeness, usually, and would shake his hand, gaze tenderly into the office as if looking at the forbidden kingdom. Occasionally Julia would show up and apologize. Then Bob would return to his desk, stare at his screen a few moments, and either Matthew or Lenore would be back again, rattling the door.

He kept his Scotch bottle in his bottom drawer, had a glass on the bookshelf behind the desk. He wasn't trying to hide anything. A moderate amount of drink was known to calm the nerves, help with the writing. Just the feel of the heavy glass in his hand was reassuring, and he was the kind of person who liked to know the glass was mostly full. So he kept it that way.

He was composing a letter to Sienna. His monitor was well away from the door and he had a certain amount of privacy, but whenever the rattling started he would flip his computer screen over to his notes on Poe's final days and pretend to study them for a moment before standing up and walking once again to the door. "My dear Sienna," his letter began.

I must tell you that nothing has seemed real since I stepped on the plane home last night. My subsequent life has been an interminable interlude before seeing you again. The memory of your remarkable eyes, the scent of your skin, just the thought that you are out there, my own, such extraordinary beauty. I do feel blessed.

My dear Sienna, we must stay quiet. There is a jealousy in life that seeks to rob us of whatever strength we have – our youth, our wit, our beauty, our minds. You don't feel it yet but I do, and that is why being with you is like

That's as far as he'd got. He had sent her e-mails before, short notes about interesting articles she might consider, when to meet for lunch, once a risqué joke he regretted almost immediately. She didn't reply to that one; he was afraid that he'd stepped over the bounds, had been too forward too soon.

But she met him at the cafeteria afterwards wearing sparkling black leggings, and though she didn't refer to the e-mail he felt it was all right.

He sat at his computer most of the afternoon rereading his words, dreading the next interruption, trying to finish that last thought: "being with you is like . . ."

ഗ

Dinner was chaotic. Matthew wouldn't eat, but howled, sputtered, screamed whenever Julia brought a spoon near his lips. Then Lenore put her elbow in her soup, seemed to be imagining she was testing the bathwater for the baby. Julia was a hovering wreck, constantly up and down, running out for wiping cloths and retrieving cutlery from the floor. She spilled her own drink late in the meal. It was the worst moment: red wine dripping through the cracks of the table onto the hardwood floor, which hadn't been properly urethaned because Julia didn't want toxic poisons killing her child, so now the wood was badly stained. Julia was inconsolable. Nothing Bob did was right: trying to wipe up with a napkin, running for a towel, barking at Lenore, who started spooning the red wine into the child's bowl.

"Don't you yell at her!" Julia suddenly screamed, at *him*, for God's sake, when he was only trying to protect their son.

"I didn't yell, but I thought it might be a good idea –"

"*Go to hell!*" she shrieked, but he was already there. This was hell, right in his own house, the evening hours painfully ticking by. It was diaper change and storytime, Jack and the Bloody Beanstalk, now and forever. It was Lenore blundering in flustered, rubbing her hands, announcing, "The contractions are ten minutes apart!" and Julia rushing after her, saying, "Mom, it's all right, calm down," in such a shrill, harried, uncalm voice that anyone would begin to hallucinate after a time. It was Matthew peeing out the side of his diaper as soon as Bob had him done up, soaking his pyjamas completely and then running away. It was Lenore breaking down in the hallway, saying, "Why, *why* won't you let me go home? I *never* wanted to come here," with Julia kneeling beside her, shaking with frustration.

Bob had one little private thing he needed to do tonight. Just something on his own. But getting a baby and a grandmother to bed takes two adults three hours and counting. He just wanted to slip into the bathroom, to lock the door and be by himself for a period of time. He deserved it, he needed it. But Matthew would not go down, he was too excited, could sense his father's impatience. "Fee fi fo fum," the story required four consecutive readings. "I smell the blood of an Englishman." Then endless songs and another diaper change, then Lenore, in her nightie, bent over, muttering, came and kissed the boy and pulled him out of bed and said she was going to take him to bed with her.

"No, no, Lenore, you sleep downstairs," Bob said, but Julia contradicted him.

"Maybe just for now," she said, desperately. "*I'm going to call tomorrow,*" she whispered to him. "*They have to take her back. Let's just get through tonight.*"

"Fine. Do what you want," Bob said and walked into the bedroom, pulled the little plastic McIntyre's Pharmacy bag out of his dresser drawer, and went downstairs to his office, poured himself a glass and drank it down for sanity's sake. He refilled the glass at once and held it, circling the amber liquid soothingly. He could hear Julia's footsteps on the stairs. He drank it down, then stepped out of his office and into the bathroom before she could stop him. He locked the door. I don't have to do anything, he thought. My options are completely open. The door is locked, I am standing here, I have the bag in my hands, but nothing has *happened* yet. Nothing.

Sometimes, he knew from some book he'd read a long time ago, actors wake up in the middle of the stage, their mouths open – words are pouring from them, but they've suddenly become conscious of being in the bright lights in front of hundreds of people, in someone else's body, saying their words. Their brains lock, their eyes go huge, they become rabbits in the headlights. The trick is to avoid waking up, to burrow deeper into the situation. Then great things can be accomplished. You become whoever you want to be and people will see only what you want them to see. That's how Niagara Falls gets crossed on a tightrope – by not looking down. Too much self-awareness is disastrous. You'll never leave the cliff-edge, then, never achieve flight.

The door was locked, he had the bag, nothing had to happen. If he thought about it too much then nothing would. So he didn't, it was a conscious act of will. He took off his clothes and started the bathwater, then fit a new razor blade into his little plastic shaver. He looked at himself in the mirror: black curly hair everywhere, though with touches of grey now, some in his chest and underarms. None in his pubic hair yet, thank God. That would be the next degradation.

"Bob! Are you having a bath?" Julia called from the other side of the locked door.

"Yes!" he said, raising his voice above the sound of the falling water. "Is that okay?"

"I guess," she said doubtfully. He never had a bath in the evening unless he was sick. Though sometimes, in the old days before the insanity of parenthood, they used to bathe together, bring out the oil and the scented candles and wine. He could hear both questions in her voice: Are you sick? Or are you trying to be romantic – *now*?

He didn't know how long he was going to take. He was just doing what he had to do and he didn't want to resist. He stepped in the hot water, soaped his calf thoroughly, took a clean, bold stroke with the razor. He'd never shaved his leg before, and now his skin showed a little rectangle of pink. He cleaned the twin blades in the bathwater with two brisk shakes – this will be very quick, he thought – and then stroked twice more before the blades were again clogged with hair.

He sat on the cold edge of the tub, turned off the water when the bath was two-thirds full. The room fell immediately silent, and he became nervously aware of the slight but distinctive scraping sound of the razor. He took several more swipes, tried to be as quiet as possible, but the quieter he got, the more noticeable the sound seemed to be. And the blades kept getting stuffed with his curly black hairs. The bathwater too was turning black and hairy, even though he'd only cleared a small section on the back of his calf. He could hear Julia in the kitchen or living room now saying, "I don't think we should call her now, Mom. It's too late. Time for bed."

Bob stepped out of the bath. His leg still looked nearly untouched. If he quit now, not even Julia would notice. But she wouldn't notice anyway, he thought. He'd leave a bit at the top of his neck, to show out of his pyjamas. He could finish the job in the morning. If worse comes to worst – which it probably would, he thought, with Lenore and Matthew – I can sleep on the couch in my office. No one would blame him in the midst of this chaos. He towelled himself lightly and took out the package of SilkenSkin Slinky Soft Hair Removal Creme with Baby Oil. The glowing, gorgeous woman on the box in the skinny towel was both looking away from him and checking him out of the corner of her eye. "Depilatory Creme," the package said, with "Finishing Creme" and "Silkystyle Puff." He looked in the box and saw two small tubes and a heart-shaped piece of foam. The description on the side of the package read: "Creams away hair naturally with the silken smoothness of blended baby oil, for sensational, sexy results."

The instructions inside the box listed five easy steps to achieving "a bare, sexy look." Step one was to thickly smooth the depilatory creme onto areas with unwanted hair. Bob squirted creme on his right calf, the one he'd begun shaving, and spread it out with his fingers – it had a sharp, chemical smell – then squirted more and spread it until most of his leg was white and gluey, and a great deal of the tube was empty. He should have bought several packages, he realized. Step two told him to wait four to five minutes and test a small area by removing the creme with the foam puff to see if the hair came off. He didn't have a watch, so he counted seconds. His skin felt tingly, alive, and he started to get erect when he thought about what he was doing – preparing his legs to step into silk stockings. Then he heard Julia say, "Matthew! *Oh!*" in a frantic tone of voice that in her current mood could mean anything: that he'd fallen out of bed and his arm was hanging lifeless out of its socket, or that he'd simply woken up and asked for a bit of nubby.

"Bob, are you going to be long?" she asked, exasperated. She was calling from somewhere upstairs. He didn't answer, continued to count in his head. "Because I could really use some help," she said. The subtext was that if he didn't drop everything and come right away then she was going to be in a horrid mood for days. But he couldn't drop what he was doing. He didn't call out and she didn't say anything more.

He counted to three hundred, then gently took the heart-shaped foam, wetted it and wiped away a bit of his leg hair. It came off like loose dirt, leaving the skin beneath smooth and pale. He rinsed the puff in the bath and took off some more hair. After several minutes of wiping and rinsing, most of his leg was bare. It looked strangely white and naked and much smaller, without the fur, but still not particularly female. It was not shapely or strong, but lumpish, with underlying stringy muscles and gnarly knees and his feet were still hopelessly enormous and bony. He felt an initial sense of frustration and disappointment, and he looked at the SilkenSkin box as, he felt, so many women must review it after the operation. Why couldn't I be curvy and voluptuous like her, he wondered, and not simply naked-looking, like a plucked chicken? Because now his leg was pimpling, like chicken skin, and turning red, and then his eyes skipped down to Step Five which said in bold letters: "Some individuals may experience skin-rash or similar negative reactions. Before initially proceeding make sure to test a small area of skin. If rash, discoloration, abrasion, irritation, blistering, or allergic reaction occurs, wash affected area gently but thoroughly with lukewarm water. Do not soap. If condition persists, consult physician."

Bob quickly sat in the bath and splashed water on his leg. Some of the old loose hair floating on the bathwater was now restuck to his skin, as if mocking him. He pulled the plug and watched the water drain sluggishly through the hair. He pulled a bunch of it away from the drain with his fingers but it was replaced immediately by more. He had difficulty getting it off his fingers: the only way seemed to be to wash his hand in the water, but that left the hair heading back for the drain. He got out of the bath, dripping, his bottom half newly coated now in his own discarded fur, and reached for some toilet paper, which he wet and used to wipe clean his hand and part of his leg. But that was slow too, and the hair didn't stick to the toilet paper but drifted off. Now there were little curly black hairs on the floor and the walls, on the sides of the toilet, on the bath mat, crawling up the shower curtain. He freed the drain once more and wiped his hand, put the wet wad of toilet paper into the toilet. Hair on the tiles and the washcloths, loose hair sticking to his body, hair in the sink when he hadn't even been close to it. Hair on the ceiling and the windowsill and on the curtains.

Bob let the bathwater hairs go down the drain, used his fingers to force them past the little steel guard. His shorn leg was covered in stinging, itchy red dots now. Water helped for the instant it was on, but the discomfort only seemed to increase afterwards.

"Bob. Please! *What* is going on in there?" Julia called through the door.

"I'll just be out in a bit," he said calmly. "Don't worry. Everything's fine." He took a rag from the tiny utility cupboard underneath the sink, wet it, and began wiping around the tub. In a minute he had a wet, hairy rag that itself could not be easily cleaned. He tried picking the hairs off and putting them in the toilet for flushing, but that was tedious. Julia seemed to be camped out on the other side of the door. He could hear her seething.

"I was hoping you could be of some help," she said with angry exactness.

"In a *minute*, I said," he snapped back. He threw the rag in the toilet and flushed. It spun round and round doubtfully, then just before he reached his hand in to retrieve it the toilet swallowed it successfully. There were no more rags, so he used more wads of wet toilet paper. He wiped the tub and the curtains, the walls and floors, the shelf where Julia kept the shampoo and conditioner, her facial scrub and bath beads. He wiped behind the toilet and he picked off individual hairs that had become stuck to the mirror, and he flushed down wad after hairy wad. He wasn't aware of when she went away, but at some point he realized she was no longer there. He looked ridiculous with one leg shaved and the other not, and he reasoned that Julia was going to be angry with him whether or not he spent the extra time. So he sat on the edge of the tub and ran the water and slowly, carefully soaped and shaved his other leg, pausing to clean off his razor straight under the tap rather than dealing with another tub full of hair. He soaped and shaved his thighs and then his stomach, his chest and neck and shoulders and arms. He didn't know how to deal with the hair on his back. He tried reaching around behind him, cleared a few patches on his shoulder blades and on the back of his ribs. But he couldn't get it all. He inserted a new set of blades to shave under his arms. That was nerve-wracking, but he was less tender than he expected, and the milky whiteness of his newborn skin made him feel suddenly female and desirable. When he lifted his arm and looked in the mirror, there he was, remade. He was flabby enough to have small breasts anyway, and the hairlessness was transforming, felt for the moment like the most delectable costume he'd ever tried on.

If I lost some weight, he thought, if I went to the gym every day, and was careful about my food . . .

He hadn't left the top of his chest curly. He'd thought about it, but it was hard to resist the momentum of the moment.

He took a last wad of toilet paper and carefully began a final wipe-up. There were still quite a few stray hairs. On the doorknob, even, on the funny ceramic knobs at the base of the toilet, behind the faucet and in the medicine cabinet, and still more on the mirror. He wasn't going to get them all. But he got as many as he could and when he ran out of toilet paper the bathroom was pretty clean, as far as he could tell. The toilet was a bit over-full, but he flushed anyway. Wads of toilet paper circled sluggishly, but finally went down. He washed his hands and spread skin creme all over himself – the full tube of SilkenSkin Finishing Creme, and then quite a bit of Julia's vitamin E skin lotion. Even his red and itchy leg felt soothed. Then he stood blushing and elated, looking quite thin already without all that hair.

23 ⌒

Julia sat in silent fury propped up in bed. She had a book open on her lap and the reading light was on. She'd put on the flannel pyjamas that Bob hated and she was looking at the page without having any of the words register. Matthew was asleep. Her mother was in bed, at least for the time being, and quiet, with the door closed. Apparently Bob was finally through in the bathroom. He'd been in there for hours, it seemed, mysteriously mucking about. She didn't know what he was up to and he wouldn't explain. He'd been hiding from Matthew and her mother all day, hadn't helped one iota. She could hear him coming up the stairs. One heavy foot after another. Loud enough to wake the baby. When he walked through the bedroom door she put her head down and read. She was feeling too angry to speak first.

But he didn't speak either. He walked into the bathroom and closed the door and she thought, My God, what now? But she heard the sounds of running water, brushing teeth. Then he peed for twenty, thirty, fifty seconds, a loud, long stream. He'd flushed the downstairs toilet dozens of times. Why did he need to pee so badly now? She could hear him flush this toilet twice, then a third time, and it sounded tired, as if it was broken. When he walked out she immediately looked back down at her book.

He pulled open a drawer, took out his pyjamas, didn't look at her. Then he walked to the door and said, lightly, as he was leaving, "I have terrible gas. I don't want to bother you. I'll sleep downstairs tonight." And he gently closed the door.

Bad gas? She hadn't heard him, hadn't smelled him. She listened now to his heavy feet descending the stairs, heard him rummage in the main-floor linen closet then tread into his office and close the door. The house settled uneasily, unbelievably into silence. So that was it? A few muttered words of explanation, not a glance in her direction?

She was fuming but she wouldn't go down and give him the satisfaction of seeing her lose her temper. Yet she couldn't sleep either, not like this, so she decided to do something useful, something that would hurt him rather effectively, in a completely different way. She'd sort through her clothes, gather together for donation everything that she had no hope of fitting into again.

She opened her closet and immediately found a beautiful linen skirt that no longer easily zipped up the back – she didn't even have to try it on. The mauve suede pants that Bob had misguidedly bought her just weeks after she'd given birth, and a size too small at that – gone. And the formerly form-fitting green velvet Christmas dress that Bob used to salivate over. But she hadn't worn it for two years now so out with it. She was in no mood for mercy.

Back to the drawers to root out those ridiculous bits of lingerie Bob kept buying for her. There was the pretty, skin-coloured satin camisole she could no longer pull over her shoulders, and various issues of thong underwear that became uncomfortable within seconds of donning them, an assortment of lacy bras too small to contemplate, and bodysuits that made her sweat and feel self-conscious. She hated to think how much money he'd sunk into these items, had never had the courage to just dump them before. But now was a good time.

Where was the purple silk slip? It was Bob's absolute favourite, but it had never fit properly. She knew exactly where it ought to have been, but it wasn't there. She hadn't worn it in ages, it wasn't in the laundry. Where was it?

There were so many things she wasn't going to wear again. The more she looked, the more she found: T-shirts that were too small, or too milky; torn pantyhose; a wide-style belt that fit none of her remaining pants; the spandex tights that she used to go running in, but that showed too much of her belly now (not that she could ever imagine going running again, in her present state of maternal incarceration, joined at the hip to Matthew). Silk scarves, sweaters that needed airing. This time she pulled nearly everything out of her drawers.

Then she stopped, looked around, suddenly conscious of the absurdity of what she was doing. And just as suddenly as she had started, she left the drawers and piles as they were and turned out the light, climbed into bed. She clamped her eyes shut, willed herself to relax. In strained stillness she wondered what she was going to do, was intensely conscious that she didn't know; she felt as if she were outside herself, watching. Would she go downstairs and give him the royal shit he deserved? Or just continue to lie here in the relative peace, though overwound, ready to explode?

Julia thought of her parents and their bitter, dark nights, her mother's voice shattering all peace, her father angrily silent, responsive as stone, while Julia listened in the black of supposed sleep. When they fought it was usually over her father's drinking. He wasn't a raging, uncontrolled drunk, but a steady, purposeful imbiber who, as the years passed, slowly gave himself over to a dulled, deadened evening state, who in later life tended to push aside those things that might distract him, that would spoil the solitude of his drinking. It became a matter of resentful, eventually silent resignation for her mother. But when Julia was young, when the pattern was just beginning to establish itself, there were awful fights. Julia remembered a lamp smashing, and little Alex rushing to the stairs to peer through the banister down into the murk of the living room. Julia had urged him back.

"No, don't worry, it's all right," she'd said, and it was – in the morning the debris had already been cleaned, the broken lamp was safely in the garbage and another one had been brought up from the basement to replace it.

Was tonight about Bob's drinking? Julia wondered. She recognized some of the signs from her father. He had his bottles in certain places; no day passed when he didn't drink. But somehow he always seemed to know when he was over the line. But what else would he have been doing in the bathroom for so long, and why did he feel he needed to hide? Then again, she hadn't smelled a thing, and she usually could.

Julia rolled restlessly in the bed, the time dragging painfully. Finally, when she knew for certain that sleep like this was hopeless, she got up, walked in the darkness into Matthew's room and lifted him out of his bed. How heavy he was getting! Without even opening his eyes he reached out, his mouth open. In her bedroom they snuggled into the big bed together, lying on their sides. She latched him on and held him, stroked his impossibly fine hair. He wasn't really hungry at first. She had to coax him, wake him a bit before he began to feed in earnest. Then it was almost as if he were cleansing her, pulling the jangle out of her thoughts, slumbering her limbs; as if together they were the centre of everything, this nucleus, right now; that nothing else mattered, really; that the sweet milk of deepest sleep would soon be on its way.

It was almost, almost enough.

24

Donny pressed the bell, leaned on his right palm against the door frame, waited. It was cold this early in the morning; he shivered in his light jacket. Everything looked different in this light, too. The last time he'd been here . . .

Well, he wasn't exactly a guest.

He pressed the bell again. He expected Julia, was ready to search her eyes to see what she remembered, if she at all remembered his touching her that night, massaging her back and shoulders and arms, naked in her bed. But it wasn't her, it was her father, a hefty man in a suit, in a hurry.

"Yes?" the man said, looking like he knew Donny was here begging for money or something.

"You must be Mr. Carmichael," Donny said. "I'm Don Clatch, I'm here to do the –"

"Who?"

"Donny Clatch. Julia hired me to –"

"I'm not a Carmichael," the man said, and Donny looked at him in confusion, then in slowly dawning disbelief. Oh shit, he thought.

"I'm sorry," he said and looked again. It wasn't her father, it was her husband, this older, heavy, angry guy in the suit. Donny had to stop himself from shaking his head. Why did Julia Carmichael have to pick someone like that?

Then Julia was there – in her bathrobe still – making the introductions, smoothing things over. "Donny helped me the other night with my mother," she said to her husband as they were all walking back to the kitchen. "He drove me around, and carried Matthew. He even came to the hospital." She said it with no hidden meaning, looked Donny straight in the eye for a moment. So she didn't remember, didn't know. A switch must have flicked in her brain when they'd gotten home.

In the kitchen, Donny could see the mother endlessly opening and closing drawers, and little Matthew playing with the dishwasher buttons. Things got quiet suddenly between Julia and her husband. When Donny looked at them he could see them glaring at one another, this silent argument happening in front of him.

Finally Julia broke the gaze, looked at Donny and said, "Do you fix toilets?"

"Yes. Sometimes."

"Ours has stopped draining," she said, and pointed down the hall.

The husband said, stiffly, "I have to go." He stayed where he was though, watching, for a terrible moment, before finally turning away while Julia watched him, furious about something.

Donny excused himself and walked to the bathroom, took a preliminary tug at the toilet handle. Water filled the toilet bowl and circled dispiritedly without draining. A bit of soggy toilet paper lolled at the bottom. There was a plunger by the side of the tub. He tried not to listen, though it felt as if his whole body had turned into a pair of ears. But he didn't hear anything else between them. He used the plunger several times without success, then returned to the kitchen. Julia's husband was gone. Julia was wiping the counter angrily, Matthew was still banging away at the dishwasher buttons. Julia's mother had gone into the living room. Donny could see her tugging at the drawers of the side table.

"I've got a snake in my truck," he said. "Did anybody put anything unusual down the toilet lately?"

"Bob was sick last night," Julia said. "He might have used a lot of toilet paper, I guess."

"The clog might just be in the trap," Donny said. He went out to his truck and got the twenty-five-foot snake, which he kept neatly coiled near the back. Then he returned and spent twenty minutes freeing the trap, but that didn't solve the problem; the water still didn't drain. He tried the sink and the bathtub, and they didn't drain either. He walked back to the kitchen, but no one was there. They all seemed to be upstairs. Donny waited for another moment, almost raised his voice, thought about walking up to talk to Julia. Finally he decided to just go down to the basement on his own.

He looked for the stack on the main sanitary drain. Normally it would be in the floor close to the water meter and it afforded access so the pipe could be rodded out all the way to the sewer. But older houses could be full of surprises. This basement had a low ceiling and he fumbled for a few minutes trying to find a light. Finally he found a pull-string on a naked bulb near the central beam. It took a while for his eyes to adjust.

The laundry room was neat and orderly, had a worn but warm green rug, a new washer and dryer, an ironing board set up in the corner. There was another room beside it with just a concrete floor, boxes and old furniture piled haphazardly. The third section of the basement was the furnace room, which was packed, also chaotically, with garden tools, old lumber, more boxes, ski equipment, a mouldering set of storm windows, and other junk lost in the shadows. Donny tried to find the light for the furnace room, finally gave up and walked back out to his truck, then returned with his flashlight. There was no working light for the furnace room. The one fixture he found by the fuse box had no light bulb in it.

And there was no stack. He checked all around the water meter and followed the natural line of the drain to the connecting upstairs pipes, moved boxes and an old rocker, a trunk, some lawn chairs, scraps of lumber and ancient kitchen tiles. Nothing. The plumbing seemed to have been constructed without thought to the possibility that the drain might someday become blocked. The pipes were cast-iron, and Donny reluctantly sized up where he would have to split them to put in a proper stack. He took out his tape and pad, made a little diagram and took some measurements.

Then he went back upstairs to the kitchen, which was still empty. He waited, and finally walked up to the second floor. They were all in the baby's room. Julia had changed into pants and a loose sweater, was on her knees on the floor sorting piles of baby clothes. Matthew was on the bed playing with a toy truck, saying "Brmmmm!" and sending it off the edge and onto the floor. The old lady was opening and closing dresser drawers.

"It's a bit more complicated than I thought," Donny said. "I'm going to have to crack the pipe because there's no stack."

"No what?" Julia asked.

Donny explained it to her, slowly, because she didn't seem to be following very well. He told her that all houses were supposed to have an access stack to the main drain, that he needed to build one so he could rod out the clogged area, clear the pipe to the sewer. He said he'd done it several times before, could save her quite a bit of money over a plumber or a drain service. He even had a drain rodder he'd bought in a used-machine shop. It had a fifty-foot flexible rod and four-inch cutters, so he should be able to get whatever the problem was, even tree roots. "Unless the pipe has collapsed. That happens, sometimes, with older pipes. But we'll have to see."

Julia nodded. She looked washed out. "If you could look after it," she said numbly, "I'd really appreciate it."

"I'll have a try, anyway," he said. "I'll have to go to the hardware to get some more pipe."

"More pipe?" she asked.

"To put in the stack," he said, and she said, "Oh, right, of course," as if he'd been talking nuclear physics or microbiology.

ᔕ

You don't win a woman by putting your hands up her toilet, Donny thought in the truck. You're not going to win the woman anyway, he thought. You never win the woman. Some guys always do, some guys never. He wasn't going to impress her by cleaning out her drain or fixing her floor either. If he had any brains at all, he'd charge her plumber's rates and walk away, not worry about it. He drove to the hardware and picked up his supplies, then back to his shed for the rodder. When he got back to the house they were gone, but Julia had left him a note. So he let himself in by the back door, rigged up a temporary work-light near the pipes, and set to work.

Julia returned around noon. Donny found her in the kitchen awkwardly clutching four white plastic grocery bags while Matthew squirmed in her arms. He reached to take the child but hesitated because of his filthy hands, and Julia nearly dropped everything, sank gracelessly to the floor, and let the child climb off her. Julia's mother was right beside her, obsessively picking at something on her hand. Julia's face was hard with tension.

"Fallowfields is going to take my mother back," she said once she stood up. "Tomorrow. Which will be fine, right, Mom?" she said, turning finally to face her.

Julia's mother said, "I think I have to get rid of it, otherwise I'll never get out."

"How's the drain?" Julia asked Donny.

So Donny gave her a complete account. While he talked he was conscious that not only were his hands filthy, but his clothes reeked and his face was probably smeared with grease. He told her about installing the stack, about rodding out the pipe, about how for a while he'd thought the pipe had collapsed after all, which was common enough in the fall with the ground freezing and thawing, shifting around. But it wasn't that. He told her about pulling up wad after wad of toilet paper and rags jammed with hair. She didn't seem to know what to say. "If you have some green garbage bags," he said, "I'll just bag it up and throw it out for you." But she wanted to see it, so he showed her. She brought Matthew down, left him to play for a moment in the hamper in the laundry room, then followed Donny into the gloom by the furnace, where he'd installed the drain stack. He was hoping she'd take notice of the way he'd rigged up his own light, since there wasn't one back in this corner, and of the rodder. She might not realize that most general handymen didn't have one in their power-tool collections. But he was invisible again. She just stood over the plastic tub and looked at the hairy paper and didn't say anything.

"I don't know if somebody got a haircut, or what," Donny said. "But if you could get some green garbage bags . . ."

"It doesn't matter," she said sharply.

"You don't want me to clean it up?"

"Oh, that. Oh yes, please. If you could," she said, and then she turned around and walked off, came back in a minute with the green garbage bags.

"Sometimes these things just accumulate," Donny said. "There's a lot of grease, too, lining the pipes. You might try putting coffee grounds down the drain. Anyway, its clear now." His voice trailed off. She didn't seem to be listening. She just kept looking at the hairy filth in the garbage bag. Finally she straightened up.

"You're right," she said. "Sometimes things just accumulate."

25 ⤸

Students entered the lecture hall talking, laughing, some of them yawning, as if 1:30 in the afternoon were still too early for any sort of intellectual challenge. Bob watched them and tried to stay calm. One boy sheepishly handed in a paper that was two weeks overdue, mumbled something that Bob missed completely.

"I beg your pardon?" Bob said, looking down at the paper where it lay on the front desk.

"Um, sorry it's late, Professor Sterling," the boy muttered.

Bob adjusted his glasses and read the name on the title page, "Clarence Boyd," then noticed that his own last name was spelled incorrectly.

"I'm not sure I can accept this," Bob said. He meant to say, "*I can't accept it*," but his voice disobeyed him. Rachel Billswell – reedy, pale as a root, looking like she lived on coffee and cigarettes – was watching from the front row. He had the absurd thought that she would know exactly what was going on – that he was tense and nervous in anticipation of seeing Sienna and of what they were going to do after class, and that's why he was being so hard on this boy with the late paper.

The boy looked unconcerned, disconnected from the moment.

"Well?" Bob barked. He was normally easygoing, but two weeks late was unconscionable.

"I'm sorry, sir. My father died. In an accident," the boy mumbled.

"*Oh, for –*" Bob began, and he really did mean to lash into him. If he only knew how many times over the years Bob had heard that sort of outright lie . . . but then Bob gazed at the name on the paper again and something clicked. He *had* received a memo about this from the dean. Clarence Boyd. His father had been killed recently on the 416 by a drunk driver in a panel van.

"I'm sorry . . . Clarence," Bob said awkwardly, and the boy dipped his head, turned back to sit down.

Calm down, calm down, he thought. He longed for a drink. His shaved skin itched beneath his suit. He had a bottle back in his office for emergencies, had already taken a few sips in the morning just to get his body running normally. He paced impatiently on the raised lecturer's platform in front of the large green chalkboard. Where was she?

Nearly everyone was in now and the clock showed several minutes past 1:30. Students were often late after lunch, and he usually tried not to start on time, and then to finish early, so that they could get to their next class comfortably. He was expecting Sienna, though, anticipating her arrival, could barely breathe for thinking about it. His plan was to retrace Poe's final, tragic, chaotic days – what was known for fact, what remains of the historical record, what sorts of conjectures and re-creations scholars had come up with. It didn't really fit now since he hadn't finished with Poe's work yet. But it was usually one of his finer lectures and he wanted to impress Sienna, today most of all. He wanted her to sit in the very front and hang on his words, to be entranced, to smile at him secretly now and again but be caught up in the story, admiring him for his grasp and his scholarship and delivery. He wanted her to be there so badly that he wouldn't start without her. But the minutes passed and there was no sign of her. He stood behind the lectern and silently reviewed his notes. He picked up Clarence Boyd's essay and read with dismay: "The ninteenth century had alot of writers, but the scariest of them all was none other than Edgar Ellen Poe."

After fifteen minutes the natural roar of conversation among the students had died down to a respectful, anticipatory lull, and it really was time to begin. But there was no Sienna. What could that mean? He could hardly think about it – it didn't seem possible that she would miss this particular class. Bob looked at the wall clock, glanced at the door, felt filled with sudden, bitter disappointment. He slapped his notes onto the table and on the spur of the moment announced an immediate assignment: to write the first three paragraphs of an Edgar Allan Poe story in a contemporary setting. Groans were soon replaced with looks of disbelief, even horror, at having to produce something creative and thoughtful right now, on the spot, without a computer or a guide to follow. There were the usual protestations and questions, and Bob raged at them. "Pretend it's cold and you're starving and a story you've already been paid for is due in an hour, and you've spent the money anyway and owe a lot more besides. Use your imagination. Pretend you have one!"

Reluctantly, students began opening notebooks, some sharing paper, others begging, receiving, thanking. One young woman didn't even have a pen, but three spare ones were thrust at her. Soon most bodies were bent to the task, words began to flow onto paper. Bob tried to look calm and professorial, as if he'd planned this exercise and knew it to be beneficial to their long-term development. But his heart suddenly was leaden. She'd stood him up. Why? Obviously, she'd changed her mind. Of course she had. That was part of being young and brilliant and beautiful, the ability to eventually dissect situations and realize when a man is a middle-aged, burnt-out slump with a ridiculous fetish, and a wife and child to boot. Of course she'd decided to back out. What could he expect?

Unless she'd been in an accident, he thought. That could happen any time. It happened to Clarence Boyd's father. She might be lying on the cold road right now somewhere. Bob caught himself looking out the window at the street, as if she might be there.

His itchiness flared up. He scratched his chest and arms through his suit jacket, then saw Rachel Billswell looking at him so he stopped. She smiled – my God, as if she knew every detail of his thoughts – then she became absorbed in the assignment again. Some people were racing along, filling up page after page. And now Bob was going to have to mark all these assignments. Rina Stendardo asked how long the three paragraphs were supposed to be, and Susan someone asked if it could be longer than three paragraphs, and a weasel-faced boy who'd never said anything in class before asked if the buried-alive theme was required, or could he concentrate on simple madness or murder?

He gazed again at Clarence Boyd's late paper, but couldn't concentrate, decided he would give it to his grad student, Rosalie . . . who could mark *this* assignment, too, he suddenly realized. If her hours were up already then perhaps he could dip into next term's. She could certainly use the experience.

Bob left the classroom, trudged down the hall, let himself into his office, closed the door. He took his bottle out of his filing cabinet and poured a taste, just half a glass, and drank it down. He had a view of parkland and water from his window, but the sky was unbearably sad, and he felt the weight of every book on every shelf in his little space. They were stacked to the ceiling, here, with the remnants of old projects poking out of file folders, dog-eared, computer-spewed bits of paper with polite, polished, lined-up, constipated words, signifying nothing.

He drank another half-glass, checked his watch. The class didn't finish until 3:00. He should head back now, though, he thought, shouldn't leave them all alone with their assignment, but he couldn't face them somehow, felt as if his body had turned transparent, that they could all see into him. He refilled his glass, just to have the confident feeling of knowing there was more, but then he carefully poured the Scotch back in the bottle, wiped the glass out with a tissue, screwed the cap back on. His hands were much steadier . . . but shaved, clearly; anyone could see if they looked closely. How long would it take for the hair to grow back? Weeks, maybe months. It was a miracle Julia hadn't noticed it this morning. If she'd been any less angry . . .

Everyone was still writing when he got back to the classroom. What have I unleashed? he wondered. He paced up and down on the speaker's platform, looked out at the grey street. Sienna hadn't been hit by a panel van. She'd come to her senses.

When the period ended, half the class was still writing and they gave up their papers unwillingly. Someone asked if he could take his story home and work on it overnight. "I'll have it completed by morning!" he begged, but Bob said no. He felt inflexible, brittle, didn't want to have to deal with students handing things in at different times.

The papers bulging and ungainly under his left arm, Bob walked out in near-misery. Three students were waiting for him with questions; he couldn't even muster the energy to listen to them. "I'm sorry, I'm very late!" he said, waving his hand, walking past. The corridor was jammed with people. They were going to overwhelm him any minute, he felt it suddenly.

And then there she was, standing demurely by his office door, with her long hair tied back sweetly, and wearing a pair of sensible, warm pants, a long dark woollen coat, a knapsack over her shoulder . . . a bulging knapsack. She stood so quietly, watching him, with such a secret smile on her face that the black clouds of the hour were dispelled with one blast of radiant sunshine and Bob had to fight to keep himself from flinging the horrid papers to the academic winds and running to her wildly. My God, she was beautiful, and his heart soared, and he actually slowed his walk because the moment was too pure for hurrying.

26 ᶺ

"Donny, look, thanks so much for fixing the drains," Julia said. She tried to perk up, but felt like she was pushing her voice through fog. The fatigue hit her suddenly. They were standing in the hallway by the door. Donny had his tool chest in his right hand, was sweaty and had a black smudge on his right cheek. His hair was plastered down on the left side of his head and bumping up on the right. He looked endearing, in a way.

They stood in the doorway talking about the drain and the kitchen and how it didn't make sense to have Donny start ripping up the floor while her mother was still staying there. Donny said that he wouldn't mind at all coming by and staying with her or with Matthew sometime, just to give Julia a break. Whenever she wanted, in fact, all she had to do was call him on his cellphone. He wasn't very busy that week, except until Thursday when he was starting a basement renovation.

"My own mother is ill," he said.

Julia leaned against the wall. Matthew was playing in the boots and shoes in the front vestibule, and her mother was opening and shutting every drawer in the kitchen for the hundred thousandth time while rubbing her hands and muttering to herself. Julia said, "Oh, I'm sorry to hear that" – about Donny's mother – but she had difficulty concentrating on his words. He couldn't seem to tell a story straight without continually veering off into accounts of several friends and relations, only the first few of whom had anything to do with the original story or thought. He'd obviously been living alone too long, was starved for conversation. But Julia nodded her head, made affirmative noises as if she had been following. She just wanted to lie down for a few moments, clear her head.

"Anyway –" he said, stopping suddenly, as if he realized she wasn't with him at all. "My mom's in bed, but she's together mentally. I don't have to keep an eye out all the time the way you do. Do you want some help bringing her back to Fallowfields tomorrow?"

"No. No, thank you. I should be all right," Julia said. Just a quick nap. She'd curl up with Matthew in bed with the big red comforter. He could have some nubbies and they both could drift off. She'd lock the doors and make sure the knives were put away so her mother wouldn't hurt herself. Just for ten minutes or so.

"She sure is hunting for something," Donny said. Her mother was approaching a fever pitch of panic, slamming the kitchen drawers, not even bothering to stop and look for whatever it was she wanted.

"Mom. Mom!" Julia said, and ran her hand through her hair, stopped to pull it for a second, just to wake herself up. "Mom, please. Just calm down!"

She turned to Donny and thanked him again, told him she would be fine, saw him out and then shut and locked the door. Then she went to her mother and embraced her from behind, around the waist and under the arms. "Please," she said softly, hugging her, trying to sound loving and reassuring. "How about some cake?"

"Well, I hardly ever am allowed!" her mother said.

"You're allowed cake," Julia said tearfully. The hands wouldn't stop, they were either pulling at drawers or else wiping themselves off. This is my *mother*, Julia thought. This woman so wretched, delusional, broken. Every so often it hit home with unbearable weight. This woman who stood so tall when they buried her husband, who planned the funeral, managed the estate, composed personal cards to everyone who called or wrote or sent flowers or even mentioned in passing how sorry they were. This woman was now reduced to pawing invisible things off the backs of her hands.

"I have some cake in the freezer," Julia breathed. "I'll have to go down for a minute and get it. And then I'll be up, all right? Do you want maple syrup on it?"

"We were all turnips," her mother said.

"You *love* maple syrup. You used to drink it from the bottle when you thought we weren't looking. Daddy would say, 'Lenore, for God's sake!' Do you remember that?"

Her mother looked quite nostalgic for a time, then suddenly seemed to be reminded of something far more important, and began again to open drawers and shut them. Julia raced down the basement stairs, got halfway to the freezer then remembered that she'd left Matthew playing in the front hall closet. She didn't want him alone with his grandmother, so she raced up again, got him, carried him down to the basement, and retrieved the large wedge of chocolate cake she'd frozen some months ago after Bob's birthday. Then she carried the boy and the cake back up to the kitchen, defrosted the cake in the microwave, and poured maple syrup on it.

"Cake! Cake!" Matthew said.

"Shhh, you," Julia said to him. "Look, it's your favourite," she said to her mother. But her mother wouldn't look. Julia had to wave the cake under her nose, then take a spoonful of the maple syrup and dribble some on her lips before her mother got distracted from the task of opening and shutting drawers.

"Mmmmmm," her mother said finally, and a distorted sort of pleasurable expression came over her face, as if she couldn't quite remember how to do it. "Oh, what was that?"

"Cake! Cake!" Matthew said. "Want some too!"

"It's dessert, Mom. You deserve dessert. Won't you sit down and have some?"

"Oh golly." She seemed torn, reluctant to leave the drawers and yet drawn unbearably to the cake and syrup.

"Pleeeese! Pleeeeese!" Matthew whined.

"Just try a bit for now," Julia said. "Then you can get back to your hunting later. That's what you're doing, isn't it? You're hunting for something?"

"That's a good idea," her mother said, and she left a drawer pulled out, as if to remind her of where she was in her labours. Then she followed Julia into the dining room and sat at the table, delicately pulled a napkin onto her lap.

"Would you like some tea?" Julia asked.

"Pleeeese, mummy!" Matthew said.

"Shhh, you, I'm going to give you nubbies in a bit," Julia said.

"Ohhh, ohhh, pleeeeese!" he moaned.

"I just want quiet for ten minutes," Julia said, plugging in the kettle.

ᔕ

Upstairs, after cake, after settling her mother onto the pull-out for a nap that Julia knew wasn't going to last more than a few minutes, after nubbies and listening to her mother get up and start pulling out and slamming drawers again, Julia closed her eyes and allowed herself to drift. She had a dream of visiting the gentle place. She was running, a little scared, through cold, dark woods, but then there was the familiar clearing. The grass was so green she almost melted into it, the air so warm and soft, and her body was so light. There was the huge, kind willow with the cool shade down by the brook. Matthew was with her, he was tall and strong, so beautiful. He said he wanted some nubbies but Julia told him, "You're much too old." He wanted some anyway, he could be so charming, and Julia felt sad, he'd grown up so quickly. "That's how it is," he said, walking ahead of her. He had tanned, strong legs, wasn't wearing anything. She meant to tell him that he couldn't go to university like that, but it was all right for the nice place.

"You'll get hair soon," she said to him. "You'll get hairy like your father," but he said no, he'd wash it off, put it down the drain.

It was a funny dream. She wasn't deeply asleep. She could feel Matthew tugging at her breast, playing with the nipple, sucking hard for a time and then letting it go, as if he were playing a fish on a line. She could feel him and yet still dream about him diving into the brook with complete abandon – it looked so shallow but he knew what he was doing. Where he was diving it was twelve, eighteen, a hundred feet deep, and so cool and clear. She could almost taste the water of that dive, and yet also she had an ear out for her mother working those drawers. She never took anything out, she just opened and closed. Sometimes with a whack, but it didn't startle her. Julia was deeply relaxed. Rare enough for her. It felt wonderful. She was . . . multi-tasking. That was the right word. It was a higher form of consciousness achieved only by extraordinary mothers in extreme states of fatigue.

It was so warm in the nice place, and he smiled. She told him, "Don't smile like that. All the girls will fall in love with you." But it didn't matter, he smiled even more warmly. His smile took some of the green away from the grass, it was too beautiful. She warned him again. She said, "Matthew, please," but he didn't stop. He drank up all the green from the grass, and it turned brown and crisp. And then the grasshoppers came out, they buzzed loud as hornets, they loved the dry, brown grass. "Matthew," she said, but her voice was quite weak, her throat dry now, she could barely hear herself above the din. She called out to him but it was hard to breathe, it was getting so hot, and she was coughing. She rolled over and opened her eyes and baby Matthew was crying beside her. My God, she thought, what time is it? She'd only been out a couple of minutes, ten at the most, but when she looked around everything was black, it looked like the middle of the night. She fumbled for her watch. She'd put it on the table by the bed. The air felt so oddly hot, and smelled horrible . . . and then Julia was completely awake, far too awake for her own taste, the smoke alarm was sounding almost in her ear. She grabbed Matthew and ran through the haze to the bedroom door. "Mom!" she cried out. "Mother!" And she put her hand on the knob, which was warm, not hot. She had a sudden thought that she should keep the bedroom door closed. She recalled some safety film from the dim recesses of her memory, how you weren't supposed to open doors in a fire, the sudden influx of oxygen might cause a flame to roar up and engulf whoever was standing there. She found her way back to the phone on the bedside table, tried to dial 911, but there was no tone. She didn't panic, and yet without really knowing how she was suddenly lunging down the stairs, grasping Matthew to her chest so powerfully she thought she might crush him, but felt unable to loosen her grip even slightly. The stairs were not on fire. The banister was not crackling with heat. She brushed her arm against it by mistake but didn't feel any burn. She thought, It might be the adrenaline; I might be unable to feel the heat. And she made it to the bottom of the stairs thinking, My God, I am putting my child in danger.

"Mother! Mother!" she yelled, but she could see no one in the kitchen. The smoke was terrible. She fell to her knees, still grasping Matthew, and crawled down the hallway – where she knew the hallway to be – until she reached the front door. And there was her mother, bent over, with a lighter, flicking the flame again and again at the doorknob.

"*What are you doing?*" Julia screamed, and stood, knocked the lighter out of her mother's hand. Her mother looked up, startled, and slapped Julia across the face.

"That was our escape, young lady!" her mother sputtered, and immediately bent to look for the lighter on the floor. "No dessert for you!" she snapped.

Julia pulled the sleeve of her sweatshirt over her hand, grasped the door handle and opened it cautiously. "Come on!" she yelled, but her mother was intent on retrieving the lighter. "We're free! We're free!" Julia screamed, and pulled Matthew and her mother out the door to fresh air.

～ 27

Clarity comes in a flat yellow tablet, which is rough on the tongue, porous, a bit crumbly. It tastes like vinegar and onions, not sweet at all, but bearable. It works best when you let it soak in the back of the mouth, like a throat lozenge, so that it seeps slowly. Too much clarity coming on too fast is overwhelming, like stumbling into direct sunlight after so much time down in the cave. You turn away from it, feel dizzy, crawl back to your little crouch in the darkness. Clarity is best in small doses, little drips spreading gradually so that the heart and eyes and mind have a chance to adjust to so much silver and translucence, so many reverberations.

The sound of the key in the lock. The trembling of the hand, his perspiration, the worried edges of his voice. They all get magnified, every breath and gesture, the hairs on the back of his neck standing up and his little nipples hardening under his shirt, they become your own. There is no single body with clarity, the lines begin to erase and fall away. You walk so softly, breathe as quietly and smoothly as you can. Waste no movement or thought.

"I was worried you wouldn't come," he says, his eyes awash with relief and expectation, and so you reach out to embrace in the middle of the office even while you seem to be staying separate. He keeps looking at the knapsack, at what you've brought, hurrying, but why ruin it? It must be done slowly, must be tasted and savoured, fully understood. That's the hard part, getting to the bottom. Cutting through the murk and incoherence. Reaching clarity.

If you relax and let the fluids soak, softly, then the vinegar-and-onion taste recedes. Or maybe it's that you adjust, become accustomed to the power of it, the rhythms, the milkiness that fills your body, the beauty of everything you sense around you. You know what to say to help others . . . because you *are* the others, you start to see that. And the others are you. You're sharing your self in the most selfless way possible, helping them to *become* you, and, in a way, you become them. Just a little.

You say, "I think you should take off your clothes." Softly, with a low purr in your voice. It's the right thing to say, because you don't want boundaries between you.

You say, "Don't be afraid. The door is locked and the blinds are closed. No one will know." And you stay where you are, by the bookcase, stand relaxed, not anticipating. Not looking, but not looking away either. He is very quiet and his fingers are trembling but you don't go to him physically. You lend your essence. That's the way of clarity. Send your essence across the room and his jacket comes off, his tie and shirt. He bends down to take off his shoes and socks, hesitates. The phone rings and you don't say a word, just turn your head slightly, the least possible movement, but he knows to leave it. When it stops ringing he turns the phone off completely, without one word from you. It's essence communicating with essence. Everything becomes smooth and co-ordinated.

"You are lovely," you say, and you mean it, it's exactly what he is. His skin so babyish and new. He's standing in his underwear, doesn't know where to put his hands – in front or behind, on his hips, where? They keep moving. He's a little cold, you sense that, in this heightened state; he's shivering but he won't admit it, and he's too afraid to ask what you've brought him. It's so sweet. He can hardly talk above a whisper, but a whisper is perfect. You say, "I've brought you a few things," and his underpants spring to attention; it's marvellous, now he *really* doesn't know where to put his hands.

Clarity is humorous. That's the unexpected thing. You think it's going to be serious, a heavy trip into deeper meaning, but there's a stage when it all looks funny. You can't give in, that's crucial, it has to be a secret humour, a more profound, cosmic laughter. You can let the lightness into your eyes, but you must show it as love and affection, an embrace of this comic world, a celebration of the essential silliness of humanity.

"We need to do your back," you say, again in a soft purr. Let the laughter resonate inside, but remain still. "I brought a shaver," you say, and you open your pack.

Whatever is happening now is happening forever. Not just now but for all time. Your fingers are pulling open the zipper. Your hand is taking out the shaver. You say, "Where is a plug?" and he turns, this large, nearly naked man, and starts to look for an electrical outlet. This pause in the dance, or is it? No, it's *part* of the dance as well, his awkwardness in not knowing where the outlet is. He walks to the corner of the room, peers under his desk, looks along the far wall. Like a bumblebee searching out flowers, flying this way and that, confused, circling. He's a big, hairless bumblebee, except for his back, which he wasn't able to shave by himself. There's a lamp and a computer on his desk; they must be plugged into something. But he doesn't realize this right away. You watch, see everything so clearly miles before it happens.

"There. I've got it!" he says like a little boy, standing there in his underpants, so excited and trusting. It's a different moment than before, and so you change directions.

"I've brought some proper panties for you," you say, and because the boundaries are being erased, and you're becoming him in a way, you feel such tenderness when his heart jigs. It's such a little thing, but to him everything. What wouldn't we give to those we love? And clarity is, above all, love. A taking-unto and soaking in the soup of our common consciousness. That's why you have to be so careful. It erases all the lines, and so you could lose yourself, you feel so close sometimes, wonder if when he lifts his foot and pulls the fabric up his leg, and then the other side, is he going to walk away as you, and will you walk away as him? Will you put on the masculine suit and the black socks and frumpy trousers, the heavy body with such big, soft hands? Will you walk away thirty years older, in another life, with a woman and child waiting at home? Will you roam through the attic and the crawl spaces of his professorial mind? All those books, so much learning and wisdom. Would there be any room for who and what you've brought with you?

"There now. That's better," you say when he stands up to show you. You haven't stinted. Black satin with French lace edging, extra large. "How does that feel?"

He doesn't have to say anything, you can *see* how it feels. "Mmmmm," you say, and you want to touch him right there but you don't. He wants to tell you all about it, but you put your finger on his lips. "Later," you whisper. "There are some things first." So you turn him, have him put his hands on the desk, and then you flick on the shaver. The head is a little cold; you're sorry, but it's in a good cause. You use the large head first, which shears the long hairs, then switch to the smaller head, which clips off the bristly ends, brings it right down to skin. "There," you say, in a dance, in a poem. "Now I can see you."

"Thank you," he whispers. He knows better, now, what is happening. That he is becoming you.

"Would you like to put on the top?" you ask, and he nods, just barely. He doesn't want to admit it, how *much* he wants it. So you pull it out of your bag. Very slowly, there's no hurry at all, and the blood shoots to his face, he's so suddenly crimson and near-desperate, but he stays quiet somehow, you love him for that.

It's one of the hardest things to get used to with this level of clarity: how much you love, how deeply, how you feel like you'd do anything to satisfy and serve.

"Do you want me to put it on you?" you ask. Coyly, just a hint of a smile. His heart is bursting out of his chest, he wants it so much. But he doesn't want to ask. "Just nod your head a little," you say, standing so close to him but not touching.

He nods his head, closes his eyes, lifts his arms a little so you can slide the black satin in place. You try not to brush against his nipples but it's difficult; he shudders once when you do and you want to do it again but your fingers smooth the straps instead, arrange the lace around his flesh. He does have some of the right flesh, and there is padding in the satin.

"How is that?" you breathe, and he moans, a low, weak noise of pleasure.

"You can touch yourself," you say, because he's still so shy. "Arrange the fit." But he doesn't move. He's transfixed, floating in a pot of pure honey.

"I'm going to do up the clasp at the back," you say. "You tell me if it's all right." He doesn't move, doesn't make a sound, so you fit the hooks in place and he stops breathing. "Is it too tight?"

Not a sign. Then, slowly, a trembling sigh.

"I'm sorry," you say, still purring. "But I'm going to need some financial assistance for these things I've bought for you. Did you bring a chequebook?" He doesn't move at all, seems locked in a trance, and there is just a moment of uncertainty, a bittersweet reminder of the normal muck and drudgery of existence.

But then he says, "Oh, of course," and he moves around to the other side of the desk, the professor side, which you are inheriting just as he is sliding past the boundaries into your young skin. You walk around to stand behind him, on the professor side, and you can't help yourself, you reach down to play with his nipples, like a professor would, pluck the fruit, it's there for you. He stops what he's doing so you stop, then he finds his chequebook, has a hard time filling out the date and your name. It's becoming his name, now, too. He's sitting in black French satin lace with his shaved legs crossed and a hand on his breast.

You tell him the number and he pauses. He doesn't understand. "It's so expensive being a woman," you say. "But it's worth it, don't you think?"

He does, and he writes the number with a flourish, hands over the cheque.

"Do you want to see what else I've bought?" you ask, and he does. He can hardly contain himself, but you tell him there are a few things to do first. "I need to anoint you," you say, "it's part of being a lady. You've done such a lovely job with your body hair. It's a shame about your eyebrows." And he stiffens, he's full of doubt and fear, you can feel the water running out of the moment. So you say, "It's all right. You mustn't resist. You will never become a lady if you resist." And you wheel him around in his professor chair so that he's facing you. You pull out your tweezers and little scissors and straddle his lap. "You mustn't resist," you say, and it doesn't take long to arch him properly, to snip and pluck. "No one will notice," you say. "I'm the only one who'll know."

And then you do his face. You kiss him once, for luck, and take away his sideburns, then bring out the foundation and blusher, the liner and mascara, eyeshadow and lip gloss. You straddle his lap and every so often your breast brushes against his bra, you rock against his rigid centre. And you say, "I think you need to tell me your story," so sweetly, so softly. He doesn't want to talk, and yet in a way he does want to, you know he does, and you need to hear him. If you're going to become the professor, you need to know his words and remember them. "Please," you say, wheedling, rubbing yourself against his satin, just briefly, just the tiniest touch. "Tell me what this is all about. Please tell me so I'll be the only one who knows."

So he starts. While you're working on his face, transforming him, he tells you about the woman who came to visit one summer when he was thirteen. "She was only eighteen, the daughter of my father's friend from Germany," he says, his eyes down, manner grave, he is so relieved to be telling this. "Mariana. She came to learn English for the summer, and to look after me when my parents were at work. She had enormous blonde ringlets and a wide, healthy, beautiful face, and big shoulders. She might as well have been thirty, she seemed so beautiful, unattainable. I didn't have any sisters or brothers. I was fascinated with her. I had no clues about my own body, you see, but I was just beginning to wake up. We did things together. She wanted me to talk to her all the time in English, so I did, I jabbered, and secretly I read books way beyond my years. Henry Miller and *Lady Chatterley* and Simone de Beauvoir. My parents stocked the house with modern literature and I sought out all the dirty bits to learn about life in the adult world."

You dab and brush and cream him, soothe the spots that have just lately been made naked, and when he pauses you say something small, to keep him going. "And Mariana?" you say, and he starts again.

"We went to the beach one time," he says. "It was a hot, hot summer day, just the two of us, and she had on a wonderful red one-piece bathing suit with a little skirt at the bottom. It seemed to hide nothing, especially when it was wet. I could see the outline of her rigid nipples, her areolae. I could see the indentation of her belly button and where the fabric stretched between her legs. She didn't shave her underarms. I was shocked. She looked so manly for that, I thought. But she also had fluffs of black pubic hair showing between her legs, on her swimsuit line. I couldn't keep from looking. It had never occurred to me that women could have hair there too. All I knew was from the few *Playboy* centrefolds I'd seen, which back then never showed any private hair, it was pink glossy skin all the way up and down. The pubic area was always coyly hidden, but I never knew that. It was a rude awakening. I couldn't believe it. I thought she must be a mutant or something."

Brush and daub, careful with the colour. You pull the wig out of your bag, slowly too, so he can see and enjoy every stretch of it, get his mind around it: the long black curls, a little crimped in the pack, but they'll brush out well. His eyes widen, he can't find the proper words, but sits still, very lady-like, while you fit him and then brush. "Mariana," you whisper again, and he doesn't want to talk any more but he must. It's part of the package.

"When we got home she hung her bathing suit in the bathroom to dry," he says. "I took it down off the bar just to examine it more closely. It didn't look like much. It seemed small, as if it might fit a child. I made sure the door was locked, and I didn't know really what I was doing, but for some reason I stepped into it. You see, we were about the same height, although I was much skinnier. I pulled it on and stretched the straps over my shoulders and looked at myself. I was so turned on, I didn't know what was happening, I just started touching myself, rocking back and forth . . . and then . . ."

You brush and wait.

"Then, of course, I came right in Mariana's swimsuit. I thought somehow I was peeing, but it wasn't that, it was utterly, utterly sweet, and I was terrified about the mess. I rinsed it out and rinsed, but the semen was so sticky, of course. I tried soap and hot water. I scrubbed. Mariana was asking me through the door if I was all right. I was fine, I was brilliant. I never recovered." He says it ruefully, a touch of a smile and of sadness, and you can't help it, you love him for it, and you love Mariana, that's the clarity working in your mind.

"You look so lovely," you say, "you need to see yourself." But there is no mirror in his office; it's a male professor's office. "Will you trust me a little more?" you murmur, still brushing his hair out. "I'd like you to be able to see yourself." Yes, he trusts you, he's already taken his heart out of his chest and placed it shivering in your hands. So you pull out your camera and he tightens. It's a terrible, frightening moment, both of you on the verge of shattering right there. "It's all right," you say, "don't worry. It's digital. There's no developing. I just want you to see in the viewer." So you snap, quickly. You're nervous, despite the clarity. The glassiness of the moment is still sharp in your gut. And you show him. It's so tiny, the LCD screen, but it's something. He's transfixed by his image, like Narcissus. And all of a sudden it's the perfect thing, the camera, it's absolutely what's needed, he can't get enough of it.

Every new bit of clothing you bring out, he wants to see himself. You pull out the strapless spandex body liner. He squirms into it, can hardly keep his hands from running up and down himself. You almost forget the stockings, he's so excited, you're so excited. He wants the red leather dress, my God, he's paid for it, he wants it, he's almost drooling in anticipation. He almost skips the stockings but you get him to slow down, not be time's fool. It will be over in a second anyway, in half a thought; you have to linger, not be taken in by the rush. "A lady is allowed to be late," you say. And so he stretches out his leg, points his toe, and you roll the stocking up to his thigh, then do the other, and he's a little disappointed you bought stay-ups, no need for a garter belt. But it isn't serious. When he's had more time as a lady he'll realize the fasteners are tedious, that the thick, lacy elastic hugging your upper thigh is far sexier.

"I want this to be a Mariana kind of moment," you say to him. "I want it to reverberate through the rest of your life." And he smiles, is speechless, but it's perfect. "I want you to replay every moment, to have this in your mind forever. Is that too much to ask?"

"No," he says, barely.

"Is this a power thing?" you ask him. "Are you one of those CEO types who gets tired of so much responsibility, you really want to give over power to someone else for a while? It feels so wonderful to sublimate, to hand yourself over?"

It's as if he hasn't understood; he is still so soaked, so molten.

"I'll tell you for myself," you say, because clarity is for sharing. It isn't, can't be, all one-sided. "I love this feeling of power. I love it when you give me control like this. But I want you to tell me, I need you to share: is it the sublimation? Or is it risk-taking, is that what stirs you? Breaking taboos?"

He's sniffing an interview so you run your hands lightly up

his silken leg, tickle his spandex middle. "You need to tell me," you whisper. "I need to understand." Because it's a sharing. "Please," and you kiss his lips, lick lightly, to taste him but not disturb the artwork.

"No," he says, eyes closed, and you wait. His thoughts are moving at a different speed now, are travelling along new corridors. So you must wait.

"It isn't power," he says finally. "It isn't . . . risk-taking." His voice candid, calm, subdued. "It isn't even that I want to become a woman. It's more this sense . . . ," and he searches for the word. You know it already, want to say it for him, but wait. You cannot put the words in his mouth.

". . . of transcendence," he says finally. "That is the most erotic thing for me. To move beyond, completely outside my usual life. To be someone else, in fact, absolutely different. Just for a while."

And then there are no words. It's enough, you think. The moment is so full there is no more room for words. You pull out the red leather dress. It's not so different, in a way, from the red bathing suit of so many years ago. You can feel that, since you are becoming him, he doesn't have to say it. And he doesn't need help stepping into it. It's tight around the hips . . . but yes, it's fine. His spirit was already in you when you were shopping, the boundaries had already begun to melt. He smoothes the waist into place, and you help him with the pull-straps in the back. They're a bit like on the old-fashioned corsets, when ladies would need a maid or a sister to help them tighten the laces. He wants them tight, that's why you bought it, though you didn't consciously think of it at the time. His spirit in you recognized what he wanted. So you pull and you pull, you place your foot on his buttocks and you pull harder, and then when he's perfect you fix the knots so that they won't slip.

"Oh, my God, you are so lovely," you say, and out with the camera again. He loves it. This is it, the Mariana moment, it's going to echo erotically through the rest of his life.

And then, disappointment. There is a smudge in everything, that's the way of life in this reality. You've forgotten the shoes. They were right there in your room by the door. They wouldn't quite fit in the pack, so you were going to put them in a separate bag. You looked for the bag, and then Ricky needed attention, she was getting brittle. She needed stroking, and time played its tricks, fast-forwarded the hour until you were running out of the residence, praying you wouldn't miss out completely.

And you left the shoes by the door.

So you say, "I have to go get one more thing. I'm so sorry. I will be back in fifteen minutes. Will you wait? Will you keep the door locked and wait?"

Will he wait? Absolutely. He'll wait across decades for you. The look on his face says it all.

"I'll knock three times, and then twice more," you say. "Don't open up for anyone else." And you would kiss him again but you want it all clear, no smudginess, you want everything to stay this exquisite for as long as it can.

You take your pack and the camera, step out and away. The halls are empty. It's turned into late afternoon already. You're hungry, suddenly, and so tired, the clarity drains so suddenly, it's heartbreaking, you can feel it leaving your mind and body as you step away from the professor's door, like shedding a skin or leaving your coat behind. It's so cold, you walk faster, but you know it's no good. Nothing will help. The faster you walk the faster it drains away. Everything's cold now, your brain is cold, your heart and lungs and legs and toes, cold, cold. There was no transcendence. It was fake, a show, so stupid to take a whole tablet without eating. The inside of your skin feels scratchy, like thin, dried-out paper. Hurry, hurry, but the faster you go the worse it feels. Your stomach is now roiling and the edges of your vision are blurry, the faster you go the muddier it all seems.

28 ✒

Bob stood still in his office, tingling from the red dress, from the wig and stockings, poised, listening to the passage of time. He was leaning against his desk, looking at the closed door, waiting for Sienna to return. It was suspended time. It felt like a hiatus. He thought precisely of the definition – a break between two vowels coming together but not in the same syllable – and then more generally of a pause, of being left in suspended animation. He didn't want to switch his phone back on. He didn't want to turn on his computer and check his e-mails. He absolutely did not want to look at the Poe story assignment he had foisted on his class. He wanted nothing to take him out of the present fantasy, to remind him of his other, parallel reality.

Besides, he couldn't sit down. The dress was too tight; he would have had to hold his breath, suck in his gut unbearably.

But this was bearable. Standing in a red leather dress, leaning against his desk, waiting for Sienna to return. She wanted him to remember this afternoon forever. He felt like he couldn't possibly do anything else, that life had changed course irrevocably, that nothing else would make any mark on him the way this had. And he was still in the moment, in the middle, in hiatus, waiting. He waited while his feet began to grow cold from lack of circulation, so he walked around for just a few minutes, back and forth, being careful not to catch his stockings on the cold floor. He walked until his head began to feel light, probably also from lack of circulation, and then he stopped again and leaned back against the desk and looked at his watch. Six thirty-eight. Was that possible? He didn't know how long Sienna had been gone, but it probably wasn't more than twenty minutes. She said she'd be back in fifteen, so there was no sense in panicking. A lady is allowed to be late.

Then someone knocked and he froze. He went silently to the door, waited, hoping. "Bob, are you there?" It was Helen, the departmental secretary. She knocked again, then went away.

Six thirty-nine. Julia would soon be wondering where he was. She might have been the one who called earlier, and perhaps she'd tried Helen after that. She knew he had only the one class on Mondays. Probably he should phone and tell her he was eating out with some of the grad students, trying to plan the work schedule for the next term. He put his hand to the phone but dreaded the task. Julia wasn't part of this world, this experience. It would spoil things somehow. So he didn't call.

Six forty-five. Bob stared at his watch. His feet were very cold now. He walked some more, but the tiles made him even colder; he couldn't bring himself to pull on his old socks, much less his shoes. He was starting to get a cramp in his side from so much shallow breathing, and he felt even more light-headed, like he would after a long day of wearing his tie too tight. He needed to get out of these clothes. They were wonderful, but now it was time.

How long had Sienna been gone? Perhaps half an hour by now. That really was unusual. Something had happened to her.

He didn't want to rush away, yet he couldn't wait forever. He just needed her to unstrap him, free him from this red leather dress, which was cutting into his back now. He could feel his muscles cringing in protest.

One thousand, three hundred and six dollars, and twenty-seven cents. That's how much this outfit had cost him. It really was outrageous; he wasn't sure how he was going to hide the expense from Julia, since they had a joint account and she examined the monthly statements closely. It was about the only thing she looked at closely these days.

At seven o'clock Bob looked up Sienna's number in the directory of students. The phone rang and rang and then Sienna picked up.

"Hello. Hi!" Bob said, breathlessly. "It's me."

"Who's me?" Sienna barked, and it was so rude, so unexpected that Bob didn't know what to say. He hung up, then looked at the directory again. Probably he'd dialled the wrong number. He tried again. This time the phone was picked up on the first ring and Sienna growled, "It's you again!"

It wasn't Sienna. Of course it wasn't. Bob remembered now, she had a roommate. So Bob said, "May I please speak to Sienna?"

"She's sick right now," the roommate said. "Sorry." And then the line went dead.

Bob put the phone down and considered his position. He didn't panic. How could she have fallen ill so swiftly? It didn't make sense. Yet in a way he felt calmer, knowing that Sienna would not be coming back. At least she hadn't abandoned him; there was an explanation for her tardiness. He hiked the dress up to his waist but it went no further; he was stuck solid. He reached around behind and tried to grasp the knots of the laces, but his flexibility was limited on the best of days; he felt especially wooden now, strapped in so mercilessly. He couldn't reach anything, could barely touch his sides, and certainly couldn't extend his fingers behind his shoulders or to the middle of his back. He spun in his office trying to catch the laces like a dog chasing his own tail.

He tried to wrench the dress around his middle so that the laces would be in front of him but it felt welded in place. He lay down on his back, rocking like an upset turtle, then stood and leaned against the wall, writhing and groaning. He rubbed violently up and down against the bookshelves to try to loosen the dress. But nothing worked. It was sturdy leather and the laces were like steel. Sienna had obviously spared no expense, had bought only the finest materials.

By eight o'clock his silk stockings were in runs. He'd taken off his black satin French-lace panties and the wig lay abandoned on the cold floor by his desk. He was sweating like a desperate amateur escape artist. The dress was bunched around his waist and partly off his shoulder, but he was nowhere near free, and he admitted it to himself. He reached for the black-handled aluminum scissors on his desk. It broke his heart, but enough was enough. It's only money, he thought. He took the hem of the dress, opened the blades. The hem was thick, and the scissors quite dull, they were only made for cutting paper. But he persisted. He worked the handles back and forth, squeezed as hard as he could; then the rivet between the blades gave way and the scissors clattered to the floor in two pieces.

Bob looked at them helplessly, blinked several times, waited, vainly hoping that his eyes were deceiving him. But the scissors really were broken. He picked up one blade and tried sawing through the material, but the blade now felt duller, more useless than a butter knife. He threw it away in disgust, took the seam in his hands and pulled as hard as he could, grunted enormously, swore when his shin shot out and caught the underside of the desk. The seam held. He could feel the dress now like a living opponent, a python squeezing him tighter the more he struggled. The room started to go fuzzy. He wasn't getting enough air. He tried one last time to rend the seam but it was a joke now, his fingers were feeble, he felt as if he couldn't even tear the cardboard cover off a notebook.

I'm going to die here, he thought. The dress is strangling me and the janitor is going to open the door in three days and find me cold and blue in these ridiculous clothes.

He pulled open his desk drawer, took out his bottle, drank down three gulps, which helped enormously. He looked at the bottle with interest. Of course! He could smash off the neck, use the jagged glass to cut himself to freedom! But the bottle was still half-full; it would make a terrible mess. He would have to finish it first or else pour the Scotch out the window.

No, he wasn't that desperate. He put the bottle back in his drawer, closed it, and tried to order his thoughts calmly, clearly. He needed to return home and get a proper pair of German scissors, which he knew to be on his workbench in the basement. Then he'd cut himself out of this unlikely straitjacket. It was evening, the halls were silent; he could put on his regular clothes over the dress and drive home and, if luck was with him, if there was a God, then he would be all right.

At some point he would still have to come up with an explanation for why he had no body hair, but with skill and some luck that could be postponed, perhaps even long enough for his regular hair to grow back. Then he thought of his face: almost mask-hard now with thick make-up. He'd never be able to wipe it off properly in his office. It would take soap and water and reams of paper towels, a mirror to make sure no traces were left. With horror he realized that he'd have to leave his office to go to a washroom to deal with his face.

Much better to have another drink. To finish the bottle, smash it, cut himself out! He opened the drawer and drank down what he could, paused, poured himself another glass. Steadily, carefully. He could imagine the janitor running into the room when he heard the sound of smashing glass. He could imagine Scotch being spilled, running all over the floor, and just try to explain that, Professor Sterling; and by the way, why are you in a red leather dress with black stockings?

This being a female even for a few hours was head-bangingly complex, was beyond him, in fact, he realized it now. How stupid he'd been!

There was only one thing for it – the men's room was down a flight, so he would have to try the ladies'. The department would be deserted this time of day, except possibly for the janitor or Barbara Law, the young twentieth-century specialist who often worked late, trying to reach tenure. Only the very worst of luck would see either one in the hall or the wash-room this particular moment. He straightened out the dress, rearranged his stockings, re-donned the panties and wig, pulled the long black curls over his face as much as he could. He could claim it was a costume party. Of course. A pre-Hallowe'en affair. If worse came to worst there was always an explanation.

But as soon as he put his hand on the doorknob he heard brisk, short, noisy steps in the hall. They passed within a few feet of his door and his heart sounded throughout the building. How could it not be heard? He didn't know, but the steps didn't slow down, they hurried past. Bob waited, barely breathing, while the noise subsided. He heard the sound of a heavy door in the distance, opening and closing. He waited.

Then in a fury of sudden will he ripped open the door and fled down the hall. He moved so quickly he actually passed the ladies' room by two strides, had to slide to a stop in his stockinged feet, turn around, slam open the door and lunge inside. He'd kept his eyes down, wasn't certain at all whether there had been anyone watching. But the ladies' room was empty, of course it was. Spinningly empty. He had to wait precious moments while his head cleared, then he searched briefly for a lock on the door, found none, ran to the nearest sink and turned on the water. Suddenly he realized that he'd forgotten to bring his male clothes. He was going to have to clean up and return to his office to become Bob again. He splashed water onto his face wildly, lathered and scrubbed in a panic, grabbed several paper towels and wiped himself off, looked at his reflection just long enough to check that his face was clear. It was still long enough to see that he was hideous: a fat, aging man in a leather dress, a horrible wig, torn stockings. He couldn't be more ludicrous if he tried.

In seconds, taking no time to think, to listen at the door, to worry or wonder or plan, he finished, then plunged back into the hall and tore back to his room.

He looked up just before reaching the door. He had a sense of being alone in the hall, felt the beginnings of relief. He was a little dizzy but not out of control. He wasn't going to run right past the target again. He slowed appropriately. It was going to be all right. His hand reached the knob, and then his heart sank. For a moment he felt as if he might expire right there, because in his panic and stupidity he'd locked himself out of his office. He tried the knob again. It didn't seem possible, and yet he knew at the same time it was absolutely possible, it was practically predictable, in his state, with his luck. If only he hadn't panicked! If only he'd brought his male clothes with him to the ladies' room – his office key was in his pocket. If only he hadn't let Sienna go, if only he hadn't been such an idiot in the first place, if only, if only . . .

If only he weren't dithering in the English-department corridor wearing a red leather dress, torn stockings, and a hideous wig! With a prodigious effort he rattled the door, threw his considerable weight against it, again and again, as if this were a movie and the door made of cardboard meant to look like wood. But it was solid, his shoulder was getting sore. He roared in anguish then, a terrible, unearthly cry that resounded through the wing. As soon as he uttered it he felt washed in regret, in the suffocating certainty that everything he did now was a mistake. He tried to think clearly but it was no use. Panic had brought him this far and he had nothing left with which to combat it. Before he knew what he was doing, he was running, his feet slipping on the cold, institutional tiles like a dog running on ice. He passed Barbara Law's office and too late realized her door was open. She was sitting at her desk, hunched over a book, classical music playing on a tiny radio, her face lit by the desk light. She looked up to see him. He just had time to see her face go from a warm, expectant smile to a perplexed squint, and then he was past, through the hall doors, flying down the stairs two and three at a time. It was mad, wildly dangerous; he had no footing, could have fallen half a dozen times and cracked his skull. But he couldn't stop himself. He could barely breathe and yet he ran like a landslide was behind him. He tore outside into the cold, sobering night air, his feet getting pricked on sharp pebbles.

He had no chance, he knew it, and yet he wasn't done yet, all wasn't lost. Quite possibly Barbara Law hadn't recognized him. No one was standing by the doors outside. He didn't know where he was running, but his body knew to take him to the little-used west entrance, to the dark side of the parking lot. And he was lucky. No one was there. He didn't even realize until he arrived that he was searching for his car. But then it made sense, and he found it, his beautiful little black Porsche. He grabbed for the nearest door, the passenger side, but it was locked . . . as he knew it must be, obsessive as he was protecting his Porsche. He felt the earth closing in around him. There was one last, faint hope, the driver's-side door. It seemed pointless even to try it. Yet, unbelievably, it was unlocked! In his eagerness to get to class, to that class in particular, he'd left his Porsche unsecured. His stupidities were cancelling each other out! He flashed inside, slammed the door shut, very nearly began weeping on the steering wheel in gratitude.

But there was no time to lose. He pulled on his seatbelt, and then his fingers felt down for the key in the ignition. He looked and then he froze in terror and dread, felt his stomach heave in protest as the thought trickled through. Of course there was no key in the ignition. The key was in his trouser pocket, locked in his office along with the rest of his clothes and his office key and pretty well his entire life.

Bob howled in a paroxysm of rage, disbelief, frustration. It didn't matter. The parking lot was deserted. There were only a few other cars sitting lonely and cold, barely lit by dull lights shivering this fall night on rickety wooden poles. He was alone in the universe, he could howl as long and as loud as he liked, it wouldn't matter. When his throat was sore he began a low, throbbing moan. Some time later he realized he was banging his head against the steering wheel. Not violently, but almost ritualistically, in time with his moaning. He could feel the steering-wheel ridges indenting his forehead. And slowly, slowly, he began to reassess his situation.

I am not dead yet, he thought. Hopeless and ludicrous as it

might look, I am not yet finished. His house was only two miles from the university. One if he cut through parkland. He'd want to do that anyway, avoid streets as much as possible. But how could he walk that far without any shoes? Wait a minute, he did have a pair of rubber boots in the trunk – the locked trunk, but which he could unlatch from the inside. Not dead yet! He got out stealthily, found and put on his boots with a growing sense of relief and confidence. He was lucky. Not only were the boots in the trunk but also an old blanket that he could drape over himself to stay warm and hidden. It was all going to work out.

As Sienna had said, he would remember this day as long as he lived.

He headed for the shadows immediately. Two students were smoking in front of the engineering building. He could see them now, their blurry outlines a hundred yards away. But he was calm, focused. They couldn't see him. He stayed in the shadows, skirted the parking lot away from the engineering building, crept from shadow to bush, crouched in hiding at building corners and beside stairs until he felt the way was clear. It was nerve-wracking but exhilarating, too, to fight his way back from the brink of certain personal and professional ruin, to hang on with the tips of his fingers, even to gain ground. He had a fixed idea now. He needed to make his way back to his house. He would break into the basement through the loose window at the back. He could slide onto the workbench and then down and find his good German scissors and free himself of these ridiculous clothes. Then he would steal into the laundry room, where he knew he had a pair of pants hanging up and possibly even a shirt. If there was a God, then a shirt would be there too. Even a dirty one, it wouldn't matter.

Through the shadows, along darkened paths, his head down but ears keen. Wrapped in the blanket, a huddled, darkened figure. He squatted behind a tree and held his breath while a campus patrolman – a sleepy-eyed old man with a flashlight – walked past humming something badly out of tune. Bob slipped down by the water and crossed under a major street by stepping carefully, fitfully over the slippery stones along the shore of the bridge rather than exposing himself to the glare of traffic. Now he was into the neighbourhoods. He stayed on a bicycle path – wonderfully deserted at this time of night, this time of year – passed by an angry barking chained dog outraged at the huddled figure in the night. When he saw a dim light approaching in the distance he quickly stepped off the path and crouched in a thicket, watched as a young helmeted woman blithely pedalled by. He waited there, still, roiling with fear and concentration for what seemed like hours until he was brave enough to venture on.

Closer to home. Even with the blanket his arms should have been cold, but he was feverish. He cut through backyards now, climbed fences, hiked up the dress and pulled his legs over, scurried along hedges like an urban raccoon. He was lucky, he felt it now from the inside. The dogs that barked were either inside or tied up. No one came out to investigate. When he had to cross a well-lit street and hurry up the sidewalk for half a block, no one saw him, no one was around.

It was eerie how deserted his own neighbourhood felt. Surely not everyone is huddled inside, he thought. It's not the dead of winter yet. As he went along he could hear people in the distance. They were out somewhere, at an event perhaps. A street party? It was possible, he supposed. He had a sense of something happening but didn't know what it might be, and when he got closer to his own house, where there would be a greater likelihood of being recognized, he decided to approach from the back along the parallel street, cut through the adjoining lot and then through the big cedar hedge.

It was odd to navigate the private property of others, and yet he felt as though he'd slipped so many boundaries already that this was natural somehow. Of course he could steal up someone's driveway, plunge into their garden, crawl and crouch and pull his way along, past fences, more boundaries, from shadow into greater darkness and then shadow again.

Into such bright light. He was so focused on the next step, where to put his foot, his hand, he almost stumbled onto his own property without realizing what was happening. It was bright and warm. And crowded. Here is the event, he thought, peering through the cedar hedge, and he cursed his luck again under his breath. *The event is at my house!*

But then he saw it wasn't an event; it was a fire. His house was burning! Fire trucks crammed the street and driveway, crowds massed, flames licked lazily out of the kitchen window. He saw Julia and Matthew and Lenore almost immediately: they were in the front row of the people watching, he could see them through the carport. Safe. They were safe.

And what he did next he did without thinking. The backyard was deserted; everyone was in the front or at the sides of the house – the firefighters, the neighbours, and police. So Bob recognized his opportunity. He raced across the yard and found the basement window. It was loose, he knew it was loose; Julia had been on him to fix it since the spring. He opened it and climbed inside, reached his leg down to the workbench in the darkness. It was terribly smoky. He knew even as he entered he was probably going to die. Somehow he thought it didn't matter. He had to get in. He coughed and sputtered and felt the workbench tipping over. All the tools went clattering on the floor. It didn't matter. There was a general uproar anyway: the upstairs was on fire, he could hear the timbers crackling, the whoosh of the wind, could feel the terrible heat. If only I'd stayed in the car, he thought. I would still be alive.

Bob fell on the cement floor, reached out with his hand to brace himself, and miraculously felt the familiar German scissors in his fingers. He shut his eyes against the smoke and began to cut blindly, trusting that his fingers would know what to do. The scissors were terribly sharp and expensive, a gift from his father-in-law years ago. They cut through the leather easily, slid right up his front, and for a terrifying second Bob felt the tips get hung up in the black satin panties, felt the hot steel beside his testicles. But the female clothes fell away from him amid the clamour and destruction and turmoil all around. He took off his boots and freed himself of his stockings, of everything, then found the blanket and boots again and climbed towards where he knew the window must be. "Help! Help!" he cried now, as loudly as he could, blindly reaching. The heat was suddenly unbearable. He'd been so focused on his task before he hadn't even noticed, but now he truly felt as if he had flung himself into hell. He screamed, but he could barely hear himself. There was a terrible crash up above and he felt the house shudder. The window wasn't there. Please God, he prayed, pawing, coughing, unable to open his eyes. Please. Please God.

And then he found the window. He scrambled up the wall without the help of the workbench, without air or aid. He pulled himself out of the basement and through the loose window, back into the world.

He didn't have the blanket any more. He didn't have anything except the gardening boots. He staggered, gasping, past stunned firefighters and gaping neighbours.

"Bob! Bob!" Julia cried when she saw him, and opened her arms, of course she did. "Oh! Your hair!" she said, and there was a God. It was clear, there was a forgiving and merciful God.

"It's been singed off," Bob gasped as he fell into her arms.

29

Cold, cold, and evening had come on so blind. Sienna stalled in front of the dormitory doors, watched them spin and stop, spin and stop, which was odd, because she knew they weren't spinning doors, they were the in-and-out type. But these had been changed and she was wary.

She squinted, willed the doors to stop spinning. The left one never did, but the right co-operated finally, began to look like itself again. Then someone brushed past her and pulled the right door open and Sienna bolted through behind her and it was fine. The lobby was itself: there were sofas still arranged around a lonely TV, and at the desk Marian the Librarian was studying a clipboard as if something was written there. Her name wasn't really Marian and this wasn't a library, but she had thick glasses and her long, tied-back brown-grey hair hung dead as an old rope. She gazed up just as Sienna looked away. She had a crush on Sienna. It was awful and it was entertaining, in a minor sort of way, and Sienna usually tried to hold Marian's gaze for one penetrating moment every day. But not now.

She paused on the stairs, felt as if she were folding when in fact she remained upright. It was the wrong place to stop;

Marian would be behind her in just a small lag, asking what was wrong. So Sienna forced herself to keep going. The stairs had a greenish glow that Sienna wasn't used to at this stage. She tried to ignore it. This was the worst re-entry she could remember.

Third floor, down the hall, step by step. Her own door was locked. She was clumsy with the key, but oddly the camera kept pace with this reality: if she looked through it, it held the door sane. That's how to get back to Sterling, she thought, but vaguely, as if remembered through layers of packing foam.

And the shoes weren't there. If only they'd been in the bag by the door, but the bag was gone and so was Ricky. Then the floor tilted like the slow, warning start of a carnival ride, and Sienna staggered two steps before regaining her balance. She wondered if that was the shoe bag by Ricky's computer, but by then she was lurching towards her bed.

I'll get up in a minute, she thought, and clutched the pillow round her ears, drew her knees to her chest, turned to the wall. *In a minute, in a minute*, it became a tiny song in her head.

Now the bed was heaving too, a different part of the ride, late to be activated. Sienna made herself as small as possible, tried to wait things out.

At some point Ricky came in. It was all wrong. She said, "*So?*" and stood over the bed as if she had the divine right of immediate explanation.

Her eyes still closed, Sienna felt as if she could see Ricky anyway. "I can't talk now," she said thickly.

"You fucked him," Ricky said. Her hands were on her hips, her face was in shadows; she was breathing like an animal a moment before rage – all this was clear in Sienna's mind.

"If that's what you think," she heard herself say, "if you can't get your mind past that."

"Oh, *shit!*" Ricky said, and Sienna couldn't help her. It was too crawling-along-gravel, but she felt so weak, couldn't think of how else to go. "You fucked him," Ricky said again, a growl that broke at the end, became pitiful. "I knew you were going to do it. I knew it." Sienna could feel her kneeling by the bed, her hands were clenching the sheets.

"If that's what you think," Sienna heard herself repeat.

"You said you wouldn't but you did. He's different to you, I *knew* he was," Ricky moaned.

"Screw you."

The phone rang.

Sounds were muffled, it was all slow now, useless. Sienna knew she had to get up and put it right, that there would be a way. When she was herself again. Some plausible combination of sounds would march out so that Ricky would understand, so that she herself would understand. Just what had happened back there? To have come so close . . . and then feel it all turn to shit.

The phone rang again. Ricky got it. Ricky could talk. In a different language, it seemed; Sienna heard the words – they were angry in a way – but couldn't process them. Her brain was limp, her muscles gelatin. It would have taken all her energy to turn and rise from bed, so she didn't. Sienna knew it was sometimes the downside of clarity, that's all. You wait it out like the flu, stay small and try not to make it worse.

She slept for a time, then opened her eyes groggily in the darkness, turned over and gazed across the room. Ricky was glowing in the unreal light of her monitor, hunched over it almost like a cavewoman huddling by the fire. Sienna didn't think she could speak yet. All she could do was watch. Impossible not to, really, like watching a film of certain disaster, a cliffside giving way in slow motion, a tree now leaning, tumbling, then a sidewalk, a roadway, the supports of a bridge collapsing now, the tiny cars spilling helplessly, the silent sickening slide of the whole structure into the murk.

"Don't!" Sienna wasn't even sure she'd said it. Ricky didn't respond. Her fingers were on the keyboard making everything worse. Sienna could see her own things on Ricky's desk, could feel it, the awful unfolding, the irresistible suction of this most unnatural disaster.

"Don't!" she tried to say again.

Then the film changed and Sienna could see him in a purplish, bruised light. He was naked to the night, twisting slowly, his tongue swollen, eyes lost, knotted at the neck by what? By a few strands of Sienna's clothing. Every time she tried to avert her gaze he turned to match her, this way and that, a grotesque dance, and she felt powerless to stop it. She tried to raise her hand to save him – oh, anything to cut him down – yet her arm felt as though it weighed a thousand pounds.

But *later*, she thought – so clearly it was almost frightening – *later I will know what to do.*

30 ⤳

Everyone had come. You'd think it was fireworks, you'd think they'd shot the president and had a parade. Tires and driving and people standing around, standing. Nobody knew anything. The men came in their big trucks and twirled about with their hard heads and the big ones, the long ones, those things. Like a big parade. They had them then, before, whenever it was. Daddy used to take everyone, and she'd sit up on his wiggle-waggle, way up, and watch. The big men with their long things, like other things, it got so you couldn't tell them apart.

And some men were naked. Completely. They ran out like they were on fire, no cucumbers, just bare and running. The one man was like that. He was so poor, it was a disgrace.

"Well, I think that's enough," Lenore said, but no one was listening. Everyone seemed to think it was her fault. It was awful, she'd never heard such nonsense. People acting like elephants.

They weren't going to blame it on her. Men running and hard heads arriving. It wasn't fair. They take one look at you, if you're over a certain time, that's it, sorry! Well, Lenore thought, if they're sorry, how do they think I feel? One little mistake. You get the code wrong and then the whole parade lands on you!

All gone. They didn't excuse you so you had to excuse yourself. If they want to stay, that's fine. But when you get to a certain time you say, "Thank you. Thank you so much. That was lovely. How very kind." Shake hands with the young ones, too. Don't speak down to them.

The hostess was very busy with the naked man. Well, that was their business. If that's how people lived nowadays. Begging on the street instead of digging ditches, which is what Daddy did. Along with all the soupers. They ate bread in the line, accepted no cheese, they were very proud. They ate and they ate.

She meant to say thank you properly, that it had been lovely, but the fat man was crying on the ground, he was so drunk. He'd never seen a parade. He was that poor. Sometimes they would come to the door, the naked ones, and Daddy would hand them a shovel and tell them about the ditches. There were always onions in the cold storage. Once her brother had locked her in.

She tried to say goodbye to the hostess. She said, "Lovely. Just lovely," and stuck out her hand, quite properly, but some people are brought up badly these days. They cling to naked men. Spoiled, battish little children. Blaming everything, *everything* on you.

"Well, I never shot the president," Lenore said, and it was true. She remembered exactly where she was. She was walking past the TV appliance store, that one on the street, with the big sign. There it was. She was walking past when Walter Klondike came on in the window and everyone stopped. Cars, everyone, they just pulled over. People were weeping, just like now.

"*Ffffghh*," Lenore said and she cleared her throat. These people had no idea.

"Mother, I'm going to take you back to Fallowfields. We're going to go to a hotel. The house has burned down. Do you understand that? You've set fire to the house and burned us all down!"

"Well," Lenore said. And she turned to go. You can't just blurt it out if there's no paste. But they take you by the wrist, that's what they do. They put you in the back of the wagon. They don't wait for your attorney. And Trevor still gone! That man! He was going to be furious. With the baby so young, no one should get away with such truck.

A long, noisy kerjangle to the prison. The baby screaming, Lenore trying to get to her, it was awful. Pleading, scratching at the door, but she was scuffed and roped, no one could escape. The fat man, the real murderer, riding with them. They'd brought him clothes. A guard's uniform. My God, he was going to be in charge of her! Just awful. His face so white, hands zickering. No one would believe her. "I didn't kill him! It wasn't me!" she screamed.

"Mother, please, calm down!" the other guard said. Speeding the paddywack a hundred miles an hour. And the baby screaming. How could they put a baby in prison?

"Please. Please, for the love of God!" But there was the prison: the big glass doors, the cream cakes inside. Those frightened eyes.

"I demand a recount!" Lenore yelled. They can't do it, just lock you up and throw away the tree.

But they can. They can and they do. They take you away when you were just passing the store, it wasn't you. You *saw* it but you didn't do it. But how can you fix them? They know from the pictures. It's all been arranged. The warden tells you – she's an enormous, frusty woman – she takes you under the arm and says, "Lenore, now, you've had a shock."

She uses those words. She pulls you away from your baby. You're never going to see her again. When it wasn't your fault, you tell her again and again and she agrees with you but it doesn't matter. She doesn't understand. And now Trevor doesn't know where she is, he'll never think to call the referee. He won't even realize till dinner and then he'll be furious. He won't care, he'll just keep on in the sauce and buy new socks when the old ones get woollen.

"I didn't do it," Lenore said, weeping against the warden. "I was there but I didn't do it, and now they're throwing it all out."

"No, they aren't, Lenore," the warden said, stupidly.

Lenore looked at her, turned her head, looked at all of them, tried, tried to understand why everything had turned so crimsy.

ဢ

Ages later. The prison smelled of toilets and dying people. It looked vaguely familiar. That was the awful thing, like this terrible dream. And then it was a dream. They didn't make things like this in real life. The smell. The green prison grass. And bars on the windows. Everyone out of their minds. Mumbling, old dead skin, dribble lips, awful white hair. Lurch and bent people. Smelling and toothless and dressed so old. There was the television. Everyone parked around it like cows.

Lenore started crying then, it was the only thing she could do. She fell on her knees and wept because of everything so gulch – her baby gone and Trevor hungry, waiting. For all that. It was so soon after the surgery, no wonder she made mistakes. Anybody would, it wasn't fair.

"Lenore. Lenore!" They were saying her name. But just wait, she thought. They came for me, they'll come for you. Put you with cows. Make you so weak and tired and the pills do you crimsy, nothing is right. Just wait. It won't be long, she thought.

31 ⌐

Julia was sweating, her heart wouldn't slow down. She knew she was driving too fast but she couldn't help it. Matthew was shrieking in the seat behind her. He'd been crying non-stop since they'd all got in the van. What if it's smoke inhalation? she thought. The paramedics had checked them all outside the house, he was fine then, but what if it's a delayed reaction? Clearly she should just drive straight to the children's hospital, get him checked out. Maybe his lungs had been burned, he wasn't getting enough oxygen. Babies don't cry without a reason. Everyone knows that. And you don't leave an Alzheimer's patient unattended. What was she thinking? Crawling off to have a nap. She'd put away the knives but had she put away the lighter? No! It was in the sideboard drawer, naturally her mother had found it. Julia should have known what she was looking for. She should have known better not to leave her alone. Now the house was burned down.

"Have you got your lights on?" Bob asked beside her.

"Of course I do," she said irritably, but in a moment she could see that she didn't. And for an instant she lost complete track of where she was going. She was speeding them along a twisty road at night in utter darkness!

Julia pulled the lights on – that was better – and took a deep breath. "The house has burned down," she said as if trying out the news, not really believing it. But she'd been there, she'd almost fallen victim. And Bob! He'd been in the house all the time, had come back after his class and had a lie-down in his office, had been drinking, she could smell it on him. "Didn't you see her?" Julia asked angrily. She tried to slow down but the van wasn't co-operating. "When you came in? Didn't you see her looking for the lighter?"

"I didn't know what she was doing," Bob said. Softly, as if from a distance. He was far too calm for someone who was almost burned with the house. He'd had to go to the basement to escape the flames, fling off his clothes, crawl out the window. "I saw you were sleeping and I thought she was all right," he said.

They were hurtling along Colonel By Drive, following the canal to the heart of the city. The large glass balls of the canal lights glowed like small moons and the sky was purplish black with dark, muscle-bound clouds hunched above the shadowed cliffs and Gothic towers of Parliament Hill. Julia pumped the brakes twice, then a third time, and the van slowed to what seemed like a crawl: sixty kilometres an hour, the speed limit. It didn't stay there more than a few seconds – she was up to eighty, then ninety again and had to hit the brakes for a red light. Then she sat waiting in unbearable stillness, and it was only when the light turned green again – a decade later, it seemed – that she realized that Matthew was finally quiet. She turned back and saw him slumped forward in his baby seat, motionless.

"Oh my God. Oh my God!" Julia said and quickly unstrapped herself and stretched back to feel under the baby's nose. "He isn't moving!"

"What are you doing?" Bob said. Julia shook Matthew until he woke up. A car behind her honked so she started them forward again. Matthew began once more to cry. "It's all right. He's fine," Bob said, gently, putting his hand behind Julia's neck. "We got away with it."

It was an odd thing to say, but she knew what he meant. It could've been much worse. They could've all been killed, or burned badly. It was a miracle they weren't. They were lucky, or someone was watching over them, even while she couldn't watch over her mother. She was too tired, she didn't deserve to have a child, she couldn't handle the responsibility. But she'd gotten away with it. The house was ruined but at least the family was still intact.

She drove them to the Chateau Laurier, beside the Parliament Buildings. It wouldn't be the cheapest hotel – was probably the most expensive, actually – and Julia didn't know what the insurance would cover, hadn't even contacted the agent – all the papers were in Bob's study, probably incinerated. She didn't want to think about it. Tomorrow. A hundred thousand details for tomorrow. For tonight they could afford some luxury, they needed it, deserved it after what they'd been through, and she simply decided for them without discussion. In this Bob seemed content to follow along. He looked so odd in the clothes that their neighbour Ray had been able to scrounge up for him: pants quite tight and a little long, a turtleneck that stretched badly over Bob's middle, an old, battered blue Toronto Maple Leafs hockey jacket, and Bob's own rubber gardening boots that he'd managed to find in the basement in his scramble to get out. He was and he wasn't Bob, at the same time.

Julia parked in the underground lot, then they walked out the vehicle entrance to Wellington Street, which looked shabby in the night, a number of lanes shut down by unending construction. The front steps and doorway of the green-towered, castle-like hotel, however, were a fairy tale of red carpeting, gleaming marble, polished brass, and the lobby was cavernous, the walls and ceiling crowded with ornate carvings. It had been years since Julia had been there – her father would meet her there for lunch sometimes when she was a teenager. She was immersed suddenly in the memory: her father so much older than most of her friends' fathers, and yet dapper in his suit, his hair so short and neat. He would hurry in from some office tangle and then relax, soak in the slow, measured, aristocratic tread of the place. She remembered the soft bright-white linen napkins and table-cloths, how beautifully ironed they were, not starched and stiff but possessed of a certain firmness anyway, a sense of decorum. She remembered the heavy silver cutlery and the delicate teacups, and her father downing that first drink, the tension draining from his face. His refuge. How silent he was at home, withdrawn. But here he was just as likely to open with a question debating the course of history – "What if Truman hadn't dropped the bomb?" – as he was to bear down and say, "I don't want you to rush into marriage. You need to wait, establish yourself, figure out who you are on your own terms." Julia all of fifteen, feeling galaxies away from getting married.

"So you don't want me be like Mom?" she'd joked once, and she remembered the way the old man's eyes narrowed, his teeth chewing on the inside of his cheek.

"I will not a hear a word against your mother. Not from you. Not from anybody." And how quickly the gravity of the moment had changed, Julia's juvenile attempt at humour buried beneath the earthen weight of her father's will and conflicted emotions.

"Just not rush into marriage," she'd said after a terrible awkwardness, and how grudgingly he seemed to accept the attempt to recover.

"Exactly. Because they're going to come knocking, you'll see. They're going to be lining up three deep." This small, tough, steady-eyed, balding man, her father in his business suit, soberly settled into drink, trying to tell her, to get something into her pretty head.

Now Julia stared at the huge marble statue of near-naked cherubs that dominated the hotel lobby. The one on top was reaching up, drinking from some sort of conch shell, while the one below knelt on a nasty-looking fish – all teeth and smiles, like a sea monster from a centuries-old map.

Julia asked Bob to sign them in but he didn't even have his wallet! He stood in front of the check-in counter patting his pockets in a helpless fog. People in the lobby were looking at him, his odd clothes.

"Do you have your cards?" he asked. His eyes were glazed.

"No," she said. Her purse was gone, like everything. If she hadn't had her keys in her pocket, they wouldn't even have been able to get out of the driveway.

"What should we do?" he asked. He stood very still, waited like a child for her to find the solution. Julia looked at the impeccable young woman behind the counter who seemed to embody a world where not having money was never an issue.

"I left a spare card in the glove compartment!" Julia announced, and waited for a spark of something in Bob's eyes: Reproach? Relief? How many times had he told her it was just asking to be stolen if left there? And what if she'd followed his advice? But there was a dull nothing in his gaze.

"What's wrong with you?" she whispered, but received only a look of surprise, as if she were the one acting strangely.

Julia explained to the desk clerk about the fire and their situation, handed Matthew over to Bob, then returned to the parking garage and retrieved the credit card. When she brought it to the desk everything was fine. The clerk put together a courtesy kit for them with toothbrushes, toothpaste, razors, combs, spare diapers for Matthew.

It was going to be all right. Hard to think otherwise in the stately surroundings, the acres of soft carpet, the old, moneyed gleam of the place, the elegant displays of Inuit carvings, of large oil paintings for sale at undisclosed prices. Even the elevator had the comforting, substantial feel of confident wealth: the dark-brown wood interior, the small, tasteful, gleaming crystal light fixture above their heads. She felt as if she were slowly emerging into daylight. Then, while being lifted so smoothly she could barely register the motion, the slumping, exhausted Matthew now back in her arms, she suddenly said, "Bob, your car!"

He looked at her, startled. "What?"

"Your car! I didn't see it in the driveway. That's why I was sure you weren't in the house, your car wasn't there when we got out."

"Oh," Bob said, and looked down suddenly, then looked up again. "Well, my car," he said.

"Do you think somebody stole it? My God, what *else* could go wrong?"

"Oh no, no," Bob said quickly. "No. It isn't that." But he didn't say what it was. He looked instead at the lighted numbers above the elevator door.

"What was it then?" Julia asked. She felt almost as if she were talking to her mother. She wasn't sure he understood what she'd said. She felt her anger rising, found herself looking down to keep from lashing out at him.

The elevator doors opened, they walked out into a wide, chandelier-lit corridor. Bob strode ahead, missed the sign that pointed the correct direction to their room. Julia told him but he didn't seem to hear – he walked all the way down the hall, then returned and walked past her, finally found the right door.

The room was expansive, high-ceilinged, dominated by two large beds, but with many fine touches that Julia forced herself to appreciate: the warm rust-coloured carpet and peach walls, the colour of both picked up in an understated, single dark strand of the ceiling moulding; the elegant curtains decorated with wildflowers on a sepia background; the two splendid pictures of ancient globes with antique gold-coloured frames; the marvellous wall mirror also framed in antique gold. And, most glorious of all, real windows that actually opened. Julia threw them open, but the view was disappointing: gnarled, tortured Wellington Street, past the Conference and Arts Centres, with the Rideau Canal splitting them, the white lamp globes now looking like touristy gimcracks. The sound of traffic spilled in and she closed the windows reluctantly, laid the exhausted Matthew on the nearest bed, changed him, then tucked him under the blanket. He seemed tiny, extraordinarily fragile, was sleeping like an angel.

"So," Julia said, "what about the car?"

"Uh, the car," Bob said, as if he'd forgotten most of the conversation.

"It wasn't stolen," she said.

"No. Oh no," he said. "I lent it to a friend. To one of the students, actually, who is moving."

"You lent your Porsche to a student who's moving?" Julia said. Bob wouldn't even let her put a potted plant in his precious car, he thought it might stain the seats.

"Special circumstance," Bob said quickly. "His name is, uh,

Boyd, Dennis Boyd. His mother was killed in an accident recently, and he needs help . . ."

"He's *your* student?" Julia said. "I read about that accident. Just awful. A drunk driver in a panel van. Wasn't the boy's name Clarence? And I thought it was the father who was killed. I didn't know he was your student."

"Yes. Yes," Bob said vaguely. "Anyway, he drove me home, and he's just using it for tonight."

"Do you want to call him?" Julia asked. "He'll drop it off and find that the house is –"

"No. It doesn't matter," Bob said.

"But he's going to be wondering –"

"I told him to keep it till tomorrow," he said. "Anyway, I can't face people tonight, too much has happened." He was standing by himself in the middle of the room, terribly still and alone, in his ridiculous borrowed clothes, looking at her with such sudden longing – artless, helpless, almost childlike in his need and want. She felt her anger subsiding, which she fought against.

"You've been drinking today," she said, her voice having more edge than she'd wanted, but there it was, she was upset, she couldn't disguise it.

"For God's sake –" he started.

"The faculty lounge?" she said. "You came back completely smashed. You must have. I was *exhausted*. I was dead on my feet. I just went to close my eyes for a few minutes –"

"Julia."

"But you! You probably could have stopped her if you hadn't been so out of it. You could have called up to me –"

"Listen –"

"Don't you understand how I feel? Our house has been destroyed, I've had to take my mother back to Fallowfields, the one place I never wanted to put her again. And you, you've been acting like –"

"Let's not do this now," he said.

"When do you want to do it!" she screamed and Matthew awoke.

"Not now. Not now," he said, his head bowed, as if too heavy to hold up.

She went to her son, comforted him, rocked him against her breast until he was calm and sleepy again. Bob stayed where he was, a mournful statue in the middle of the room, facing the wrong direction.

She put Matthew back in his bed, walked into the bathroom and shut the door. The house burned down, she thought. The one time I close my eyes.

"I'm sorry," came Bob's voice from outside the door. "Let's not fight."

She ran the cold water in the sink, splashed her face. If he said anything, she couldn't hear it. She kept the water running while she dried herself with a towel. When she finally shut off the faucet he waited a breath or two. "Let's not fight," he said again, almost a whisper. "It's a disaster. We need each other. This isn't the time to fight."

She found herself shedding her clothes, stepping into the chilly, austere, old-fashioned tub, running the water full blast. Her feet felt oddly numb, cold from the night, not yet used to the heat of the water. In a minute. She adjusted the taps, had a hard time finding the right temperature. When the tub was full she shut everything off and lay back in the silence, her ears under water, her head at an uncomfortable angle because of the steep slope of the tub. Was he still hovering outside the door?

She thought of her mother screaming in the Fallowfields lobby, hair wild, the anguish on her face. She remembered holding the pen with too much force, signing so violently that she couldn't recognize her own signature.

"You have a drinking problem," she said, and lifted her ears out of the water, adjusted her posture to a slightly less awkward position. "We never talk about it. This would be a good time."

Silence.

"You spend too many afternoons boozing in the faculty lounge. I smell it on you a lot. How am I supposed to trust you to look after Matthew when you can be like this? You probably could have stopped my mother but you were too drunk to notice. It might be you someday out of control on the highway smashing into someone's parent. Did you ever think of that?"

No answer. She submerged again, wet her hair completely, then sat up and scrubbed her face and body with hotel soap. How many times had her mother screamed at her father about his drinking? How many times did Julia swear she would never be in that same position?

Bob mumbled something outside the door.

"What?"

"You're right," he said simply.

"What?"

"You're right. You're absolutely right. I had too much to drink. I will never drink again in my life."

"Fuck off," she said.

"I'm not being facetious! You're absolutely right. I had too much to drink, I wasn't alert when I got home, you were exhausted, we could've all been killed. I will never drink again. I swear it absolutely."

Julia didn't comment. She pulled the plug, stepped out and dripped onto the bath mat, wrapped herself in thick, warm towels. She didn't want to go out. But she wasn't going to spend the night in the bathroom either.

When she opened the door he was standing inches away. He looked utterly ridiculous, still in his silly Leafs jacket. She pressed forward, eyes down, had to pause and press forward again before he got out of the way. She grabbed the bag of extra supplies from the dressing table, returned to the bathroom and brushed her teeth. Then she snapped off the bathroom light and the main light as well, plunging the room into darkness. In a few seconds she was between the sheets, towels discarded on the floor, thinking, Just try it. Just try getting into bed with me tonight.

She could hear him moving about the room, starting this way, going another, as if unable to decide what to do. Her eyes were clamped shut, she held her body as still as possible. She heard him sit down on the edge of Matthew's bed then move off. For a while she couldn't hear him at all, wondered if he had slipped out the door somehow. But there he was on the edge of her bed now, a voice in the darkness.

"This isn't entirely my fault," he said. "We don't know for sure what started the fire. It could've been your mother. Could've been something else. Maybe, maybe right now it doesn't matter. Maybe what's important right now is that we were all spared. We had a terrible shock, an extremely close call, but we all have our lives, lives that we took for granted. We're all right really. We get another chance." Bob fell silent. Julia could hear his breathing – serious, a bit laboured – a deep bass beside Matthew's shallow, sweet breaths.

He shifted his weight on the bed. Julia braced herself, but he didn't try to come any closer.

32

The morning was so brilliantly sunny. Bob steered the van cautiously along the tree-lined street – few leaves left aloft now, the branches were mostly bare, looked like sharpened, dark fingers piercing the magnificent blue. The night had been . . . long, tense. But at breakfast, Julia was surprisingly upbeat and forward-looking. She gave him the directions now and he followed them soundlessly, turned into the neat asphalt driveway of the unfamiliar house, a little red-brick bungalow with a black roof, a tiny garage, an enormous blue tarp wrapped around the corner bush as part of the winter preparations. Bob turned off the engine but sat motionless while Julia took the child out of the carseat, brought him around to the driver's side for kissing, then carried him, with carseat and extra diapers, up the walkway. Bob watched while Julia pressed the bell and waited, jiggled the boy, blew into his face and smiled. Then the door opened and a young woman named Brenda in a red fleecy reached out and embraced both Julia and Matthew. Bob knew her from the department, where she had been a student with Julia – her best friend, really, and not particularly in favour of Julia's romance with her professor. After graduation she'd stayed on in the department as a research assistant working part-time for a meagre wage. She acknowledged Bob now – half-glare, half-wave – and Bob nodded back.

The two women stood talking on the doorstep, the baby somehow balanced between them, not quite handed over by Julia, still unreceived by Brenda. Bob could hear snatches of the conversation: "I was so worried" from Brenda, "saw it on the news" and "so glad you called, what else can we do?" and from Julia "this is so great" and "we were so lucky, it could have been worse." And then they were going over parts of it again, repeating key phrases, standing in the cold wind on this brilliantly blue day while Bob sat in someone else's ill-fitting clothes, painfully aware of his good fortune. It was as if in the middle of an intoxicating dream he had awoken to find that he had in fact just sleepwalked his way around a building ledge without falling.

Julia headed back to the car, stopped on the walkway to blow a kiss to Matthew and to thank Brenda again for taking him for the day. When she got in the car her face was flushed with an odd energy. "She is so nice," she exuded. "Do you know, she asked if we wanted to stay in their guest room. I told her no, we were fine, but if the insurance doesn't come across, you know, we might think about –" and on she went, recounting almost all of the conversation she had just had – twice – with Brenda. Bob backed the van out, nodded, smiled.

The house was only a short drive away. Julia talked animatedly while he drove. She was full of energy, as if she'd been awakened by this catastrophe, was focused now and coping brilliantly. She was the one who'd phoned the insurance people, who'd remembered the agent, looked up the phone number, described what had happened. She had also thought to call the contact at the fire department who was going to meet them at the house this morning. She was rattling off plans now: the logistics of replacing credit and identity cards, of getting cash, clothes, food, where to stay, what they might want to do with the house since they were going to have to renovate anyway. She chatted on, bright-eyed, hardly stopping for breath.

When they rounded the familiar corner he was unprepared for what he saw. The house appeared much the same as it always had been: the same brown stone walls, darkened windows, steeply sloping slate roof, the same dried ivy and crumbling driveway and porch that needed painting. In fact, it looked so astonishingly untouched that Bob thought for a moment that this too had been a narrow, miraculous escape. He'd been expecting a charred hole in the ground, blackened timbers, walls caved in, smouldering embers, piles of rubbish being picked over by scavengers and sniffing dogs.

But the place was still standing, looked surreally normal, unexceptional. Some of the windows were broken and had been covered. The front door had a board nailed over the gash down its centre. The lawn was chewed up by hundreds of muddy footprints – the firefighters trampling the place in their eagerness to save it. Yellow plastic hazard tape was stretched all around the property. But there were no crowds of neighbours, no dogs or kids, just a small red van with an unlit cherrytop. Bob parked on the side of the street. He let Julia get out first and greet the fire-department official. Bob hung back while she began to talk to him, gesture at the house, communicate her thanks. Julia made the introductions when Bob finally approached. The official was a short man, well into his fifties, with unkempt grey hair, a face of old shoe leather, friendly, compassionate eyes. He shook hands with Bob, and Bob immediately forgot his name. He felt sluggish, slow, inadequate.

"It really doesn't look so bad from out here!" Julia said, in almost too sunny a way, somehow able to rise to meet the situation.

"In the end it was a fairly contained fire," the official said. "It could've been worse. If we'd been called fifteen minutes later, I could see the whole place going up. There's a lot of smoke and soot damage, though, and water. I'm sorry about that, the guys can't really help it. I was through it this morning: most of the beams are still sound, but you're going to need to replace your wiring. Some of the pipes have melted, and we've shut off the water, of course. The integrity of the kitchen floor is suspect, too, and your appliances are shot. You should be able to get a lot of the work done before the first snow, though, if you start right away. Have you got someplace to stay?"

"Temporarily," Julia said, and she explained that the insurance agent was coming out any time now.

"We could wait for him," the official said, looking at his watch. His face betrayed no sense of hurry.

"Can we have a look now?" Julia pressed, so they went in. At the door, Bob was almost overpowered by the lingering, acrid stench. Though near-normal from a distance, inside the house looked like a nightmare: a chaos of wet, charred walls, soot-blackened windows, baked carpet, singed paint, bubbled and blackened varnish, sodden, smoke-darkened coats in the cupboard, and on the floor a smashed mirror, gooey cobwebs of soot streaming from the ceilings, the kitchen a fallen, sullen cave littered with pieces of dishes, heat-warped cutlery, little melted plastic blobs that might have been anything, charred cupboards, the broken, reeking skeletons of the fridge and stove, burnt pieces of the ceiling dripping down.

Julia stood on the edge of the kitchen gaping while the fire official shone his flashlight into the darkest corners. The smell was awful, it made Bob's lungs feel papery and brittle. "I've seen worse," the man said. "Believe me, I've seen worse!"

Outside again, Bob stepped under the pine tree in the front yard, leaned over and retched thoroughly. His body shuddered and he felt a cloud of dizziness engulf him. He stood after a moment and felt Julia's hand on his back. She handed him a rag and he cleaned himself slowly.

"I have to tell you how sorry I am," she said. "It was your house, much more than mine. I should never have brought her home, left her unattended . . ."

"Stop," he said.

"I just kept making mistake after mistake, and then I blamed you, and I almost killed us all . . ."

"Shhhh. No. We all made mistakes," he said.

". . . and I'm just so sorry. I am so, so very sorry." He tried to hold her but she was wound up, suddenly and dangerously over-stretched, a spring about to snap. She stepped away, seemed ready to continue the harangue against herself. But then her gaze swept up and down the street and she said, "Your car isn't here. What's-his-name forgot to drop it off. Clarence Boyd."

"Ah," Bob said uncomfortably.

"I hope it's all right. I hope he didn't take it for some joy ride and abandon it."

"Actually," Bob said quickly, "I think he might have brought it back to the university."

"Why would he do that?" Her eyes narrowed.

The fire official came out of the house, then marked something in the notebook he kept in his back pocket.

"Because I asked him to, I guess," Bob said.

"That's not what you said last night."

Bob stood still. Last night. Last night was the edge of the abyss – the pulling back, rather, the salvation.

A small blue car pulled up beyond the pine tree and a tall, thin, intense-looking man in a grey overcoat got out. Bob recognized the insurance agent from years ago when they'd changed the policy on the house after his divorce.

"I was concerned about other things last night," Bob said. He knew that he should look her in the eye but he couldn't, ended up gazing slightly over her head. He couldn't let everything unravel now.

The insurance man ducked under the yellow hazard tape, was stepping towards them.

"Were you?" Julia asked. She looked at him too long, had not turned her gaze away even when the insurance man was nearly upon them.

"Bruce McCutcheon," he said, and held out his bony hand. Bob took it gratefully. "Looks like a hell of a mess," he said gravely. Julia continued to stare at Bob.

"You know what?" Bob said suddenly. "I've got to get to the university."

"*Bob!*" Julia said.

"I just remembered, I think I left my wallet in my office after all, not in the house. It would be really useful to have some cards and cash. Don't you think?"

"*Bob*," she said again, her tone edged in ice. "We have to deal with the insurance right now."

"I know. I know," Bob said. "I wish I could. But I think I left my office unlocked. I'm afraid somebody will just see my wallet there on the desk."

"You can't be serious," Julia said.

"I'm just –" Bob hesitated, looked in embarrassment, in some hope of aid, at Bruce McCutcheon, then lowered his voice. "My house has just been burned to shit, I almost lost my life, I think I'm doing pretty well, considering."

"I can run you over to the university," McCutcheon said, too helpfully. "After we're done here."

"I think . . . I think maybe I should just go," Bob said. "I'll be a few minutes, that's all. I'm sorry, I feel like I have to do this now. I'll be back before you know it." He stepped off then, felt for the van keys in his pocket, knew they were staring at him.

ᔕ

Bob set his teeth, tried to get his heart to slow down. He felt suddenly plunged back into darkness, yearned for a quick, stiff drink to set him right again. There was a bottle in his office, and Julia would be thinking that was why he'd run off – of course she would; he'd given her no reason to think otherwise.

He parked the van in the empty departmental slot beside his fine little Porsche, got out, thought vaguely that he didn't have a parking permit for the van. A very aggressive towing company had won the surveillance contract. They checked every couple of hours, ruthlessly towed anything without a permit and dumped it in a dreary compound in darkest Gloucester, then charged one hundred and five dollars to relinquish the vehicle. Gerry Calcavecchia had had to pay even though he'd *had* a departmental sticker – it just wasn't in the right spot on the windshield, and it would have taken a battery of lawyers to win a case against the towing company.

But what did it matter? Bob shoved his hands in his borrowed pockets, walked away. Everything was in ruins, was drab and done and unchangeable now. If they towed the van it would just be one more thing to deal with. Julia would take it in stride. She was so much stronger than he was now.

How quickly this slide into blackness, he thought. But I will not have a drink.

He wandered, distracted, up to the English department. The halls now were crowded with young people, with fresh energy, hopes and dreams, wearing sloppy pants and baseball hats turned backwards, with knapsacks and pimples and loud, brazen voices, with too much life. He felt like a heavy black rock in the current that he only now realized was sweeping past him.

And now everyone seemed to know it as well. Voices stilled, conversations took silly little hops, eyes turned. To see what? An engulfed weight. He felt their gazes, it was remarkable, all these students who weren't his own. At least he didn't think they were his. And they were stopping to watch him; the whole flow changed when he went by.

Whispers and subtle laughter and stares, outright, almost rude, the closer he got to the department. His heart began to jiggle nervously, remembering the night before. He almost felt as if he were still caught in the leather dress, that he was that conspicuous. It's possible, he thought, that Barbara Law *had* seen something, had told someone . . . possible, but not likely. Not likely that *everyone* would know.

Perhaps it's these borrowed clothes, he thought. But the gardening boots, the trousers so tight, sleeves too long, were hardly more outlandish than what some of the students were wearing. Still, he was a professor, the standards were different.

"Fire," he said lamely, but people turned away.

He hurried into the departmental office and sought the refuge of Helen's friendly face. She had a wonderful sense of humour, would laugh with him about his outfit. And there she was, absorbed in something on her computer screen, didn't look up immediately when he walked in.

"Helen," he said, happy to say her name, to ground himself in something familiar and secure. She looked up then, but her smile didn't follow. She appeared startled, almost frightened, as if she knew him to be a ghost. It couldn't have just been his altered appearance. It occurred to him that there must have been a mistake – maybe the local news had reported him dead in the fire, that was what was behind all the whispers and stares.

He waited for her to recover, to say something about the fire or his clothing, or perhaps even about his continued existence, to cry out in joy and relief. But she didn't, and she wasn't her usual graceful self. She turned her eyes down quickly, her face looked strained, as if there were a sudden bad taste in her mouth.

"What? What is it?" he asked. "You heard about the fire? My home has been destroyed, it was a disaster, we could have all been killed."

Even when he said those words her reaction was muted.

"Are you . . . are you all right?" she asked.

"Yes! Fine! We're all fine!" he announced, too loudly, over-compensating. "I can't stay long – insurance, everything to work out. Could you cancel my classes for this afternoon? And I'm afraid I've locked myself out of my office. I think you have an extra key, don't you? Or am I going to have to track down the –"

Gerry Calcavecchia poked his head in the office at that moment and then did a cartoon double-take. Bob thought he was fooling, waited for the punch line. But Gerry couldn't deliver it. Instead he dropped the papers he was carrying, then didn't bend down to pick them up.

"*What is it?*" Bob implored.

"Bob, I guess you haven't heard," Helen said then, her voice so thin, the moment tight as a wire against his throat.

33 ⤳

"I suppose you get used to it," Julia said, not feeling used to it at all, but opaque and otherworldly. She was sitting in the passenger seat of the insurance man's light-blue sedan – Bruce McCutcheon – who did seem used to it, tramping through burnt-out houses, picking over the ruined remains of flooded rooms, soggy carpets, cracked paintings, smoke-blackened drapes, melted toys, computer carcasses, splintered doors, of collapsed cupboards and blistered furniture and potted plants blasted across the floor by jets of water. Julia had two things in her hand: a water-stained photo album and Matthew's cloth snake, Willy, damp and slightly singed, though with a still fully functioning rattle.

"At least there were no deaths," Bruce McCutcheon said, and he wiped his big hand back through his thinning hair. "It's when they bring the bodies out you can't get used to it." His fingers were long and bony and looked terrifically strong. Julia could imagine him in another era tightening the wire on a fence or pulling a horse to the barn in a snowstorm – chin down, face out of the wind, those fingers in the harness strong as sprung steel. Now he was guiding a ballpoint pen along the lines and boxes of a carbon-sheeted form. There were other papers spread out on the top of his briefcase, a pamphlet in blue and white on her lap: *When Disaster Strikes! Your Guide to the Insurance Process.*

"What's the worst you've seen?" she asked.

"You don't want to know the worst thing," Bruce said. He looked up from his form. He wore a wedding ring and his left pinkie was badly scarred, bent a little the wrong way.

"I do," she said. "I really would like to hear." And so he told her about his first case, a family he'd sold a policy to just weeks before the fire. "It was a winter night, thirty below, and the house went up in seconds – either a leak from the gas stove or else a burner had been left on and a spark had set it off. The mother was at bingo, it was her first night out in months, and the father was drunk in the living room. The place blew up. The father was thrown back against the wall, the couch rolled on top of him. He was out of it anyway, he'd been drinking very hard. Three little girls upstairs in bed. They tried to get to the window but it was frozen shut." He had a little voice, odd in such a large man, and when he talked his mouth barely moved, his eyes stayed down at the form. "It was frozen," he said, "and then they were roasted, and when the mother came home the walls had all but collapsed. She ran in right past the police and the firemen. They had to go in after her and drag her shrieking from the building. I was trying to comfort her and all she wanted to do was die with her family. Besides that, they'd made a mistake in their coverage. The husband had sworn he was a teetotaller – he got a break in the premiums for that – but there were bottles littered all over the living room, and the autopsy showed blood-alcohol of .38 or something."

"So there was no coverage?" Julia asked.

"Technically it should have been nothing. We had absolute proof. But I got the brass to spring for a reduced pay-out. She never thanked me. She killed herself later on anyway. You asked."

Julia had asked and now she felt rotten. This wasn't anything she wanted to think about. It was awful, too raggedly close to what she imagined could be her own life. She looked at her watch.

"Do you want to call him?" Bruce asked, his hand on the car phone.

"No," Julia said quickly. "I wouldn't be able to get him in his office. He's probably on his way back now anyway. He said he'd be just a few minutes. I'm so sorry for this." Bob had been gone over an hour. He was the one who knew all about the computers and the piano and the value of most of the furniture: old, beautiful pieces which had come from his family. He'd be heartbroken to view them, but she needed him to see the process through. They were going to have to account for every belonging in their possession, to give it a name and description and replacement value. "You didn't videotape everything?" Bruce had asked with resigned skepticism. "Everybody does it now," he'd said. Well, if everybody did it why did he look that way, as if everybody *ought* to do it but nobody whose house actually caught fire had *ever* done it? There was a box of soggy papers in the back of the car, salvaged from the study, Julia and Bob's files of receipts reaching back a few years at least. Pure luck they hadn't gone up in flames. She was going to have to go through them systematically, account in detail for their material lives, and she didn't want to do it alone.

Bruce looked at his own watch, but patiently, with no sense of irritation or hurry, then wrote a few more things on the form on his lap. It was warm in the car in the sunshine. Besides the salvaged box of receipts there was a baby seat in the back and a single child's hockey glove; the side pockets of the passenger door were stuffed with disposable diapers, and the floor under Julia's feet was littered with cassettes – a smattering of Spanish-language tapes mixed with blues, folk, reggae, and Cajun music.

"I guess we can wait a little longer," Bruce said.

Julia heard a vehicle approach and turned to see a familiar, beat-up red truck. Donny Clatch was driving. He didn't seem to see Julia in the car at first but peered at the house, the yellow hazard tape, the empty-soul appearance of the broken windows. He parked the truck at the side of the road opposite Bruce's car and Julia excused herself, got out to talk to him.

He stood at the edge of the tape and stared wide-eyed, his mouth hanging open a little. "Is everyone all right?" he asked, and Julia told him the whole story. Throughout he shook his head, turned away in amazement, said over and over, "Is that right?"

"We were lucky," she said for what seemed like the millionth time. "We all got out. Nobody was hurt."

"So where are you staying?" he asked, and she told him the insurance would pay for a hotel, not the Chateau Laurier where they'd stayed last night, but something more downscale.

"They have a list. We have to choose. And we have to get started on renovations," she said. He asked her when and she said as soon as possible, asked him if he would be available.

"You'll want a whole team working on this project," he said. "I'd have to get some guys together."

"The insurance company wants us to get three bids," she said. "But I'd love it if you could do it. I just, I want someone I can trust." And then for the first time she really noticed how he looked at her – like he was ice cream dripping down the side of a cone and one more moment in this heat he was going to fall over, go *splat* on the sidewalk at her feet. "We need the three bids," she repeated, a bit flustered, he seemed so moved and embarrassed, almost unable to speak. "Anyway, as soon as you can I need you to board up the remaining broken windows. The fire department did the main ones last night, but I noticed damaged panes in some that they didn't do. The raccoons are going to move in soon with the cold weather and I'm afraid of looting and kids getting hurt playing inside."

"Sure. Absolutely," he said, and took out his notebook. "I have to feed my Mom some lunch, then I'm installing a dishwasher, but I could get to this after."

"Thank you. Thank you so much," she said and stepped in quickly and kissed his cheek. She couldn't think why she did it except to see him nearly burst with pleasure, to feel what a wonderful thing that is, even in the midst of disaster.

"God. I'm glad you're okay," he said.

Julia used Bruce's phone after all. She got machines at Bob's office, at the departmental office, and even in the faculty lounge, left curt messages for him in all three places. Donny had to leave then and Bruce and Julia shared Bruce's meat-loaf sandwich on brown with mayonnaise and tomato. Then Bruce asked her if she wanted him to drive her to the university to try to find Bob, but she said no. "I've got to check on Matthew anyway." She thanked him as politely as she could, given how bitter she felt inside to have been abandoned like this. Bob really wasn't a brave man, she knew it in her core. He was squeamish and fussy and he hated unpleasant things. That's why he was so bad about helping with Matthew. And why he drank so much. She could picture him now in some dark corner, in the middle of an intense academic conversation, hiding from his family responsibilities, dulling himself with Scotch.

Something else nagged at her – another possibility she really didn't want to think about. What if Bob had early-onset Alzheimer's? It was rare, yet it happened, and Bob was fifty-four, certainly old enough. She knew that the early stages could be very difficult to detect but involved subtle changes in behaviour, memory lapses, problems with words and simple tasks, confusion. Stress could bring it on, and she had a secret fear that he was stumbling around right now, lost, the way that her mother had before anyone realized anything was wrong – driving aimlessly in the van, perhaps, or trying to remember what had happened to his car. That part was especially bothersome. She didn't for a minute believe his story about lending his Porsche to Clarence Boyd to help him move. He seemed to have simply made it up in order to fill a void, either caused by a drunken blackout or something else.

Or something else.

So many things could go wrong. It was shattering to think how fragile anyone might be. She hoped it was just the drinking – *just the drinking* – but she struggled with the thought that the problem might be much worse.

She told Bruce she would work on the forms at Brenda's house, gave him her number there, said that she wanted to walk, needed time to think and breathe. He understood. They made a tentative time to meet again later to do more damage assessment.

"I'll call first," she said.

"The longer we leave it the longer you'll have to wait for your settlement."

"Yes. Yes, I know."

She didn't want to leave the place unlocked, but Bob had her keys, so she went around to the back, found the spare house key they kept in a film canister behind a stone in the garden, locked the doors and pocketed the key. Then she left, walked off, worried. The more she thought about it the more likely it seemed to her that Bob was unravelling somehow, that the drinking was a symptom but not the root cause. Ever since her mother had started to come apart, she'd been more aware of how vulnerable anyone's mind might be to depression, to chemical changes signalling the onset of some horrible disease. Was that it? Were these the early stages? She was carrying Matthew's Willy, the rescued photo album, and the wet box of old receipts, and with each step weariness invaded her limbs. She felt abandoned, suddenly and single-handedly responsible for a wilful young child, a failing mother, and a fading husband. It seemed as if the heavens were against her, had burned out her house, plagued her life. And why? Because she'd stolen him, that's why. He was already married, she had no right responding to his overtures the way that she did; she should have kept her distance rather than wrecking their home.

ഗ

"You must be devastated!" Brenda said at the door, looking at her face, then hugging her ferociously. "I can't imagine!" she whispered.

Julia was confused for a moment – Brenda knew all about the fire already. "It's not so bad," she said, when they'd separated. "The house is still standing. I like the insurance guy, he's going to be all right to deal with." Brenda was looking at her with blazing intensity. "*What?*"

"You don't know," Brenda said, and Julia had a sudden, sickening premonition, a vision of a car wreck, of Bob's body crushed inside ruined metal. She felt faint, had to lean against the railing by the door.

"Tell me," she said. Matthew was playing in the hallway with plastic men – safe, thank God.

"It's the weirdest thing," Brenda said, "I don't know what to make of it. But everyone with a university e-mail address got this message. I just read it an hour ago."

"What message?"

"About Bob and . . . and one of his students."

"What about Bob and one of his students?"

"Come in – oh, I'm sorry!" Brenda suddenly said and held the door open.

"Brenda, just tell me!"

"Julia, it's so strange. It's either a prank or . . . or your husband has been having this . . . bizarre affair. It's hard to describe. Maybe . . . you need to see it. I'm sorry. I'm so sorry for this," she said. "Come in! Don't stand out here."

Julia felt her feet carry her into the living room.

"Let me get you something," Brenda said. "I have coffee, I have alcohol –"

"Willy! Willy!" Matthew said, and Julia numbly let the snake drop into his hands.

"What do you mean he's having a bizarre affair?"

"Well, given his history, do you think it might be –?"

"Brenda, I don't know what you are talking about!" Julia was shouting now. "He's been impossible lately, but –" She didn't know how to continue. She felt smacked in the face, as if she'd walked straight into a pane of glass.

"I'm sorry. But you need to see this," Brenda said.

Julia followed her into a small room with a single bed, a dresser, a desk and computer. There was only one chair. Brenda sat in it and Julia sat on the edge of the bed. She could see the screen clearly, waited with a sense of mounting doom while the machine warmed up and Brenda clicked the appropriate icons. "I didn't bookmark the site. I'm sorry, I was just so astonished," Brenda said.

Julia could hear Matthew playing happily. She had a strange sense that everything was whirling apart despite her sitting so still and composed. That she had control over nothing except taking one breath and letting it out.

"Come on. Come on!" Brenda said. The modem was dialling, but kept encountering a busy signal. "This is one of the worst times," she said. "The traffic just builds and builds all through the afternoon."

Brenda tried a different number and it was busy, tried the first again and it was busy. Then she tried a third, a slower line, and got through. In a few minutes she had the letter on-screen.

THE SEXUAL PROCLIVITIES OF ENGLISH PROFESSORS:
PRELIMINARY RESEARCH

An inquiry into the sexual fantasies and practices of male professors of English literature by poetical and sexual anthropologist Sienna Chu. Preliminary findings are now available. Comments, discussion, corroboration, and debate are all welcome.

"Poetical and sexual anthropologist?" Julia said.

"You don't want to see this. Believe me," Brenda said, but she'd already clicked on the icon. The Web page was coming.

There was the title again in bold black lettering. The explanation followed.

Poetical and sexual anthropologist Sienna Chu presents preliminary findings in a study examining the sexual fantasies, histories, practices, and inclinations of a sub-group of male English literature professors. Featured today: Dr. Robert Sterling, Associate Professor of English literature specializing in 19th century American letters. This extraordinary, candid, and deeply original portrayal eschews more traditional, western, linear textual modes of exposition while revealing fascinating glimpses and sub-texts regarding highly individualized sexuality, as arranged and imagized by Ms. Chu, a pioneer in the nascent field of poetics and sexual anthropology.

"Everyone at the university was notified of this?" Julia asked.

"Everyone on-line," Brenda said. "It seems to have been a bulk mailing. There are supposed to be spam guards, but this chick knew what she was doing."

There was more text, but by then a picture had arrived on-screen. It was a grotesque, partially blurry image of a fattish, aging man wearing a hideous black wig and garish make-up, and stuffed into the most awful-looking hooker-style scarlet mini-dress. He was leaning against a desk in some professor's office – in Bob's office; Julia recognized the pen and pencil set her mother had given him years ago, and the window behind, the chair and the books . . .

It was Bob's office, and the sorry-looking Hallowe'en figure with the gash of red lipstick, the gaudy face, the stockings, for Christ's sake, his legs apart as if he wanted people to look up his dress . . . it was Bob. Unmistakable, but she couldn't believe it. She fought down a rising sense of nausea.

The expression on his face, almost drugged, and yet . . . so ordinary, too. A shy little smile. Bob a bit embarrassed. Bob as if gazing up from a funny article in the Saturday *Globe and Mail*, a particularly nicely phrased review lacerating some overrated author.

Brenda said, "That's enough, I think."

Julia said no. "It says there are more pictures. I want to see all of them." So she sat through them all. Twelve grainy photos, the colours leaking over the edges of things, like in impressionistic paintings or tabloid exposés. Bob standing, his arms – hairless, big meaty jokes coming out of the ludicrous dress – crossed in front of his chunky bosom. Bob's back and rear, his skin bulging out of the lacing of the dress, clues of underwear poking out – a black bra strap, the edge of some sort of slip or something. Then there he was just in a black bra and panties. Bob trying to cross his legs, Bob standing as if in a police line-up, staring blankly. Bob with his hands on his hips. Bob sitting on the corner of the desk, his tongue resting on the edge of his painted lips.

"There's text, too," Brenda said. "It doesn't make any sense."

"I want to read it," Julia said. She felt deeply focused, angry but cold. Weak, but holding on somehow. She promised herself she would only look this once. She wanted to see everything once.

The text read:

> *we bob and we see   we cohabitate*
>   *we shed*
>   *we lie in the lingering lake of the dead*
>   *we welter, we slag   we are*
>   *Dietrich in drag*
>   *we reach for a live wire*
>   *a razor*
>   *a rag*
> *a lifeline   an item   a something to be*
>   *we are naked in lustre in bluster*
>   *in creed*
>   *we see and are seen   we step and we strut*
>   *we worship and wonder and ache*
>   *when we fuck*

we lionize   levitate   liberate
eviscerate
we horn and we act and we shine once a life
we float like a fissure
we soar like a wife
a pen   a rifle   a
sickening thought

we fall first in likeness
we gloss up our nails
we are hiding in silk and satin and tales
we are teaching your children
mouldering their minds
we are leaning over backwards
and spreading our legs
we bob and we see
we

we

we

are unravelling strange
the way that we look
the breast of the wind the twist
of the hook

Julia could barely move. She felt suddenly pumped full of some heavy, hot, debilitating liquid, as if she were in an old-fashioned diving suit that had filled up suddenly and now was holding her sickeningly on the bottom.

"It must be a joke," Brenda said. "It's so awful. I can't believe . . ."

"Her name is familiar," Julia said. She tried to think. Sienna. *Sienna?* Oh, Sienna. Oceana. Oh my God.

Brenda was hitting the BACK button now, flipping once again through the horrible, horrible pictures. Julia said, "She must be his student." Undoubtedly she was his student. Who else could she be?

Matthew came in then dragging a yellow plastic bulldozer and making flapping noises with his lips. He turned his little head to look at what Brenda and his mother were so intent on, and Julia shrieked, she threw herself at him, banged her shoulder on Brenda's chair as she went down. "Ow! Ow!" he said, holding his knee, his face full of outrage and surprise.

"Oh, baby. Oh, baby, I'm so sorry!" she said, and cuddled him, smothered him against her, held his struggling head away from the monitor. "*Turn it off!*" she howled. "Please, Brenda, get rid of it!" and she ran with Matthew out of the room, the plastic bulldozer bumping behind as the boy held on, craning his head to see what was so interesting.

~ 34

Bob felt his vision narrowing, a circle of blackness closing in, everything else superfluous except for what was on the screen. Helen's fingers did not let any single picture dwell for long. They flitted by with just enough force to shatter his life. One, two, three – by the fourth one he had to turn away, reeled against the window frame, against the figure standing there.

"Whoa! Hey!" the man said. It was Gerry Calcavecchia – Bob knew it was, but it didn't look like him, his face was so distorted and blurred. Everything at once was different. Bob felt awash in malfunctioning sensations that turned the air grey and the floor blood-red, that squeezed all meaning out of sound.

He cried out something anyway and would have hit the man, the hand that was leaden on his shoulder. But he spun instead, heard his name strangely, found himself in the hall lurching like a madman, bouncing off one person and another, then running, running . . .

Where?

He didn't know.

Outside. Fleeing, stumbling on, for how long he couldn't tell. He glanced around in a panic, found himself inside again, somewhere, he wasn't sure how he'd got there.

ᔕ

"The last days," Bob said. It was later, but how much later he couldn't say. He didn't even know where he was, if it was the same room he'd crashed into or a different one, if he'd been there an hour or a minute. He stumbled on the little platform but kept his feet. The lights were on now. They must think I'm drunk, he thought. Whoever they were. The empty faces, the generations, such a sorry lot, a tiny blur of them in the large lecture hall.

"The last days," he said again, louder, because they weren't listening. They were whispering amongst themselves and looking at him. Mocking him, he could tell. The bloody ingrates. "In the last days," he said, and then he became very still, waited for the rest of the words to come. He felt his back bump rudely against the green chalkboard at the front of the lecture hall and bounce away; he staggered towards the lectern.

"Excuse me, sir, this is Biology 211," someone said. Bob stared at him until he shut up.

"Poe knew," he said gravely, trying to get them to understand. "He knew that the marriage to Elmira Royster was never going to happen. He knew that he'd be selling out his soul. You can see it in his face in the last portrait – *Excuse me, do you have a problem?*" Bob boomed out.

Whoever it was said, "No, sir, no," and shut up.

Such a stupid, cloying clot of sheep, huddled, heading for the door.

"*He was damned and he knew it!*" Bob yelled. His fist slammed the lectern. "He was dishevelled and baggy-eyed, his clothes were a wreck, this fastidious man – *What are you laughing at?*"

"Nothing. Nothing, sir."

"Are you laughing at me?"

"No. No, sir. It's just that this is Biology . . ."

"I will not tolerate snide remarks!" Bob said, and his hand slipped from the side of the lectern. He hadn't realized how much weight he'd put on it because he started to fall over and had to catch himself. There was a gasp from the students.

"Have you never seen a man in desperate straits?" he asked quietly, and sat on the edge of the platform, put his face in his hands. They were deserting him, nervous little lemmings. He straightened and sat back, his head now against the base of the lectern. They were leaving and others were coming in but stopping at the door when they saw him. Stopping the way you do on the sidewalk when you come across someone stretched out and filthy, lost in the bottle.

Lost in the bottle. Such an evocative phrase. Bob hurled it at the ones by the door. *"Lost in the bottle!"* he said, and laughed. They didn't get it, of course not. Students now, they are blank fucking slates. Little sheep people who have no idea. Astonished, uncomprehending faces. Of course they couldn't know. Poe spent at mid-life, exhausted, reeling about in the rain, lost in the bottle in Gunner's Hall in Baltimore, dressed in a vagrant's clothes, staring out at nothing with blank stupidity. A last sensible thought in the hospital, to ask his friend to blow his brains out. Bob looked up. Some bespectacled man in a tweedy jacket was approaching, white hair sprouting from his nose and ears, a look of idiocy in his eyes. "Dr. Sterling," the man said, smiling like a caricature, a demented professor. "Can I help you? Maybe you need some rest."

Bob looked at him, waited for him to start to shimmer and then melt, disappear. Waited for everything to disappear.

Waited to wake up and find it had all been a gut-wrenching dream that now was over. Julia would be beside him, Matthew sleeping nearby, and it would be summer, no classes, the air would be warm and in the light of day all the ugly details would evaporate into groundless little fears.

Bob waited but the professor with the white hair in his nose kept leaning over, his hand beckoning, smile cracked and almost maliciously innocent. "Just a bit of rest," the professor said like some kindly, rumpled old children's-show host. "Just a bit," the professor said, and took his arm so gently.

ᔕ

Bob was resting. He was sitting alone in a nursing station he hadn't even known existed. It was a closet-sized space with no windows, just barely enough room for a single bed, made up severely, with starched white sheets and a thick green blanket, a pillow too fluffy and white and perfect for someone's head. There was a locked cabinet with first-aid supplies, mostly triangle bandages and little packets of disinfectant. A safe-sex poster was yellowing on the wall. It showed a cartoon packet of condoms running along, huffing and puffing, with a message balloon overhead saying, "Don't forget me!" There was a dispenser for condoms on the wall but it appeared to be empty. Bob imagined the room overwhelmed with young couples ducking in for an afternoon quickie until the unionized care staff, or whoever, complained about the constant upkeep: the sheets to be changed, the condom dispenser to be refilled.

They were already locking the toilet-paper rolls in the washrooms. It didn't surprise Bob that this nursing station was kept such a dark secret.

They were coming for him and he had to wait where he was. There was going to be herbal tea in the morning and a ruddy-faced eighty-five year-old was going to teach them Tai Chi and someone else was going to do flower-arranging and at night people would scream in the dark. It would be bedlam, but most of the staff would be home in their own beds trying to forget.

There was nothing to do but wait.

He felt terrible. He felt shocked and numb and exposed, blown apart. He felt like he couldn't move. What was the point? The whole world knew, or thought they knew, his most private thoughts and yearnings. There was nowhere he could go. This was the safest place for now, this airless, sterile little nursing station with the huffy-puffy condom cartoon. He was exactly where he needed to be. He didn't feel like he could move a limb to help himself. He was just supposed to wait.

He imagined the ambulance roaring along the main routes, the impatient drivers pulling over, wondering what was the disaster this time. Those efficient, smart, strong men and women in white. Coming in great haste to clean him away, wipe up all traces of this messy personal meltdown. They were coming and he was waiting and it was simply a matter of time.

Just to experiment, though, to try something out, he got off the edge of the bed and went to the door. He turned the handle to see if it was locked. It wasn't. He opened the door an inch, and then he shut it and went back to the edge of the bed, sat down again. The men in white were coming. It would be a relief, no more explanations. He felt so tired anyway. He didn't want anyone to look at him, much less ask him a question.

He should have seen what Sienna was up to. What had she done, really, to earn his trust? But on the other hand, how could he have been expected to know what she was capable of? And why him, of all people? Why?

How had she seen through him in this way? She must have set out from the beginning to take away everything of value in his life. First his home had been ruined, now his reputation, his career, probably his marriage – of course Julia would find out about this; everyone in the university knew. And he remembered now with a dull, drumming ache that he had left the remnants of his female clothing in the basement, where Julia and the insurance man, what's-his-name, were probably picking over them this minute. Because everything wasn't burned. With his luck, the red dress, the incriminating underwear, would probably be among the most prominent surviving items. So if Julia didn't know now, she would find out very soon.

And why had this all happened? The Sienna he knew was a caring, decent, sensitive person, not a sexual predator, this monster of the Internet. He had denied her nothing. Why would she possibly want to destroy him?

Someone came to the door. Bob watched dully as the handle turned. He was expecting people in white and so sat fooled and stunned for a moment when no one in white entered at all. It was a square woman: she was wearing a dark-blue suit, her head was square and topped in square grey hair, her glasses were heavy and square. And he knew her. It was Dean Rudd. She said, "Bob, this is most upsetting. How are you feeling?"

Bob said he was fine, he was really quite well. He said, "I had no idea this room even existed. How long have I been teaching here?"

"Yes," she said. The dean looked at him as if she wished she were wearing a white coat and could lead him out the back way to the waiting ambulance. She said, "Bob, some very serious things have happened." He nodded his head. "Have you heard at all from your student, Sienna Chu?"

The dean had fat legs and was a leading medievalist now turned to processing forms, trolling for endowments, managing student flow, and coping with disasters. Bob had never been a disaster before. Even when he was breaking up with his wife in order to be with his student, Julia, he wasn't a disaster. He'd been on top of the situation, a consummate professional. Whole sections of the department had had no idea that anything out of the ordinary was happening.

"I think probably the whole school has heard from her," Bob said. Listless and exhausted as he felt, he still had a hard time keeping the anger from his voice.

"Bob," the dean said, carefully, like someone chewing a mouthful of fish bones. "Sienna tried to kill herself. She's resting now in hospital. I just got a call from her parents."

"Suicide?" Bob said. Now the room seemed criminally small, like some tiny cell reserved for the most repulsive offenders. The walls themselves seemed to be squeezing out the remaining air.

"There were drugs involved, an overdose. She appears to be all right. Most of the problem seems to have been caused by an admirer, a Ricky, who did the number on you on that Web site. Sienna has confessed that the photos were fakes."

"Fakes?" said Bob numbly.

"Taken from transvestite home pages," the dean said. "There are thousands of them, apparently. Middle-aged men who dress up and post pictures of themselves. This Ricky combined images from those pages with scanned pictures that Sienna had taken of you in your office. Do you remember her photographing you for the yearbook?" Bob nodded automatically, tried to understand the improbable words, the enormity of these new lies. "They can play amazing tricks with photos these days," the dean said. "We're still trying to track down this Ricky. What you need to know, Bob, is that there is a very good chance of a full retraction and apology here. I know you're probably eager to see your student, but I think it would be best for now if you held off until this is all cleared up. Are you following me?"

Bob blinked, tried to think of what his reaction ought to be. "An admirer . . . decided to make a fool of me on that Web site?" he asked.

"A jealous computer-science whiz," the dean said. "All we have is a name, Ricky. But we'll find out more. I can't have my staff feeling this vulnerable. But it does seem to be a student prank, if you want to think of it in that sort of category. You know," she said cautiously, shifting gears, "this stuff, it's not so unheard-of any more. I've already had the campus Gay, Lesbian, and Transsexual Society contact me about your rights. So if you were –" She faltered, seemed to be searching his face for some sign as to how to continue. "I'm sure this is all the last thing you needed after dealing with the fire in your house last night," she said finally. "I think you should take some time off, Bob. I'll contact you later, and we can discuss whether you want to lay charges, what sort of disciplinary actions might be taken. I expect an apology will be forthcoming, and as far as I know the Web site has been taken down."

"Is she okay?" Bob asked finally. "Is Sienna really okay?" It was hard to know what to believe. If she could lie this elaborately about the photos, then the suicide attempt might simply be a ruse as well. But why? All this just to damn then save him?

"She seems to be resting. Again, given the circumstances, Bob, I have to feel that it would be imprudent for you – Bob?"

"I need to go home," he said.

There was a crowd outside the nursing station, a thicket of heads gathered to watch the continuing collapse and self-destruction. He pushed through them. There was something he desperately needed to do: return to his basement and collect the only physical evidence of his old, irrational, deluded self.

His mind working furiously, he raced down to the parking lot, but the van was gone – towed. Of course it was. He ran back to the department, burst in on Helen, demanded the extra key to his office, which he hadn't collected before in the shock and confusion of first seeing what Sienna had wrought. Barbara Law was standing by Helen's desk, the two were deep in conversation when Bob arrived. They looked up, startled, guilty. "It wasn't me," he sputtered when he saw their looks. "I need my key," he said. "Immediately!"

Helen was flustered, took too long trying to find it. Barbara didn't seem to know where to aim her eyes. It didn't matter. It would all be cleared up. Bob grabbed the key from Helen when she finally produced it and as he was turning away she proffered a note – a phone message. "*Please call your wife*," it said rather baldly, and there was a phone number underneath that he didn't recognize. It must be Brenda's, he thought. Julia has probably gone back there. And probably she has heard. She has heard, but there's no proof. He sprinted to his office, fought the door open, burst in upon his clothes rumpled on the floor. He didn't care who was looking from the hallway. There were no female things in sight. It could all be explained. He grabbed his wallet and keys from his trousers pocket, didn't change into his own suit, there wasn't time, but bundled the clothes under his arm. He rushed down to the parking lot again, and into his car.

Home, home. It was only a five-minute trip. He hit all the lights, changed lanes at exactly the right moment to avoid someone plugging traffic by turning left, sped through a section of construction without slowing. He swerved to avoid a young man who was crossing four lanes of congested traffic on foot like an unshaven immortal, his jaw slack, his lips turned up in a dopey half-grin, and he saw himself, his old self, whistling on the edge of disaster.

No one was at the house. Both the insurance man's car and the fire-department official's vehicle were gone. The yellow hazard tape fluttered in the chilly wind. Bob parked on the street and walked to the porch, called out but got no reply. "Thank you. Thank you," he said softly, and let himself in. It was so much darker than just that morning. It was afternoon now, the sun had moved around to the other side of the house. He entered the hallway carefully, had to wait for his eyes to adjust.

In the kitchen the floorboards protested under his weight and he imagined himself falling through, getting skewered on some blackened rafter. The basement stairs looked shaky too, possibly a bad bet. So he turned around. He had a safer route, the same one he'd taken at the height of the blaze.

He walked out the front door again and was headed towards the backyard when he caught sight of his neighbour, Ray Little, standing on the edge of the hazard tape, looking at him.

"How's it going, Bob?" Ray asked. He was a fortyish man, soft-spoken.

"Okay," Bob said. He wanted badly to just head for the back window, to complete his mission. But now that Ray had seen him he had to walk over and chat. "I haven't had a chance to thank you for the clothes, Ray," he said.

"Yeah, sure. Hope they're not strangling you." Ray attempted a laugh. "Hell of a blaze."

"We were lucky," Bob said. "Lucky we all made it out."

And they talked about it for several minutes, Ray asking about the support beams and the wiring, and whether the insurance company was being decent about it all, and he mentioned that his parents' place in Bells Corners had burned down four years before. "That house had been in the family for four generations. It had to be gutted. All the old furniture was ruined. We had letters that were over a hundred years old, pictures. It doesn't matter how much money you get in settlement, you can't replace those memories."

"That's so true," Bob said, and he felt it in his bones. And how good it felt too, to stand and have a normal neighbourly conversation.

"My mother and father never recovered, really. I mean, they were safe, but the shock of it, the stress. Their health started to go almost immediately."

"That's awful. Just terrible," Bob said.

"But you know those insurance guys, they're just trying to rip you off most of the time. The one who handled my parents' file, you won't believe this, he insisted –"

Bob cut in. "You know, I have . . . I have a thing I have to do," he said vaguely. "In the back. But I'll catch you later."

"Do you need any help?" Ray asked. Patiently, in a friendly way, in no hurry to move.

"No. No, I have to do it myself. But thank you, you've been a wonderful help, we really appreciate it." Bob shook his hand and it felt true, it felt warm and connecting in an unfamiliar, grounded way. He turned and waved and walked off and Ray stood watching him, smiling, just beyond the tape.

Bob headed to the back of the house, then when he was safely out of sight darted to the basement window. It was cracked; part of a pane had fallen out – probably broken in his mad scramble to escape the night before. He bent down gingerly and pushed the window open, cautiously reached his right leg in while trying to avoid the bits of broken glass. The workbench had toppled over, he knew that. He knew he was going to have to ease himself in, balance the window open while gently lowering himself without the benefit of being able to step on anything on the way down. He was set in his mind to do that. He knew he shouldn't take much time, but he couldn't hurry, either, and while he was thinking that he shouldn't hurry his support foot slipped on some mud and he fell about three inches onto the windowsill. It wasn't far, but his legs were split and the point of contact included his testicles, which his full body weight slammed. The pain was immediate and shocking: he gasped once, wildly, for air, and managed a low, terrible moan, and clutched awkwardly even as he was falling, his body helpless as a bag of wood, and struck his head almost soundlessly on the concrete floor lost in the darkness below.

~ 35

"I wish you wouldn't keep missing me!" his mother said, and she turned her head just as Donny got the spoon to her lips.

"I'm not missing you," Donny said.

"You are. You're preoccupied!" she said. She raised her eyebrows and flapped her gums. "I wish men would talk about things."

Donny wiped her chin with a napkin.

"Your father was a great man for the silent treatment!" she announced. Then she said, "This is terrible, by the way. You might as well shoot me now if this is the sort of rubbish you're going to feed me."

"You liked it yesterday," Donny said. It was mashed cauliflower soup with mushrooms and carrots and a light touch of garlic and a secret vitamin E tablet crushed up and hidden.

"It's baby's mash. I would *kill* for a steak and a glass of wine."

"It would kill you," Donny said, holding the spoon patiently in front of her, waiting for the right opportunity. "Besides, you need teeth to eat steak."

"You could just put it in the blender!" she said. "It's what you do with everything else anyway!"

"There *is* a steak in here," he said. "Can't you taste it?"

Her mouth fell open and he shoved the spoon in, wondered for a moment if the mush would come sputtering back in his face. But she swallowed it down grimly.

"If you took away the hockey scores," she said, "he could go for days without talking. Men are extraordinarily shallow."

She accepted another spoonful, then another and another. Then she had a small sip of water.

"Where do you go at night?" she asked finally.

"I have to go do a dishwasher pretty soon," he said, another spoonful ready. She looked at it with slightly crossed eyes.

"This is Pablum," she muttered. "I thought I was through with that when I turned *one*."

"You have to boost your immune system," he said, and she made a noise with her lips, *Bppbbpptt!*

"I asked you something," she said. "And you just changed the subject. I hate to think what you get up to when you go out."

He stopped talking. They were both looking at the spoon, balanced now in mid-air. She finally took it in her mouth. He wiped her cheek again, handed her the glass of water.

"It's become quite cold," she said.

"I don't do anything at night," he said. "I walk around, that's all."

"Because some men," she said, "some very lonely men –"

"I know."

"I don't think you do. I *hope* not! There are men who will pay for –"

"I know, Ma."

"Thank God your father was never like that."

"Yes."

"He could out-silence Gibraltar, but he was never that way."

"I just go walking. I think a lot and I walk."

"So you are *pining*," she said, corkscrewing the word. "I have to tell you, in all honesty, there is nothing more pathetic to a woman than a man who is pining and mooning and a hopeless Milquetoast."

"I know."

"You will *never* get anywhere with a woman by –"

"I *know!*"

"Then why do you *do* it?" she said in exasperation. "You know and you know and yet there you are walking about in the middle of the night."

"I'm just trying to make sense of things," he said quietly. "I know it's not smart and not attractive and it's clumsy and stupid, but it's what I know to do. I'm not a complete idiot. Are you going to finish this or not?"

"I've had quite enough," she said, and pushed the tray away. "I met your father at a dance," she said. "It was a cold, wild night and he was terrifying the way he looked at me. Don't young people go to dances any more? I was just so frightened. But I stared right back at him. I was shaking like a leaf when he walked over. I thought I was going to overturn the table, my hands were so wobbly. And he was a wreck. He told me later on. He was more afraid of that particular moment than any time he spent on scaffolding twenty storeys above the ground. But he went through it. He blurted out the words and took my hand and he mangled my feet till past midnight, I thought we were both going to burst. It wasn't like dancing today. We were hot as the sun in mid-August. You either stand up to it or you melt away."

"I know," he said. "I know," and nearly dropped the tray in his hurry to get out.

∽

The course of one's lifetime is like a great, winding river, and the individuals who are maladapted, who fight every turn, try to flow uphill, who overreach or fail to stretch at critical times will end up wasted in some inappropriate, rocky field or stagnating in some dark place, crowded with silt and cans of beer. Donny was thinking about one of Waylun Zhi's most recent lectures. He was on his belly on Mr. Hopkins's filthy kitchen floor checking the water hook-up under the new dishwasher and thinking about Julia, too, about how terribly much he wanted her and so the passion was unbalanced, it would never come to fruition. He would always be forcing or running away. It would never again be like that night when he had simply walked into her bedroom and there she was, half-asleep, naked, waiting, and she wanted him to touch her and he did, because it was a mistake, she didn't realize what was happening. It was just a matter of timing and it would never happen again, because Donny Clatch doesn't get Julia Carmichael. He doesn't get her when she's Julia Carmichael and he doesn't get her when she's Julia Sterling. He doesn't get her because he never knows the right time to act.

He got up on his knees and pressed the button on the electronics panel to start the machine, then he went down on his belly again to check for drips. He was almost finished. He wanted so much to be on his way, to hurry to the lumber store and buy the plywood then head over to Julia's house to work on the windows as she had asked. He really wanted her to be there, just her, without insurance men or husbands, just Julia. She'd asked *him* to work on her house during this difficult time. She'd stepped up and kissed him on the cheek and she'd looked so vulnerable, like she'd wanted him to embrace her.

He rarely was in real life, but when he was standing for long periods, when he was careful about his breathing and how he held his arms, when he could feel the energy circulation in his body, gentle and deep, the way Waylun Zhi described it – when all those things were happening he did have a slight sense of being somewhat nimble. Perhaps. An inkling. Of balancing. Of having a vague idea of when might be the right time, of what might be the right thing.

That powerful, effortless sense of flow.

There was no leak. The motor ran fine. The dishwasher was in place and level, he hadn't scratched the walls or the floor, he'd followed the building code and hooked the machine through the drain at the sink, even though it had meant outfitting new pipes over what the last idiot had done, which was to drain separately using pipes too narrow for the job. He screwed the bottom panel in tight and offered to take the wood and cardboard crate away. Mr. Hopkins, a retired auditor suffering from some kind of health problem that made him wear a scarf around his neck, even indoors, thought over the matter with painful deliberation.

"It doesn't matter," Donny said amiably. "Most people don't like to keep the crate. I can take it away for you, or if you like I can put it in your basement."

"What would *you* use it for?" Mr. Hopkins asked. He stood leaning on a dark-brown cane and the dome of his head was flaking.

"I just recycle the cardboard," Donny said cheerfully. "I usually keep some of the wood. I've got so many little projects on the go. Sometimes I make wooden toys for the kids of friends. That sort of thing."

"Do you want to *buy* the crate from me?" Mr. Hopkins asked, and then he coughed into a wrinkled grey handkerchief that he pulled from his drooping grey pants, gobbed up and coughed again. He looked at Donny with pressing eyes.

"No. No," Donny said, trying to stay friendly and light. Trying to think of the right thing at the right time. "It's just if you *want* me to take it off your hands."

"I'll sell it to you for twenty-five dollars," Hopkins said.

"No. I'll take it downstairs for you if you like," Donny repeated. "Or I could just leave it right here. Your machine's working. Nice and quiet."

"You've got no dishes in it," Hopkins said.

"I'm just running the cycle," Donny replied.

"How do you know it's working if you didn't put dishes in it?"

Donny looked at him, grinned, knelt down, and started to collect his tools. "I don't know how well it *cleans*," he said. "That's up to the manufacturer. But it's hooked up. All wired and ready to go." He closed his metal tool box, stood up again. It was a tiny, dark kitchen with warped counters, a sink full of dirty dishes, ashtrays on the countertop overflowing with cigarette butts. The curtains were ancient yellow chintz, evidence of a wifely presence from years ago, perhaps, or maybe a last feminine touch from the previous owners.

"You are not going to charge me the full hundred dollars," Hopkins said. He had his chin out as if daring Donny to take a swipe at him. "There's a scratch on the corner there. You did that!"

Donny looked at where the old man was pointing with his cane. There was a mark, but it wasn't a scratch; it was a bit of glue stain left over from the manufacturer's sticker. Donny told him, but he refused to believe it, said it was a bad scratch that ruined the value of the machine.

"You can just wipe it off!" Donny said. "Here. Have you got a rag?" He looked on the counter, in the dirty sink, on the stovetop. There was days-old soup and hardened remains of spilled sauce and a topless, fuzzy jar of jam, but no rag, nothing to wipe with.

"I don't supply the plumbing materials!" Mr. Hopkins said. "This is outrageous."

Donny bent down and rubbed hard with his thumbnail until most of the alleged scratch had disappeared. Then he stood up again and said, "It's just glue."

"Well, you only worked on it an hour," Hopkins said. "I'm not going to pay you a hundred dollars for only an hour's work. Do you even have a university degree?"

Donny swallowed hard, ran his tongue over his front teeth, took a deep breath. "It would have been a hundred dollars if I'd taken three hours to do it," he said calmly. "It's a flat rate. When I install a dishwasher it's a hundred dollars. You might find someone who'll do it for less, but they might do a crappy job, too."

"I'll give you seventy," Mr. Hopkins said. He shuffled a bit on his cane, appeared to be looking around Donny at the dishwasher to see if he might find some other supposed scratch or dent to bring the price down even further.

"It's a hundred dollars," Donny said quietly. "I quoted you the price, you agreed to it. It's a flat rate, and I've done the work."

"Seventy," the old man said, and shook his head as if disgusted to have to pay that much. "And you can take the crate if you want it." His lip was trembling, and his skin was chalky grey, the colour of death. It was probably a battle for him to stay on his feet that long.

"It's a hundred dollars," Donny repeated. "I'll take the crate off your hands if you want me to, but I'm not going to buy it for thirty dollars. I dare you to get twenty guys with university degrees and have them hook up this dishwasher and see if one of them – *one of them* – does it right without flooding your kitchen or electrocuting himself."

"That," Mr. Hopkins said, "is a bad attitude."

He put his head down. He was reaching in his pocket, he was going to bring out his money, but Donny had suddenly had enough. He said, "Forget it," and walked past the man, had to keep himself from upsetting the cane with his foot.

"Come on!" Hopkins said, and Donny could hear the rustle of bills behind him. "You'll never get anywhere with that kind of attitude. Here's seventy dollars, you've earned it!"

"Keep it," Donny said. "Buy yourself a hooker!" and he slammed the door behind him, nearly broke the window.

5

It had been a while since he'd been jerked like that. He was angry driving, angry in the lumber store, he wanted to calm himself before he got to Julia's, but he couldn't. Not with breathing, not with soothing thoughts, not with roaring break-neck into traffic and leaning on his horn. He'd never get any-where. Old Hopkins knew it and Donny knew it. He was pathetic. He had no hope. He'd be screwed and overlooked and forgotten every day of his life because he never got the hang of the right time, the right thing. He was disjointed, awkward and out of step, unco-ordinated; even when he was in the right time and doing the right thing it was because of a mistake, it wasn't *really* what was supposed to happen.

When he got to Julia's house she wasn't there. No one was there. There was a sleek black Porsche on the road that he almost backed into, he was so angry and out of sorts. That was the kind of neighbourhood Julia lived in, black Porsches parked on the street. He got out of his truck and walked past the hazard tape to the door, looked at the first of the windows that needed his attention, began to measure with undue precision – they were Julia's windows, he wanted somehow for her to look at his work and think about him.

It was getting cold, so he went back to the truck to put on a jacket and got the plywood while he was there. He measured and sawed with grim efficiency, looking around every so often in case she arrived, in case it suddenly became the right time. But it didn't. He could've simply nailed the boards in, but he screwed them instead because it was more secure, more meticulous . . . even though she'd never notice the difference. It was an absurd, hopeless little detail.

Some kids came by and stared from behind the yellow tape and a cat investigated him when he was in the backyard. It took him nearly two hours and he would charge Julia one hundred and twenty dollars, which was fair, since the lumber had cost sixty-five. He was giving her a break on his hourly rate. It wasn't her fault that her house had burned down, that she used to be goddamn gorgeous, that she'd married stupidly – lots of women did that. Donny wasn't going to say a thing. He'd just look at her and maybe, maybe she'd see somehow that he was a decent guy, a fair guy, with a good heart and strong hands, and he wasn't educated but he knew a thing or two, he wasn't stupid or full of himself. What was wrong with all that?

Nothing except the timing, which he would never get right.

36

Julia looked at the caverns and craters in her face, the gaping pores, the sickly age marks, the dried, shocked, drained, ravaged, pale, washed-out, horrible skin exposed in the mirror before her. She was sitting in Brenda and Doug's guest bedroom, at the little girls' mauve vanity in the corner with the chipped pink ballerina music box and the tarnished antique silver comb-and-brush set. Matthew was somewhere; perhaps Brenda was feeding him. He seemed to have made himself completely at home. If Julia really set her mind to it, she could say where he was, and what time it was, and whether or not she'd eaten dinner herself. But she didn't set her mind, she let it fall and float in the ugliness of the present moment. It was the only way she could think of it: the desperate ugliness of this reality. Her plain, unadorned, abandoned face. She used to be pretty, she knew it; she used to restrain herself in her choice of clothing, in her presentation, since she didn't want to be judged just by the lustre of her skin and hair, the symmetry and fashionableness of her face, the size and shape of her breasts. It was her mind she wanted to count.

Her mind! Where was her mind? What was she thinking when her husband was clogging up the drain with his body hair? When he was parading around in women's clothing? Some of it must have been hers, she realized suddenly – her purple slip, of course, and other things too had gone missing. Where was her mind when he was carrying on with some undergrad "poetical and sexual anthropologist," whatever that was? All her brain cells were dripping out through lactation, they were sliding into Matthew's hungry mouth, she was drifting along in a dopey fog and had to have a friend show her *on the Internet* exactly what her husband was up to.

He hadn't called. Everyone else had. Julia had asked Brenda to make a few discreet inquiries, and now the stories were pouring in – a dozen friends connected to the department had phoned to report that Barbara Law had seen him running through the halls in drag, that he'd been drunk and incoherent in front of his students, that Sienna Chu was fucking half the department, that she was bisexual, that no one had seen her. That Bob had bolted, no one knew where he was either. That he'd run off with Sienna, that they were driving to the States, that the bitch had gone to New York with him last weekend to the Poe conference, everyone knew . . .

Everyone! It was common knowledge. Bob and the slut had been carrying on for ages, Julia was the last to realize. And the Poe conference! Bob had pretended that he wanted Julia to go, but it was going to be so intense – his word, *intense*; now she knew what he meant.

The phone rang downstairs and Julia stiffened. She waited while Brenda answered. There was the smell of cooking from the kitchen, something garlicky. Something that Bob, if he were here, would wolf down between long gulps of red wine while carrying on three different conversations and laughing, lecturing, pausing to chat up the hostess, tell her what an extraordinary culinary gift she had and ask her, in front of everybody, if her juices were always this succulent . . . and get away with it. Why did people always forgive him?

Footsteps on the stairs. Julia glanced again in the mirror, saw how utterly plain and blown apart she looked, her eyes so small, hair limp, the life siphoned from her face. There was a knock at the door. She wiped her eyes, said, "Uh-huh," and the door opened. It was Doug, short and bony, who had a thick beard and a quick laugh and eyes too penetrating for the moment. Julia didn't want to be looked at that deeply.

Doug said, with gentleness, "Dinner's ready. Come and have something to eat."

"Did someone call?"

"Brenda took it," he said, and he didn't say more.

She hated herself for asking. But she asked anyway. "Was it Bob?"

"I'm not sure. I don't think so," he said.

Julia followed Doug down the stairs. Brenda had seated Matthew in a brand-new high chair in the kitchen. She'd bought it the year before when she was pregnant for the first time, and kept it despite the miscarriage. Then she'd gotten pregnant again in June but had lost that one as well. Julia had been a pillar during her disasters, and she realized ruefully that it was good in a way for Brenda to have this disaster of Julia's to deal with. Brenda was being magnificent: cooking the pasta and sauce, stepping over joyfully to spoon some mushed broccoli into Matthew's waiting mouth, singing along with the radio.

"Are you *famished*?" Brenda asked when she saw Julia. Then without waiting for a reply she said, "Food will help. It always does. Doug, could you pour the wine?"

"Oh," Julia said. "I left my glass upstairs." She'd been drinking all afternoon. Brenda said it didn't matter. Julia accepted a new glass of wine, sipped a bit, and sat with Doug and Brenda in their cheerful little kitchen. Doug was being clumsily conscientious: getting up to retrieve missing pieces of cutlery, leaning over Brenda to get the breadboard, trying to be an attentive husband.

"I ran into someone from my high school the other day," Julia heard herself blurt, apropos of nothing. "He's a carpenter now. He used to –" She stopped. It was pointless. Why was she talking about this?

"What?" Brenda asked, too insistently.

"He had a major crush on me." She stopped again. They were looking at her too closely. She felt as if she'd turned into her mother and everyone was analysing her speech.

Her poor mother.

"Oh well!" Brenda said. "A carpenter! Good hands?" and she laughed too brightly. She was feeding Matthew mushed banana now and Matthew was taking everything from her.

"Who was that . . . who was that who called?" Julia asked, fighting to stay on top of things, to not break down. "It wasn't Bob, was it? You would tell me?" She hated the way her teeth clattered together, her fingers felt so drained of life, her centre so exposed.

"Of course," Brenda said. "But it wasn't him." She picked up a piece of paper. "It was a Bruce McCutcheon –"

"Oh shit!" Julia said. "I forgot to call him. I was supposed to meet him again at the house. About the insurance."

"You can call him tomorrow," Brenda said.

"Yeah. God knows what's going to go wrong tomorrow!" Julia said. She had a sense of water flooding over the dam, of cracks and fissures widening. She couldn't trust herself to speak. She rose awkwardly, struggled with the seat straps, clutched Matthew against her, closed her eyes.

Brenda said, "Oh, I'm sorry!" and Julia said, "No, no, it's all right." Matthew's little arms hugged her back and shoulders and he started patting her, saying, "Okay, Mommy. Okay."

Julia peeled his arms off her, handed him over to Brenda, left the room to the sound of his wails.

ᔕ

Sitting in her borrowed room, Julia could hear the sounds of the bathwater from just a few feet – a single wall – away, of Brenda playing with Matthew, getting him to put soap on the washcloth and scrub out his ears. The breath was entering and leaving her body, and for a moment she didn't know how it did that. She became acutely aware of how little she knew about herself, of how little control she exercised over the course of events. Somewhere buried inside her chest, her heart was beating away as if nothing had happened. She was conscious of not knowing the first thing about how or why it worked. It just did, sent blood scurrying around her body through channels she didn't know. And her brain kept the thoughts ticking over, somehow, despite the utter ruin of the universe. She was still able to hear Matthew say, "Where's the ducky?" and "Sometimes I poo-poo."

Julia had the rescued photo album on her lap, was looking at a picture that her mother took during Bob's first dinner with her parents. He wasn't "Bob" then but "Professor Sterling," her married American-literature professor, who was taking an unusual interest in her work. Her father had been stiff and furious during dinner, though outwardly coldly civil. When Bob made a big show of clearing the table for dessert, her father followed him into the kitchen then blasted him. Julia heard bursts from the other room like, "My God, man! What are you thinking?" and, "She is half your age!" They were lovers already, and Julia was appalled at her father's paternalism but stayed riveted in her seat, unable to move. It was her mother who went in to break things up, not by confronting the men at all but by flapping about like a flustered bird. "Well, I really think it's time for a picture!" she announced.

So there in the photo – amazingly intact, despite fire and flood – was her father, glowering, eyebrows furrowed, looking away, a cigarette in his hand, standing as far from Bob as he could and still fit in the narrow frame of her mother's ten-dollar camera. Bob was in the middle, large, oblivious, slightly drunk, his arm around Julia in too familiar a way but not caring a whit for appearances, only for the moment. And Julia finally, staring up at him – how dewy-eyed she looked to herself now. Trying so hard to care just for the moment too, for what he seemed to promise.

37 ⤺

Bob opened his eyes slowly. He shifted stiffly, looked around at nothing, at darkness . . . smelly darkness, heavy with the stench of . . . what? Of charcoal and ash, of not-so-ancient disaster. Where was he? What was he doing? He couldn't remember. He felt the strongest pull to return to sleep, but he didn't want to do that now. He'd been doing that off and on for what felt like ages. But it was so difficult to climb out. Just to raise his hand, he had to concentrate fiercely. But slowly, slowly, the feeling eased, and he came to realize that he was in the basement, that this was what was left of his home. He turned his head cautiously – oh, it hurt badly – and felt for his hands . . . but his neck was rusted solid and he couldn't feel his hands at all, he seemed to have lost them. He rocked his body and the pain stabbed from his knee straight through the roots of his teeth, and he bit his tongue so badly he tasted blood. He tried to turn over and then a thousand pins inserted themselves up and down his arms, which had been asleep, the circulation had been cut off in his awkward position. He freed his arms and shook them, felt them vibrating like loose, hurting rubber.

Though he couldn't remember any of it, it occurred to him that he'd fallen somehow, may have suffered a spinal-cord injury, that he should stay motionless and wait to be rescued.

Instead he panicked. He was on a pile of spilled tools, a hammer had been clawing at his back. He tried to stand, but his right leg buckled and he eased back down.

What I am doing here? he wondered. He remembered the fire. He remembered meeting the insurance man in the morning, and then the shock awaiting him at the university. And then he knew: he had to find and get rid of the cut-up clothes to be finally free of this nightmare.

He moved on his hands and his left knee in the darkness, the right leg dragging behind him. He could feel his Phillips screwdriver, his adjustable wrench, his power drill, the edge of the upended workbench. He'd hurt himself coming down through the window, of course, that must have been what happened – though he couldn't remember it at all, there was a blurry hole in his memory. He looked up slowly, trying not to strain his neck, but he couldn't see the window, couldn't see anything. It was black upon black.

He began to search about with his cold, painful, waking hands, tried to concentrate on his sense of touch. He fingered glass jars of nuts and bolts, a ball of twine, a dead windshield-wiper blade, an old metal tackle box. Eyes opened or closed, it didn't make much difference. Scraps of wood, a chisel, the German scissors, there they were! The clothes should have been beside them but weren't. An old fork, scattered drill bits, a cord and then his sander, a splinter that drove itself painfully into the side of his hand.

Something odd. A plastic bag split open, a ball of fluff . . . a wet ball, then more. It smelled disgusting, of sewage. A huge hairy ball of risen sewage. What was that doing there? He tried to brush it off his hands. He shook them and frantically pulled the sticking strands away from his fingers.

He felt some more with his hands in wider and wider circles, found another rag and then something else, and then his hand hit leather – unmistakable, soft, thousand-dollar leather – and he chortled and gasped in surprise and relief. There they were! The sliced bra and the stockings and the leather dress and panties and wig, the limp rag of a body slip – everything was there. He couldn't see a bit of it but he could feel with extraordinary clarity, as if he'd been blind his whole life. Safe! He was safe! He hugged the soft garments to his wounded face and for the first time realized he had a gash on his forehead from his fall.

A tiny price to pay, he thought. Now to get out. He manoeuvred around, started to scramble back to what he thought must be the position of the window. He hit his good knee on the invisible edge of the upended workbench, then crawled over it more carefully. There was no great hurry, no fire from which to escape. What time was it? It was unnaturally dark, even for blackest night, he thought. He'd find Julia at Brenda's, or Brenda would know where she was. And even if Julia had seen the Web site, he'd be able to explain everything. Just as soon as he got out and disposed of these ridiculous clothes.

What to say about Sienna? It was unfortunate, he'd explain, she'd become overwrought about, well, about being in love with him, a terrible crush. Julia would have gotten upset if Bob had told her, so he'd kept quiet. But of course he'd refused Sienna. Then the whole Internet nonsense had blown up – he would explain about the jealous boyfriend if she hadn't heard already. And today he'd tried to call, but the number Julia had left in her message was wrong. Helen must have made a mistake transcribing it.

But why was he so late? Bob tried to formulate his story while he found the wall, inch by careful inch, and then felt up to where the window should have been. Where was it? He was clutching the clothes and wig now to his chest in a well-guarded ball. He would stay patient, would right the work-bench and carefully climb up, crawl out the way he'd come.

He reached and he felt and at last, as he knew he would, he found the bottom of the window. He swung it open – it was hinged at the top – and stretched up just to feel if there was something he could grab on to, use to haul himself out without having to bother with righting the unwieldy workbench. But he didn't find anything; he found instead a wall of wood where there should have been open air.

"Jesus!" he said and recoiled. The window swung shut with a bang. He reached up again, reopened the window, once more encountered solid wood. It felt three feet thick. He pounded it with his fist and hurt himself. He tried in vain to account for this new, disturbing fact. Someone has nailed me in here, he thought. They've nailed the lid on my coffin and I'm going to die here, there's no other way out!

But of course there was another way out. He could go up the stairs the normal way. No one was in the house. The stairs might be in a fragile state – that's probably why he came in through the window – but he could try them, and the back door was right there. Once he made it to the landing he'd be home free. But where were the stairs? They were somewhere in the black. He turned around slowly, shaking with cold and fear but still in nominal control. The stairs were on the other side of the furnace. He'd have to go around to the left then turn

right and then the distance was only three normal steps: he'd
be at the foot of the steps.

He held the bundle to his breast, felt again carefully to make
sure he hadn't dropped any little thing, a stocking or part of a
bra. He took a tentative step to the left. For a moment he had
to put weight on his right leg and he went over, crashed into
tools again, felt the imprint of tiny screws and nuts on his right
side before he came to rest.

He moaned in pain, then moved slowly, crawled over a chaos
of skis and lawn chairs and again the corner of the downed
workbench until he found the dead furnace and then manoeuvred around it. Here the crawling was easier, just the grit of
the concrete grinding into points of contact. He rounded the
corner, kept the furnace on his right. Now it was just the equivalent of a few steps . . . and he felt the base of the stairs. Thank
God! He was just twelve feet from safety. He began to climb,
but after a moment the stairs cracked like a rifle shot. Bob
stopped and hung on, felt his whole aching body petrify trying
to keep the stairs together. They seemed weaker, looser, precarious. He wondered if he should retreat, ease back down, try
the window again. He could find that hammer that had clawed
his back while he lay on the floor. It would be noisy but he
could probably slam his way out. No, he could find his power
saw, cut his way out . . . except the electricity was off, and a
good thing, too, he thought, because he was such a shaking
wretch he'd probably end up slicing off body parts. No, he'd
have to race up the steps, one quick burst, grab the landing
before the stairs collapsed. He stayed monumentally still,
frozen in consideration, and then the wood moaned, a weak
little gasp compared to the gunshot of a moment ago. He
lunged up, pushed with his left leg once, then twice, and then
a third time, made the landing just as the stairs began to fall

away below him. He hung on desperately, pulled himself up. He stretched his arm for the handle of the back door, found it, but just then the landing gave way too and his grip failed. He was pitched in silent agony backwards into the depths of the cave. He felt himself bounce once and then again as something ripped in his leg.

38 ⤳

It was past midnight. Julia was on the bed clutching Matthew, who was asleep now at her breast. Brenda and Doug's house was cold and dark, the bed small and strange. She heard every creak. The first wintry winds were whipping through the branches, practising their howls. Everything had changed. Matthew's milky breath, that was the only familiar thing.

Where was Bob? She'd heard nothing. Julia couldn't help it, awful images were invading her brain. Bob and Sienna Chu were fucking in a sleazy, rat-trap motel just off the highway. There were sixty rooms and five guests and the baseboard heaters rattled, the bed squeaked with rust, when they turned on the light the cockroaches scattered with revolting little clicks. The wallpaper was mouldy beige, curling at the seams, the carpet was full of cigarette holes, the sheets smelled of traces of other people's body fluids. He was humping her, they were sweating like pigs in the desperate, electric heat. Julia could picture her, this Sienna Chu, eighteen years old, a nearly prepubescent body, almost titless, tiny hips, a belly like a boy's.

She opened her eyes. The wind toyed with the little house.

Brenda and Doug couldn't afford proper insulation, were still dealing with Brenda's student loans. Julia got out of bed, left Matthew asleep under the covers, walked to the window that was shivering in the breeze. It really was cold. Cold enough to snow. This early? It happened sometimes in Ottawa. October snow.

She looked out the window at the black-grey clouds – they looked like snow clouds – and even with her eyes wide open those ugly images were there still, haunting her thoughts. Damn him! Why was he so cock-driven, so impatient to throw away everything that they'd built? For what, younger flesh? How young does it have to be? How kinked-up and bizarre? How humiliating for them all?

For him too, she thought, despite herself. He was a proud man, would be mortified with this kind of exposure and attention. He might have simply fled on his own in disarray, in need of help.

Julia went to the bathroom down the hall and tried to not look at herself in the mirror. But she had to flick the switch to find the sink and the light was flat, awful, her face ghastly pale with black circles under her eyes.

Now that she'd found the sink she snapped off the light, splashed water over her face in the dark. She sat on the toilet and peed and mentally saw herself walking down the hallway, knocking gently on Brenda and Doug's door, whispering, "Brenda, it's me. I'm going out for a walk. I'm sorry. Matthew won't wake up. He's deeply asleep."

Deeply asleep. Something she would never be able to manage, not this night, impossible. It might be months, years before she could sleep soundly again.

She wiped herself and didn't flush, walked out of the bathroom. She meant to go down the hall to Brenda and Doug's door. She took one step and then stopped. They were so quiet but she heard the rocking, the murmur of their breath, a little moan that sounded like Brenda far away, in some other state. They were trying to be silent. Julia turned around, her heart breaking.

In the guest bedroom she dressed quickly and watched her child sleeping in such peace. He was exhausted, poor thing. He'd been so good in spite of all the disruptions. She couldn't hear Brenda and Doug now. Her own breathing sounded harsh and unpleasant. As she pulled on her things she had the unreal feeling that she might never be back. She might never see her child again. She didn't plan on leaving, but the whole universe was off its moorings. Nothing could be counted on, houses burned down, people lost their minds. Husbands changed their skin and absconded with sexual anthropologists.

ᔕ

Julia was walking quickly, grinding her teeth, trying not to think. The frigid wind blasted her face, cut through the flimsy defences of her borrowed coat, sought out her fingers, which were plunged deep in her pockets. She wanted every step to hurt just a little, to stab *this is real, this is real*. Because she'd been living in a haze for years, she knew it now and wanted nothing more of it.

She approached the house with trepidation. She hadn't meant to walk this way, but wasn't surprised in the end when her legs took her there. The sky was cloudy in patches, the wind pushed the clouds along at a terrific rate. They weren't keeping their shapes, either, but were rolling and changing like an avalanche in the sky, burying one another, reappearing, hurtling past. Some stars poked through the empty spaces: she could see Orion's belt, and the bottom of the Big Dipper, but not the handle.

The house looked dark as a tomb, sombre, desolate, a black shadow compared to most of the other houses on the street, whose porch lights were still burning even though it was past midnight. New boards were up on the remaining broken windows – Donny had come; she'd forgotten completely that she'd asked him. The wood was bright and new, a contrast to the dark, soulless eyes of the undamaged windows. Ironically, the house now looked as if it were undergoing a renovation, as if it would be transformed into something fine and beautiful in just a short time.

As if the family inside hadn't fallen in upon itself.

She walked closer and was so preoccupied with the house that she didn't notice the black car until she was just about next to it. It was nearly lost in the gloom cast by the neighbours' Manitoba maple, but when she saw it the cold wind faltered a moment and a surge of heat and anger – and strange relief – ran through her. Bob! But he'd taken the van. What was his car doing here?

She approached the house, listened intently. Was he in there? What was he doing? Was Sienna with him? It didn't seem possible, yet all kinds of unbelievable things had happened. She stood still on the front porch, strained to hear anything unusual. Then she tried the front door – still locked. She took the key from her pocket and opened the door, peered into the darkness.

"Bob?" she called out. "Bob, are you there?" Her voice sounded strange in the altered house, larger than usual though edged with fright.

No reply, just the complaint of charred rafters, the dripping of water somewhere. She reached to pull the door closed again – her house was scaring her like this. But she heard a noise that made her pause.

"Bob?"

"Julia. It's me!"

Oh, thank God, she thought. "Are you all right?"

"I'm fine. Really, I'm all right," he said, but he sounded far away, she could barely hear him. "I've had a bit of a fall."

"Where are you?"

"Down in the basement, almost directly under the back door. The landing collapsed. I'm going to need a little help."

"Stay there," she said. "I'll go around."

And she closed the door, her mind storming as she walked to the rear of the house. She took the key from her pocket, slotted it in the back-door lock, opened the door, and, standing on the sill, tried to see him.

"What the hell have you been doing?" she demanded. It was all blackness.

"I'm all right," he said again, sounding much closer now. "It's nothing major. But you're going to have to get help. Someone's going to have to lift me out."

She waited for further explanation and to gather her own thoughts, to let her heart stop galloping, trampling her brain. But he didn't say anything else. He was a long silence somewhere down there in the black.

"How bad are you really? Are you bleeding?"

"No," he said after a time. "A bit maybe, it's hard to tell. My leg is twisted. I can't get up."

"Why in God's name are you here in the middle of the night? Didn't you get my messages? Where did you go?"

"I was too long at the university, I'm sorry. When I got back you weren't here. So I just wandered in and then –"

"What do you take me for? How stupid do you think I am? I know all about it."

That stopped him. She could hear the panicked intake of breath.

"What do you know?" he asked flatly.

"What I know half the fucking world knows," she said. "But perhaps you can start by telling me about Sienna Chu."

"It was a prank!" he blurted. "There's going to be a retraction. Sienna has a jealous boyfriend, he did the whole thing. He went on the Internet and found all these photographs and then he substituted my face. But they confessed to the dean –"

"*Bob*. Stop it!" she said. "You know you're lying to me. I won't have it any more. You're living another life I know nothing about. How do you expect me to trust anything you say? You took her to New York, for Christ's sakes!"

She knelt down on the door sill. Her body felt tired and heavy and part of her was yearning to just step over the edge, follow him to wherever he'd plunged. Another part wanted to close the door, abandon him to his fate.

"This is awful," he said. When she started to tell him how bloody awful it really was, he said, "Just be quiet, please, and I'll tell you. Please."

So she stayed quiet. She sighed, shifted so that she was sitting now, most of her body huddled out of the direct wind, the backs of her thighs resting against the ragged ends of what used to be the landing, her calves and feet dangling in mid-air.

"I was smitten by Sienna," he said. "I will tell you freely, I was dazzled and confused. But nothing happened, not really. She did come to New York, but she stayed in her own room. There were a few . . . embraces, it was heady and stupid, but I'm now over her, irrevocably. Apparently she's telling people she's overdosed – she's in the hospital, but is all right. God knows what the truth is with her. But I will not be seeing her again.

And what I said about the dean was no lie. There is a retraction coming, if it hasn't been sent already. The Web site has been shut down. So the only wound left, I suspect, is with you and me. It's a terrible one, I know. I regret everything that happened." He was silent for a time, and she was about to tear into his pitiful excuse of a story when he said, "I need to tell you something else, I'm sorry. I came back here this afternoon in a panic to try and retrieve some things I'd left. Some . . . incriminating things, which I was trying to hide from you. No one was here. I have a . . . kind of a . . . fantasy. It's a . . . private thing."

"Oh my God!" she wailed.

"Shhh. I need to say this."

She went rigid, trying to stay quiet.

"It was something that I've held inside and kept all to myself. It should have stayed that way. I was perfectly happy. Except someone stumbled on it –"

"What do you mean *private*?" she asked. "How about me? How could you keep something like that from me? You think you can just go around trying on ladies' underwear and –"

"*Shhhh! Shhh!*" he said.

"What, you don't like me saying it out loud? Who's going to find out who doesn't already know? It's been broadcast across the fucking planet!" She tried to calm down but she couldn't. It was outrageous. He was down there still trying to hush everything up, to prevaricate like a bloody politician caught with his cock up his secretary's skirt.

"*Shhhh*," he said. "This is very difficult for me."

"What do you think it is for me?" she said. "This was no prank really, was it? How could you let this happen?"

"It was meant to be private," he said again. "And I was weak, vain, stupid, I have no excuses. I was in a daze, I let her lead me around. I don't know what I was thinking of to trust her and not you with my secret, if I was going to trust anyone. But I was afraid of how you'd react . . . needless to say."

He sounded subdued, defeated. He said, "I am so sorry. I would give anything – *anything* – to be able to rewind this week. Just wipe it out, try it again."

"Do you really want to go around wearing women's clothing?" Julia asked. She felt sad, low, still.

"I don't want to go around at all," he said, almost dispassionately. This flat voice in the darkness. "It's just a quirk of my wiring. I don't like to think about it even, it's not for public consumption. I know, I know, it is public now, but I never gave permission. I don't know why I let her take the pictures. I was in a state of . . . temporary insanity."

"So they weren't fakes?"

"No."

"Oh, Bob," she said.

He was quiet for a time. The wind now was worsening and Julia could feel on the back of her neck the first wet, miserable flakes of snow coming down. She didn't want to be there. She felt disoriented. It was some sort of answer to have everything out in the open. But what was she supposed to do with it?

"I know you feel bitter," he said after a time. "But please don't abandon me. I will be lost and worthless without you."

"You mean if I divorce you over this, the whole world's going to know for sure."

Another silence, and Julia felt as if she'd ground her heel into his wound, but she couldn't help it. She felt as if she'd been wounded, too.

He said, "Julia, try to be reasonable. That's not what I meant. And anyway I don't care about the whole world." His voice was finally rising with a sense of purpose. "I care about you and Matthew." He fell silent again.

"It's going to take time for me to absorb all this and figure out where we are," Julia said at last.

"Yes. Yes!" he agreed.

"All right then." She suddenly felt how cold her hands were, how uncomfortable it was on the perch. "All right," she said again, as much for herself as for him. What's next? "Bob, I'm going to go across the street to ask Ray to call an ambulance," she said.

"Good. Thank you."

"Are you okay?"

"Yes. I'm just – I seem to be bleeding a little more than I thought."

"Oh, Bob! Hang on!" she said and turned quickly to go. Her legs were stiff and she felt shaky, cold to the core. She started to run. Snow filled the air now, was melting on the ground. She pounded along the driveway and across the quiet street, forced herself to focus on getting to Ray's door.

∽ 39

Bob suddenly felt flushed, as if some block in the radiator pipes had given way and now he was wrapped in liquid warmth. Yet it wasn't liquid, turned as in a dream to heated sand, to something he loved – that was it, the warmth of familiarity, as if he had walked back into his childhood home, miraculously restored, unseen and yet preserved all these decades later.

It was brown – not the home, which he couldn't visualize so much as sense somehow in his blood and bones – the feeling was brown, was comfortable, soothing. And she was there, so close now he had a hard time seeing her; she was out of focus, a blur of brownish skin. She'd been lying in the sun, that was why she was so warm and brown. He saw her in a vague way, her nose, the curve of her eyelids, the haze of her hair. His eyes were so close he was conscious of the shadow of the end of his own nose, would pull away in a moment to see her better. But it was fine too to breathe together like this.

How long had it been? He couldn't remember, but it felt like centuries, slow accumulations of time, of not recognizing each other. "Hello, you," he said tenderly, but she didn't reply – didn't look quite at him, but didn't look away either. Their bodies were very close. Of course, they'd been making love, they were still immersed, it was hard to know where the one ended and the other began. That was an important part of the feeling, Bob thought, this comfortable, easy joy of knowing, of not really being separate. *And so you are this and we did that.*

She turned then, rolled like an ocean wave, and they were quiet spoons in the soft, warm sand. Her hair smelled of salt and wind, of sweet sweat, of the remnants of desire. She closed her eyes and Bob could feel her almost immediately settling into sleep, the way that she did, holding his hand over her breast, which was as perfect as it was ordinary. It was as familiar as his own body, might have belonged to him at another time, he thought. They'd been together, possibly even been one another in different ages. The idea seemed quite natural, something known but sometimes forgotten, the way that so many important things are forgotten in the mists of living.

"Stay with me here," he murmured, trying to make it into a little song, something that might slip through, last somehow. "Stay with me here."

In a moment she was on her feet, was brushing the sand off her perfect, her ordinary body, and walking away. He propped himself on one elbow to watch her, and she knew, so let herself sway a bit more than she would have all alone. It was this dance they did. He thought of calling out her name but stayed silent, watched her instead as she waded into the water, not slowing for the first bite of the waves, not speeding up either to put distance between them.

He wanted to see her face. He knew who she was, of course he did, her hair fluttering now in the breeze, golden brown, down her backside. But he wanted to see her, to memorize her; he wasn't sure how long it would be until he saw her again. Turn, turn, he thought. He held his breath, waiting.

She paused, dipped her shoulder as if to do it then, to plunge, but straightened instead and turned to meet his gaze. His smile was reflex, was out of the cage before he could withdraw it. Something was wrong. Her hair was quite dark now, a trick of the light perhaps, but black, actually, and her face, her eyes . . . her eyes wouldn't meet his, one went this way and the other was . . .

Then she disappeared without a ripple. The water betrayed nothing, no churning of strong legs and feet, no trailing bubbles. He stood then and watched, but the sand, the water, the sun were all harsh as glittering diamonds, and the wind told him nothing. He ran to the edge of the water, felt the splash on his legs as he ploughed forward – cold, but not impossible. A wave hit and he fell, was soaked now, taken by surprise by the saltiness. He tried to gain his feet but where were they? It was hard to know where the beach was, the sky, the world had turned to a turmoil of pounding surf. He spat out a mouthful of water, coughed.

He kicked his legs – what should have been his legs – felt himself rolling, sinking, changing. The whole world was pulled inside out like an animal being skinned. He felt the corkscrewing, yearning tug of the air, scanned feverishly to find where he'd last seen her . . .

There she was in the corner of the room – it was a room, a grey box with a bed and a window, a table, a clock – she was sitting up in the gloom and he could see her *from inside*. That was the bizarre thing, how normal it felt, to look out through the eyes of Sienna Chu and to think: that man slumped in the corner chair with the balding head, the wisps of black hair, snoring in Chinese – that must be my father. And that woman in the cot next to me, curled in her sweater, the wild white mane, pale complexion – there is my mother. He saw the room from outside and from within her, as if he had stolen into her mind, was tiptoeing around as a burglar might in a sleeping house in the minutes before dawn.

He tried to poke into her thoughts, as if slowly and silently opening a door in the murk. And immediately he was aware of a strange dust, like eggshell rubbings, or as if she'd spent half a summer grinding pencil shavings into tiny particles then absorbing them into her bloodstream, the lead and the wood together, a soupy glue limping through her body. Alive but dragging, suffocating, like a huge snake that's eaten a water-buffalo calf and is bloated in the shade, stuffed for weeks now, not wanting to move, unable.

And then it was later. Through Sienna's eyes he could see half a field out the window. Half a grey field between her father and her mother. The tops of traffic, a bit of a light: grey-red, grey-yellow. He could see her parents' coats piled on a small chair, and grey flowers balanced on an absurdly small bedside table, and one-third of a doorway and a sliver of hall, fractions of people waiting for an invisible elevator to take them away in clumps.

He hadn't noticed before, but now great bricks of words lay in rubble in the room: helpless, shattered, dusty, cracked, with broken clinging bits of mortar. Words thrown at moving targets, words stuck together to try to stand up to the winds and rain, words piled in approximations of this and that: this wall will stand for that thing, that act, and over here, this section will be that person, and here is what certain thoughts look like, explanations, and over here a doorway through which we might pass. As if.

Her mother woke up, looked lost, disoriented for a moment, then the whole history of the current disaster booted up in her mind, took over her features, and she said, "Oh sweetie. Is there anything we can get you? What would you like?"

What would I like? What would I like? Here I am inside the mind, the body of Sienna Chu, Bob thought, and the world is unbearably heavy, is sad beyond measure.

"Nothing. Nothing," he heard Sienna say – a strange version of her voice, heard like this from the inside.

"Ah!" Bob said, and opened his eyes. Julia was there. She looked tired, devastated, vulnerable.

"You're awake," she said. She turned to the driver – there was a driver, Bob could see and recognize it all in an instant. There was a driver and an attendant and the lights going by were streetlights. "He's awake," Julia said to the ambulance attendant. "Lie down. How do you feel?"

How did he feel?

He couldn't say. The moment felt crammed beyond belief, as if it could not contain one more ounce of anguish, joy, relief, fear, anticipation.

"Are you all right?" she asked, her face so drained of colour, a portrait of exhaustion.

She ran her hand through her hair in fatigue, smiled for him with such emptiness – or was it concern? He couldn't tell. He didn't know. He'd been married to her for seven years, had fathered their child, had loved her forever, and yet still didn't know the first thing about her.

"Julia –"

"For God's sake, Bob, just close your eyes," she said. "Try and rest."

I'm not going to let you go. He willed her to say it. He didn't want to shut his eyes until he heard those words from her.

"We'll be there soon," she said. He could feel his heart lying limp on the floor of the ambulance. She turned to look out the windows at the rear, her face blank. And then he felt her hand on his – warm somehow, despite the chill. Her shoulders were rocking with the vibrations of the vehicle, she was still looking away, but her touch was for him. Suddenly the ambulance slowed down – they'd come to an intersection, maybe – and the siren came on, a doleful, penitent song on the underside of this strange, strange night.

↶ 40

Everybody was there: Trevor, Mary Hoderstrom, Tommy, the nephews, Babs and Dougie and the others, all of them. Mother and Father. Trevor had been late – he was always getting hung up and such. Now he was eating a banana. He was so hungry he was smushing his face down into his flat thing like it was a cigar. Not a cigar, a rollout, a section head. Just smushing. He was older. All of them were. They had brown teeth and there were cows, and the president was always getting shot, over and over, it didn't matter so much. It was something to do.

Lenore said, "Trevor!" and rapped at his forehead. She wanted him to get his face out of the smushy thing, the ligament. The ointment. He ignored her, as he always did, it was so annoying. She said, "Guests are coming!" and the big one, the Italian, said, "Don't be such a sissy!" It was so sad, Mary Hoderstrom coming down like that, the way she did, getting so old. She had fluffs of white hair and pink skin underneath, she trembled like she was spraying all the time, Dear Lord this and that. Just mottled. Her tongue went wah-wah, like a cradle-cap, muffing, little bits of prayer came down her lip and leaked onto the rug. She was never like that in school, always very

• 359

clever with her things, and such. She was never leaky. But then it changed.

Tommy too looked much older after the accident. He had claws and one eye went this way and the other didn't. He kept watching the president. This hump on his back. Quasi hoo-hoo. From before. Mary would know. She knew everything, very doctor and all. Lenore said, "Why wouldn't he want to?" but Mary ignored her. It wasn't the right question. It was something to do with the accident, the shooting, that terrible divorce. She said, "Well, if you must!" and she meant it, it seemed so sad all of a sudden. Things got that way. The glue fell out and then the wind blew it all down south. Lenore said, "Mup-mup!" and tried to ignore Trevor with the banana, but he was having a terrible time with it. Just mushing. The Italian one said, "It isn't at all like that!" but she was always that way, big and black, just dribbling.

There were cornflakes outside, they looked so white and silly, Lenore could see them through the bars. It wasn't such a bad hotel. At least they let everyone stay, and she didn't know about the tipping – Trevor took care of all that. She was upset about the stinky rooms. She'd tried to talk to the woman, but it just got lunkier every day. Lenore turned to Trevor now and said, "You talk to her! I've tried!" but he didn't say that he would. He was finishing the last of the banana, it was all over his face, he never used to be like that. He was going to ignore it. He'd go away and pretend it was all right.

It wasn't all right. Everything was stinky, the cows, the corn-flakes, the whole shipyard. But not so bad, as holidays go. She was dreading going back, actually, though she didn't want to stay. She didn't know what she was going to do. Hadn't decided at all. She couldn't even remember what the choices were. They were all back at home on the kitchen counter in the pile where she kept things. She could picture it clearly, the whole pile, papers and other important ones, a bit bulgy, and she just had to get to it. Put them away in the right order.

Babs and Dougie weren't speaking. That wasn't such a surprise. They were angrily married, Lenore watched them closely for a time. Babs had let herself go completely, she was limping up and down the cricket pitch, sputtering. That's what happened sometimes; Lenore could remember when she was like that with Trevor. Just up and down. Dougie was watching the president, he couldn't get enough of it. His neck was all loose now and turkey, he broggled a lot and didn't like the dessert. He used to be a real car. But that was before. They were all a lot less shiny.

And Mother and Father, sitting on the corner, holding hands. They just dribbled with it. Lenore had never seen them so happy. This holiday was really doing them good. Father was skinny now, thin as a lake, and Mother was a loaf of bread. Freeze-dried and such. You couldn't separate them. They didn't even say much, they didn't have to, that's what happened after a long, long time. You just hold hands and clatter.

Everyone was there and Lenore looked up, she couldn't believe it. Now everyone *was* there! She almost got to her feet, she rocked and Trevor elbowed her for help. She said, "Ouch!" and the flat thing got in her way, went crickle and bonked her back down. It didn't matter. Julia was there with the little one, and the big one with the wiggly-sticks, he looked like a humpy little balloon.

"Oh hello! Hello! Isn't this *lovely!*" Lenore said and she started to cry. Everything was perfect now.

Her daughter, the pretty one, said hello to her in Italian, it was quite a feat. Lenore shook her head, she was so happy. "I suppose that's what you'd call it," she said and she leaned forward. She wanted a kiss. She tried to say it but her lips fumbled, she said, "What about this?" and the pretty one said, "Mess of dishes!"

Trevor said, "It's shit rock. God you're gorgeous!" and Lenore slapped him on the arm.

"You remember Julia," she said.

"Aren't you gorgeous!" he said, banana all over him.

"You should kiss your father," Lenore said, then she said to Trevor, "Swipe your face!"

He grinned, he was drunk. Lenore didn't know why she hadn't recognized it before. He said, "Kiss your father!" and leaned towards Julia.

"Do you have any kids?" Julia said, hoppity, like a bird. Trevor had her wrist now. He was still a strong man.

"I'm sorry! I'm sorry!" Lenore said, and blished the flat thing at him, it went clank off the banana cheek, but he didn't let go.

"Kiss your father, sweetie!" he said.

"Trevor. *Trevor!*" Lenore said.

"It's all right. It's okay," Julia said and took her father's hand away, like folding a birthday card. She said much more, too much to tell, really, and then they were on their way, which was quite right. If he was going to behave like a triffid.

Julia helped her up. Trevor went back to his banana gunk. They walked past the sign and Lenore read, "No Smoking Please."

"Mom, that's excellent, that's really good!" Julia said. Now the other little one went hiccuffy down the way, saying, "Brrrumppp! Brrrummppp!"

They were all going sniffly-sniff, speaking loudly and Italian about it, so Lenore said, "It's the cows."

"The cows?"

"The cows! The cows!" she said, and pointed to where they were.

"Oh. Oh, the cows!" Julia said.

Scholarship student! Sometimes you have to wonder. Marrying that bear-head. Lenore wondered where he'd got to. He was a lot like Trevor, it was so sad. She wanted to tell Julia, it was really weighing on her. She wanted to tell her what a stupid mistake it was. But she couldn't find the right time. It just went and went and things came up.

So she said, now, "Where's what's-his-name?" She wanted to tell Julia when he wasn't around. Before it was too late. "The bear-head," she said.

"Who's the bear-head? Is this your room?"

Well, she should know, she picked the hotel. Lenore looked up. "I suppose so," she said.

They sat on the slab and there was a little worm in the picture, red and cross. Lenore didn't know who it was. They came with the room, all those things. And there was no door on the bathroom, she certainly hoped that would be reflected in the bill at the end. She'd left Trevor to look after it, but he was such a man, sometimes.

Julia asked about whatever it was, the thing. She didn't know whether to sit down or fly away.

Lenore said, "It's completely broken!" and the big one hipped off to have a look. Lenore asked, "Whyever does he have the wiggly-sticks?"

Julia said, "What?"

"Well?"

And Julia went on insufferably, as if she'd prevented them.

"Oh my, yes!" Lenore said. The big one was off so she took her chance. She pulled Julia to her and said, "Don't make a mistake!" Julia didn't let on. "When it's too late you'll just be worry!" Lenore said. She meant another word but her lips fumbled again. It was the cornflakes, they feed them to you so you won't be able to figure out the bill.

Julia mumbled about something else.

"Don't marmalade that man!" Lenore blurted. And more mumbly so she said, "You *know* what I mean! The bear-head!" and then she looked up and there he was. My God, she'd never been so embarrassed, she just blurted the first thing that came in her head. "Bob!" she said. "You look like a million bucks!"

"Why, Lenore," he said, sheepy as a goat. But then it didn't matter. She saw it clear as pain, as anything was any more. They were all together, it would just be a nice holiday, and if Julia went ahead, well, there'll always be another room, you try one and then another.

"It's been lovely," Lenore said. "Just lovely."

Julia said something else, sputtery and little-breathed.

"Rain and nails!" Lenore said, and Julia couldn't follow her. It was a problem now with the channels. "Worms," Lenore said, groping.

"Worms?"

"What you said," Lenore blurted. So upsetting, when the wires bulged.

Lenore didn't know what to say next, so she just curdled her baby – the big ones, they never really stop. She wasn't sure what had been led and what was trump. Ages passed, like a bad winter, Lenore was trying so hard. She tried and tried, knew there was something, but it was frozen off and away. Finally, when she gave up, it came to her. She said, "The really good thing about it all is, after a while, you ferment."

"Yes, Mom?"

"You just do. And it's lovely. It really has been. Very Christmas, you know. Forgive and ferment."

She started to cry then, she didn't know why. Julia sat up on the bed and stopped being such-like, she put her arms around Lenore and it felt close, with her and the little one, and even the bear-head. Julia said something else, softly, Lenore didn't bother to hear it so much. It all drips into the same.

It wouldn't last, couldn't, Lenore saw it now. Nothing ever did. But for just this right now it was fine.

"I wish your father was here," she said, crying again, it was so too much all of a sudden. "Instead of being such a banana." And she felt herself dozing, just like that, a gentle leaning murmur into her daughter's lovely shoulder, a soft little carpet tickle into sleep. It wasn't much of a dream – she didn't want to, these days – but it was pleasant and downhill and there were very few onions, which was lovely, she didn't want to have to worry about dinner till it was done.

ACKNOWLEDGEMENTS

The author would like to gratefully acknowledge the financial assistance of the Arts Council of the Regional Municipality of Ottawa–Carleton in the preparation of this manuscript. Thanks too to the many friends and family members whose comments, suggestions, and support have been invaluable. Finally, thanks to Ellen Seligman for her inspired editing. A.C.

ᔕ

Some sections of this novel, in different form, first appeared in *The Canadian Forum* ("Capt. Buzbie," May 1998).